Thousand Autumns

QIAN QIU

4

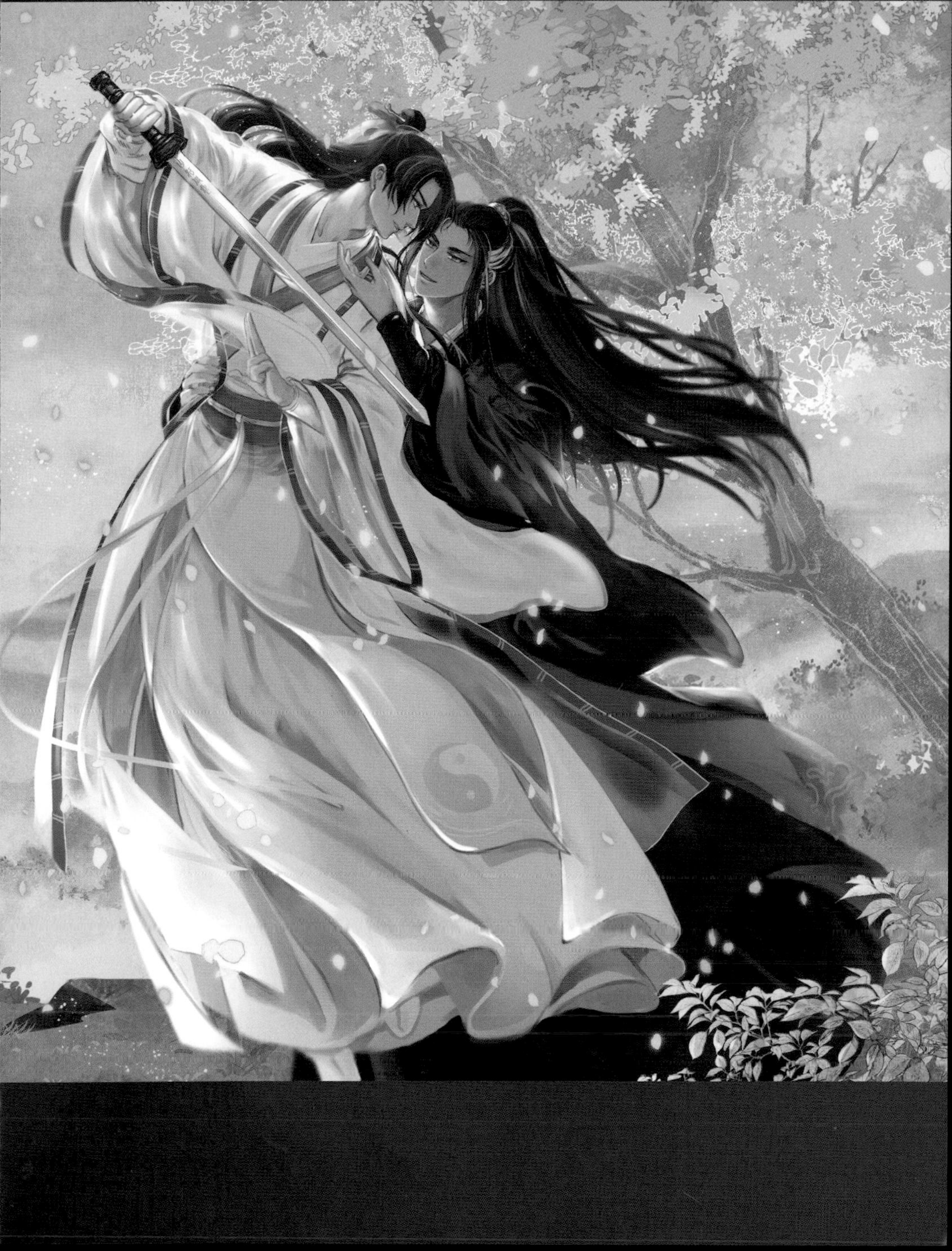

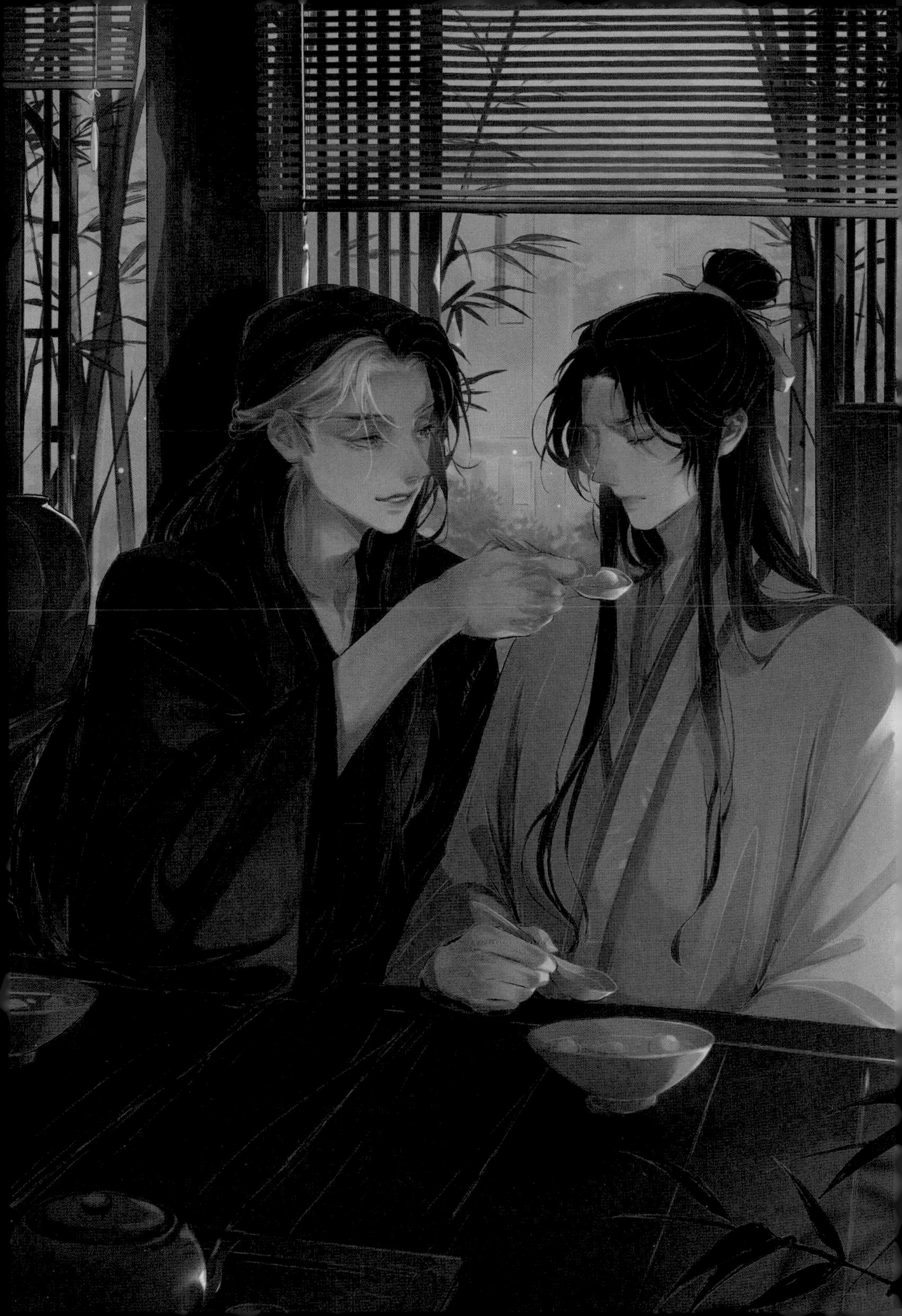

Thousand Autumns

QIAN QIU

WRITTEN BY
Meng Xi Shi

TRANSLATED BY
Faelicy

ILLUSTRATED BY
Me.Mimo

BONUS ILLUSTRATION BY
Ying

Seven Seas

Seven Seas Entertainment

THOUSAND AUTUMNS: QIAN QIU VOL. 4

Published originally under the title of 《千秋》 (Qian Qiu)
Author © 夢溪石 (Meng Xi Shi)
English edition rights under license granted by 北京晋江原创网络科技有限公司
(Beijing Jinjiang Original Network Technology Co., Ltd.)
English edition copyright © 2023 Seven Seas Entertainment, Inc.
Arranged through JS Agency Co., Ltd
All rights reserved

Illustrations by Me.Mimo
Bonus Illustration by Ying

Seven Seas press and purchase enquiries can be sent to
Marketing Manager Lauren Hill at press@gomanga.com.
Information regarding the distribution and purchase of digital editions is available
from Digital Manager CK Russell at digital@gomanga.com.

Seven Seas and the Seven Seas logo are trademarks of
Seven Seas Entertainment. All rights reserved.

Follow Seven Seas Entertainment online at
sevenseasentertainment.com.

TRANSLATION: Faelicy
ADAPTATION: Harry Catlin
COVER DESIGN: M. A. Lewife
INTERIOR DESIGN & LAYOUT: Clay Gardner
PROOFREADER: Vivica Caligari, Hnä
COPY EDITOR: Jade Gardner
EDITOR: Laurel Ashgrove
PREPRESS TECHNICIAN: Melanie Ujimori, Jules Valera
MANAGING EDITOR: Alyssa Scavetta
EDITOR-IN-CHIEF: Julie Davis
PUBLISHER: Lianne Sentar
VICE PRESIDENT: Adam Arnold
PRESIDENT: Jason DeAngelis

ISBN: 978-1-63858-944-0
Printed in Canada
First Printing: March 2024
10 9 8 7 6 5 4 3 2 1

TABLE OF CONTENTS

Send-Off

ZHANGSUN SHENG had spoken the truth: the Jade Dew Pills truly were outstandingly effective. Shen Qiao took two, and after he'd waited a few moments and circulated the *Zhuyang Strategy*'s true qi through his body, he found his meridians cleared up. His blood and qi flowed freely, and the muffled pain in his chest gradually lessened. No longer was it an immense effort to simply say a few words.

He bade farewell to Zhangsun Sheng and Dou Yi, then lifted Yuwen Song with him onto the horse. To help the boy adjust, he deliberately set the pace at a slower trot while turning his head to look back.

The city of Chang'an towered behind them, as majestic as it had always been. Although scoured by the flames of war, it still stood lofty and unshakable. However, over these hundreds and thousands of years, the people had changed, the dynasties replaced. After a couple of years, perhaps even the tragic, unjust death that Yuwen Xian had suffered would be forgotten by most.

Dou Yan held her father's hand as she watched the two leave, without blinking. Then she raised her voice and yelled, "Take care, esteemed Daoist Master Shen! Take care, Yuwen-qilang!"

Shen Qiao smiled at her, but then he noticed that Yuwen Song, who was sitting in front of him, hadn't spoken a word. He asked,

"Do you wish to take another look at Chang'an? Once we leave, there's no saying how long it'll be before we can return."

Yuwen Song was silent for a moment, then said, "It's a place of sorrow, so looking at it will only bring me more sorrow. I only hate how powerless I am, that I could do nothing but watch as my parents suffered injustice."

He was even younger than Shiwu, yet the words from his mouth were mature beyond his age. Shiwu had wept uncontrollably the day he lost his master. As for Yuwen Song, he'd cried back at the Su residence, and at this moment his voice was dull and hoarse. But his words remained clear and articulate. He was many times stronger than Shiwu. Thinking about it now, perhaps all children from the royal family were like this—Dou Yan, too, when Shen Qiao had been carrying her, had neither panicked nor struggled despite the treacherous situation she was in and thus hadn't hampered Shen Qiao as he'd faced the enemy.

Shen Qiao caressed his head. "Don't think of it that way. Originally, your father could have fled without issue, but he insisted on staying. First, because he was unwilling to leave your mother and brothers to face danger by themselves, and second, so that he could demonstrate his innocence and loyalty to the emperor and the world. Perhaps some people wouldn't understand, but as his son, you surely do, don't you?"

Yuwen Song made a sound of assent. Then, after a long while, he whispered, "In truth, Father had already made some arrangements: he wanted Mother and the rest to leave at the first opportunity, but Mother also didn't want to leave Father to face the danger alone. My brothers, too—none of them were willing to leave. I was the youngest, so Uncle Yan forcibly brought me away..."

"Yes," said Shen Qiao. "During our time in this world, everyone has to make their own choices. Some will choose to preserve their lives at all costs, and some will choose to give up their lives for their reputation or to demonstrate their innocence. In all cases, there is nothing to criticize. Only during the darkest hour will one's true self emerge. So many people were willing to secretly assist the Prince of Qi, and the Su family was even willing to stand up for him against the emperor. Clearly, everyone knew how moral the Prince of Qi was. No amount of slander would be able to change this.

"Since someone has entrusted me with this duty, I must ensure that you arrive somewhere safe. Do you have any relatives you can turn to?"

He'd originally planned to bring Yuwen Song back to Bixia Sect on Mount Tai, but having seen that this child had his own views despite his young age, he decided to ask his opinion instead of making the decision for him.

Yuwen Song shook his head. "The Yuwen family's relatives are all from the royal family. Even if someone was willing to take me in, if the higher-ups pursue the matter, they'll eventually end up implicated. Yuwen Yun has already killed my father and three other members of the royal family who were all prestigious and respected, so he'll have no scruples about killing more to strengthen his authority. I'll go wherever you go, Daoist Master Shen."

"All right," said Shen Qiao. "Then we'll head to Bixia Sect."

"Where is Bixia Sect?"

"On Mount Tai."

Sure enough, Yuwen Song's interest was piqued. "Mount Tai, as in the first of the Five Sacred Mountains?"

Shen Qiao smiled. "Correct. Mount Tai lies within a mountain range, the finest in all the world. The red clouds at sunrise are peerlessly beautiful. If you see them in person, you'll never regret it."

Yuwen Song was still young, after all, so he was easily distracted. Though he was heartbroken, when he heard Shen Qiao's description, he couldn't help the look of slight anticipation that tinted his face.

Yuwen Yun had always feared Yuwen Xian's prestige. Fearing that dragging things out could lead to disadvantageous changes, he first dispatched his men to surround the Prince of Qi's residence, forcing Yuwen Xian into hiding. Everyone else only took this to mean that Yuwen Yun was still unwilling to kill him, and thus dropped their guard. No one expected that Yuwen Yun would suddenly launch an attack and have Murong Qin kill his own uncle. Unwilling to endure humiliation, the entirety of the Prince of Qi's residence had committed suicide in front of the messengers. This news had already spread, and the entire city was now in shock. As everyone mourned Yuwen Xian, they also began to send memorial after memorial indicting the emperor's underlings—Chen Gong and the others. This was an implicit accusation toward the emperor as well, and there were also people secretly doing their utmost to keep the emperor occupied to prevent him from dispatching men outside the city to capture Shen Qiao and Yuwen Song.

As a result, Shen Qiao and Yuwen Song did not see a single pursuing soldier for many days on their journey out of Chang'an.

As for the people of Hehuan Sect, Shen Qiao had killed two of their elders at once, and there was now a deep blood feud between them. Even if this hadn't happened, there was still the incident where Sang Jingxing had forced Shen Qiao to destroy his martial arts, then been left gravely injured by Shen Qiao's counterattack. The hatred between them had long been planted. Things were peaceful for now, but there was no guarantee it could continue forever.

Though Shen Qiao was currently injured, he was no longer the same man he'd been before. As long he didn't have to deal with Sang

Jingxing or Yuan Xiuxiu, he'd be able to handle any attacker while protecting Yuwen Song. So, when they arrived in He Province, he slowed their pace, choosing not to take the shortest route to Bixia Sect—instead, he headed south. Not only so he himself could recuperate but also to give Yuwen Song a diversion.

This journey continued for over three months. The two of them traveled and rested, rested and traveled. Whenever they entered a city, they'd seek out a Daoist monastery to recuperate in, then Shen Qiao would take Yuwen Song to broaden his horizons—either by enjoying the local scenery, or wandering through the streets and alleys, observing the town and various happenings.

"The vicissitudes of life each hold their own meaning. Within the happenings of this world also lie many truths—from the great Dao springs forth many thousands of paths, but even if there are millions of variations, they never stray from their source." The more Shen Qiao saw, the clearer his heart became, and this benefited his sword and martial path as well.

His current self was long changed from the betrayed, down-trodden sect leader on Xuandu Mountain, but even after being mired in the dust of the secular world, not only did he lack even a hint of crass materialism, he actually seemed more transcendent than ever. Dark hair and blue robes, a longsword on his back, his complexion lustrous, bright like a shining moon. He looked like an immortal among humans, subtly giving off a sense of unapproachable, lofty abstinence.

As for Yuwen Song, he was able to mitigate most of his sorrow and melancholy through these sights and sounds. For one so young, if his heart were immersed in gloom for long periods of time, it would shorten his life. Shen Qiao had given this matter much thought, and, accordingly, spoke little of theories or philosophies.

Instead, he simply took the boy out to wander around, wanting him to see and consider more of the world. This way, he could open his mind and broaden his horizons.

"I must let this Daoist Master know—the two of you came at the perfect time. Today is Master Huang's banquet to celebrate his sixtieth birthday. All the city's officials and famous gentry have come to offer their congratulations. If you're planning to climb the mountain to sightsee, why not wait until tomorrow to do it? It would be a shame to miss the birthday banquet!"

After they arrived at Runan's border, Shen Qiao had brought Yuwen Song to an inn. The concierge, having noticed that they weren't locals, gave them this recommendation.

"Master Huang?" Naturally, Shen Qiao was unable to discern the man's identity just from this title alone.

"Yes, yes. Master Huang's real name is Xidao. He's an illustrious scholar of this city—seems that he's well-known among both the jianghu and the scholar class. My young self cannot claim to know much, but Master Huang's reputation within this city is indeed thunderous. His esteemed self is extremely hospitable—anyone can stop by for a drink, no invitation required. I heard that the renowned lute player, Master Du, will be playing a piece in his honor at the banquet, and that many people are going to hear him play. Even if they can't get inside, just listening outside is enough to cleanse the ears..."

The concierge prattled on and on. Shen Qiao recalled that name, Huang Xidao—Yan Wushi had mentioned him before. The man was from a noble family in Runan, and he was both a master of music and accomplished in martial arts. But due to his family background, he couldn't count as a full member of the jianghu.

Yan Wushi had no time for martial artists who were the slightest bit lacking. He'd brought up Huang Xidao solely because the man could not only infuse his music with bitter desolation, but also perform sounds so beautiful that birds would flock by the hundreds to listen. He shared some similarities with Fajing Sect Leader Guang Lingsan, but though Huang Xidao couldn't compare to Guang Lingsan martially, he might surpass him when it came to music. And so, Yan Wushi had briefly mentioned Huang Xidao, while talking about Guang Lingsan.

Yuwen Song's eyes shone, and he tugged on the corner of Shen Qiao's robe. When Shen Qiao bent down, he whispered, "I've seen the lute player he mentioned. His name is Du Yun. He entered the palace to perform before, and it's true: he's so skilled that any piece he plays seems to linger for three days."

"Do you wish to go listen?" asked Shen Qiao.

Yuwen Song bore a yearning expression. "Can we?"

Shen Qiao gave a small smile. "Of course we can. Since Master Huang is hospitable, I'm sure he won't mind having the two of us as additional uninvited guests."

This inn wasn't far from the Huang residence. When they arrived, a man dressed in a steward's uniform was standing before the gates, personally welcoming the guests inside.

When he saw Shen Qiao and Yuwen Song approach, he dutifully asked for their names. To avoid trouble, Shen Qiao used an alias. "This one is Shan Qiaozi, a wandering Daoist. I heard that it was Master Huang's birthday, so I specially came to congratulate him."

It'd be too rude to come empty-handed, so he'd purchased a small gift on the way, which Yuwen Song now presented with both hands.

The steward thought little of this small gift—many people arriving at the Huang residence today were here for free food and drinks, but the Huang residence was large and well-off, so a couple extra freeloaders wasn't an issue for them. However, they did separate the banquet-goers based on status, grouping them and assigning them to different areas. There were seats for those from the jianghu, as well as seats for scholars.

The Huang residence's steward had seen all sorts of people and had thus long developed a keen eye. When he saw the long weapon-shaped cloth bundle slung over Shen Qiao's back, he grew more cautious. "May I ask if this Daoist Master is from the jianghu?"

Yet Shen Qiao shook his head. "I only know a little martial arts—I can't be considered a man from the jianghu."

Seeing how extraordinary his demeanor was, the steward dared not classify him as an ordinary person. He also noticed that while Yuwen Song was young, he was similarly elegant and collected. Hence, he immediately had someone take them to where the scholars were seated.

Shen Qiao wasn't acquainted with the people at the banquet, but he was gentle and good-natured, as well as amicable to everyone. When the others saw his Daoist dress, they couldn't resist asking him about Daoist matters. After answering a couple of their questions, Shen Qiao was already friendly with the people around him, and he also knew that they were all illustrious scholars from the city, with some reputation among the scholar class. They too had come for Master Du's performance—their esteem was evident in their words.

The guests had yet to finish arriving, and the host was greeting them elsewhere. The atmosphere was fervent but a little noisy as the crowd quietly chatted among themselves, and Yuwen Song listened intently to the discussions of music around him. Shen Qiao involuntarily raised his head and caught a familiar silhouette out of the corner of his eye.

So familiar, in fact, that he couldn't resist making a noise of surprise.

87

Seeing Yan Wushi Again

THE PERSON SHEN QIAO saw was not just anyone, but the Fajing Sect Leader Guang Lingsan.

In the past, Riyue Sect had split into three, and Fajing Sect moved their operations to the distant lands of Tuyuhun. But as the current world was in turmoil, Guang Lingsan had interfered with the jianghu of the Central Plains several times—even participating in the ambush on Yan Wushi in order to secure a share of the spoils. That day, the moment the news of Yan Wushi's death began to spread, Fajing Sect's authority immediately began to expand eastward. They quickly replaced the influence Huanyue Sect held in Zhou near the borders of Tuyuhun, solidifying their own power at the same time.

Speaking truthfully, Shen Qiao didn't have too many dealings with this Fajing Sect Leader, but as he was a fairly special man, being the head of a sect, it was hard not to notice him. However, as Guang Lingsan rarely made any public appearances in the jianghu, few people around him recognized who he was. The man simply drifted past the crowd beneath the colonnades, dressed in his wide sleeved robes, just like an utterly ordinary guest taking a stroll.

Shen Qiao instructed Yuwen Song to sit still and not move, then rose from his seat, walking in the direction where Guang Lingsan had vanished.

Though Shen Qiao looked like he was idly strolling, he was actually crossing vast distances as if they were mere inches, like he was traipsing on clouds—elegant and otherworldly, leaving behind nary a trace. The Huang residence maid passing by him had the feeling someone was there, but by the time she turned her head, Shen Qiao had completely left her field of vision.

Only someone who had trained "A Rainbow Stretches Across the Heavens" to transcendent perfection could manifest Xuandu Mountain's qinggong to such an amazing level.

Though Guang Lingsan also looked like he was on a carefree stroll, he too was walking at a very swift pace. Shen Qiao turned a corner and arrived at a fork that split into three: one led toward the main courtyard, another to a scenic cobblestone path that was part of the garden, and the last to a pond in the backyard. The Huang residence covered a good deal of land in Runan, and the area ahead was surrounded by rockwork, which blocked the view. Guang Lingsan had already disappeared from sight, making it hard to determine which path he'd taken right away.

Shen Qiao stood in place and pondered for a moment. Then he gave up on taking the middle path, which held the highest chance of finding Guang Lingsan, and instead picked the last one.

The Huangs were a powerful local family. This garden was attached to a building next door, originally where the host would serve guests. Normally, people were free to go anywhere they wished, but as the host might still have live-in guests to serve, most people wouldn't charge into the backyard.

As Shen Qiao walked toward the pond, keeping his footsteps and breathing as quiet as possible, he suddenly heard the faint murmurs of conversation from afar. One of the voices caused his heart to sink heavily, as if he'd received a harsh blow. Even his breathing became harried and disordered for a moment.

It was only for a moment—an average martial artist wouldn't have detected such subtle changes, but that didn't hold for experts who'd climbed past a certain level. Upon entering any environment, they'd be able to sense the movement of qi within their surroundings, to the point that they could even affect it by mobilizing their own true qi. The slightest disturbance was enough for them to immediately realize that something was off.

A leaf shot toward Shen Qiao, its caster unknown. It sliced through the air with incredible speed, but without a sound. Any martial artist who was even a little mediocre wouldn't have been able to react before it reached them. But fortunately, it seemed like the attacker hadn't wanted to kill anyone while at the Huang residence—it only swept past Shen Qiao's hair, obviously meant as a warning.

If the target had been a manor servant or even an average practitioner, they'd involuntarily gasp in shock and dodge backward. Or perhaps they'd rush to flee, knowing that their skills were inferior. In any case, they'd definitely make some noise.

Guang Lingsan had assessed that this was but a trifling Huang family birthday banquet—thus the practitioners who'd arrived were also mediocre, without any standout characters. However, not even the slightest whisper followed this leaf of his, as if it were a stone sinking silently into the ocean. That was strange.

He couldn't help but jolt, wondering if there was someone incredible here after all, a crouching tiger or hidden dragon. To think that a grandmaster-level expert unknown to him would appear here...

"Which venerable gentleman has graced this place, who somehow doesn't know to 'hear no evil, see no evil?' It's rude to eavesdrop."

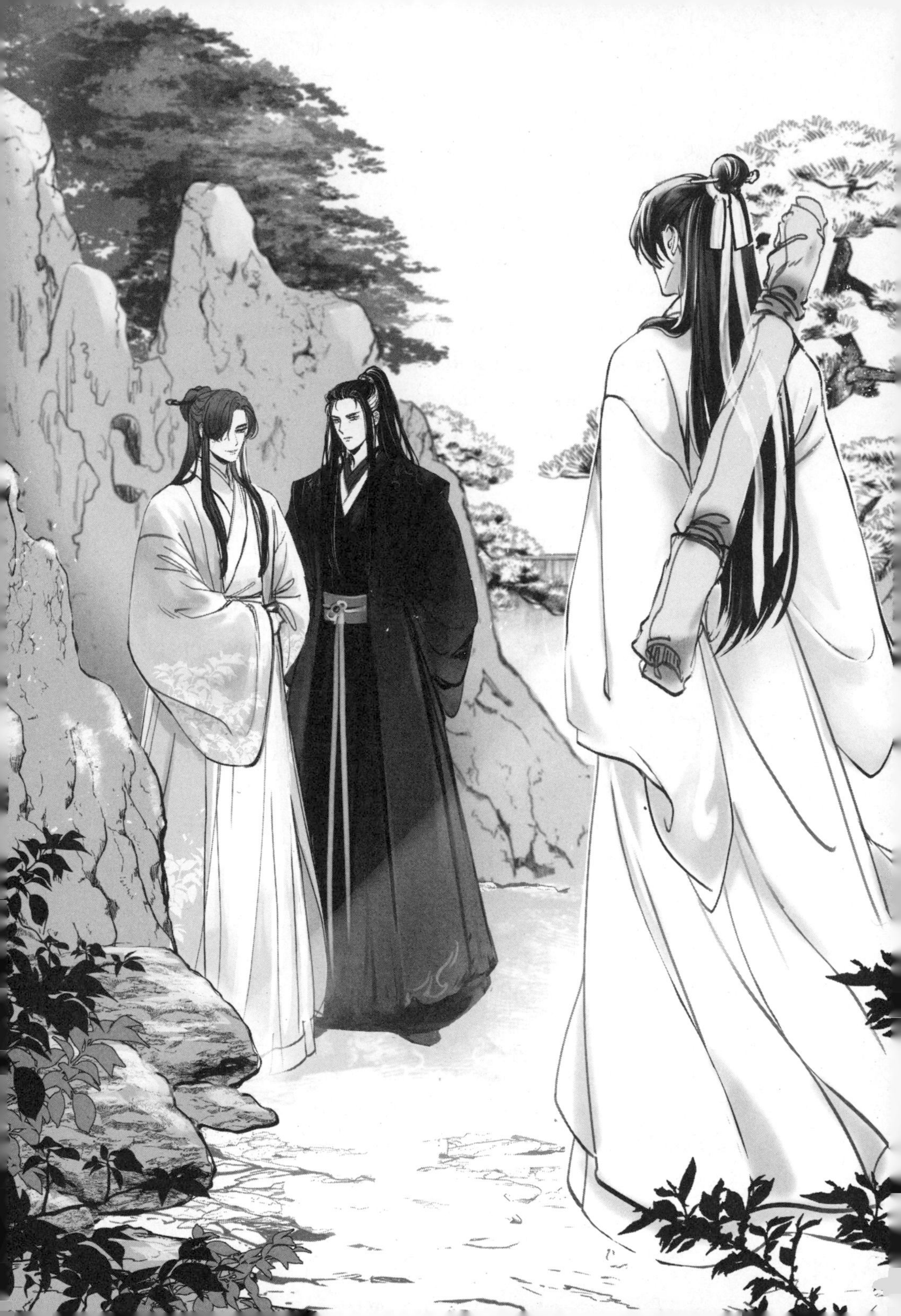

Guang Lingsan's voice was bright and clear as he slowly stepped out. Now that the rockery was no longer blocking his line of sight, the man behind it also came into view.

He'd barely finished speaking when a look of surprise crossed his face. Although it lasted only an instant, it was enough.

"So, it was Daoist Master Shen." They'd parted on unpleasant terms last time, but now that they'd met each other again, Guang Lingsan wore a smile as before, as if it had never happened.

Yet Shen Qiao's attention wasn't on him but on the man next to him.

For the person standing next to Guang Lingsan was none other than Yan Wushi.

He stood with his hands clasped behind his back, his temples peppered with white. His countenance shone like jade, and there was a faint smile at the corner of his lips, his imperiousness apparent. Just like when they'd first met.

Even at Yan Wushi's most downtrodden, Shen Qiao had never seen even the slightest hint of mental collapse from him. His self-confidence and conceit were obvious, and he'd always been this way.

Since Yan Wushi had lured away Sang Jingxing when they'd parted at the broken-down temple and Shen Qiao had headed to Chang'an alone, over four months had passed, and much had happened.

Four months was neither particularly long nor particularly short. For a martial artist, a single day-night cycle could be enough for a breakthrough. However, if they couldn't make any progress, then even years and decades would be nothing to them.

Yan Wushi had always been a martial arts genius. Having obtained three volumes of the *Zhuyang Strategy,* including the one related to the demonic discipline, he'd told Shen Qiao before that he already knew how to repair the flaw in his demonic core. It wasn't inconceivable for him to show up, four months later, as healthy and whole as he'd been in the beginning.

But a question remained: that night, his martial arts had yet to recover, so how exactly had he managed to escape danger at Sang Jingxing's hands?

And Guang Lingsan was one of the five martial experts who'd ambushed him—he'd even played a crucial role—one could say that he'd been directly responsible for aggravating Yan Wushi's flaw and was the ringleader who'd ultimately caused his defeat. So why was Yan Wushi with him?

Furthermore, the two of them seemed to be chatting; they were smiling, painting a rather harmonious picture, even. It didn't seem at all like they could draw their swords on each other with one wrong word.

Shen Qiao's heart was heavy with doubts. For a moment, he wasn't sure which he should do first: ask Yan Wushi if he'd fully recovered or deal with Guang Lingsan.

Seeing his reaction, Guang Lingsan smiled. "Looks like Daoist Master Shen is confused that I've shown up here at this time?"

Shen Qiao pulled himself together. The moment Yan Wushi had appeared, his mind had all but fallen into chaos, shaking his Daoist core. So he took this moment in the conversation to settle his emotions, then said, "The Huang family's banquet is open to everyone, so it's natural that Sect Leader Guang has come as well. This humble Daoist isn't the host—of course he has no right to intervene. But he wishes to know why Sect Leader Yan is also here."

Guang Lingsan looked at Yan Wushi, then said with a smile, "Shouldn't you give Daoist Master Shen an explanation, Sect Leader Yan?"

However, Yan Wushi gave a slight sneer. "Who is this? Is he someone my venerable self must know?"

It was as if a basin of frigid water had been thrown over his head—Shen Qiao's heart instantly became ice cold.

He scrutinized Yan Wushi carefully. Not only was his lack of recognition plain on Yan Wushi's face, there wasn't a hint of familiarity hidden in the depths of his gaze. Shen Qiao didn't even see the sense of closeness expected of a reunion between old friends, let alone the joy of seeing someone after a long separation.

The man who'd smiled and sighed at the broken-down temple, calling him "Foolish A-Qiao" still seemed to stand before his eyes, and those words still seemed to linger in his ears.

Ever since they'd met at Banbu Peak, it was as though their fates were tightly bound by an invisible string.

If one said that Yan Wushi had saved Shen Qiao's life in the beginning, then, afterward, Shen Qiao too had risked his life to protect Yan Wushi several times. He'd pulled him back from the brink of death, yet Yan Wushi only considered him a tool, treating Shen Qiao without the slightest hint of sentimentality. He'd even pushed him into the flames himself, nearly causing Shen Qiao to suffer a calamity of calamities. On careful analysis, Yan Wushi was the one who owed Shen Qiao more, but matters of the heart couldn't be treated like transactions—they couldn't be weighed and calculated so clearly. After repeated entanglements, past kindnesses and grudges had all blurred together, impossible to delineate.

That is, up until that moment in the broken-down temple, where Yan Wushi had placed him within the buddha statue, then drawn Sang Jingxing away by himself.

Then everything seemed to change.

But right now, the man he'd been unable to find had suddenly appeared before him, and he was even fraternizing with an enemy.

Exactly what had happened since then?

It shouldn't have been like this.

It shouldn't have been like this...

These words sounded several times in Shen Qiao's heart, and he suddenly recalled when the other man had first awoken after his grave injuries and entered qi deviation. He felt even more certain in his judgment: Yan Wushi had probably yet to fully recover, and his personality had changed drastically again, causing him to lose his memories. Guang Lingsan had taken this chance to get close to him, and he must have said something to make Yan Wushi trust him.

But even when met with such an unexpected incident, Shen Qiao was able to quickly calm himself, then begin pondering the most appropriate strategy of response.

"Sect Leader Yan's memory is quite terrible," he said. "To think he's even forgotten his own savior?"

"Savior?" Yan Wushi's tone was full of mockery. "My venerable self would like to see what you're made of, that you dare proclaim yourself my savior!"

As he spoke, his figure flitted forward, and he clawed at Shen Qiao with lightning speed.

A martial artist's every movement, every word, would all reflect their prowess. Yan Wushi didn't underestimate Shen Qiao—he put around six to seven-tenths of his full strength into this palm strike. Even if his opponent's skill was comparable to his own, he'd still be forced to draw his sword and meet him accordingly.

But Shen Qiao was already prepared. He was unwilling to fight Yan Wushi in front of Guang Lingsan, much less fight him at someone else's house. He instantly flew back several yards, then floated back around the rockery. His figure flitted about, feather-light and lovely, as if he were a piece of drifting duckweed. Seeing such a display of qinggong, not only was Yan Wushi a bit surprised, even Guang Lingsan couldn't help but shout in praise.

"Very few in this world can match Daoist Master Shen's qinggong, I believe! 'A Rainbow Stretches Across the Heavens!' Truly outstanding! Xuandu Mountain has indeed earned its reputation!"

"Sect Leader Guang is too kind." Shen Qiao's expression was cool. "This is the Huang residence, and this humble Daoist is only here as a guest. It wouldn't be right to stir up trouble at someone else's birthday celebration. If Sect Leader Yan wishes to fight, please set another time and place. This Daoist would be pleased to keep you company then."

"That's true," said Guang Lingsan with a smile. "Though there's no one here, it'd be far too unsightly to disturb the hosting family. Wushi, since Daoist Master Shen wishes to reminisce with you, why not set a new time?"

Shen Qiao's eyes twitched.

Yan Wushi sneered. "My venerable self doesn't even know him. Why should I meet with him to reminisce? If everyone used this excuse to come knocking, does that mean I'd have to keep each and every one of them company? While his qinggong is decent enough, his internal energy is completely average, supported only by a couple of sword techniques. He'd lose to me within a hundred blows. Why should my venerable self give this kind of opponent a second glance when a single one is enough to see through him completely?"

These words truly elicited a sense of déjà vu. Shen Qiao recalled what he'd said that day: "My venerable self doesn't need friends. Only one kind of person is qualified to stand as my equal: an opponent."

Shen Qiao realized that now, no matter how awful of a situation he found himself in, he too had learned the art of self-deprecation and mockery.

"If you don't fight me, how can you know that I'm beneath you?" he asked Yan Wushi.

His desire to provoke Yan Wushi into a duel was all for the purpose of finding a chance to be alone with him, to warn him that Guang Lingsan was a foe, not a friend.

Unfortunately, Yan Wushi couldn't be bothered to spare him another glance. He said to Guang Lingsan, "I was already growing impatient with staying here. You're the one who insisted on coming to listen to music."

Guang Lingsan was all smiles. He didn't refute him. "Yes, it's my fault."

"Go listen by yourself," said Yan Wushi. "Come find me after you're done. You know where I'll be."

"All right," said Guang Lingsan. "Then you can leave first; I won't see you off."

The two of them seemed familiar with each other, yet also like strangers. Shen Qiao, wholly unable to intervene, could only watch from the side, completely superfluous.

Teaching a Disciple

DU YUN'S MUSIC was indeed extraordinary. The notes of his lute reverberated within the Huang residence and, in an instant, even the birds flying overhead seemed to stop and listen. The lively Huang residence suddenly quieted down as all noise of conversation vanished. Only the scant notes of the lute remained, drifting about the rafters.

Yuwen Song had grown up living a luxurious life, which had left its mark. Combined with his outstanding gifts, his appreciation for music went far beyond that of others his age. At this time, he was fully immersed in the music with his entire being, all the way until the performance finished and Shen Qiao sat down by his side. Only then did he return to himself.

"You're back?" Yuwen Song noticed that Shen Qiao's expression was a bit off, and he couldn't help but ask, "What's wrong? Did your esteemed self see something?"

Shen Qiao frowned slightly. "I met an old acquaintance, but it seems that he's completely forgotten me."

"A friend?" asked Yuwen Song.

Shen Qiao smiled. "Rather than a friend, he's more like a foe."

"Did your esteemed self fight him?"

"No," said Shen Qiao. "He's insolent and arrogant by nature, and he usually does as he wishes. He can switch between good and evil without a second thought. At first he saved me, but then he threw me into the hands of an enemy."

"Ah," said Yuwen Song. "Then, have you sought revenge on him yet?"

Shen Qiao shook his head. "Afterward, out of happenstance, he and I again spent some time in each other's company. Once, he ran into a common enemy, and he sealed my acupoints before hiding me in a safe place, then went to meet the danger himself, luring away the enemy who presented the greatest threat to us."

Yuwen Song was perplexed. "He doesn't sound too evil, then? So why would he ignore you now?"

He was still young, after all. Regardless of how mature his speech was, there was a limit to his experiences, and so his words carried a slight hint of childishness.

Shen Qiao thought this amusing and patted his head. "I don't know either. Perhaps some things are better left unknown."

After these last couple of exchanges, a good amount of his confusion and disappointment had faded as well.

Yuwen Song took the initiative to ask, "Shall we leave, Daoist Master?"

Originally, Shen Qiao had thought that since the Huang residence was a prosperous household and the image of luxury, Yuwen Song would have been nostalgic for this kind of environment, being from the royal family himself. He didn't expect that the child had truly only come for the music, without any other thoughts.

"The banquet has already begun, and we've presented our gift, so no one can say we came empty-handed," Shen Qiao said. "The delicacies and wine here might not compare to what's in the palace, but it should be many times better than what's at the inn. Don't you want to eat before leaving?"

Yuwen Song shook his head. "There are too many guests here. An oversensitive person might grow suspicious. I was already indulging myself by coming here to listen—you've indulged me so much, and I can't keep recklessly taking advantage of it."

As he said this, he once again seemed to stop being an ordinary child. Shen Qiao knew that the deaths of the entire Qi residence had been a heavy blow to him. Ever since they left the capital, Yuwen Song had remained vigilant and wary, his every word and action exceedingly careful. He avoided talking to strangers as much as possible. Coming to listen to this performance could already be considered one of his most "excessive" requests for the entire journey.

Shen Qiao recalled the chance encounter just now. Guang Lingsan probably hadn't shown up just for Shen Qiao, but he knew that Shen Qiao was here now. If he wished to investigate further, it'd be easy for him to discover Yuwen Song.

Guang Lingsan ranked as one of the world's top ten martial artists. His martial prowess itself wasn't particularly outstanding among the top ten—rather, it was his identity as the leader of Fajing Sect that earned him a seat. But Shen Qiao knew that he absolutely couldn't underestimate any member of the demonic sects. Demonic practitioners were demonic practitioners precisely because they never showed their full selves to outsiders. They'd use layer upon layer of crafty tactics, unpredictable and inscrutable. Regardless of one's martial skill, it was easy to fall into their trap the moment one became careless.

Though Yuwen Song was of little use to Guang Lingsan, who knew if the man would do something on a passing caprice? On top of that, there was Yan Wushi...

Shen Qiao nodded. "Very well. Let us go then. It's still early—we should still be able to order something when we get back to the inn."

They'd come to the birthday banquet, but they'd failed to manage a meal and had only gotten to hear music. It was simply too strange in the eyes of others. The concierge was shocked at their swift return.

However, Shen Qiao had no intention of explaining any details to him. The two ordered some food to eat in their room: three side dishes and one soup. Compared to what Yuwen Song had once eaten, it was really too humble, and the taste naturally couldn't compare to the dishes of the royal chefs. But Yuwen Song understood very well the situation he was in—he hadn't so much as uttered half a complaint the entire journey. Seeing this, Shen Qiao was of course even more pleased, and even began to contemplate accepting him as a disciple.

Thinking of how Yuwen Song had just suffered through a huge change, and how his emotions were probably still immersed in the grief of losing his loved ones, Shen Qiao was in no rush to propose this to him. He was prepared to wait until Yuwen Song completely emerged from the shadows within his heart.

"Is there something on your mind, Daoist Master Shen?" Yuwen Song suddenly asked.

Shen Qiao said nothing about accepting disciples. "It's nothing," he said instead. "I was only thinking about the old acquaintance I met this afternoon."

"Is he important to you?" asked Yuwen Song.

"Why do you ask?"

"If he isn't, why do you keep thinking of him?"

Shen Qiao gave a light cough. "I'm not always thinking of him."

Yuwen Song didn't say anything, but the words "you clearly are" were written all over his face.

Shen Qiao suddenly felt like bringing up this topic had been most unwise. Even if he tried to argue and lay out his reasoning, it'd be pointless.

He was about to change the subject when Yuwen Song spoke in a consoling tone, "In truth, I think that this acquaintance of yours also considers you important."

Shen Qiao was caught between laughing and crying. He really wanted to say, "Let's not talk about this any further," but it was rare for Yuwen Song to earnestly discuss something with him, so he didn't want to smother his mood. He played along and asked, "Why do you think so?"

"My sixth elder brother—Liuxiong—and I were close in age," said Yuwen Song. "We did everything together, whether it was studying, eating, or sleeping. But since he was older, he would always mess with me. Once, he even told me that there was a tree with phoenix eggs and tricked me into climbing it. I couldn't get down, and he stood beneath it and laughed at me."

Shen Qiao thought this amusing. "How old were you then? With how bright you are, I can't imagine you getting tricked."

Yuwen Song's fair and tender face tinted a soft red. It was unclear if it was due to vexation or embarrassment. "I wouldn't have fallen for a normal trick, of course. But to make sure I believed him, he had someone create a resplendent model phoenix, then in the middle of the night, he made it fly past my room several times and land on the tree. He told me that a phoenix had come to our house to lay eggs. If it'd been only once or twice, I wouldn't have cared, but after it happened so many times, how could I not be fooled? If it were you, Daoist Master Shen, surely you'd want to investigate too, wouldn't you?"

Shen Qiao held back his laughter. "Yes, of course!"

"Afterward, I tattled on him to Father. But Father said Liuxiong acted like that because he loved me, and that those he didn't like wouldn't even get a second glance. I think, perhaps, your old acquaintance is the same, isn't he?"

Shen Qiao gave a wry smile. Coming from Yuwen Song, the unpredictable and inscrutable nature of human hearts became little more than a child's playtime.

"And you said he placed himself in danger for your sake," Yuwen Song added. "That proves that he cares about you even more, just like Liuxiong and me. Though he often bullied me, that day, he said to Mother that I was the youngest and so I had to leave first in order to preserve the Yuwen bloodline."

If it had been Shiwu instead, he would have definitely teared up at this point. But Yuwen Song's voice only grew a little heavier as his expression strained, and a solemn cast fell over his face.

He said quietly, "Right now, I wish so much that I could return to the past. It'd be fine if he messes with me every day. I only wish this was a dream, that the moment I wake up, they'd all return to life."

Shen Qiao was silent for a moment. He knew that Yuwen Song's mental maturity was far beyond the average child, so the normal words of comfort would do little for him.

"Do you know what the Three Talents are?" he asked.

"Heaven, Earth, and Man," said Yuwen Song.

"The Dao of Heaven: Yin and Yang. The Dao of Earth: Strength and Gentleness. Do you know what comes after?"

Yuwen Song nodded. "The Dao of Man: Benevolence and Righteousness."

"Correct," said Shen Qiao. "I didn't want to bring up the past, at first, in case it would arouse your grief. But since I've already mentioned it, I might as well prattle on a bit more. Daoists cultivate tranquility, but they also value karma and reciprocation—it's not unique to only Buddhism. Yuwen Yun's perverse actions caused your entire family to suffer unjust deaths. If you wish to seek revenge, not only will I not persuade you against it, I'll also teach you martial arts. However, I do not wish for this to consume your heart. Humans are humans because they possess wisdom—that's what differentiates them from beasts. No matter how good-natured a tiger or lion might be, the moment they're hungry, they must eat, and so they must kill. But when a human grows hungry, they can endure that hunger, and they know how to use various methods to keep themselves clothed and fed. This is the basis on which Man can rank among the Three Talents. Do you understand?"

Yuwen Song truly possessed comprehension beyond the ordinary. After a moment of silence, he nodded. "I understand. The Daoist Master hopes that I can throw away the burdens of the past to become someone great and indomitable. No matter how much I hate Yuwen Yun, I cannot become like him."

Shen Qiao was pleased. "Exactly. You truly are incredible. As expected of the most promising son of the Yuwen family!"

A rare bashfulness surfaced on Yuwen Song's face. "Then, may I learn martial arts from you?"

Shen Qiao laughed. "Of course you can. My sect accepts disciples based on two things: first, their moral character, and second, their aptitude. Even if their aptitude doesn't stand out, being honest and upright is enough. Furthermore, your aptitude is exceptional, and your physical qualities excellent—perfect for practicing martial arts."

Yuwen Song was delighted. He rose to his feet, wanting to acknowledge Shen Qiao as his master, but Shen Qiao stopped him. "No need to rush," he said. "We can hold an official ceremony once I bring you back to Bixia Sect. It won't be too late then, and it'll have more gravitas as well."

Of course, Yuwen Song had no objections. This one conversation with Shen Qiao had resolved many of the troubles plaguing his heart. That night, he slept soundly, sinking into dreams the moment his head hit the pillow.

Instead, it was Shen Qiao who couldn't stop his fluctuating emotions when he recalled those words. Even after meditating for a long time, he failed to completely enter the state of being one with the world.

By now, the wee hours of the night had already arrived. The bustling clamor of daytime had completely vanished, and the only sound was the ringing of the watchman's gong from beyond the window.

Now that he could neither sleep nor meditate, he didn't open his eyes either, but instead kept them closed, calming his mind and opening his senses. He keenly felt as if his entire surroundings were melding into each breath he took.

Then he suddenly opened his eyes and rose, drifting toward the window. He moved swiftly, with nary a whisper. Even if Yuwen Song had been lying awake instead of fast asleep, he wouldn't have realized that the man beside him was already gone without personally seeing him leave.

At this time, the windows were only half-open—leaving through them would be quite difficult. But Shen Qiao was like a ghost: one instant he was stretching his torso outside the window, and the next his figure was already sliding along the inn's outer walls as he flitted onto the roof.

Sure enough, on the roof, right above and across from their room, stood a man.

He was dressed entirely in black, and he wore a veiled hat, concealing his face from view.

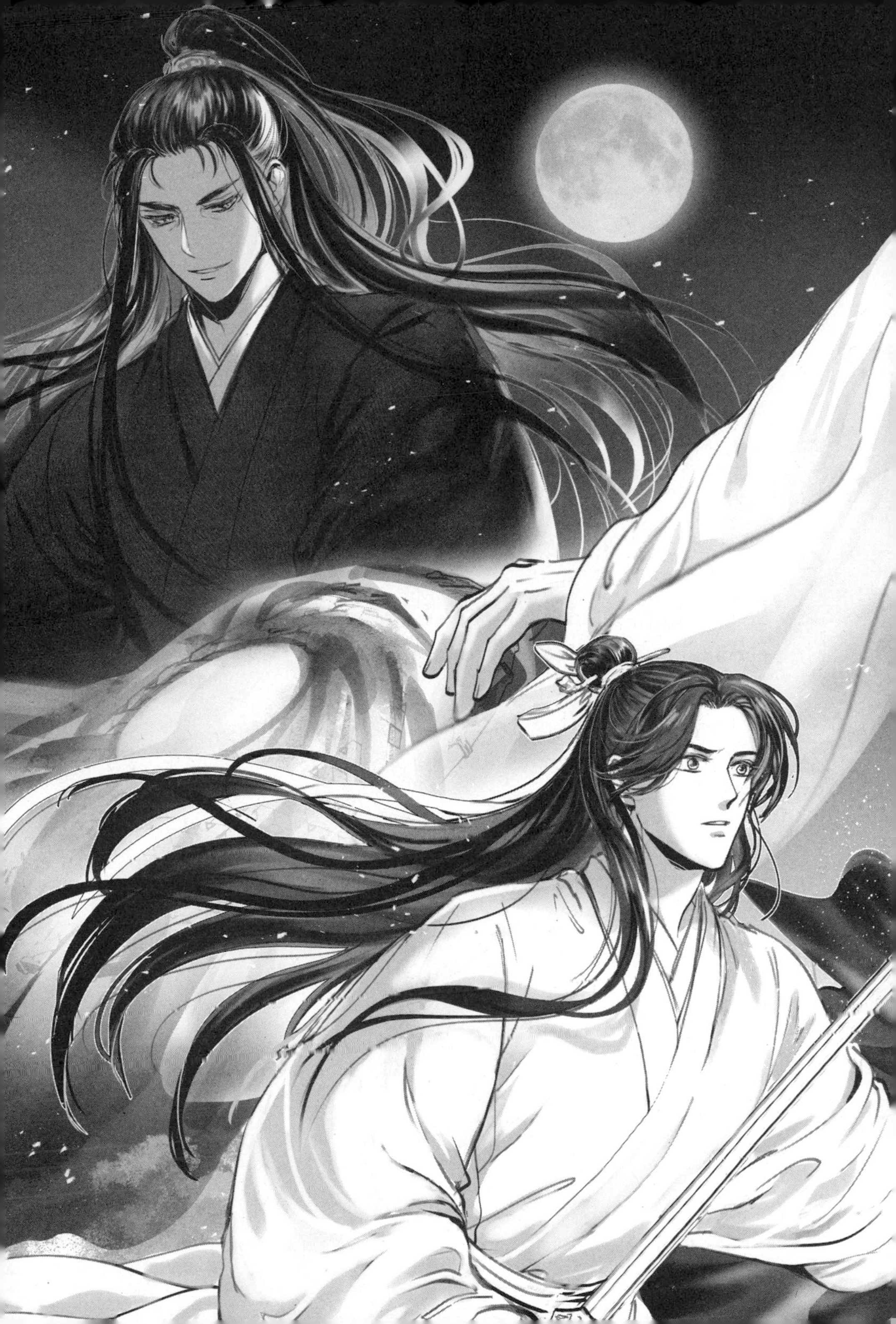

89

Listening in to a Late-Night Show

"IF THIS DISTINGUISHED MASTER is only stopping by," said Shen Qiao, "I must ask you to go somewhere else."

Though the other party didn't reveal his face, his figure appeared somewhat familiar. However, Shen Qiao couldn't be certain whether he really was that person.

He once heard Yan Wushi mention certain rules of the jianghu: When traveling outside, robbers would inevitably appear at night. They'd hide on inn rooftops and target guests, waiting for a chance to strike. Perhaps to steal money, or perhaps for another reason altogether. At this point, guests from sects ought to declare which one they were from. If the thief saw that their target was a powerful martial artist, or came from a prestigious background, they'd usually be too afraid to attack.

Shen Qiao had already displayed his qinggong. Anyone with eyes should be able to see that he was a fearsome martial artist and have second thoughts about offending him.

But the other party didn't speak—didn't even wait for Shen Qiao to finish before he suddenly struck.

His movements were profoundly gentle, as if he were only plucking flowers or willow branches, but it wasn't the Spring Waters finger technique that Shen Qiao expected. The blast from that palm was light and airy, yet halfway through it suddenly transformed, now bone-chillingly severe as it swept toward his face.

With a furl of his sleeve, Shen Qiao negated the palm strike, but the other man suddenly flashed forward, reappearing before him. His right hand struck at a key acupoint on Shen Qiao's wrist, and the left made a grab for Shen Qiao's neck.

Shen Qiao didn't retreat but advanced instead. His sleeves flapped outward like waves crashing upon the shore, and he sent a heavy strike at his opponent's left hand. Meanwhile, his own left hand nimbly turned itself over, slipping out of the other's grasping range, then grabbed for the man instead.

"Yan Wushi?" he ventured, if only because those hands looked somewhat familiar. The martial arts, however, were completely different.

The man in black still didn't answer. Instead, he made another soundless strike, but it didn't seem like he wanted to kill Shen Qiao— rather than fighting, it was more like the two of them were sparring.

Even if it was only a spar, every move was expertly executed and profound.

The current Shen Qiao was already extensively experienced—at least, he possessed an understanding of the martial arts from the various sects. For a martial artist of his level, if he'd seen moves that were similar in style, he'd recall them completely. But this black-clad man's movements were an utter mystery—one move would seem like it came from Qingcheng Mountain's Chunyang Monastery, but then his next would appear in the style of the demonic sects. Shen Qiao found himself at a loss.

Some powerful martial artists might not care for battle, but any who were willing to chase after goals on the martial path would possess a love for the arts themselves. No matter how uncompetitive or indifferent to reputation Shen Qiao was, he couldn't resist the thrill of excitement upon seeing an unknown yet equally matched opponent, and he was itching to duel him.

Having gained so much experience while in the jianghu, he no longer dropped his guard so easily. He was also wary that the opponent might be trying to draw him away from the inn, to target Yuwen Song while he slept in the room.

Once someone attained a certain level of martial prowess, they could determine a person's location just by the sound of their breathing, and Shen Qiao possessed this ability. Though he was currently fighting this man, he kept a sliver of his attention on Yuwen Song, and he could tell that the boy was still sleeping as soundly as before, completely unaware of the fight taking place on the roof.

They'd exchanged several blows, but neither side had used their full strength. His opponent's goal was unclear, and his moves only grew more varied, innovative, and unpredictable. Shen Qiao took the opportunity of an opening to grab at his hat, and his fingers caught the black veil, thus exposing the man's face.

It really was Yan Wushi!

"Sect Leader Yan?" Shen Qiao frowned. "What are you doing here?"

"A-Qiao, you're so callous," said Yan Wushi. "I almost died against Sang Jingxing for you, and yet the first thing you say is a frosty 'Sect Leader Yan?'" His voice was teasing and full of laughter. There was no trace of the estrangement he'd demonstrated earlier in the day.

"You remember everything?" With their meeting that day, Shen Qiao had already mentally prepared himself for Yan Wushi losing all his memories. To think that the man would be exactly the same as before upon opening his mouth! He couldn't help but pause in his astonishment, his movements also halting.

And with this slight pause, Yan Wushi's finger had already struck his shoulder, and Shen Qiao fell limply into Yan Wushi's outstretched arms.

"Shh!" Smiling, Yan Wushi made a gesture, telling him to be quiet. "No need to worry. I'm just bringing you elsewhere."

Before Shen Qiao could react, Yan Wushi also struck his mute acupoint. His use of the Spring Waters finger technique was incomparably dexterous—there was no sign that he'd suffered any decline in martial arts.

Shen Qiao thought that he'd been quite watchful, yet somehow he'd been tricked anyway. Before he could drive himself to frustration, Yan Wushi had already picked him up in a bridal carry and leapt off the inn's roof. His figure fell and rose, elegant and strong, his black clothes melding into the night. Carrying a second person didn't slow him down in the slightest.

Yuwen Song was still back at the inn...

Shen Qiao couldn't speak, but Yan Wushi seemed to guess his thoughts. "The Yuwen family has nothing to worry about now that Yuwen Xian's gone. Yuwen Yun is the only one who wishes to slaughter them all; no one else will care about a single Yuwen-qilang. It might have been different right after Yuwen Xian's death, but to travel thousands of miles and drag him back at this point? It's pointless."

These words implied that Yuwen Song was safe.

Upon hearing this, Shen Qiao knew that Yan Wushi had never lost his memories in the first place, let alone undergone any personality shifts. But he had no idea what had happened in between. Why had he been talking and laughing with Guang Lingsan? Shen Qiao's many doubts hadn't vanished with Yan Wushi's reappearance— if anything, they'd increased.

Yan Wushi had no intention of explaining—at least, not right now. He carried Shen Qiao as he flew from rooftop to rooftop. Before long, the inn was far behind them.

Though his body couldn't move, Shen Qiao's vision was still fine. He suddenly realized that Yan Wushi's destination seemed to be the Huang residence they'd been at earlier in the day.

"We're going to see a fun show," said Yan Wushi. "However, you're not to move, else I won't bring you out to play again." His voice was light; it sounded more like he was coaxing a child.

Regardless of how good-natured Shen Qiao was, he couldn't resist internally rolling his eyes.

The Huang household wasn't a poor, humble family—guards were patrolling, both within the gates and without. However, their martial abilities were naturally insufficient to discover Yan Wushi, and he might as well have been carrying Shen Qiao through a public square— no different than if he'd been strolling around his own backyard.

Shen Qiao noticed that the place he'd landed seemed to be the back garden where they'd thrown the birthday banquet earlier. Shen Qiao had encountered Guang Lingsan and Yan Wushi around the rockery. In order to reach this yard, one had to loop around the rockery first, so they should be near the yard's pond.

Unlike before, Yan Wushi didn't stop on the rooftop—instead he chose a spot near the pond with dense vegetation, which happened to be in a blind spot around a turn in the walls. The cover provided by the shadows of the colonnades and leaves helped conceal their figures completely, and with their martial prowess, they could easily adjust their breathing. There was little worry of them being discovered.

The building near the wall they were pressed against was lit by candlelight. The faint, flickering glow poured out through the cracks in the window, accompanied by the scattered sounds of conversation.

Shen Qiao had no idea why Yan Wushi had brought him here to eavesdrop. Even after they'd waited a while, the man appeared to have no intentions of unsealing his acupoints, so he could only prick his ears to listen to the sounds within that room.

The conversation was very quiet, but by using his true qi, he could still hear a little.

One person was panting harshly, their breaths interspersed with the occasional teasing word.

Another person moaned, their voice sweet and fawning.

It was true that Shen Qiao had no experience when it came to romance between men and women, but even someone who'd never eaten pork would still know the word "pig." Hearing these noises, of course he knew what they were doing.

Daoism extolled a life of purity and integrity, but if one wanted to pair cultivate, there were Daoist methods for it. There was no outright ban, making it different from Buddhism, which enforced both abstinence and vegetarianism. However, knowing about it was one thing; actually listening to people rolling about in bed was another. Perhaps some people would enjoy eavesdropping on the lovemaking of others, but Shen Qiao was a modest and upright gentleman. He was instantly uncomfortable and longed to burst his acupoints open right then and run.

As if he'd noticed Shen Qiao's thoughts, Yan Wushi sealed two more key acupoints on his back, utterly laying waste to Daoist Master Shen's plan.

Shen Qiao would have had nothing to say even if he'd been able to speak.

"Only an immoral man will see immoral things," said Yan Wushi, using the Sound Transmission technique, "while the pure will remain pure. Don't you know that, Daoist Master Shen?"

His tone was leisurely, leaving Shen Qiao speechless.

At this moment, the couple were in the throes of passion. The woman was completely bare, reclining on her back with her legs wrapped around the man's waist. Her soft and pliant body delighted the man so much he was loath to let go, and he quickened his pace.

"Yun-niang, Yun-niang..." The man repeated the nickname of the woman below him, his body soaked in sweat from his vigorous thrusts. Panting ceaselessly, he teased her in a rough voice: "Though you're a little older than me, I couldn't have imagined how arresting you are without your clothes. If only I'd known earlier..."

Since Shen Qiao's acupoints were sealed, rendering him completely immobile, he could only steel himself and continue listening. Yan Wushi had placed him by the wall, while he himself stood behind him, holding him up, supporting what seemed to be most of Shen Qiao's weight. But even as the lovemaking continued within the building, Yan Wushi didn't stay still either. The arm holding Shen Qiao slowly began to wander, and he even whispered in Shen Qiao's ear, "A-Qiao, I don't see how she's so arresting. She's only average. If anything, you have a waist more slender than hers..."

Spring nights were crisp, but Shen Qiao's internal energy had slowly recovered, and he no longer feared the cold as before, so he only wore a single Daoist robe. Right now, separated only by a thin layer of fabric, Yan Wushi's body heat was searing hot. It almost felt like it was pressed right to his skin.

"A-Qiao, you're shivering," Yan Wushi said, mouth against his ear. "Are you wearing too little?" Laughter laced his tone, and he had almost trapped Shen Qiao within his arms.

I'll stop shivering if you let go! Shen Qiao raged internally. He didn't know whether it was due to shameful anger or embarrassment, but his face also grew increasingly warm.

The conversation within the building continued.

"What would have happened if you'd known earlier?" The woman's voice was a little hoarse, but it only added a touch of charm.

"If I'd known earlier, I'd have dragged you into bed sooner!" The man laughed, gloating. "Is your Guild Leader Dou as skilled as I am in bed?"

The moment he heard the words "Guild Leader Dou," Shen Qiao jerked to attention. He paid no further heed to Yan Wushi's provocations and focused all his energies on listening to them talk. Yan Wushi silently lamented this, but his teasing ceased.

The woman was displeased. "Enough with that nonsense. There's nothing between him and me. If not for the rapport we shared, why would I do this with you? What kind of trash do you take me for? Do you think the lofty deputy leader of the Liuhe Guild is so eager to humiliate herself?!"

The Liuhe Guild's deputy leader, Yun Fuyi!

Shen Qiao had already thought this woman's voice sounded familiar, but he'd been unable to recall it. It was only when she spoke her own title that he saw the light.

Was this not Yun Fuyi, whom he'd met once before at Chuyun Temple?

When the man heard the subtle anger within her voice, he quickly smiled apologetically. "I misspoke, I misspoke. Don't be angry! My love for you is sincere!"

After this brief interlude, the building was once again filled with sounds of passion. Shen Qiao had no mind for embarrassment— he replayed their conversation in his mind.

The man's voice sounded fairly young—he definitely wasn't the Master Huang who'd thrown the birthday banquet earlier today. Perhaps he was from the second generation, or even the third.

The Huang household was wealthy and could be considered a famous noble family in the area, but by the standards of the jianghu, they were only average, their martial arts mediocre. Why would Yun Fuyi show up here and involve herself with them?

Regardless, Yan Wushi couldn't have brought him to this wall to eavesdrop for this long, just so Shen Qiao could witness the passion between a couple in love.

But Yan Wushi didn't give him much time to think—once again, he picked Shen Qiao up by the waist, then took him around the garden. They passed through the rockery and arrived at the cookhouse within the yard.

Naturally, as it was the middle of the night, it was silent. There was neither smoke nor the aroma of food. In fact, other than the couple from earlier who'd snuck into the garden for their affair, the members of the Huang household mostly stayed in a neighboring manor, which had its own kitchen. The master of the house and his female servants also had their own cooking areas while the food served at the banquet earlier had been ordered from inns. This kitchen was mostly for decoration, and few people visited.

Yan Wushi put Shen Qiao down and unsealed his acupoints, restoring his freedom. Of course, Shen Qiao didn't start yelling, nor did he make a run for it; by now he'd realized that Yan Wushi must have brought him here for something important. He followed him as he pushed open the door of the cookhouse and entered.

"Did you realize anything?" Yan Wushi suddenly asked without looking back.

Shen Qiao thought for a moment, then said, "Everything here is neatly put away. Seems like it's rarely used."

Yan Wushi shook his head. "If it's been a while since it was last used, with the windows shut so tightly, there should at least be some dust. But there isn't even a speck of it. Don't you find that strange?"

Shen Qiao realized he was right. "That's true. So that means people must come here often?"

"Correct," said Yan Wushi.

He approached the stove and effortlessly lifted the iron pan. There was no wood-burning stovetop beneath but instead a pitch-black hole—an entrance.

Yan Wushi vaulted up the stove and into the hole. Shen Qiao followed closely, his hands braced against the stone wall. Initially, he'd thought that this would be a long, deep tunnel, but he unexpectedly hit the ground right after leaping in. Looking at the room below, it seemed to be a cellar, but there were no stairs.

The glow of fire flickered to life—it was the torch in Yan Wushi's hand.

Shen Qiao looked around, his expression shifting to surprise despite himself. This hidden room wasn't very large; at most it was the size of a main hall. However, other than the one they'd entered against, the remaining three walls were lined with weapon after weapon, all neatly arranged. There were spears, sabers, and bows and arrows. An expert could tell at a glance that these weapons had been forged from high-quality woods and metals. Roughly estimating, there were around one to two thousand weapons here in total. No matter how wealthy the Huang family was and how many guards they employed, this was far beyond what they needed. It would have been excessive even if they were used to lay siege to this city.

Shen Qiao couldn't help but ask, "The Huang family wishes to revolt?"

Yan Wushi didn't answer his question. Instead, he said, "The man who was together with Yun Fuyi is called Huang Gefei. He's Huang

Xidao's second son. The eldest son is sickly, so this second son is likely to succeed the family."

The two of them followed their original tracks out of the room and returned the iron pan to its original spot. It was as if they'd never been here; nothing was out of place.

The two of them walked toward the inn after leaving the Huang residence. Runan had a curfew in place, but this meant nothing to the two of them—they naturally had many ways to avoid the night patrols.

Yan Wushi chuckled. "A-Qiao, I can see from your face that you're bursting with questions."

Shen Qiao indeed had many questions, all intertwined with each other like tangled silk threads, impossible to separate. He could only start from his simplest, most pressing one.

"How did you escape Sang Jingxing that day?"

"I never fought Sang Jingxing that day," said Yan Wushi.

Shen Qiao thought, *Don't tell me that he lied to me back then?*

Yan Wushi seemed to realize what he was thinking. "I didn't lie to you. Before I took you to that broken-down temple, I contacted Guang Lingsan to tell him that I wished to make a deal with him."

He purposely paused. Shen Qiao was no fool, just a bit slow when it came to figuring out schemes. Now he followed Yan Wushi's train of thought and found the answer. "The *Zhuyang Strategy* scroll?"

It was simple. Since the *Fenglin Scriptures* contained a flaw, anyone cultivating from the book would run into the same obstacle. That was why Yan Wushi had wanted the scroll, Hehuan Sect had eyed it covetously, and Fajing Sect too, naturally, could never let it slip by.

After Guang Lingsan had allied with four other martial artists to ambush Yan Wushi, one would expect a deep grudge between the two. But when human machinations were afoot, things could never be that simple. The three demonic sects kept each other in check, and so, with the threat named Sang Jingxing looming ahead, Yan Wushi had chosen to form a temporary alliance with Guang Lingsan. It was sensible.

Praise colored Yan Wushi's tone. "Indeed. I told him that if he was willing to help me out of this situation, I'd pass the entirety of the scroll's contents to him."

However, even if Yan Wushi had calculated correctly, he couldn't be certain that Guang Lingsan would arrive in time, or even if he'd show up as promised. Hence, he'd still chosen to go ahead by himself and leave Shen Qiao at the temple.

Although he didn't give Shen Qiao a direct answer, with this, Shen Qiao's doubts were resolved.

For some reason, when he received this answer, it felt like a weighty stone had been lifted from his heart, which was no longer suspended in midair.

Yan Wushi mocked him then. "Did you still doubt me, deep down inside? Did you think I'd abandoned you in order to escape?"

Of course, Shen Qiao would never admit that he'd wept at Yan Wushi's retreating back. "Sect Leader Yan has always been this way. This lowly Daoist dares not let down his guard."

Yan Wushi gave a scoffing laugh but didn't say anything else.

After thinking for a while, Shen Qiao brought up another question. "Demonic practitioners have always been mistrustful. Why would Guang Lingsan believe that you'd hand him the real thing and not something you'd scrambled or modified?"

"You've also read the scroll," said Yan Wushi. "You should still remember that it was only a commentary on Riyue Sect's various martial arts. Tao Honging wrote down his understanding of the demonic core's flaw but not any details on the martial arts themselves. All he did was offer several of his opinions on how to repair the flaw. Anyone familiar with Riyue Sect's martial arts would naturally be able to tell if the contents are complete or truthful. It's immensely difficult to tamper with."

Plainly speaking, no concrete martial arts were listed within the scroll—one couldn't cultivate with it. Each person would have to patch the flaw based on their own understanding. Whether or not they could make a breakthrough ultimately depended on their comprehension. Since it was a matter of life and death, even if there was only a strand of hope, Guang Lingsan still had to try. After all, no one would be willing to stagnate forever as a martial artist.

Shen Qiao nodded. "That's why you showed up at the Huang residence with Guang Lingsan?"

"I told him the scroll's contents," said Yan Wushi, "but as he can't trust me completely, he wanted to find Chen Gong's version and compare the two. During this time, I found a place and entered secluded cultivation, but I didn't expect that the moment I left, I'd hear that Yuwen Yong had already passed."

Shen Qiao sighed. "That's not all. The newly enthroned Emperor of Zhou unjustly slaughtered Yuwen Xian's entire family. Yuwen Song is the only one left."

Yan Wushi didn't seem the least bit surprised. He went on, "After Guang Lingsan verified the contents of the scroll, he met up with me and told me this news: the Huang family of Runan is raising a private army and secretly colluding with the Göktürks."

These were tumultuous times. One might sit on the throne today, but tomorrow, another would sit there instead—this wasn't anything new. Only in the last couple of decades had the situation in the world at large stabilized somewhat. It was no surprise that there were still people ambitious enough to rebel, wanting to be crowned king. However...

"Though Yuwen Yun's killing of talented ministers makes one's heart heavy, the foundation Yuwen Yong laid out for him still exists," said Shen Qiao. "Zhou has also just annexed Qi—they're at the peak of their power. These weapons of the Huang family can arm at most one or two thousand soldiers. Even if they can occupy Runan, I fear it'll still be useless."

Yan Wushi's expression was uncanny. "That's where you're wrong. The Huang family has no need to revolt. They're only the Göktürks' dogs; as long as the Göktürks toss them some scraps, they'll be able to gorge themselves endlessly."

Shen Qiao found himself uncomprehending and a bit perplexed. "Forgive this humble Daoist for being so slow."

"Now that Yuwen Yong is dead, the Göktürks have lost one of their greatest enemies," Yan Wushi explained. "They support the abolished royal family of Qi, planning to divide the north once again. Yuwen Yun completely lacks the ability to hold on to what his forefathers left him. Meanwhile, Runan has a potent military, who have always protected the rightful bloodline of Zhou. Now the Huang family need only stall Runan, and the imperial court would have their hands full. Especially since Yuwen Yun has already eradicated his capable generals, like Yuwen Xian. Under these circumstances, the Zhou Dynasty will be unable to stop Qi from reviving."

Shen Qiao thought, *Why are you so happy when the Zhou Dynasty is suffering misfortune?*

"Didn't you support Yuwen Xian's ascension to the throne before?" he asked. "Now he's gone, and Huanyue Sect's authority has been uprooted entirely. What are you going to do?"

Yan Wushi blinked at him. "My good A-Qiao, are you worried about my venerable self?"

Though his face didn't reveal his age, this man was already past forty, and he was still trying to act cute. It was really...

Too shameless.

Heartfelt Sincerity

SHEN QIAO WASN'T A GOOD LIAR, so he vacillated a while between the replies "yes" and "no" before finally shaking his head.

But this momentary pause was enough for Yan Wushi to know his real answer.

"Daoist Master Shen," he said. "There is one matter that puzzles this venerable one. He asks for enlightenment."

"...Please, go ahead." Shen Qiao had never heard him speak in such a grave and serious tone. For a moment he was almost terrified.

"Buddhism asserts that monks must not lie. Does Daoism have a similar teaching?"

Shen Qiao didn't understand what he was getting at, and he began pondering the question earnestly. "Daoism doesn't have restrictions as severe as those of Buddhism, but whether it's the three schools or just the average person, being truthful is a virtue for anyone with moral integrity."

"Then why did you shake your head when you were clearly worried about this venerable one?" said Yan Wushi curiously. "Does this not violate your principles? Daoist Master Shen, it seems you've learned all sorts of cunning after spending so long in secular society. If this continues, I fear that you'll soon be an expert at swindling and cheating others, even!"

He was messing with Shen Qiao. Seeing that he refused to respond, Yan Wushi knew he'd successfully ruffled Shen Qiao's feathers with his teasing. Finally satisfied enough to move on to proper topics, he said, "Yuwen Xian was the only descendant of the Zhou Dynasty qualified to inherit Yuwen Yong's mantle. If he became emperor, the Zhou Dynasty would have flourished for another twenty years. Unfortunately, Yuwen Yong was too short-sighted and didn't heed that advice. He insisted on passing the throne to his son and brought about the situation today."

"The father passes it to his son, and the son to the grandson," said Shen Qiao. "This is the cycle anyone with descendants inevitably falls into. If we take a look at history, any emperor with sons never considered passing it to his brother, no matter how talented or virtuous he was."

Yan Wushi sneered. "I used to think that Yuwen Yong was the exception, but it seems I overestimated him. With his unwillingness to pass the throne to Yuwen Xian, and Yuwen Xian's reluctance to scheme for it, the current situation makes complete sense. All it means is that the Yuwen clan's legacy will end here. With Yuwen Yun, the Zhou Dynasty has passed its peak and will inevitably begin to wane."

Shen Qiao nodded. "Since that's the case, you must have predicted this situation long beforehand and made your preparations in advance. No wonder the manor within the capital was already deserted when I arrived."

He didn't mind that Yan Wushi had held information from him. Instead, he was happy that there hadn't been more losses.

"Because Bian Yanmei followed my orders and withdrew early, all that's left for Yuwen Yun and Xieting now are a couple of abandoned estates," said Yan Wushi. "It wasn't worth mentioning. You were able to leave the capital safely and without trouble because he contacted his old acquaintances in the imperial court who secretly provided assistance."

Yuwen Yun was determined to eradicate Yuwen Xian's entire family, and Yuwen Song was a fish that'd escaped his net. The most dangerous part of Shen Qiao and Yuwen Song's journey had been when they were just leaving the capital. The farther they got from Chang'an, the safer things became, because by that time Yuwen Yun had realized that his fish had slipped into the vast oceans—it'd be too difficult to chase them down.

Shen Qiao was no fool; after pondering to himself a moment, he understood what Yan Wushi was implying. "So, you have no more hopes for the Yuwen family. Then you must have already chosen a new candidate for emperor?"

Yan Wushi laughed. "Why didn't you guess that this venerable one would want that position for himself?"

Shen Qiao shook his head. "You wouldn't."

His reply was so decisive, even Yan Wushi couldn't resist probing him curiously. "Why not?"

Shen Qiao thought to himself, *You might be mercurial and egotistical, but if you wished to become emperor, you'd have already unified the three demonic sects and infiltrated Northern Zhou, then found an opportunity to usurp the throne. Why would you have fooled around until you burned even yourself and ended up being ambushed by Xueting and the others! It was obvious that you were only acting on your whims. Even the throne means little to you.*

However, if he said this aloud, Yan Wushi would certainly mock him endlessly. So, he offhandedly said, "Take a guess?"

Yan Wushi didn't reply.

It was rare for Shen Qiao to leave Yan Wushi awkward and speechless. He couldn't help but smile, inordinately pleased. Not a sound accompanied this smile; it came whisper-silent. When Yan Wushi saw it, the upward curve on his own lips slowly faded.

This man was far too tenderhearted, and he'd only remember kindness, not enmity. A thought suddenly surfaced within Yan Wushi's mind: *If the one who'd found Shen Qiao beneath Banbu Peak hadn't been Yan Wushi, but Sang Jingxing or Duan Wenyang, what would have happened to him?*

Yan Wushi didn't believe that it was human nature to be kind. In the past, with the goal of toying with this man's heart, he'd tested him again and again for the single purpose of unearthing the darkest parts of Shen Qiao's personality. But even after all he'd been through, with his martial arts destroyed, on the brink of losing everything, and forced to start over, Shen Qiao had never changed. It was as if no matter how many trials were forced upon him, they would never crush him.

No, there were still some changes.

At the very least, he now knew how to judge the best course of action, and his understanding of people and situations had sharpened.

Or perhaps you could say that those various trials had been no more than a whetstone to Shen Qiao—they'd slowly ground away all the rock concealing the lovely jade within, and now it'd blossomed to its full glory. And this "lovely jade" was none other than Shen Qiao's Daoist core.

Even after thousands of temperings, his Daoist core had remained the same.

Shen Qiao noticed Yan Wushi had stopped walking, and that the man was looking at him contemplatively. Confused, he asked, "What is it?"

"Nothing," said Yan Wushi. "Just now, I finally understood something."

"Hm?" said Shen Qiao.

Yan Wushi smiled but didn't speak.

Before, he'd loathed "Xie Ling's" influence, thinking that those thoughts weren't his own. He'd tried to suppress that strange feeling numerous times, and he'd believed that the moment he repaired the flaw in the demonic core, that feeling would vanish with it. He hadn't expected that Shen Qiao's smile would reawaken everything.

He was unwilling to admit that he, who'd looked down upon everyone in the world, would one day find that a name had wormed its way into his heart.

Human hearts were filled with malice. Some people were traitors, turning their backs on all integrity; some were ingrates, repaying kindness with enmity. There were also those who'd abandon their spouses, who were willing to do anything for wealth and glory. Yan Wushi had seen many, and he'd thought nothing of them because he, too, was a selfish, callous human. He only categorized things based on whether they deserved his notice, and to him, there were no actions that fell beyond a line that could not be crossed.

However, now Yan Wushi was forced to admit that Shen Qiao was unique and that he couldn't change him. Though the world was vast, there was still only one Shen Qiao.

"My venerable self suddenly thought of something amusing," he said. "Would you like to listen?"

"No," said Shen Qiao.

Yan Wushi turned a deaf ear and started talking anyway. "Once upon a time, there was a man who found a stone in a heap of gold and jewels."

Shen Qiao's mouth twitched. Didn't he just say that he didn't want to listen?

"But he couldn't believe that it was only an ordinary stone. He thought that since it'd been piled together with the mass of treasures in that room, it must also be a treasure. So, he brought it everywhere with him, and even had it examined and polished by many. But every single person, without exception, told him that it was only an ordinary stone, that there was nothing special about it. Guess what happened in the end?"

Shen Qiao's face was both lost and bewildered.

"In the end, he finally believed that it was indeed a worthless stone. But in his eyes, compared to the room full of gold and silver treasure, even if it was only a stone, it was still one of a kind—a stone out of a million."

Shen Qiao was silent.

Why did this story sound so bizarre? It was indeed unusual to hear such a normal story from such an abnormal person.

He couldn't help but say, "Even thousands of gold pieces cannot purchase happiness. Some people care little for wealth—they only wish to seek out things that other people find worthless. In my opinion, that man already liked that stone more than the other jewels and treasures, but he was trapped by his preconceptions and unwilling to admit it."

Yan Wushi laughed. "That's true, you're very correct. Thousands of gold pieces cannot purchase happiness."

There seemed to be a deep significance within these words.

"But why did Sect Leader Yan suddenly start telling me a story? Does it have something to do with the Yuwen clan?"

"Not at all," said Yan Wushi. "This venerable one was bored and wanted to tease you, that's all."

Shen Qiao said nothing. He truly regretted his actions somewhat. He should have just let Yan Wushi ramble on by himself—why had he replied to him in good faith?

Enough time had passed during their conversation for the two of them to walk from the Huang residence all the way back to the inn. It was still the wee hours of the night, so the inn's gates were naturally closed, and Shen Qiao returned to his room from that same window he'd left by. Only when he saw Yuwen Song still slumbering away did he finally relax.

Yan Wushi followed him. He laid eyes on Yuwen Song upon the bed and made a surprised noise. "This is my first time seeing him. Looking at the boy now, he indeed possesses an incredible talent for martial arts. His physical bases are spectacular."

Yan Wushi's standards were immensely high. For him to say "his physical bases are spectacular" was incredible praise.

Shen Qiao smiled. "Yes, he's indeed a promising youth. If he turns his energies to the martial path, he will definitely achieve great things in the future."

Yan Wushi tapped Yuwen Song's gate of sleep, and the child fell into an even deeper slumber. Like this, their conversation would not wake him. "It's enough that you know that Yun Fuyi has been in secret contact with the Huang family," he said. "You need not concern yourself with it any further."

Shen Qiao frowned. "The Huang family have dealings with the Göktürks. This means that the Liuhe Guild are also involved. Since Dou Yanshan was willing to ally with Duan Wenyang to attack you, they must have been in contact for a while?"

"That's a separate matter," said Yan Wushi. "Whether it's news by land or water, the Liuhe Guild controls most of it through cargo escort and boat travel. The south is full of waterways, besides, so the Liuhe Guild has always been close to the Chen Dynasty. Unless there are mutual benefits, like when they joined hands to take care of me, Dou Yanshan would never agree to work together with the Göktürks."

Shen Qiao understood. "So, you're saying that there's discord between Yun Fuyi and Dou Yanshan?"

Yan Wushi made a sound of agreement. "Ever since Yun Fuyi lost the *Zhuyang Strategy* scroll to me back at Chuyun Temple, Dou Yanshan has been dissatisfied with her. Yun Fuyi has noticed, and as she's unwilling to be reduced to a figurehead, the two of them have been fighting in secret inside the guild. After all, Yun Fuyi is only the deputy leader—not many people would be willing to leave with her, so she naturally needs to secure outside support."

"So that's why she went to the Huang family," said Shen Qiao. "She wishes for their help in wresting power from Dou Yanshan, and through them, she also must have spoken to the Göktürks, promising her allegiance, cooperation, and a share of benefits, things like that."

"Correct," said Yan Wushi. "I, too, share a grudge with Dou Yanshan—now I can sit on the mountainside and watch the tigers battle. I'll let Yun Fuyi realize her wish. She wants to become guild leader, but even if the Göktürks support her in secret, she still needs to eliminate the guild members who are loyal to Dou Yanshan. Once she takes the leader's seat, the Liuhe Guild will suffer from a shortage of manpower—there won't be enough new talent to take on the work. When that time comes, I'll give them another push. I trust that there are many people who'd leap at the chance to carve up the Liuhe Guild's authority like they would a melon. They'll collapse like a house of cards, all without me lifting a finger. Isn't that wonderful?"

"But once they achieve their goals, the Göktürks might also choose to get rid of Yun Fuyi and expropriate the wealth the Liuhe Guild has accumulated over the years," Shen Qiao pointed out.

"Indeed," said Yan Wushi. "It'll depend on the methods each side employs."

Shen Qiao felt a little helpless. "Since Guang Lingsan also knows you don't have amnesia, why did you pretend in front of him earlier during the day?"

"First, my venerable self doesn't want Guang Lingsan to know that we're close," Yan Wushi replied leisurely. "This is to keep you safe, so you should thank me."

How are you and I close? Shen Qiao thought to himself, but he played along. "I'm grateful for Sect Leader Yan's care. What's the second?"

"The second reason," said Yan Wushi, "was naturally to see your dumbfounded, disbelieving, and utterly lost expression. It was quite entertaining, wasn't it?"

Shen Qiao didn't respond.

Playing Weiqi

YUWEN SONG HADN'T THOUGHT that he'd wake to another person in the room. He even thought that he must still be half-asleep. He blinked several times, then rubbed his eyes, unable to help himself. Only then did he tentatively ask, "...Sect Leader Yan?"

This entire trip, he'd behaved himself like a miniature adult, and it was rare for him to do something so childish. Shen Qiao was secretly amused and said gently, "I trust that you know this man. He's indeed Huanyue Sect Leader Yan. You should greet him properly."

Yuwen Song cupped his hands and bowed. "The junior Yuwen Song greets Sect Leader Yan."

Yan Wushi made a sound of acknowledgment, which was already quite obliging coming from him. "No need for courtesies," he said. "We last met two years ago, but a glance from me is enough to see that you've grown quite a bit."

"I'm grateful to Sect Leader Yan for his praise," said Yuwen Song.

"In that case, would you like to apprentice under my venerable self?" said Yan Wushi.

Shen Qiao stared at him.

Yuwen Song was dumbfounded. "Huh?"

A faint sullenness came over Shen Qiao's face. "How unkind of you, Sect Leader Yan. When did you sink to the point of stealing someone else's disciples?!"

Yan Wushi gave a leisurely smile. "Look at his reaction: he didn't immediately refuse. In fact, he even hesitated after hearing this suggestion of mine. It's obvious he'd rather be this venerable one's disciple than yours!"

Yuwen Song rushed to declare his loyalty. "I'm grateful for Sect Leader Yan's favor, but this junior has already told Daoist Master Shen that he'd follow the Daoist discipline. The word of an upright gentleman is no different from a swift horse: once spoken, it cannot be reined in. I beg Sect Leader Yan's understanding!"

Yan Wushi raised an eyebrow. "What's so great about being his disciple? You can't do this, have to cherish that. If you apprentice under my venerable self, your two shixiong will both be over twenty years your senior, so in the future my venerable self might even be able to pass you the position of sect leader. Huanyue Sect is wealthy, and no matter what happens, you won't be required to wear a Daoist robe all year round. Looking at things this way, aren't there plenty of perks?"

Shen Qiao was angry. "Could Sect Leader Yan have followed this humble Daoist here just to steal my disciple?"

"If there was no demand for him, that'd be evidence of his inadequacy. Me trying to steal him from you proves that you have a good eye for disciples, so you should be thanking my venerable self."

Shen Qiao finally understood: Yan Wushi could twist each and every reasoning under the heavens to justify himself if he so wished.

Yuwen Song silently rubbed his forehead. He couldn't stand seeing Shen Qiao in this speechless state and leapt to help his future shizun out of this quandary. Attempting to draw Yan Wushi's attention back to himself, he said, "Daoist Master Shen and I intend to head to Bixia Sect. May I inquire as to Sect Leader Yan's plans?"

"Very well," said Yan Wushi.

"Huh?"

"Didn't you just invite this venerable one to Bixia Sect as a guest?" said Yan Wushi, perfectly composed. "This venerable one accepts."

Yuwen Song was dumbfounded.

Wait! No, that's not what I meant! he cried in his heart. He couldn't resist pleading for Shen Qiao's help.

"Sect Leader Yan," Shen Qiao said quickly, "Bixia Sect is currently on the wane; it's no longer of high status. I fear that it's unworthy of your regard."

"Ah," said Yan Wushi. "No matter, this venerable one does not mind."

The corner of Shen Qiao's mouth twitched. "But I'm not a Bixia Sect disciple. When under the roofs of others, we shouldn't overstep."

"No matter," said Yan Wushi. "Once they see my venerable self, I'm sure they'd dare not refuse me."

Shen Qiao was speechless for a moment. Finally, he couldn't take it, and said, "This humble Daoist is puzzled greatly over something: Bixia Sect and Huanyue Sect have no relationship, and the former is on the decline, so it has no benefits to offer Huanyue Sect. So why does Sect Leader Yan insist on going?"

"Naturally, it's for you," said Yan Wushi. "Why else would my venerable self grace that tiny sect with my presence? And once they see me, how could they dare refuse? They'll be falling over themselves to welcome me."

It was truly impossible to continue this conversation any longer!

Shen Qiao was about to spit blood in rage—it was like Yan Wushi was acting oblivious and perplexed on purpose. What he understood even less was Yan Wushi's subtle shift in attitude after some time apart.

The more he ruminated on this, the more it disturbed him.

After a long period of silence, he could only force out a single sentence: "What if I refuse to let Sect Leader Yan come along?"

Yan Wushi was astonished. "Just now you said you had no right to decide anything, so how does your permission matter? Why are you being so unreasonable, Daoist Master Shen?"

Shen Qiao gave up.

Yuwen Song gazed at his future shizun, his eyes full of sympathy.

Then Yan Wushi suddenly turned to him. "Do you really not want to be this venerable one's disciple?"

Caught off guard, Yuwen Song shook his head back and forth like a rattle-drum. Yan Wushi didn't say anything—he only gave a faint smile, as gentle as water. But with this smile, a shiver traveled through Yuwen Song's body.

And just like that, the traveling party of two grew to three.

When faced with someone who didn't understand "no," who couldn't be chased off, and who Shen Qiao probably couldn't even fight off, he could only choose to ignore him.

However, Yan Wushi's entire existence was, intrinsically, quite difficult to ignore. As the three walked together, his face—so handsome it bordered on supernatural—would instantly draw the notice of others. For example, when they were staying at inns or enjoying meals, practically every concierge considered them a group and assumed that Yan Wushi would be paying the bills and calling the shots, so they all rushed toward him. Shen Qiao made many fruitless attempts to correct them, which left him physically and mentally exhausted.

Like right now.

The three of them had already arrived at the foot of Mount Tai. The sky was dark, so they planned on staying beneath the mountain for the night before making the climb.

It was the best season for sightseeing trips on Mount Tai. The inns at the foot of the mountain were usually full, and it was clear the innkeeper hadn't expected guests to arrive at such a late hour. He quickly came out personally to greet them, then had the concierge serve them enough hot food to fill the table. Smiling apologetically, he said, "I'm truly very sorry. These days, there've been a great many guests who wish to sightsee, so we only have one room left. Will this be acceptable?"

Yan Wushi sent Shen Qiao a glance. Shen Qiao had already given up on correcting others who assumed they were traveling together—he didn't speak but let Yan Wushi respond instead.

Faint amusement flashed through Yan Wushi's eyes. He leisurely replied, "That works. How large is the room?"

"Not that big," said the innkeeper with a laugh. "There's only an inner section and an outer section, but it's elegantly furnished. Once your esteemed self sees it, I guarantee your satisfaction. There is no inn in the surrounding ten miles that's comparable to ours!"

Yan Wushi nodded. "Then bring us a weiqi set."

At this time of year, most of the sightseers were literati. To cater to their preferences, the inn had made some preparations, so the innkeeper smiled and said, "Yes, yes!"

He also threw in some flattery: "My lowly self assumed that the three gentlemen were men who wandered the jianghu; never did I expect such intellectual hobbies! Masters of both pen and sword, truly outstanding!"

Shen Qiao really couldn't figure out why Bixia Sect held any appeal to Yan Wushi, so he had been forced to conclude that it was a whim. However, he hadn't expected that this whim would send Yan Wushi tagging along for the entire journey, saying nothing about going their separate ways. Now that they were about to enter

Bixia Sect's gates, Shen Qiao felt his head throbbing nonstop, fearful of what trouble this fiend might unleash upon the sect. He tried again and again to get rid of him, but it was to no avail—instead, he spent the entire journey being messed with, which left him thoroughly despondent.

Upon hearing that all the inns within ten miles were full, Shen Qiao couldn't help a slight frown as he considered whether they should climb the mountain that night. After all, Bixia Sect was located just halfway up the mountain. If he hadn't been considering Yuwen Song's youth and frailty, a small distance like that would have been no issue.

Yan Wushi seemed to have read his thoughts. "Why don't we let Yuwen Song sleep on the bed, and the two of us can play some weiqi outside?"

Shen Qiao gave a wry smile. "Is Sect Leader Yan still unwilling to tell me? Just why are you going to Bixia Sect?"

"My venerable self has already said that it's for you," said Yan Wushi. "But you didn't believe me."

Shen Qiao shook his head. Of course he wouldn't believe him. "I'm still gradually recovering my martial arts—currently I have around eight to nine-tenths of my past strength. But it'd be a bit of a stretch to say that I'm your match. If I fight you, my chances of victory are slim, so I'm still unworthy of being your opponent."

Yan Wushi raised an eyebrow. "Daoist Master Shen, your beloved Daoist path of cultivation emphasizes spiritual tranquility and non-interference, yet you carry around thoughts of murder and battle day in and day out. If you're so full of wrath, how many eons will you take to attain Daoist enlightenment?"

His gaze swept over Shen Qiao and Yuwen Song, whose expressions were equally speechless. He casually threw in another line:

"I heard that there's a peerless beauty at Bixia Sect, whose name is Yue Kunchi."

Shen Qiao was stunned. "That's the sect leader's shixiong, and... and he's a man. You actually...?"

"That sect leader should be a woman?"

"That's right..."

"Then let me try again," said Yan Wushi. "I heard that the Bixia Sect Leader is a peerless beauty, whose appearance surpasses even Yuan Xiuxiu's. My venerable self has admired her for a long time, so I wish to meet her."

Shen Qiao stared at him.

You don't sound like you've admired her for very long at all.

Whatever the case, Yan Wushi insisted on coming, and Shen Qiao was helpless to stop him. Without understanding his reasons, he couldn't very well take it upon himself to deny him entrance, breeding enmity between Yan Wushi and Bixia Sect for no reason.

After they finished their meal, the concierge took the three of them to their room.

The room was indeed as elegantly furnished as the innkeeper had claimed. Leaving aside Shen Qiao, who was easy to accommodate, even Yuwen Song revealed an expression of delight. For the sake of his future disciple, Shen Qiao felt that sacrificing a night here was worth it.

Yuwen Song was quickly urged into bed, but Yan Wushi grabbed Shen Qiao. "Let's play a game."

Shen Qiao gracefully declined. "This humble Daoist isn't a skilled player."

Yan Wushi said coolly, "Back when your eyes were bad, you even played blind against yourself."

Shen Qiao hadn't expected him to remember so clearly—how embarrassing. Unable to refuse any further, he could only sit down.

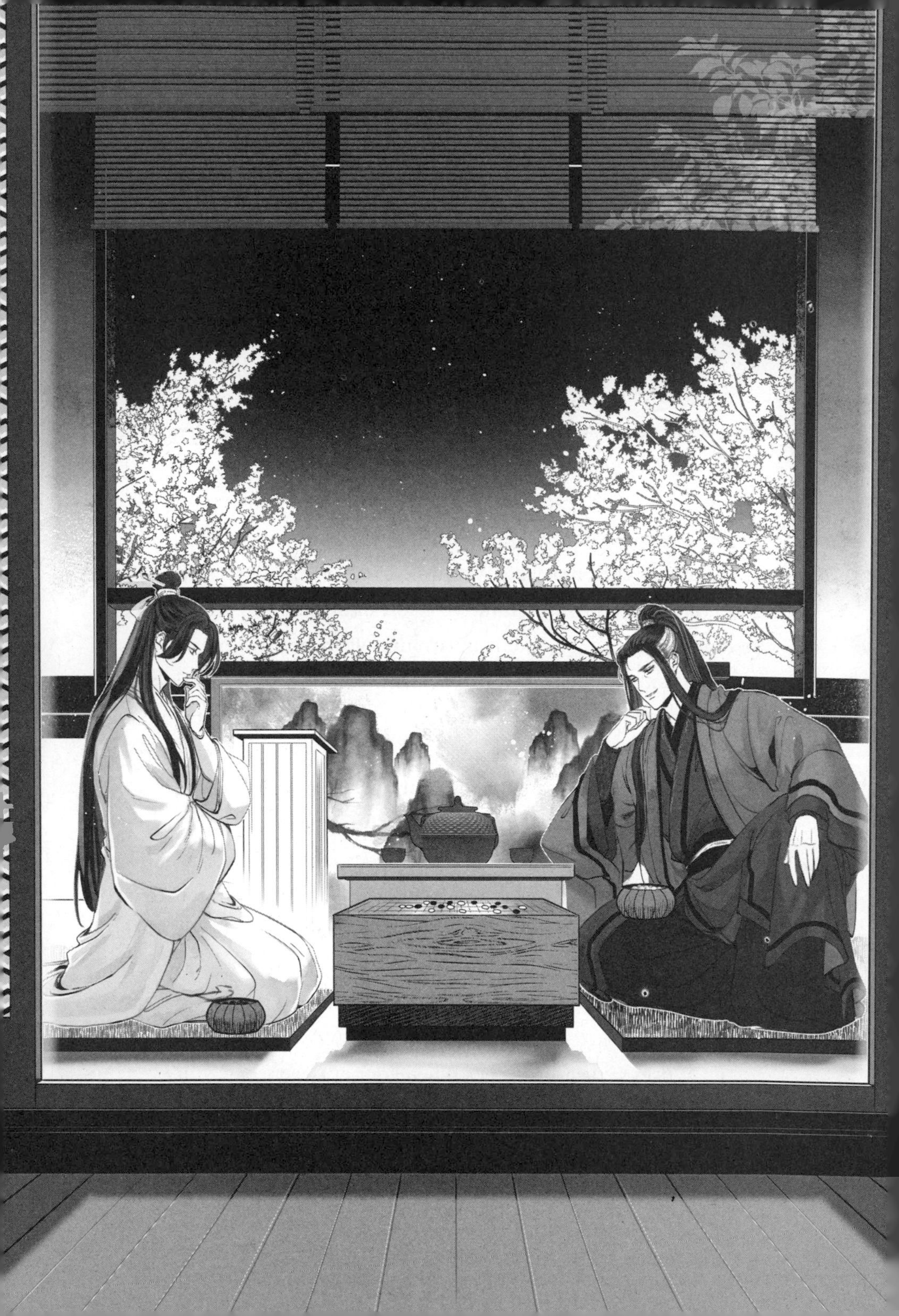

The first match, Shen Qiao eked out a small victory.

Yan Wushi told Shen Qiao, "Your skills and mine are about equal, and this time I lost due to a couple of mistakes. You should let this venerable one have a chance at victory as well; that's only fair."

Shen Qiao had wanted to meditate and train, but when he heard these words, he ultimately couldn't bear to. "All right, then let's play another."

In the second match, Shen Qiao lost to Yan Wushi, but it was by an even smaller margin than the first—practically only a single move.

Yan Wushi gently consoled him. "It was only because I had the advantage of going first. You can make the first move this time."

Shen Qiao frowned as he stared at the board, thinking that something seemed off, but never having been the competitive type, he responded right away. "Let's stop. Wins and losses are unimportant. You won once and I won once; with this, we're even."

"The game is akin to the sword," said Yan Wushi. "Did you gain any insights?"

Shen Qiao was taken aback, then scrutinized the board for a moment before shaking his head. "Forgive me for being slow. I don't see it."

"Let's play another game," said Yan Wushi. "This time, appreciate it properly: advancing and retreating are akin to swinging a sword at an enemy. If you grasp this, the rest will follow."

Shen Qiao had always admired his insight into martial arts. He immediately agreed and approached the game with greater seriousness.

He's really too gullible, Yan Wushi thought. *Spin any sort of nonsense and he'll believe it.*

With their third match, the two of them finally played to a draw.

By this time, the ends of the pitch-black sky were now edged in a faint gold.

Shen Qiao stared at the board for a long time before he finally couldn't take it anymore. "I've heard that the board is like a battle-field, and one can thoroughly understand the hearts of men and the art of war through it, but I can't see anything related to the sword here. Did you lie to me on purpose?"

As if nothing was amiss, Yan Wushi said, "Of course not. You misunderstood."

Naturally, he wouldn't admit that he'd only done it because he found the sight of Shen Qiao struggling as he deliberated incredibly entertaining.

"Then may I ask Sect Leader Yan to explain the insights he gleaned so that this humble Daoist may grasp them as well?"

Yan Wushi stood up. "The sun's risen. This venerable one will wake Yuwen Song. Without carving, jade cannot be made useful. He should practice the sword."

Shen Qiao was speechless.

92

Giving Pointers

SHEN QIAO BROUGHT Yuwen Song up the mountain. Yan Wushi remained behind him the entire time, neither close nor far as he looked around, his manner leisurely.

After the tragic incident, Bixia Sect had very few men left, but as they still needed to patrol the area, they couldn't spare any sentries for the foot of the mountain. Shen Qiao's entire climb went smoothly and unimpeded—it was only when they were almost at the mountain gates that they saw a silhouette walk toward them, carrying a sword.

"Which lofty person graces Bixia Sect with their presence?!" Only after saying this did he see Shen Qiao, and his expression immediately transformed from wariness to surprised delight. Even his tone changed completely. "So it's you, Daoist Master Shen!"

Shen Qiao laughed. "Yuanbai, your skills have improved yet again. Truly worthy of celebration!"

Fan Yuanbai was Yue Kunchi's disciple, so naturally, he was Shen Qiao's junior—there was nothing wrong with calling him by name. Back during Shen Qiao's duel with Kunye, everyone from Bixia Sect had been there as witnesses, making them all keenly aware of his abilities. So, when Fan Yuanbai heard Shen Qiao's compliment, he grew even happier. "I'm deeply grateful for Daoist Master Shen's praise. Please enter. Your esteemed self has always remained in

Shizun and Zhangmen-shishu's hearts. With you gone for so long without news, they sent people to try and find some. We heard that you fought two of Hehuan Sect's elders in Chang'an and that they perished beneath your blade. The entirety of Bixia Sect was overjoyed. Your esteemed self is truly formidable!"

He never spoke much in front of outsiders, but the moment he got to know someone, Fan Yuanbai had the tendency to chatter endlessly. Shen Qiao smiled, eyes crinkling as he listened. He didn't cut him off but let him speak as much as he wished.

Bixia Sect had much fewer disciples, but their hearts had grown more united. Even after such great losses, after experiencing all those sorrows, everyone's faces shone with smiles, and their relationships had grown more harmonious as well. On their way in, the group encountered only a few insignificant disciples. But Shen Qiao had performed the grand deed of rescuing Bixia Sect from a crisis, so upon seeing him, those disciples had the same reaction as Fan Yuanbai. And because of Shen Qiao, neither Yan Wushi nor Yuwen Song were subject to interrogation as they climbed the mountain with him.

It was just that Yan Wushi's appearance was too eye-catching, and he inevitably received much curious scrutiny. In contrast, Yuwen Song was rather inconspicuous.

Zhao Chiying just so happened to be discussing matters with Yue Kunchi. When she heard that Shen Qiao had returned, she quickly went out to greet him personally.

Though it'd been some time, Zhao Chiying was as elegant as ever. She couldn't be considered a peerless beauty, but she was fair and lovely nonetheless. Her status as sect leader had also given her a graceful composure no common woman could possess. Shen Qiao had never seen such a bearing on even Hehuan Sect Leader Yuan Xiuxiu.

Zhao Chiying cupped her hands and smiled. "Daoist Master Shen has finally returned. Mount Tai is on the coast of the Eastern Sea, thousands of miles away from Chang'an, so news was slow to arrive. We heard of your one-on-three battle in Chang'an only a short time ago and were astounded by your magnificence. Never did we expect this: speak of Cao Cao, and he will arrive!"

Shen Qiao returned the greeting. "I was gone for quite some time and left Shiwu here. I've given Sect Leader Zhao much trouble!"

"Daoist Master Shen exaggerates. Shiwu is a good child—he might be young, but he possesses great discipline and never needs prodding from others. Every day before sunrise, he attends morning classes with the rest of the disciples. He is ceaselessly diligent, day in and day out."

Hearing this, Shen Qiao was naturally thrilled, and he turned to exchange pleasantries with Yue Kunchi as well.

Zhao Chiying had already noticed the people standing behind Shen Qiao, one tall and one short. Now she smiled and asked, "And who are they, I wonder?"

Shen Qiao gave a slight cough. "One is Huanyue Sect Leader Yan, and the other, younger one is Yuwen Song. He's a child I brought from Chang'an."

Being from Chang'an and having the surname Yuwen, anyone who'd heard about how Shen Qiao had fought Hehuan Sect rescuing a Yuwen clan orphan from the midst of a thousand-strong army—would quickly surmise who Yuwen Song must be.

However, everyone's attention was instead ensnared by the first introduction Shen Qiao had made.

A man's reputation was like the shadow of a tree. Once his identity as Huanyue Sect Leader was out, everyone had the same reaction: their hearts gave a small jolt. The numerous curious gazes aimed at Yan Wushi instantly became complicated: there was awe, fear, and shock—and some disbelief.

Most of Bixia Sect's disciples had never seen Yan Wushi in person, but that didn't stop them from hearing a great many stories concerning him. To them, Qi Fengge and Cui Youwang were more or less figures of myth, and Yan Wushi, who matched their strength and had nearly fought them to a draw, was practically a legend as well.

Under an assortment of measuring, scrutinizing gazes, Yan Wushi stood with his hands behind his back, his expression relaxed. There wasn't a hint of discomfort about him—it was obvious he was used to this.

Shen Qiao had left the mountain to save a man, and during this trip he'd experienced all sorts of ups and downs, twists and turns. Zhao Chiying had heard of some of it, but with the distance so vast, her knowledge wasn't very detailed. She hadn't expected that Shen Qiao, in going to save someone, would bring that very someone back. She was stunned for a while, then just barely managed to recover and cup her hands. "Sect Leader Yan's illustrious reputation precedes him. Bixia Sect Leader Zhao Chiying respectfully welcomes the esteemed Sect Leader Yan to visit. Our sect is but a humble one, so if our hospitality is lacking in any way, I must ask your forgiveness!"

As Zhao Chiying was a sect leader, the attitude she showed now was already incredibly earnest and polite. After all, Yan Wushi was famous for being capricious. Zhao Chiying did not wish to upset him over potential discourtesies that might arise over minute details.

"Sect Leader Zhao handles matters with great equity and possesses rigorous moral standards," said Yan Wushi. "I have heard much of you. On the way here, A-Qiao also praised you highly. Now that we finally meet, I can see that your reputation is well-earned. I hope that my unexpected visit will not bring Sect Leader Zhao any trouble."

Eh? This was a fairly normal response!

Not only was Zhao Chiying surprised, even Shen Qiao was a little astounded.

Yan Wushi wore a slight smile, his demeanor gentle and polite. From head to toe, he radiated an aura of amicability. One couldn't see even a hint of the arrogance and scandalousness typical of the demonic sects.

The only issue was that "A-Qiao," which sounded a little too intimate, but having heard it so much, Shen Qiao was already numb to the name. Everyone else found it strange, but they couldn't say why. They only thought that Shen Qiao and the Huanyue Sect Leader must share some remarkable relationship.

With such a good start, everything that followed also went smoothly. Everyone gave their courtesies and took a seat. Having heard the news, Shiwu ran over. The reunion between master and disciple made for a moving scene: Shiwu was overcome with emotion and threw himself into Shen Qiao's arms, in full view of the onlookers. Shen Qiao was very gratified to notice that he'd grown somewhat taller.

On the side, Yuwen Song examined this future shixiong of his. He was curious, but also a little disappointed.

It was obvious that the other boy was older than him, yet his words and actions were even softer than his own. Being so reliant on Shizun, just when would he be able to gain independence?

However, he'd forgotten about the days right after he left Chang'an, when he was racked with anxiety. Every night, he'd needed to see Shen Qiao's figure before he could slip peacefully into sleep.

Separate from these childish matters, Zhao Chiying said to Shen Qiao, "Daoist Master Shen's return was perfectly timed. The Bixia Sect's numbers have fallen greatly, and we're in dire need of more disciples. My shixiong and I were worrying over this matter—could Daoist Master Shen help us with ideas?"

"Sect Leader," Yue Kunchi said tactfully, "Daoist Master Shen has just arrived after a long journey; he must be exhausted. Wouldn't it be better to let him rest before discussing?"

Zhao Chiying became a little embarrassed. "Shixiong is right. I was too impatient. I'll have Yuanbai take you elsewhere so you can rest first. Would the house you stayed in last time be acceptable?"

Shen Qiao nodded. "That would be excellent. I'm sorry to have troubled Sect Leader Zhao. Qilang can stay in the room next to Shiwu's; that would also help to build their relationship."

"Very well," said Zhao Chiying. "On the eastern side of our sect is a bamboo building reserved for honored guests. If Sect Leader Yan does not mind, he can stay there."

The house Shen Qiao had stayed in last time was meant for elders of the sect, which also demonstrated that Bixia Sect didn't see him as an outsider. However, if they had Yan Wushi stay there, it would look like a snub instead.

Yet Yan Wushi said, "No need to trouble yourselves so. I'll stay with A-Qiao."

Zhao Chiying's expression faltered. "Huh? Won't that be an inconvenience?"

Yan Wushi raised an eyebrow. "Why would it be inconvenient? We used the same arrangements during our travels. My venerable self has stayed in the same room as him more times than I can remember."

It was true, of course, but the words coming out of his mouth seemed to carry a different connotation. Shen Qiao couldn't help but say, "Urgency is a priority while traveling, so it was fine then. But now Sect Leader Yan will be able to enjoy a more comfortable stay. If you refuse, you would be brushing off Sect Leader Zhao's good intentions."

"No matter," said Yan Wushi. "My relationship with A-Qiao is no ordinary one. Since he has such a high opinion of Bixia Sect, you lot need not treat my venerable self as an outsider either. Be at ease. Does his house not have a single empty one next to it?"

Though he was smiling as he spoke, Zhao Chiying could feel a palpable, intimidating pressure from him. Under that kind of gaze, even her scalp seemed to tighten. Before she could ponder more, she already found herself replying: "There... There is..."

Yan Wushi gave a slight smile. "Then all is well."

This smile was different from the one just before. Zhao Chiying could tangibly feel the pressure on her body lifting. She silently breathed a sigh of relief and quickly called for Fan Yuanbai, then had him take the party away so they could rest.

Once Shen Qiao and the others had left, only the shixiong and shimei pair remained within the council chamber. Yue Kunchi's expression transformed into one of great relief, like a heavy burden had been lifted. "Just let Sect Leader Yan stay next to whoever he wants. It's not as though we lack for empty houses. From what I saw, Daoist Master Shen didn't make any firm objections—that means tacit approval. Just now I wanted to tell you not to go against Sect Leader Yan's wishes, but I couldn't have imagined that I'd find myself almost unable to speak."

He didn't know that the reason Shen Qiao hadn't given a firm objection was because even if he'd tried to, it would have been pointless.

Zhao Chiying gave a wry smile. "Shixiong can make fun of me, for I was little better. Bixia Sect and Huanyue Sect have never had any dealings—our small temple cannot house such a great Buddha. I also have no idea what he intends by coming here. Could it hurt our Bixia Sect?"

Yue Kunchi was more optimistic. "With Daoist Master Shen here, I doubt anything would happen. It's said that Yan Wushi is mercurial, but we only need to keep a bit more caution and tell our disciples to be careful with their words and actions so as not to offend him."

Zhao Chiying nodded. "That is true."

Elsewhere, Fan Yuanbai had brought Shen Qiao's party to the house where they would rest. As it was cleaned year-round, it was pristine, and there were even water bamboo and bluegrass orchids placed within—remarkably tasteful and refined.

"If Sect Leader Yan and Daoist Master Shen need anything, please send word. I am always at your service." Fan Yuanbai had wanted to speak some more to Shen Qiao, but when he saw Yan Wushi standing to the side, he couldn't speak a single word more. He stiffly finished his speech, hurriedly ending the conversation, then turned tail and fled.

Shiwu was still young, and thus not particularly sensitive. He'd waited a long time for Shen Qiao to finish talking with Zhao Chiying so that they could have a private moment to themselves and catch up. So even though Yan Wushi and Yuwen Song were nearby, it didn't stop him from tugging at Shen Qiao and voicing his yearning. "Shizun, you were away for far too long. This disciple missed you dearly."

Shen Qiao patted his head. "While this master was outside, he naturally missed you a great deal as well. I heard that you've been doing well at Bixia Sect, and it seems you've grown taller too?"

Shiwu nodded somewhat shyly. "The shixiong at Bixia Sect are very kind to me. Since Shizun left, I've been practicing the sword every day so as not to disappoint you. Now I can even execute the entire set of the Azure Waves sword techniques!"

The tone of these words held a hint of childish sweetness and yearning for long-unheard praise. Yuwen Song couldn't resist pouting to himself. *He's even a couple of years older than me,* he thought. *Am I really supposed to call him Shixiong in the future?*

Shen Qiao smiled. "Is that so? Then you can show me now."

Shiwu hesitated. "Will it disturb Shizun's rest?"

"We already rested last night at the base of the mountain," said Shen Qiao, "and it's not yet noon. The day is still early—this master is not yet tired."

Hearing this, Shiwu happily went to retrieve his sword.

He'd studied the sword for less than a year, still but a beginner, so he wielded a wooden sword rather than a real one.

Beneath the attention of three people, he stood and bowed, then stretched his arm forth, twirling his sword in the manner of the first stance. His hand and sword rose and fell, and his every move was measured and systematic, structured and meticulous. Though not poor, his moves were also nothing extraordinary. Shiwu's natural talent was still a level below Yuwen Song's, but Shiwu knew that he was of only average aptitude, so he trained twice as hard. His sword techniques were already quite adroit.

"I ask for Shizun's instruction." Shiwu put away his sword and stood straight, his tone earnest.

Shen Qiao didn't want to crush his spirits, so he first chose to mention some of his strong points. "Generally, you've learned the movements well," he said. "I can tell that you must have arduously practiced—you didn't spend these days slacking off."

Then he continued, "However, some of your sword moves were executed incorrectly, which will affect their strength. This master only demonstrated the set to you once, so it would have been hard for you to remember them in full detail. Now I'll redemonstrate this set of sword techniques for you from beginning to end. Pay closer attention and, if you can, compare them to your own."

"Yes," Shiwu said solemnly.

Shen Qiao didn't use Shanhe Tongbei but instead took Shiwu's wooden sword from his hands. He gave a slight smile. "The Azure Waves sword techniques are true to their name. The great seas are boundless, their waves tempestuous. The ocean engulfs the mountain stones countless times, yet again and again, those rocks will rise above the water's surface. The radiant sunbeams, the majestic waves—they all come together to create magnificent scenery. Those who practice this set of sword techniques must be as magnanimous as the sea that accepts a hundred rivers—only then can one harness the true essence of these moves. You must climb Mount Tai to view the great seas; if you can, climb higher and look further. In time, you'll achieve your own enlightenment."

After he finished, he didn't wait for Shiwu to respond, but raised the sword!

It was the same wooden sword, but when placed in the hands of someone else, the power unleashed was on an entirely different level. Shiwu, having just started on his martial arts journey, had shown swordplay that was utterly unremarkable, so much that Yuwen Song found it dull. Yet when Shen Qiao began to swing his sword, Yuwen Song's eyes went round, unable to believe that Shiwu and Shen Qiao were using the same set of sword techniques.

A scouring wind came from the sword's swings, its blade a flurry of afterimages. Though Shen Qiao didn't use true qi, that wooden sword still seemed to shine with the brilliant radiance that accompanied his moves. Yuwen Song could almost see the tumultuous waves of the great sea, the dark clouds and scattering rain, the rainbow dipping into the waters. And standing within a thousand yards of white waves was a single man.

All his eyes could see was this man—in all of heaven and earth, this man was the sole existence.

Even after he finished the entire set of techniques, now standing still, the images from before lingered in Yuwen Song's vision. For a long time, they did not fade.

Yan Wushi was smiling. "A-Qiao has achieved transcendental perfection with regard to the sword. You have attained the echelon of grandmasters."

Shen Qiao smiled back. "I'm deeply grateful to Sect Leader Yan for his support."

Of course, he hadn't performed those sword techniques for Yan Wushi's applause, but for Shiwu and Yuwen Song. "Did you glean anything?" he asked.

"Please forgive this disciple for being clumsy with his words," Shiwu replied falteringly. "I only felt myself surging with emotion, as if something wished to burst forth from my chest. But I'm unable to give a proper description."

"It's all right," Shen Qiao said gently. "No one can achieve enlightenment with a single glance. Take your time to digest it—if there's anything you can't understand, just ask."

"Yes," said Shiwu respectfully.

Then Shen Qiao turned to Yuwen Song. "You've yet to formally join the sect, and you've only been meditating while resting for the past few days. If you can't manage a comment, that's no issue either."

"My heart is filled with words upon words, uncountably numerous," said Yuwen Song, "but I can only manage a scant few lines as description."

When he spoke, he always came across as old and grizzled despite his age. Shen Qiao found it very amusing. "Which few lines?"

"It appears as the cloud-shrouded moon and drifts like the snow carried on swirling winds. As one gazes from afar, it glows like the dawning sun, and when peering up close, it dazzles like a lotus above green waters."

This was from Luo Shen Fu, about the beauty of the Luo River's nymph.

Shen Qiao was caught between laughing and crying, but he had to say something. Yuwen Song had indeed grasped a vital thread related to the Azure Waves sword techniques: the idea that "the heart is dazzling in its ever-changing majesty, while the sword is dexterous, graceful in its agility."

Just from this point, Yuwen Song indeed possessed more aptitude than Shiwu.

Yan Wushi gave a silent sneer. "He doesn't even have the slightest foundations for practicing martial arts. Reciting Luo Shen Fu was just him seeing the surface and trying to be clever. It'd be such a waste to for such talent to be squandered on wordplay! You should let this venerable one sharpen and polish him thoroughly!"

He didn't wait for a response before his palm came down on Yuwen Song's shoulder. The boy gasped, then his body dropped involuntarily—the acupoints of his upper body were sealed!

"Sect Leader Yan?" Yuwen Song was dumbfounded, his body bent in a half crouch and completely unable to move. The worst part was that he still didn't know what he'd said or done wrong.

Yan Wushi saw that Shen Qiao was about to speak but stole ahead first. With the shadow of a smile on his face, he said, "Speaking so frivolously to your shifu would merit a punishment even in Huanyue Sect, which you take as a demonic sect. A-Qiao, you're far too gentle when teaching your disciples. Surely I don't need to teach them proper discipline on your behalf."

Shen Qiao's face was stony. "Have you finally given up on stealing my disciples, Sect Leader Yan?"

Yan Wushi said leisurely, "Out of consideration for his life, I won't fight you over him anymore. Otherwise, my venerable self fears that I'd end up killing him right after I accept him."

On that first day of their meeting, no one other than Shen Qiao and Shiwu had witnessed how Yan Wushi treated Yuwen Song, so all the disciples of Bixia Sect thought him quite amiable, completely different from the rumors.

But on the second day, they soon realized they were wrong.

After morning class finished, the disciples all gathered in the practice field to train and spar. Yan Wushi stood to the side, hands behind his back. Even in the case of a personal demonstration by Yue Kunchi or Zhao Chiying, he'd pick at their flaws, pointing them out in an airy, condescending tone.

The Bixia Sect disciples were greatly displeased and took the initiative to challenge him. Each and every one of them was sent tumbling to the ground, and in the end, even Zhao Chiying and Yue Kunchi fell in defeat. By the time Shen Qiao heard of this after exiting seclusion and hurried over, it was midday, and Yan Wushi had already fought the entire Bixia Sect from top to bottom.

Of course, with Yan Wushi's abilities, annihilating the entire sect was no difficult task. But a martial arts grandmaster pushing around a tiny sect like this, instead of picking on someone his own size? What was going on? Surely he couldn't be looking for some sense of fulfillment to amuse himself with?

If not for Shen Qiao's presence, Bixia Sect would have thought that this man was here to trash their place.

Standing before the immense field of casualties, Shen Qiao could only pull a strained smile and apologize to Zhao Chiying.

Zhao Chiying remained unexpectedly gracious as she waved her hand and smiled. "Sect Leader Yan only thought our martial skills inadequate, so he gave us some pointers. Bixia Sect is too happy to receive such an opportunity."

When she said this, everyone else began to feel that her words were true.

Many of them would never achieve martial arts worthy of a sect leader in their lifetime, let alone anywhere close to Yan Wushi's. Everyone wished to be strong—just the chance to spar with Yan Wushi once was more than worth it. Even if it had meant heavy injuries, let alone something small like getting thrashed and humiliated, it was invaluable to their journey on the martial path.

With this thought, the disciples' gazes as they watched Yan Wushi instantly transformed from fearful displeasure to reverent yearning.

Yue Kunchi had been clutching his arms and sighing about how stately his shimei was, befitting of a sect leader, when a voice nearby softly said, "How does it feel, to hold a torch for someone for decades on end while being too scared to confess? My venerable self has no experience with this—please enlighten me."

This voice was like an arrow to his heart, one that pierced right into a hidden place buried deep within. Yue Kunchi's hair stood on end, and his face twisted in horror. Instantly, he looked at Yan Wushi with the expression of one who'd seen a ghost.

Before Yue Kunchi could reply, Shen Qiao showed up and dragged Yan Wushi away.

Yan Wushi didn't fight him either—he let Shen Qiao pull him aside, a bright smile still affixed to his face.

Shen Qiao held his forehead. "Sect Leader Yan, are you bored with nothing to do?"

Yan Wushi said curiously, "What do you mean, nothing to do? Every day, I must amuse myself with you and give pointers to that useless rabble. I'm incredibly busy."

The corner of Shen Qiao's mouth twitched. He was speechless for a long stretch before he found his voice again. "You should have been in Chang'an assisting the new emperor, yet you followed me such a vast distance to Bixia Sect. I doubt you came for something as trivial as sightseeing or messing with others. Are you still unwilling to tell me the reason even now?"

"If you switch to a new address, this venerable one will consider telling you. How about that?"

Shen Qiao was baffled. "What address?"

"How about Yan-lang?"[1]

So he really was messing with me, Shen Qiao thought. Without a single word, he simply turned and left.

---

1   "-lang" can be used by married women to address their husbands.

Day-to-Day

"THERE WILL BE GREAT CHANGES to the current jianghu. If you wish to return to Xuandu Mountain, it's better to do so later than sooner."

Yan Wushi's words stopped Shen Qiao in his tracks.

He was taken aback for a moment. Then he asked, "How did you know that I wanted to go to Xuandu Mountain?"

Yan Wushi chuckled. "A-Qiao, all your thoughts are written upon your face. I know you like I know myself—how could I fail to tell?"

Shen Qiao didn't realize that Yan Wushi was messing around with him again. Instead, he believed that Yan Wushi's eyes were sharp enough to see right through his thoughts. Even if he found the man's behavior disagreeable, this ability alone was valuable enough that he wanted to learn from Yan Wushi, hoping to patch his own weakness. He earnestly consulted him: "I really can't bring myself to call you that, and even if I do, it'd only bring you brief amusement. How does that help you? I'm indeed inferior to you when it comes to judging matters and people, so I sincerely request an explanation, Sect Leader Yan. I'm willing to offer other things in return."

Yan Wushi was all smiles. "Very well then. But you must remember that you owe me."

Shen Qiao thought for a while, then nodded. "As long as you don't ask me to do anything criminal or inhumane. Nor will I betray righteousness."

"In my opinion," said Yan Wushi, "murder helps humanity—it eliminates scourges on the world who are wastes of space, hence it's not inhumane at all. So why are you so reluctant?"

Shen Qiao furrowed his brows. "If you insist on using such twisted arguments, just pretend I never asked anything."

He was about to leave, but Yan Wushi stopped him and said with a smile, "All right, all right, I was only joking with you. My venerable self will never ask you to do anything you consider criminal or inhumane. Surely that's fine?"

Their current relationship was a terribly tricky one. They couldn't be called enemies, but neither did they interact in the way expected of normal friends. At least Zhao Chiying and Yue Kunchi would never use such a tone when speaking with Shen Qiao.

He didn't even find the words intimate or provocative—no such suggestive descriptors came to mind. He only thought that Yan Wushi had always been this way, erratic and mercurial, always doing as he pleased. He was used to it now, so it no longer mattered. "Then please grace me with your insights, Sect Leader Yan," he said.

Seeing that he'd gotten all he could, Yan Wushi decided to let things go. "Do you know of Han Feng?"

Shen Qiao said, "The Han Feng who was once one of the Three Nobles of Qi with Mu Tipo? I remember that his daughter is an external disciple of Bixia Sect. I met her once in Yecheng. But as I was still blind then, I don't know what she looks like."

Yan Wushi laughed. "True, I'd almost forgotten. My A-Qiao was born so handsome, it's not surprising that she fell for you. She even took the chance to strike up a conversation, right?"

Shen Qiao was perplexed. "Why are you mentioning her all of a sudden? Just because she has ties with Bixia Sect? Is that why you came here?"

"It is," said Yan Wushi, "but not entirely. I had three reasons for coming to Bixia Sect, and she was but one of them—in fact, she's the least important one. Han Feng followed Gao Wei and surrendered to the Zhou Dynasty, but Han Eying is much more loyal than her father—she insists that Gao Zhao should take the throne, and she wishes to restore the country. Given her relationship with Bixia Sect, it's highly likely she'll arrive here to request help from her sect, to have them join her campaign to revive Qi."

"Bixia Sect took severe losses after their tragedy," Shen Qiao pointed out. "Even if they wanted to help, they'd lack the strength. Furthermore, Sect Leader Zhao is determined to keep her sect away from the power struggles of the secular world. If Han Eying did come, she probably wouldn't agree to such a request."

Yan Wushi disagreed. "Deep down, you too know very well that being in the thick of things can prevent some people from seeing clearly. You should look for an opportunity to clarify this matter with Zhao Chiying. If Qi wishes for revival, they'll need support from the Göktürks. Bixia Sect is a small sect—if they overestimate themselves and collude with the Göktürks, fate will not be kind to them."

Shen Qiao was confused. "Sect Leader Zhao has never seemed like someone so foolish to me. You seem to hold some heavy prejudices against her—has she wronged you before?"

Yan Wushi didn't answer his question and instead changed the subject. "Yuwen Yun elevated that bald donkey Xueting, but he also promoted Hehuan Sect, who are completely unrelated; he's undermining everyone, as emperors do, to maintain a balance of power.

He believes that this will make it easier to exert control, but none of them are fools. Whether it's Xueting or Hehuan Sect, they can see through his plans, and they'll take this opportunity to aggressively shore up their influence."

"Is this why you said that the current jianghu will experience great changes soon?" Shen Qiao was deep in thought. "Huanyue Sect has moved from open operations to covert ones. While it's good to lie low and bide your time, if Hehuan Sect jumps to expand their influence, they'll inevitably clash with you. Aren't you worried about the losses Huanyue Sect might suffer if they do?"

Yan Wushi smiled, completely carefree. "Foolish A-Qiao. Now that they have Yuwen Yun's support, they're like the high sun at noon. What's wrong with letting them bite and tear at each other? Why should I hop out and give them a free excuse to unite against me? As they expand their influence, they certainly won't let a gold-mine like Xuandu Mountain escape. But that shidi of yours, he's so proud and arrogant that he'd never take it lying down, so conflict will be inevitable. That's why I said there's no need to hurry back to Xuandu Mountain."

He paused before continuing, "Duan Wenyang allied with various forces to kill me. He even coordinated all sorts of offenses to have a father and son destroy one another. Do you understand why?"

Shen Qiao nodded. "The Göktürks don't want to see a powerful, united north, so Yuwen Yong has to die. And you, who support Yuwen Yong, naturally must also die."

Yan Wushi smiled. "Indeed, the time you spent in the secular world hasn't gone to waste. However, you were much cuter when you'd just awoken and couldn't remember anything, as transparent as glazed snow, and oh so trusting..."

Shen Qiao's face went dark. "That's only because I was more gullible then. You liked that, didn't you?"

"A-Qiao truly understands me so well!" said Yan Wushi with satisfaction.

This man was beyond shameless. Shen Qiao desperately wished to turn around and leave, but he couldn't bear to just yet. Yan Wushi had said quite a bit just now, and though Shen Qiao himself had already figured out a fair amount, once the other man had spoken, it was as if the scattered weiqi pieces had suddenly realigned themselves—like brushing away clouds to reveal the moon or the tides receding to expose the rocks.

"What you're saying, then," said Shen Qiao, "is that the most worrisome enemy is neither Xueting nor Hehuan Sect but the Göktürks?"

"This move from Duan Wenyang was set in motion since the day he entered the capital to see Empress Ashina," said Yan Wushi. "Perhaps it was even earlier. And the gold lotus ring he demanded from Su Wei's mother when he arrived at the Su residence too—that was no ordinary ring."

"That's right," said Shen Qiao. "Madam Qin and Duan Wenyang both said so, that it was a keepsake."

"I've been dispatching people to investigate this entire time," said Yan Wushi, "but I only received the answer a few days back. That ring is indeed a keepsake, but it's no ordinary keepsake. Rather, it's proof that Hulugu's defeated all the martial experts of the Khaganate—a symbol of his status. It can be used to mobilize some twenty-odd martial arts masters from all over the Eastern and Western Khaganate. The Göktürks occupy a vast territory, so these experts are usually scattered all over. Even the Khagan himself might have trouble summoning them. But this keepsake can do just that, and with half the effort."

"From what I know, Duan Wenyang is a first-rate martial artist," said Shen Qiao, "but they say he has Han blood, so his status within the Khaganate is not very high. I doubt that the keepsake alone would be enough to win the Göktürks' trust…"

Shen Qiao jolted. "Unless—Hulugu is still alive?"

If Hulugu was still alive, he was the only one who'd have the right to use that keepsake to assemble the twenty-odd Göktürk masters.

But if this were the case, then things had just become much more thorny and complicated.

Two decades ago, Qi Fengge had dueled Hulugu and eked out a small victory, forcing him to swear to stay out of the Central Plains for twenty years. Now, the time limit was up, and Shen Qiao's shizun had already passed on. If Hulugu were still alive, his martial ability could only have soared even higher. With the Göktürks' current movements, if Hulugu again entered the Central Plains, it would definitely not be for simple sparring and reminiscence. Once that happened, who could stop him?

"It isn't impossible," said Yan Wushi. "However, as there's no evidence yet, you need not worry about it."

Shen Qiao pulled himself out of his worried thoughts. "Before, you said that you had three reasons for staying at Bixia Sect. Just now you told me one of them; what are the other two?"

Yan Wushi gave a slight smile. "The second, naturally, is you."

"…Then, the third?"

"The third is also you."

Shen Qiao's mouth twitched. "This humble Daoist has neither the virtue nor ability. I'm unworthy of such regard from Sect Leader Yan."

"But you do possess both virtue and ability," said Yan Wushi with a smile. "Since that's the case, of course you're worthy of my regard.

And aside from those matters, there's also your beauty—you're practically perfect beyond reproach."

At this moment, Fan Yuanbai walked over and greeted them. "Sect Leader Yan, Daoist Master Shen, our sect leader has some words for you. Because we didn't expect the arrival of honored guests, we didn't have time to make proper preparations before. But today we've specially thrown a banquet, and we ask you to grant us the honor of attending."

Yan Wushi grabbed Shen Qiao's hand without waiting for his answer. "Sect Leader Zhao is too courteous. We will respectfully honor her wishes."

Shen Qiao was unable to pull his hand back. "...You act like I'm not going. What are you doing, Sect Leader Yan?"

"A-Qiao, have you never heard of 'walking arm in arm?'"

"That's reserved only for the closest of friends!"

Yan Wushi looked dismayed. "Are we not the closest of friends?"

"...This humble Daoist possesses no such sentiments."

"This venerable one saved your life beneath Banbu Peak. Doesn't that count as a gargantuan favor?"

"...It does."

"I resolutely put my life on the line to lure away Sang Jingxing, back outside the capital of Feng Province. Were you really not the slightest bit moved?"

"...I was, but don't forget, I've saved you several times as well."

"Aren't I right, then? How many people in this world have shared as many life-and-death experiences as we have? Don't you feel extremely honored to have someone as charming as my venerable self as your friend?"

"Can I say no?" asked Shen Qiao.

"No," said Yan Wushi.

So Shen Qiao said nothing.

Fan Yuanbai watched, dumbfounded. *To think that Sect Leader Yan shares such a close relationship with Daoist Master Shen—no wonder Daoist Master Shen brought him up the mountain as a guest,* he thought. *That means even the pointers Sect Leader Yan gave on our martial arts were certainly for Daoist Master Shen's sake. Some of our shidi were unhappy, thinking that he was deliberately picking a fight with us, but they really shouldn't be. When I head back, I must tell them off.*

Because Shen Qiao had a moral character, Fan Yuanbei assumed that Yan Wushi, too, must have held good intentions, but this was nothing more than a beautiful misunderstanding. If Shen Qiao had heard his thoughts, he'd definitely have told him that Yan Wushi was indeed deliberately picking a fight.

The three of them arrived at the Flower Hall, where the preparations for the banquet had long since been completed. Zhao Chiying had ordered everything—she'd specially had a chef from an inn at the foot of the mountain purchase the ingredients, then ascend the mountain to cook here. Naturally, the quality and taste of the food was higher than anything the disciples of Bixia Sect could make.

Bixia Sect had very few disciples left, just enough to fill one table. Zhao Chiying stood up and offered a toast with a cup of wine, welcoming Yan Wushi's visit and hoping that he wouldn't mind the spartan state of the sect.

Yan Wushi left her quite a bit of face himself: he raised his own cup and said, "Sect Leader Zhao need not be so courteous. A-Qiao is soft and simple by nature. When the things and people he cares about are in question, I also can't help but worry about them on his behalf."

You came of your own volition, thought Shen Qiao. *What does this have to do with me?*

Zhao Chiying also found herself wondering, *Why do these words sound so strange?*

But she didn't think too much about it and placed her cup down with a carefree smile. "Though we had a chef specially ascend the mountain to prepare this banquet, Lu cuisine is fairly different from that of Chang'an. I don't know if it'll suit Sect Leader Yan's tastes. I hope you won't mind, and feel free to eat as you wish."

After the opening speech, everyone picked up their chopsticks and began to eat. Shen Qiao recalled the matter that Yan Wushi had brought up earlier concerning Han Eying. Since he was sitting next to Zhao Chiying at the banquet, he took the opportunity to ask her a few things.

As he expected, Zhao Chiying was astonished. "Yue-shixiong took Han Eying as his disciple while he was outside, so she only counts as an external disciple. Even I have never met her myself; there's even less to be said about any relationship with Bixia Sect. Thank you, Daoist Master Shen, for telling me this. I'll ask Yue-shixiong once I get back and take note of it myself." Her tone was colored by dejection as she added, "With the way Bixia Sect is right now, though, even if she is seeking outside help, I doubt she'd pick this place."

Shen Qiao tried to think up a solution for her. "Could you head down the mountain and recruit some talented disciples?"

"Daoxiong used to lead Xuandu Mountain," said Zhao Chiying, "so forgive me for being forward, but may I ask how Xuandu Mountain went about recruiting disciples?"

"At the foot of Xuandu Mountain lies Xuandu Town," Shen Qiao explained. "Though it's small, it's quite bustling, so every year, Xuandu Mountain would send people down the mountain to find disciples. We'd set up special areas within the town—anyone interested in entering the sect could go there to apply. When the time came, we'd accept them based on their aptitudes and dispositions."

Zhao Chiying sighed. "I see. I was too forward with my question. Xuandu Mountain is the world's foremost Daoist sect, so of course there'd be no dearth of disciples coming to apply of their own volition! And Daoxiong knows about Bixia Sect's current situation as well. To be honest, there are potential disciples from farming families at the foot of the mountain who are willing to join us, but many of them are too old. Their parents see that they lack the strength for farm work, so they get sent up the mountain in search of a master. But those children are mostly of poor aptitude, and they have long passed the ideal age to begin their training in martial arts. On the other hand, those with better credentials are rarely willing to travel such long distances to Bixia Sect—they'd likely just enter another, nearer one. As time passes, the situation will only worsen."

As the sect leader, she naturally had to take into account long-term considerations on behalf of her sect. The only thing that could support a sect was talent. Without talent, the sect would die off sooner or later.

Currently, a lack of that talent was Bixia Sect's biggest problem. The disciples underneath Zhao Chiying and Yue Kunchi, like Fan Yuanbai and Zhou Yexue, were of only average aptitude. To put it bluntly, in the future, their martial skills would only be second or third-rate at best. It would be incredibly difficult for them to enter the ranks of first-rate experts. In the long run, Bixia Sect might meet its end in the hands of Fan Yuanbai and his ilk.

Shen Qiao could understand the pains she was undertaking. "In my view, Sect Leader Zhao, you're still young—you need not worry so much. Perhaps given two to three years, you'll be able to recruit some good disciples!"

Zhao Chiying gave a strained smile. "I can only continue with those thoughts in mind!"

Shen Qiao wanted to say more, but then a spoonful of soup entered his field of vision, accompanied by a tender voice: "Open your mouth."

At Shen Qiao's stare, Yan Wushi smiled slightly. "Don't forget that you still owe me," he said, his tone firm yet unruffled. "Is drinking this spoonful of soup criminal or inhumane? Or does it betray righteousness?"

Momentous Changes

N ATURALLY, PARTAKING from this spoon was not criminal or inhumane, and it certainly didn't go against righteousness. But as it would drop them into an embarrassing situation right before everyone's watching eyes, a normal person would choose to keep their mouth shut.

In truth, Shen Qiao had the vague feeling that, ever since their reunion at the Huang residence, Yan Wushi's attitude toward him had undergone some strange and subtle changes. If previously Yan Wushi had been full of malice, wanting to push him into certain death, then this time it looked more like Yan Wushi was taking pleasure in Shen Qiao making a fool of himself, wanting him to embarrass himself in various ways.

However, Shen Qiao had no idea what reason lay behind Yan Wushi's change in attitude. He could only assume that Yan Wushi had found a new avenue of entertaining himself.

"I remembered you liked fish, A-Qiao," said Yan Wushi. "This minced fish is very fresh and tender, so I'm sure it'll be to your liking."

As if to prove Shen Qiao's suspicions correct, Yan Wushi's face bore a hint of deep amusement. No matter how he looked at it, it was infuriating.

The two of them stared at each other for a long while. By now, all the onlookers had caught on to the bizarre atmosphere.

"I'm grateful for Sect Leader Yan's kindly intentions," Shen Qiao said slowly. "However, this humble Daoist possesses both arms and legs. Sect Leader Yan shouldn't squander that hard-won promise here."

Yan Wushi raised an eyebrow. "A-Qiao, you're someone who always keeps his promises, yet you're going to break your word for a request as trivial as this?"

A notion suddenly came to Shen Qiao. "That's because Sect Leader Yan was the first to speak falsely," he said.

"When did I speak falsely?"

"You have such a poor memory, Sect Leader Yan. You clearly said that you only need opponents, not friends. How, in the blink of an eye, did this humble Daoist suddenly become the closest of friends with you?"

"I wasn't speaking falsely," said Yan Wushi with a smile. "It's only that things have changed. Back then I really did think so, but a person's opinion is bound to change over time. Even if you couldn't walk away from tangren when you were three years old, A-Qiao, does that mean that you still can't now?"

Shen Qiao gave a slight snort. "I know someone who indeed can't walk away from tangren!"

He was talking about the incident with "Xie Ling."

Surprise came over Yan Wushi's face as he purposely misinterpreted Shen Qiao's words. "Truly? Such a sentimental person! Then aren't they even more suited to becoming the closest of friends with?"

This man was really too shameless! No matter the situation, everything he did was always correct!

Shen Qiao knew that he'd never prevail in a verbal debate. When he saw how everyone was watching them, he felt his face warm in spite of himself, and he suddenly thought this all ridiculously childish. He quickly lowered his voice and whispered, "We're in public, Sect Leader Yan. Have some more self-respect and save any arguments for when we get back!"

Yan Wushi laughed. "I only asked you to eat this spoonful of fish. How do I lack self-respect?"

After saying this, he continued to thrust the spoon toward Shen Qiao, and Shen Qiao moved back to avoid it, even raising his hand to push it away—but with barely a flicker of movement, Yan Wushi flipped his wrist, and the spoon somehow vanished before reappearing in his other hand, which he held out to Shen Qiao. His determination was clear.

Neither of them appeared to move at all, but their sleeves flapped, and they exchanged several blows in an instant. Everyone else stared, dumbfounded.

Many of them were still lost on what was happening. Zhao Chiying was hesitating over whether she should step in and stop the fight, but quite a few Bixia Sect disciples were taking it as a valuable learning opportunity—they watched the two men's motions with rapt attention, terrified of missing out on even a second.

The moment they started fighting, Shiwu had wanted to get up and stop them, but Yuwen Song grabbed him.

"If Shixiong can, he should watch closely," said Yuwen Song. "Shizun and Sect Leader Yan are only sparring. It's not a real fight, or else they'd have turned the whole place upside down already. How could they remain firmly in their seats otherwise?"

But Shiwu was still worried. "Things were fine just a moment ago. Why did they start fighting all of a sudden?"

Yuwen Song watched their movements with rapt attention, his tone unconcerned. "Perhaps something about Shizun displeased Sect Leader Yan, so he purposely picked a fight?"

Shiwu was shocked. "Why would Sect Leader Yan be displeased with Shizun?"

Yuwen Song had always acted mature beyond his age, but he didn't know everything—with his limited understanding, he couldn't explain. At Shiwu's question, he simply shook his head. "It seems that Shizun gave him the cold shoulder just now, which made him unhappy."

Having gained this new revelation, Shiwu carefully ruminated on these words. Yet he still felt that something was off.

The two men continued to fight. Each blow they exchanged was exquisite, and the crowd was unable to tear their eyes away. They'd even forgotten why the fight began in the first place. Yan Wushi held a spoon in one hand, using only his wrist and arm to meet Shen Qiao's strikes. With his other hand, he took the opportunity to flick several of the peanuts on the table toward Shiwu.

Seeing this, Shen Qiao naturally had to shield his disciple. His sleeve billowed as it first flapped, then furled. It made for a lovely sight, accompanied by a sense of effortless freedom characteristic to Daoism, and the witnesses felt their minds and bodies relax. It wasn't only the Bixia Sect disciples—even Zhao Chiying and Yue Kunchi revealed expressions of awe.

However, at this very moment, Yan Wushi reached out and wrapped his arm around Shen Qiao's waist, then delivered the spoon right to Shen Qiao's mouth. He struck at an acupoint with the hand on Shen Qiao's back, and when Shen Qiao instinctively tried to evade, his guard against the spoon fell. Thus, the fish soup slid straight inside.

These actions happened within a single breath; Shen Qiao had no time to react. Once finished, Yan Wushi immediately pulled back and retreated bodily. He smiled as he said, "Daoist Master Shen is so dishonest; your words don't match your heart. If you wanted to eat it, why spend so long declining and wasting my energy? If only you'd simply opened your mouth earlier."

This was really...!

Shen Qiao swallowed the fish with difficulty. He was torn between leaving the banquet in a rage, and simply pummeling Yan Wushi head-on.

But the former would be terribly rude to the host, and the latter would look like him making a mountain out of a molehill.

But this was really...too shameless! If he let even this slide, he might as well let everything go!

Do I, Shen Qiao, really look like such a pushover that you can treat me like a plaything trapped in the palm of your hand?

Shen Qiao's face went dark. This time, he was truly enraged.

However, he didn't lose his temper because that would put Zhao Chiying and the others in a difficult position. Instead, he simply nodded and said indifferently, "Sect Leader Yan, your skills are beyond mine. I am truly not your match and therefore must thank you for the guidance."

Then he raised his cup at Zhao Chiying. "I'm grateful to Sect Leader Zhao for taking care of Shiwu while I was away. I'm not good with wine, so I offer a toast of tea to Sect Leader Zhao instead."

Zhao Chiying swept a glance at Yan Wushi. His face still held a smile, but she couldn't determine the emotions behind it—they were difficult to grasp.

She spoke candidly. "Shen-daoxiong need not be so courteous. You've done our Bixia Sect a great kindness, and we share a deep friendship. Please don't take a small matter like this so seriously! Even if there were ten of Shiwu, Bixia Sect would still be capable of caring for them all. If we're talking about the amount of food, Shiwu eats even less than Yexue!"

Shiwu blushed. "You can't make that kind of comparison. Zhou-jiejie is older!"

Everyone couldn't resist laughing when they saw his face, and the tension from earlier dissipated like smoke.

Once the banquet was over, Shen Qiao bade farewell to Zhao Chiying and the others, then brought Shiwu and Yuwen Yong back to their respective rooms to rest.

After taking care of them, Shen Qiao returned to his own house but found someone standing before his door. The man's features were crystal clear under the moon's bright glow and the lanterns hanging from the eaves.

Shen Qiao's anger had yet to subside, and he was loath to say anything to him. *Even if I can't afford to provoke him,* he thought, *surely I can avoid him.* So he silently turned right around to leave.

But Yan Wushi moved faster than he did. Shen Qiao only managed a single step before his arm was caught.

Shen Qiao yanked his arm away and stood still, face expressionless. "Sect Leader Yan, please have some self-respect."

Yan Wushi was all smiles. "What, are you upset?"

Shen Qiao said nothing.

"I was only messing with you. No malice intended. If I upset you, let me make amends."

"I really can't afford to receive Sect Leader Yan's amends," said Shen Qiao stuffily. "Previously you said you didn't need friends and that this humble Daoist wasn't qualified to be your friend. I accepted that. Later, I saved you, but that was only because your life was linked to Yuwen Yong's, and the north can only be stable if the Zhou Dynasty is as well. There were no personal feelings involved, and I never expected you to thank me or pay me back. Now that you've recovered from your injuries, we should go our separate ways. Sect Leader Yan has his glorious path, while this humble Daoist will walk his lone wooden plank. I am a poor man with nothing to my name, so I don't understand what I've done to deserve your good graces, so much that you must constantly try to humiliate me. This humble Daoist asks that Sect Leader Yan be gracious: please inform me why, and I will make the appropriate changes!"

Qi Fengge had influenced Shen Qiao greatly, and Shen Qiao himself was also gracious and magnanimous by nature. He was always generous with his goodwill and kindness when interacting with others, even if it came with what should have been deep-seated grudges. Even after Yu Ai hurt him, Shen Qiao had been heartbroken and furious, but once it was over, he didn't spend day and night gnashing his teeth and dreaming of ways to bring misfortune to his shidi.

Yan Wushi was the only exception. Ever since he'd fallen from the cliff, their fates had become intertwined. The old scores between them, gratitude and resentment both, couldn't be simply broken down into who owed whom more, but as the saying went, once a man is bitten by a snake, he'll spend ten years jumping at the sight of a rope. Currently, Shen Qiao truly wished to avoid him. Out of sight, out of mind. But things hadn't gone as he hoped or expected. Even now he didn't understand—this world held thousands of people more outstanding and beautiful than Shen Qiao, and thousands of people more downtrodden and miserable than him as well. Exactly why did Yan Wushi insist on adhering to Shen Qiao and Shen Qiao only, unwilling to let go?

Various unhappy experiences had been piling up for a while, and a sense of grievance and frustration suddenly surged within his heart. But it was hard to voice.

Shen Qiao only felt thoroughly exhausted, in both body and mind.

In Yan Wushi's eyes, that aggrieved, dejected expression of his was terribly adorable. And at this moment, Yan Wushi's lips, originally curved with amusement, became stained with the gentleness of moonlight.

But this gentleness was so subtle as to be imperceptible, and Shen Qiao naturally failed to notice.

"When has my venerable self humiliated you?" asked Yan Wushi. "If I really wanted to embarrass you, I have far more ruthless tricks up my sleeve. Why would I play that kind of harmless prank?"

Shen Qiao was furious. "You call that harmless? Before everyone's eyes, you...you..." As rage exploded through him, he momentarily stumbled over his words and found himself struggling to continue.

Yan Wushi sputtered a laugh. "All right, just let me apologize. Calm down. My venerable self will personally make you a bowl of soup as amends, how about that?"

Shen Qiao turned his head away. "No need!"

Yan Wushi tugged him along. "Even if the words I said in the past hurt your feelings, there's nothing I can do. Once out of your mouth, words are like water spilled on the ground—impossible to take back. My venerable self will never do something as childish as regretting what's already happened. As an enlightened master of Daoism, are you going to act as the talentless masses do and cling to the past, unwilling to forgive? Everyone says that Daoist Master Shen is a generous and magnanimous man who lets bygones be bygones. Why do you treat this venerable one so specially, then? Or is this a sign that we're destined to be?"

Shen Qiao was so angry he laughed. "If it's destined for calamity, yes!"

Yan Wushi was unconcerned. "Destined for calamity or destined for happiness, both are still destiny. Your Daoism often speaks of working in accordance with the flow of fate, so why, when it comes to yourself, are you unable to let nature take its course?"

"From how I see it, you shouldn't be called 'Yan Wushi,'" said Shen Qiao.

"Then what should I be called?"

Shen Qiao gave an icy laugh. "Zong Youli.[2] Because you're always right, no matter what you say!"

Yan Wushi burst out laughing.

He dragged Shen Qiao to the kitchen. The chef had been using the place in the afternoon, so some fresh ingredients still remained.

"Give me fifteen minutes," said Yan Wushi.

Shen Qiao frowned. "I'm not hungry."

Yan Wushi didn't even look back. "True. You're full with rage."

Shen Qiao choked at his words.

Yan Wushi indeed moved swiftly—by using his internal energy to stoke the flames, he greatly increased his efficiency. Hot water was swiftly boiled, then fish meat and eggs scrambled with starch were mixed and shaped into balls. He cooked them in the steaming water, sprinkled some green onion and salt on top, and fresh off the stove came two bowls of piping-hot fish ball soup.

Martial artists also needed to eat and sleep. No matter how well respected a man Yan Wushi was, he couldn't always bring a servant when traveling outside, so there were still times when he had to cook himself. Shen Qiao had already witnessed his cooking skills when the two of them were hiding from disaster back then, so he wasn't particularly surprised this time either.

Shen Qiao scooped up a fish ball and popped it into his mouth.

---

2   总有理. Literally, "always justified."

It was, he found, quite delicious. Although his anger had yet to subside, he couldn't go against his conscience and say it tasted bad, so he ducked down and began to eat silently.

Yan Wushi held his own spoon out to him.

"What?" asked Shen Qiao.

"Wasn't I going to make amends?" said Yan Wushi.

Shen Qiao was baffled. "Then why give me a spoon?"

Yan Wushi laughed. "It upset you when I fed you earlier. So, now you can feed me—that way, we've both had our turn. Isn't that fair?"

Shen Qiao was speechless.

Right now, what he really wanted to do was upend this bowl of fish ball soup over Yan Wushi's head.

The days at Bixia Sect were comfortable and monotonous, yet time still passed quickly.

With Zhao Chiying and the others as witnesses, Yuwen Song officially underwent the apprenticeship ceremony with Shen Qiao. While Shen Qiao instructed his disciples, he also continued practicing his own martial arts. As days passed, his internal energy gradually advanced toward his former level, and there were even vague signs that he was approaching a breakthrough.

Though Zhao Chiying was worried about Bixia Sect's lack of new talent, she also knew that the most important matter was to properly instruct Fan Yuanbai, Zhou Yexue, and the other current disciples. Otherwise, they'd end up squandering their current saplings before they could find any beautiful jade to work with.

With masters like Yan Wushi and Shen Qiao present, it was inevitable Zhao Chiying would raise her expectations of the sect's disciples—her demands became stricter, causing everyone to moan and groan and beg Yue Kunchi for help. Yue Kunchi, that bleeding heart, was caught between his shimei and their disciples, and found himself frazzled in the daily state of chaos.

Yan Wushi had also seemed to have rooted himself at Bixia Sect—he said nothing about leaving, and Bixia Sect couldn't make him go either. Furthermore, Yan Wushi would sometimes impart to them some martial guidance, even if this guidance was accompanied by jeering more cutting than knives. Bixia Sect could only weather it, equally suffering and grateful.

The passage of time meant little within the mountains, but beyond them, the world had undergone many changes.

After Yuwen Yun ascended to the throne, he gave Buddhist Master Xueting the title of state preceptor and poured his support behind Buddhism. With the pretext of praying for blessings for his mother, he began to perform large-scale renovations of Buddhist temples. Buddhism's influence had suffered a heavy blow during Yuwen Yun's reign, but now it began to show signs of another great rise.

Meanwhile, Yuwen Yun also elevated Hehuan Sect, imitating what the previous emperor had done with Huanyue Sect. He allowed their influence to permeate the court and monitor the officials, and he also let both Hehuan Sect and the Buddhist discipline shore up their authority all over the jianghu for his own use.

Under these circumstances, both the Buddhist discipline and Hehuan Sect took the chance to undergo explosive expansions, starting from Chang'an and spreading north. Faced with this pressure, many smaller sects either submitted themselves to Buddhism or were assimilated by Hehuan Sect.

As for Lingyin Temple and Duyuan House, and other Buddhist sects relatively unknown within the jianghu, the imperial court soundlessly seized control of them, placing them under the state preceptor's direct jurisdiction.

And when it came to small sects like Taohua Pier or Pingshan Hall, Hehuan Sect annihilated them all.

Even Zhongnan Sect, which was fairly well-known, fell apart with their sect leader's death and was eventually forced to surrender to Hehuan Sect.

Almost overnight, Hehuan Sect and the Buddhist discipline rolled forth, crushing all that came beneath them like wilted leaves or twigs, swiftly expanding their power and influence and transforming into leviathans.

A little more than half a year later, the predictions Yan Wushi had made all came true.

Invitation

EARLY ONE MORNING, an unexpected visitor appeared at the foot of Mount Tai.

He ascended the mountain, sword in hand, his steps as light and graceful as if he were treading over flat ground. It wasn't long at all before he was already halfway up the mountain, outside Bixia Sect's gates.

Zhao Chiying was leading the disciples in sword practice when she heard the report from Fan Yuanbai, who was on duty. He said that someone had arrived from Qingcheng Mountain's Chunyang Monastery and was currently waiting for her.

Bixia Sect and Chunyang Monastery had a fairly good relationship. They'd had many back-and-forth dealings, but as Bixia Sect waned and Chunyang Monastery grew, the friendship inherited from the previous generations gradually faded. Though Chunyang Monastery had never looked down on Bixia Sect's lower status, the two were still separated by a vast distance. For example, when Bixia Sect experienced its previous crisis, distant waters couldn't quench a close fire. If not for Shen Qiao dropping out of nowhere, it would've been far too late by the time Chunyang Monastery received the news and came to their aid.

News of happenings below the mountain trickled in bit by bit. Zhao Chiying didn't know as much as Yan Wushi, but she had heard of Hehuan Sect and the Buddhist discipline's rapid expansion. Bixia Sect was on a remote mountain, distant from imperial rule, so for the time being they could afford to pay attention to only themselves. But now Chunyang Monastery had sent someone to them, and that meant an urgent matter.

As she was thinking, the visitor was led inside by Fan Yuanbai.

His expression was frosty, his bearing dignified. His steps were steady, and even as he walked, the grip on his sword remained firm, without the slightest quiver.

It seemed that Chunyang Monastery had found its successor. Zhao Chiying sighed to herself—she was somewhat envious.

"Li Qingyu, disciple of Chunyang Monastery, greets Sect Leader Zhao."

"So you're Abbot Yi's favorite disciple?" she said. "As expected of one of the Twin Jades of Qingcheng. Abbot Yi is truly fortunate!"

"Sect Leader Zhao is too kind."

"I was in seclusion for a long time. Even though I've exited, I still haven't had the chance to meet with Abbot Yi. I trust that his martial arts have scaled even greater heights?"

It was obvious that Li Qingyu wasn't a martial artist accustomed to exchanging pleasantries. "To tell the truth, this one came as a messenger on behalf of Liuli Palace," he said. "It regards the matter of the Sword Trial Conference."

Sword Trial Conference?

Zhao Chiying and Yue Kunchi exchanged a glance.

"If I remember correctly, the Sword Trial Conference takes place once every ten years. Isn't this only the ninth year?"

"That is so," said Li Qingyu. "However, a few days ago, someone from Liuli Palace visited us, saying that they planned to hold it early and wished to use Chunyang Monastery as the venue. Shizun agreed, so I came to deliver the message and invite Sect Leader Zhao."

Fangzhang Isle was an island, one that was impossible for most people to find. There was only one sect on that island: Liuli Sect. They were self-sufficient and rarely participated in the conflicts between the powers of the jianghu, yet they were also fond of making records of the Central Plains' martial arts circles. For example, rankings like "The World's Top Ten Martial Artists" that were so often discussed were created by none other than Liuli Palace. And they were also the ones who organized the once-a-decade Sword Trial Conference.

The disciples of Liuli Palace were neither impressive nor famous when it came to martial arts, but due to this tradition, members of the jianghu would still give them some face whenever they met. After all, that sect had little worth coveting, so there was no point in making a mortal enemy out of them. If someone was dissatisfied with the ranking, they could simply seek out the martial experts ranked ahead of them; there was no need to make things difficult for Liuli Palace.

If any great martial advancements happened within those ten years, the names on the next ranking would naturally change. As the saying went, "no first place among scholars, no second place among martial artists." Martial arts wasn't something you could obtain through deceiving others. Who was the true number one, who was stronger, those things could be determined at a glance. Even if two masters appeared to be equally matched, a single duel would be enough to distinguish victor and defeated, superior and inferior.

The Sword Trial Conference was where the jianghu rankings were determined. It happened once a decade, and invitations were sent out en masse. Anyone could participate to spar and test their skills. As Liuli Palace was in a remote area, they'd borrow a venue from a sect within the Central Plains and host it there. The sect in question could take the opportunity to bolster their reputation, so they'd naturally be willing.

As the ones in charge of the rankings, their insights were keen despite not being martially impressive themselves. Everyone trusted Liuli Palace's rankings because they were almost always free of errors. Such as in the case of Qi Fengge, who did not participate in the Sword Trial Conference ten years ago despite still being alive at that point. Even so, he remained in first place, and it was seen as deserved—no one voiced any complaints.

Over the years, as Liuli Palace rose to fame, many rankings emerged one after another. They'd yet to hold another Sword Trial Conference since the likes of Qi Fengge and Cui Youwang passed. As the next ranking from Liuli Palace would take too long, people began making their own lists of "Top Ten Martial Artists." Though Shen Qiao never used to show his face in the jianghu, they'd entered him into the rankings because he'd succeeded Xuandu Mountain. After he dueled Kunye and fell from the cliff in defeat, those busybodies also added Kunye and Yu Ai's names.

But as Liuli Palace hadn't created those rankings, many people's hearts naturally surged in excitement and anticipation the moment news that Liuli Palace would hold the Sword Trial Conference emerged. Other than rankings like "The World's Top Ten," Liuli Palace created various other lists as well, such as those for swords and sabers. Since the sword was the king of all weapons, the land had a vast number of sword users, and "swordmaster rankings" also became the focus of many people's attention.

True martial arts grandmasters who'd entered echelons occupied by Qi Fengge, Yi Pichen, and Buddhist Master Xueting didn't need to use Liuli Palace's rankings to bolster their own reputations. Their names being on the list or not didn't affect their fame at all—the ranking was merely an extra touch, like embroidering flowers on extravagant brocade.

As for Shen Qiao, he couldn't care less about these things. Even if he were still in charge of Xuandu Mountain, even if Yu Ai's plot against him had yet to happen, he probably still wouldn't have sent anyone to the Sword Trial Conference after receiving this news.

But exceptions aside, there were still many who needed to use Liuli Palace to boost their fame, and Liuli Palace also needed a way to validate their existence. Both parties benefited.

Zhao Chiying didn't crave fame, but currently, Bixia Sect needed to recruit new disciples for their long-term development. If she or Yue Kunchi managed some achievements during the Sword Trial Conference, they'd gain a fair number of admirers who'd come forth to learn martial arts from them.

"I'm grateful to Abbot Yi for sending word to us about the conference," she said, "Bixia Sect is so remote, if we waited for outside news to arrive by itself, I fear we wouldn't have made it in time."

"If Sect Leader Zhao has finished with her preparations, this one can accompany her there," said Li Qingyu. "That way I can also assist you on your trip."

"No sects you need to inform, Li-daoyou?"[3]

"Normally, Liuli Palace is responsible for informing sects across the land. But since Chunyang Monastery and Bixia Sect have always had a good relationship, Shizun had me come here. We heard that Bixia Sect suffered a crisis a while back. Because of the vast distance separating our sects, we were unable to offer our assistance in time. We hope that Sect Leader Zhao doesn't hold it against us."

---

3   道友. Literally "Daoist friend." A polite address for cultivators or Daoists.

As he was Yi Pichen's personal disciple, his status was higher than normal. Rumors said that he was likely to inherit Yi Pichen's mantle, making him Chunyang Monastery's future leader. And when it came to martial arts, Zhao Chiying might even be a level below him. His personally coming here to deliver the news was already giving Bixia Sect more than enough face. Of course, Zhao Chiying knew this, so she treated Li Qingyu with great courtesy and didn't face him with the attitude of a sect leader.

"I also know that distant waters cannot quench close fires," she said, "so I didn't wish to trouble Abbot Yi. I'm already deeply grateful that Abbot Yi remembered us regarding this matter. I'll explain things to our disciples, then we can set out tomorrow. If Li-daoyou does not mind, you may stay here for tonight."

Li Qingyu nodded. "Feel free to do as you wish, Sect Leader Zhao."

But suddenly, he seemed to recall something. "May I ask Sect Leader Zhao? Shen Qiao, or Shen-daoxiong—is he also at Bixia Sect?"

Shen Qiao had planned to guide his disciples through sword practice that morning, but Yan Wushi invited him to spar at the mountain summit. Yan Wushi said that it had been a long time since he himself had practiced the sword, so he wanted to exchange a few moves with Shen Qiao. He even borrowed a sword from Yue Kunchi. But unexpectedly, Shen Qiao remembered something. "What happened to Taihua?" he asked. "You traded with Sang Jingxing for it that day."

In the past, Yan Wushi had fought Cui Youwang and lost. His Taihua also fell into the other man's hands, which was how it ended up with Cui Youwang's disciple Sang Jingxing. But Yan Wushi was extremely arrogant. No matter how excellent the sword was, it was still a mere worldly possession, something separate from himself. If the enemy took it away, first it became a weakness that could be exploited, and second, it compounded the humiliation of defeat. So he'd decided to give up on the sword—instead he created the Spring Waters finger technique, unrivaled in all the world.

So, when he'd exchanged Shen Qiao for Taihua then, he hadn't actually cared about the sword at all—he merely wanted to take the chance to humiliate Shen Qiao, to make him understand that he was worth less than a sword. That way, he expected, Shen Qiao would sink into a state of absolute despair over the human heart.

As for Taihua, after taking it back from Sang Jingxing, he instantly tossed it to Yu Shengyan without even a second glance.

Still, no matter how egotistical Yan Wushi was, he knew very well that he couldn't speak these thoughts out loud or Shen Qiao's current placidity toward him would be utterly annihilated.

Perhaps the Yan Wushi from back then had never expected that a day would come when he'd fall into a pit he'd dug himself...

Fortunately, Shen Qiao didn't pursue the matter further but brushed it aside after asking that single question.

The two of them dueled on the mountain summit. After they had exchanged hundreds of blows, the sun peeked out, its golden rays spilling over the mountainside and illuminating their surroundings. Shen Qiao lost by a small margin, but it wasn't because his sword-play was lacking—rather, his internal energy had yet to recover to its previous highest point. In contrast, with the help of the *Zhuyang Strategy* scroll, Yan Wushi had been able to repair the flaw within his demonic core in only three short months, and his skills had grown even greater. He'd indeed been blessed with heaven-given talents—they were awe-inspiring to behold.

Those endowed with extraordinary talents were always arrogant and ambitious, and they'd find it difficult to accept the existence of people who were even more gifted than themselves. But Shen Qiao didn't have this issue—his temperament was mild, and he maintained a generous heart toward everyone and everything. Whenever he encountered a problem, he'd examine his own mistakes before blaming others. Now he sheathed his sword and straightened, then cupped his hands. "When my late master was still here, he once mentioned that Sect Leader Yan would be his equal within a few years. Sure enough, that has come true. This humble Daoist is grateful for your guidance—I have learned much."

This was no empty flattery. He truly believed that Yan Wushi was stronger than he was, and thus his gratitude was sincere as well. He felt neither envy nor fury at his defeat: a win was a win, and a loss a loss. There was no need for other emotions like resentment or anger. To Shen Qiao, things were just that simple.

Yan Wushi thought that he could look at Shen Qiao's earnest expression hundreds of times without growing bored. In the past, he'd wanted this man to fall into the pitch-black abyss, to hate and curse the world, but he now adored his warm and gentle heart with that same fervency.

He savored the other man's expressions again and again, and smiled as he said, "A-Qiao, your words are far too distant considering our current relationship."

What current relationship? Shen Qiao's mouth twitched as he forced himself once again to endure an irrelevant remark from Yan Wushi. If he couldn't stop himself from retorting, he knew that he'd be on the receiving end of another flood of twisted reasoning.

He silently lambasted him with "Zong Youli" several times but said, "It's getting late. I should return to teach Shiwu and Qilang some swordplay."

The two of them descended from the mountain summit, one after the other. The one in front walked with somewhat hurried steps while the one behind was neither fast nor slow. A consistent distance of five paces remained between them, which also reflected their current relationship.

The mood hovered between irreproachable and eerily ambiguous. Their relationship was like a snapped lotus root that, on closer inspection, remained still linked by dangling threads, heavy with words and feelings unvoiced.

When Shen Qiao returned to the grounds of Bixia Sect, he saw a man standing by his door. The person in question seemed to have also seen Shen Qiao walk toward him from afar, for a trace of a smile emerged on his cold, youthful countenance. It was an expression he hadn't even shown in front of Zhao Chiying.

"It's been a while, Shen-daoxiong."

Fish-Head Soup

SHEN QIAO FROZE, but once he realized who the man was, a smile appeared on his face as well. "Li-gongzi, it's been some time. How have you been?"

"I've been well." Li Qingyu wasn't the type to be free with his emotions—the unprecedented smile he'd revealed earlier was already terribly rare. It was a restrained smile, one that quickly vanished as his face returned to its usual placid calm, but one could still sense the delight that hung about him.

Shen Qiao, too, had a favorable impression of Li Qingyu. That day, though the other man had first shown him contempt, he'd lent Shen Qiao his sword and helped him defeat Duan Wenyang. It was clear that he actually possessed an emotional, willful personality—he just wasn't good with words and thus came across as aloof. Cold outside but warm inside.

"While I was in Chang'an, I could only fight my way out of the siege with Qilang thanks to the assistance of your shixiong's family. How is your shixiong, Su Qiao, doing right now?"

Li Qingyu nodded. "He is quite well. After Hehuan Sect forcibly assimilated Zhongnan Sect, the Su family and a couple other disciples came to Qingcheng Mountain. They're now safe and sound."

Shen Qiao breathed a sigh of relief. "That's good. It's unfortunate that Chang'an's current situation is rather dire. They probably won't be able to return for a while, will they?"

Li Qingyu made a noise of agreement. "How has the recovery of your martial arts been, Daoxiong? If you have the time to spare, would you mind giving me some guidance with a spar?"

As someone obsessed with the sword, Shen Qiao looked to him like a precious blade that had yet to be unsheathed, concealing its sharp edge and wondrous surprises. Enthralled, he practically itched to examine and ponder every inch of Shen Qiao's body, though he had no impure intentions.

Faced with Li Qingyu's blazing gaze, Shen Qiao didn't know whether to laugh or cry. "I…"

He'd only managed this one word when Yan Wushi answered for him. "A-Qiao is going to teach his disciples now. I'm afraid he doesn't have any time for you to waste. If you wish for guidance, my venerable self will advise you with a spar."

Li Qingyu stared at him. "Who are you?"

The corners of Yan Wushi's mouth twitched. "If you can defeat this venerable one, I will give you my name myself."

Li Qingyu's gaze shifted downward, and for a moment, it stopped on the wooden sword he held in his hand. Then he suddenly shook his head. "You don't often use a sword, and you possess a great jumble of skills. You aren't Shen Qiao's equal in the sword, and my internal energy is currently inferior to yours. There's no point in fighting."

Yan Wushi's smile was warm and kind. "My venerable self has never seen someone this self-aware. You are truly the first."

Li Qingyu's gaze quickly sharpened. The two of them stared at each other for a moment, then he nodded. "So you must be Huanyue Sect Leader Yan."

Yan Wushi raised an eyebrow. "You recognize this venerable one?"

"Mm," said Li Qingyu. "Rumors say that the Huanyue Sect Leader's egotism is unmatched in the world. Seeing you today, I can tell that it's a well-deserved reputation."

It was only their first meeting and the two men were already at loggerheads. It was completely beyond Shen Qiao's expectations, and he said, "Sect Leader Yan, Li-gongzi is Bixia Sect's honored guest..."

He'd yet to finish when Yan Wushi laughed. "Then let my venerable self see just how capable this honored guest is!"

He extended his index finger, the movement as swift as lightning, yet also beautifully flawless. It was the renowned Spring Waters finger technique!

Shen Qiao wanted to stop him, but it was already too late.

There was a loud clang—Li Qingyu's Qiushui had only half left its sheath, and that half a blade perfectly blocked Yan Wushi's index finger. After that moment of brief contact, Li Qingyu retreated three steps, and his sword was forced back into its sheath.

Yan Wushi withdrew his hands and stood still, utterly motionless.

The difference in strength was stark.

But this was also within expectations. Li Qingyu was, without a doubt, a martial expert of the younger generation, so of course he wasn't Yan Wushi's match yet. He too had said it just now, that his internal energy was inferior to Yan Wushi's. It was Yan Wushi who'd forced his hand, demonstrating the malicious desire to bully a junior.

Li Qingyu gripped his sword while cupping his hands, suppressing the surge of emotions within him. "Sect Leader Yan's internal energy is truly too imperious. I am no match for it."

His emphasis on internal energy meant he believed that Yan Wushi's victory was due to his powerful internal energy, and not the strength of his finger technique.

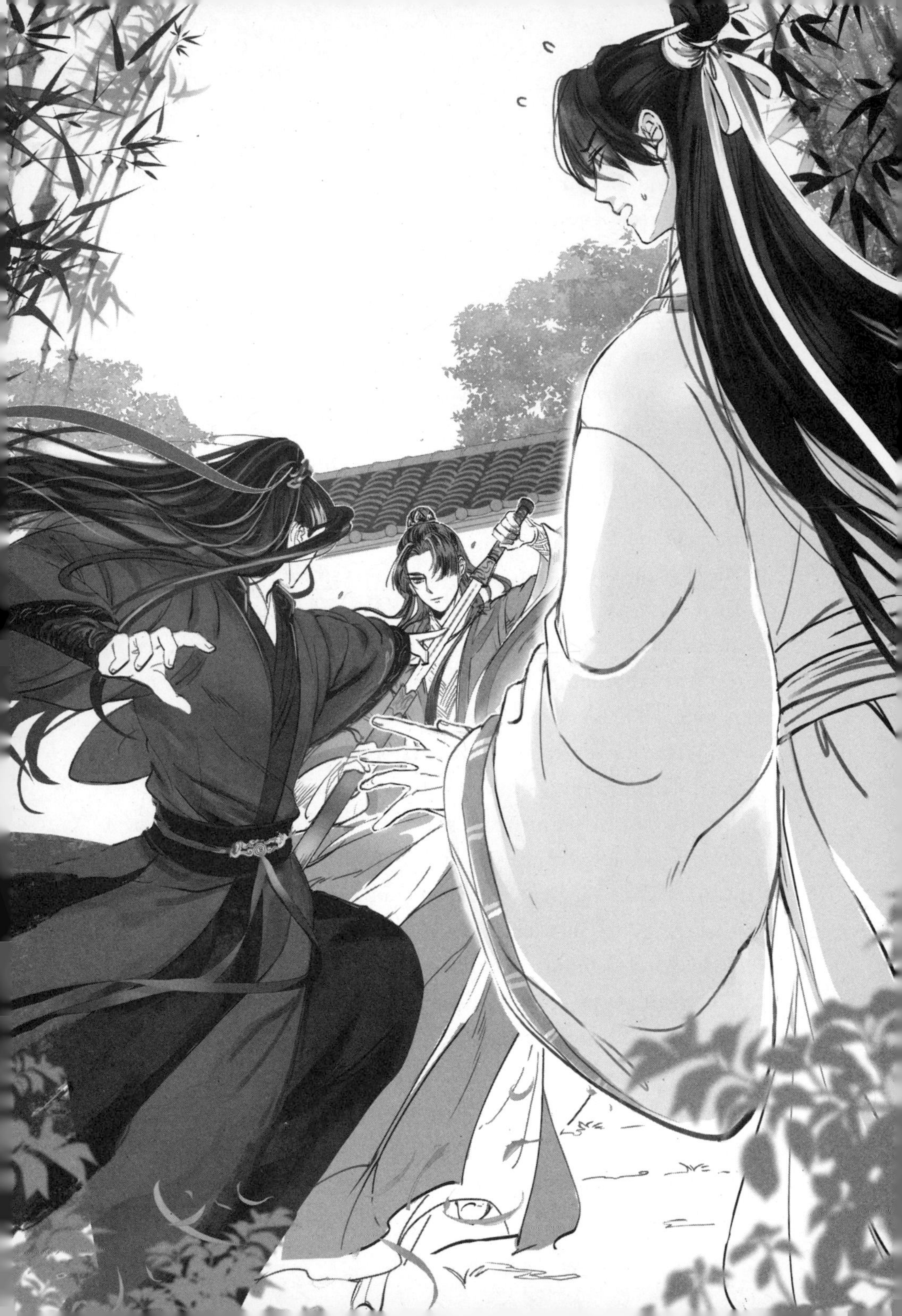

The loggerheads were about to explode.

Yan Wushi gave a sneering laugh.

Before he could take further action, Shen Qiao stepped forward. "Li-gongzi, the death of the Zhongnan Sect Leader and the sect's forced assimilation into Hehuan Sect must have made quite a few waves in the jianghu. As I wish to know more of the details, might Li-gongzi spare some time to elaborate on this?"

Li Qingyu tossed a glance at Yan Wushi, then he nodded. "But of course."

Shen Qiao gestured for him to enter the house. "Please come in."

Then he said to Yan Wushi, "Would Sect Leader Yan also like to come? Or do you have other pressing matters?"

In Shen Qiao's view, Li Qingyu was here as a guest, yet Yan Wushi had provoked him for no reason whatsoever. This was considerably unacceptable. If a fight had broken out between the two, regardless of who was injured, Bixia Sect would suffer.

Yan Wushi suddenly pursed his lips into a smile, and the frigid cold of his expression thawed, transforming into a warm spring breeze. "You two can chat. I'm a bit hungry, so I'll head to the kitchens to see if there's something to eat."

Bizarre, thought Shen Qiao. He couldn't predict Yan Wushi's temper, which often felt like sudden rainfall rolling in on a bright, sunny day. He watched him walk away and couldn't help but shake his head, then headed inside the house to talk with Li Qingyu.

Zhongnan Sect's tragedy this time had caused it to crumple completely. The sons of wealthy, aristocratic families, like Zhangsun Sheng, were fine—even without a sect, they could still return home, but the ordinary disciples who completely relied on the sect were in much greater trouble. They were forced to take sides: either submit to Hehuan Sect and become an external disciple or oppose

Hehuan Sect and defect to another sect, like Qingcheng Mountain's Chunyang Monastery. And due to the Sword Trial Conference being hosted there, dark undercurrents were now stirring beneath the peaceful surface.

In truth, Chunyang Monastery had already become the third force in a power triangle with Hehuan Sect and the Buddhist discipline. All the sects in the north that refused to attach themselves to Hehuan Sect or the Buddhist sects had sought out Chunyang Monastery for protection. In the south, the Yangtze River serving as a barrier and Linchuan Academy's position of power meant that, for the time being, Hehuan Sect and the Buddhist discipline failed to make significant inroads there.

It was the unknowingly planted willow that granted shade. Yi Pichen never expected this result, but as Chunyang Monastery had already planned to enter the secular world, he naturally had no reason to reject it. That they were hosting the Sword Trial Conference was also proof of what the public wanted.

However, in just over half a year, the world situation had undergone such an upheaval, it was truly lamentable.

"Heroes from all over will arrive at the Sword Trial Conference," said Li Qingyu, "so it's a good opportunity for everyone to exchange pointers and improve their swords. Shizun hopes that Daoxiong can attend as well, when the time comes, to discuss the friendship between Daoists."

"If I count Qilang, I've accepted two disciples," said Shen Qiao. "They've just begun their apprenticeship, so at this time, stabilizing their foundations is of utmost importance. If I'm not here, I fear that without any guidance, it'll be easy for them to go astray."

Li Qingyu was unconcerned. "When I was practicing as a child, Shizun only ever taught things once, and we were left to understand on our own. The martial path has always been inseparable from natural talent. If someone has neither talent nor aptitude, they might as well live as a fisherman or woodcutter. That would be better than squandering their remaining years."

Though these were callous words, they weren't without reason. But someone like Shen Qiao could never say such things, so he simply smiled. "Let me consider this matter. I will return and discuss this with them, then make my decision."

Li Qingyu nodded.

Shen Qiao remembered something. "Has Li-gongzi heard any news of Xuandu Mountain?"

"I have not."

The last news Shen Qiao knew of Yu Ai was that he'd participated in the group assault on Yan Wushi. Afterward, Shen Qiao never saw him again.

Yu Ai was determined for Xuandu Mountain to stand at the top of the Daoist discipline once more, but his goal had gotten off to a rocky start from the beginning. First, Chunyang Monastery had stolen their momentum, then he'd conspired with the Göktürks, hoping to use their strength to bolster Xuandu Mountain's. But such calculations were based on wishful thinking that was unlikely to come true. In the end, it was like trying to draw water with a bamboo basket and coming up empty.

After the initial shock and sorrow of betrayal passed, whenever Shen Qiao now thought about anything related to Xuandu Mountain, it seemed like a hazy, misty dreamscape, beautiful yet unreal.

"If you wish to return to Xuandu Mountain, I can ask Shizun to lend you a hand," Li Qingyu offered.

Shen Qiao shook his head and laughed despite himself. "Thank you. But only the things you obtain through your own abilities are likely to last long."

Li Qingyu saw that he'd already made his decision, so he only nodded and spoke no more on the topic.

The two of them conversed for a while. When it was nearly noon, one of the Bixia Sect disciples, Zhou Yexue, came and knocked on the door.

"Li-shixiong, the sect leader is currently discussing an important matter with our shifu. She specially told this disciple to come and invite Li-shixiong and Daoist Master Shen to the Flower Hall for lunch."

Whether they should attend the Sword Trial Conference was a vital issue to Bixia Sect, so it was imperative for Zhao Chiying to discuss it with Yue Kunchi. It made sense that she was unable to spare the time to personally receive Li Qingyu right now.

Zhou Yexue was sixteen years old, at the age where she was lovely and delicate like a flower. Li Qingyu was around the same age, and they both used swords. In terms of background, they were very compatible as partners. If affections could blossom between them, it'd make for a lovely story.

Though Yi Pichen himself had not married, he never demanded for his disciples to do the same. Chunyang Monastery had almost no female disciples. If Li Qingyu chose not to marry for the rest of his life, he could focus on the sword, and that was fine. If he wished to find a wife and have children, Bixia Sect's female disciples were outstandingly beautiful, and there was no lack of choice either. As Zhao Chiying had sent Zhou Yexue to receive them, it was clear she felt the same way.

However, it seemed that Li Qingyu had no such thoughts, for he said, "Thank you for informing us. But since Sect Leader Zhao won't be present, I won't be going either. Could you bring two meals for Shen-daoxiong and myself? I wish to ask for his guidance on the sword, so we can simply eat here."

Clearly, Zhou Yexue had never met someone so insensitive and unromantic before. She stared at him for a long while before she slowly said, "All right." Then she turned right around and left without looking back.

The one who came to deliver the meals some time later was not her but Fan Yuanbai.

As a bystander, Shen Qiao could see things clearly. He saw that the young maiden had seemed interested in Li Qingyu, but it was obvious that Li Qingyu didn't feel the same. Of course, trying to instigate anything would be too awkward, so he pretended to have seen nothing.

Today's chef was not the one from the foot of the mountain, so both the side dishes and soup tasted quite average. Shen Qiao ladled out half a bowl of the soup. He was halfway through before he realized it was fish soup.[4]

And it looked like fish head soup...

He looked at Li Qingyu, whose head was lowered as he drank.

For some reason, Shen Qiao was suddenly hit with the feeling that this was terribly comical. He wanted to laugh but also thought it'd be rather unkind, so he immediately shut the idea down.

"This soup is quite good," said Li Qingyu.

Shen Qiao gave a dry laugh. He didn't know how to reply and only said, "These vegetables are also quite fresh."

As these words left his mouth, Yan Wushi's face abruptly flashed through his mind, but he repudiated it right away. Surely the great and lofty Huanyue Sect Leader wouldn't do something so childish?

---

4   Li Qingyu's personal name (青鱼) means "green fish."

Zhao Chiying's contemplation quickly came to an end: she decided to bring Fan Yuanbai and Zhou Yexue to Chunyang Monastery and attend the Sword Trial Conference. Yue Kunchi would stay behind to oversee matters at the sect. Shen Qiao had wanted to remain as well, but Zhao Chiying herself suggested that Shen Qiao come with them. She dearly valued this friend with whom she'd weathered hardships. Currently, Bixia Sect was very weak, so it would be incredibly difficult for Zhao Chiying to stand out on her own. She indeed needed Shen Qiao's help.

Shen Qiao agreed. He assigned Shiwu and Yuwen Song some homework and told them to train properly with Yue Kunchi. Yuwen Song had grown up in a rich and powerful clan, so here on Mount Tai, he was filled with curiosity and an insatiable desire to explore— right now, he was in the phase where he could enjoy things for hours without ever growing bored. Shiwu was the shixiong, but he possessed a gentle personality and he'd usually go along with Yuwen Song. He'd only grow insistent when important matters arose. The two martial brothers got along very well, so Shen Qiao didn't worry about leaving them on their own.

The group quickly finished packing and set out on their journey.

97

Reappearance in the Jianghu

THE JOURNEY FROM Mount Tai to Qingcheng Mountain was not a short one. In fact, it spanned almost half of the nation of Zhou. If they wanted to arrive within half a month, they had to travel briskly. Fortunately, everyone, even the young maiden Zhou Yexue, had been on trips where they needed to travel through the night before. By making haste, they'd managed to pass Chang'an within ten days and arrive in Hanzhong. Five days remained until the Sword Trial Conference, allowing them to relax their pace somewhat and travel slower.

They'd spent the entire journey thus far hurrying on horseback, and even the horses could scarcely take such a strenuous speed any longer. Now they could finally stop to catch their breath, to everyone's delight. Being younger, Fan Yuanbai and Zhou Yexue were especially happy, and their faces shone with joy. Li Qingyu wasn't even two years older than them, but he was much more stolid—his face remained as cold and solemn as it'd been when they'd set out.

The news of the Sword Trial Conference had already spread throughout the land. As they traveled, they saw many jianghu warriors carrying swords. After entering Hanzhong, these types only grew more numerous with all kinds of people carrying all kinds of weapons.

Places teeming with jianghu members would of course also teem with jianghu matters. As the saying went, "a scholar disrupts the law with the pen, while a warrior flouts it through the sword." Many people who knew martial arts felt it gave them the right to look down upon the common people, leading them to arrogance and a sense of superiority, and their actions would grow more unscrupulous. Shen Qiao's party had already encountered three such conflicts on their trip.

This time, they arrived early. The sun had just begun to rise as they entered the city, and the inn still had a fair number of empty rooms. There weren't many people in the hall on the first floor either.

Zhao Chiying and the others first booked their rooms, then took their seats.

Yan Wushi was special, so almost everyone in the party kept a respectful distance from him. Zhao Chiying feared this Huanyue Sect Leader—who was neither friend nor foe—and though she didn't want to offend him, she also didn't want to get too close. The Bixia Sect disciples, having suffered his torture, were even more terrified of him—none dared to provoke him. Zhao Chiying and her two disciples, together with Li Qingyu, perfectly filled a table of four, while Yan Wushi sat alone at another table, surrounded by empty seats. Onlookers found the sight rather strange.

Shen Qiao walked over and sat down across from him.

Yan Wushi's face stretched into a smile. "A-Qiao couldn't bear to see me all alone, so he specially came to sit at my table?"

"The number of guests will only increase. Eventually there won't be enough seats, and they'll be forced to rush their customers. I just don't want to cause the innkeeper any trouble."

Yan Wushi found the words insincere and remained unbothered.

He raised his hand to pour Shen Qiao a cup of freshly warmed wine. "The innkeeper must have spent three lifetimes accumulating fortune to be blessed with a guest like you."

For a moment, Shen Qiao felt like there was a deeper meaning to Yan Wushi's words, but after zoning out for a moment, he thought that he must have perceived wrongly.

"Once I finish my meal, I'll head out first," Yan Wushi told him. "I won't be traveling with you anymore."

Shen Qiao was a bit taken aback. "I thought that you were traveling with us in order to meet with Yi Pichen at Chunyang Monastery."

Even if Yi Pichen's martial abilities weren't good enough for number one, it would still be a simple matter for him to rank within the top three. It was indeed rather strange for Yan Wushi to see such an opportunity yet not go and request a fight.

Yan Wushi shook his head. "I can meet with Yi Pichen at any time, but the chance to watch someone's downfall? That's not something that happens every day."

There was an overpowering sense of schadenfreude within his tone, and one name immediately came to Shen Qiao's mind. "Dou Yanshan?"

"The bait has been laid for long enough," said Yan Wushi. "It's time to reel in the net. How could my venerable self not watch when something this exciting is about to happen?"

"You told me before that Yun Fuyi and Dou Yanshan were only keeping up a harmonious appearance, and that sooner or later, they would begin taking action," said Shen Qiao. "Yun Fuyi's influence within the Liuhe Guild is still too weak, so she was forced to borrow the strength of the Huang family along with the Göktürks, who are backing them, and secretly execute her plans that way."

"Correct," said Yan Wushi.

"Since you're able to swiftly determine their every move, I trust that you've also contributed to adding fuel to this fire?"

Yan Wushi was all smiles. "My A-Qiao is truly so clever! Dou Yanshan is both deeply cunning and incredibly mistrustful. He won't allow those he doesn't trust to get close enough to hear his secrets. It's thanks to this prudence of his that the Liuhe Guild was able to expand bit by bit over the years, becoming the dragon's head that dominates the water routes in both the north and south. Can you guess how I broke through these defenses to plant my spies within?"

Shen Qiao's brow furrowed. He thought for a moment, then said slowly, "I cannot guess."

Yan Wushi smiled. "In truth, it was very simple. Though Dou Yanshan is indeed prudent, the people close to him may not be. He has a personal servant who's followed him for eight years. The man is clever and capable, but there's also a woman he loves deeply. That woman's family demands money from her without end. Though she was unwilling to trouble her beloved, she also had no solution and suffered greatly. At that time, I had Bian Yanmei send someone to help her resolve this issue, all while doing something else."

"You were able to control Dou Yanshan's servant through her?"

Yan Wushi shook his head and burst into laughter. "A-Qiao, you're too naive! Dou Yanshan's servant is clever and capable, so how could such a crude method work on him? Bian Yanmei simply used this matter to foster a favorable impression with that woman. He used a false identity, pretending that he was a distant relative who'd not contacted them for years. This way, he won the trust of that woman's family and is now able to move around as her distant cousin."

"That seems far too convoluted."

"Don't underestimate the power of family relations," said Yan Wushi. "No one will believe your kindly intentions if you're an unrelated stranger. Adding an identity like that into the mix will always make them drop their guard, at least a little. Within a few interactions, this woman trusted this cousin of hers greatly, and she even introduced him to Dou Yanshan's servant."

As he listened to Yan Wushi describe the steps he'd undertaken, all meticulously interlocked, Shen Qiao heaved a silent sigh.

Both the imperial court and the jianghu were mere games to this man. His contemptuous arrogance and extreme egotism had earned him countless enemies, sprouting as thickly as trees in a forest. In the end, five great martial artists had ambushed him, and he'd almost lost both his life and reputation. But nonetheless, his martial arts, capabilities, and sense of strategy were undeniable.

"According to what you just said, Dou Yanshan's servant is both intelligent and capable," said Shen Qiao. "How could that older cousin win his trust?"

Yan Wushi sent him an unruffled smile. "By offering him benefits. In this world, only common interests can bind people together, even more intimately than brothers and spouses. As that servant followed Dou Yanshan, he must have witnessed many lavish events dripping with decadence and extravagance—yet he himself remains only a servant. Do you think that a clever and capable man would be satisfied seeing this? If the woman's cousin gave him a way to earn money, meaning he could own and manage his own business, wouldn't he eventually come to see that cousin as a close friend and ally?"

Understanding dawned on Shen Qiao. "So you purposely chose someone who was shrewd, and not someone honest and straightforward? Because you knew that he'd be dissatisfied with his current situation?"

"Honest people have their own weaknesses," said Yan Wushi. "Where can you find a person who's perfect and flawless?"

Shen Qiao nodded. "That's true. If you didn't possess such an exaggerated opinion of yourself back then, always looking down on others, Guang Lingsan and Dou Yanshan would have never gotten that opportunity."

He was clearly mocking Yan Wushi, but he'd overlooked how shameless this man was. Yan Wushi simply gave a slow, dignified smile and said, "You're wrong. That was a weakness of my past self, not my present self."

Shen Qiao couldn't stop himself from laughing. "Then, this distinguished master's present weakness is a face that's thicker than Mount Tai's stones are wide?"

Though his countenance often held a warm and gentle smile, it was rare for him to laugh freely.

It wasn't a loud laugh, but the corners of his lips couldn't help but stretch upward, and unceasingly so. Even his eyes were sparkling, like jade stones soaked in rainwater, vibrant and beautiful.

"That's a strength, not a weakness." Yan Wushi was the type to act on whatever whims floated to mind. As soon as this notion emerged, his hand was already on Shen Qiao's. "This venerable one's present weakness is you!"

Shen Qiao shook his head, and the look on his face said that he'd just heard something even more hilarious. He wanted to pull back his hand, but Yan Wushi's grip was tight.

"Sect Leader Yan, some tricks are tiresome if performed more than once. So why perform them again and again? No matter what a fool someone is, surely they won't fall into the same pit twice?" Within his words lay a trace of self-mockery, something that he perhaps didn't even realize himself.

"Do you remember the tale I told you last time?" Yan Wushi's smile remained unchanged. His eyes stayed fixed on Shen Qiao, and he didn't release his hand either.

Before this point, Shen Qiao's thoughts on their relationship had never strayed to improper paths. After a snakebite, a person would fear ropes for ten years. After his experience of unrequited friendship, Shen Qiao had gained a deeper understanding of Yan Wushi's callousness. He knew this man's heart to be as hard as stone. Even if he demonstrated the utmost sincerity, it would never amount to more than wishful thinking, for it was near impossible to move this man. In truth, down in the depths of his heart, Shen Qiao no longer dared to believe him, for that memory was carved too deep. He was simply unable to trust this man again, in fear of repeating his past mistakes.

However, at this moment, beneath that scorching gaze, Shen Qiao's heart gave a thump. He felt like prey being glared at by a predator, one that wouldn't give up until it caught its quarry.

Just then, a loud voice came from a short distance away, diverting their attention. "Innkeeper, there are clearly two empty seats there. Why did you say that you were full?"

Shen Qiao took the chance to pull his hand away. He looked around to realize that at some point, without his notice, the inn had filled up and the only empty seats left were at their table. As he was sitting across from Yan Wushi, the spots beside each of them remained open.

People at this time were unaccustomed to sharing a table with strangers, and they generally wouldn't insist on sitting with people they didn't know. But some didn't mind, and, secure in their martial abilities, they'd be confident that the other party wouldn't be able to refuse. This was often a source of disputes within the jianghu.

The innkeeper was obviously reluctant to see his place become a site for such a dispute. He quickly gave an apologetic smile and tried to explain, saying that if they waited a while, some guests would finish their meal and leave, freeing up some seats.

But the loudmouth in question was unwilling to compromise, and his companions also looked like they weren't people to be trifled with. Not only had they noticed that only Shen Qiao and Yan Wushi's table held two empty seats, they also saw that Shen Qiao was dressed in Daoist robes, with a kindly face that made him seem easy to push around. Meanwhile, Yan Wushi didn't even have a weapon. Both men looked like soft persimmons, easy to crush. If it'd been two strong, strapping men with fierce expressions sitting there instead, they might not have dared to be so rash.

"I've seen those people before. They're from Taohua Pier. Ever since Taohua Pier was absorbed into Hehuan Sect, they've become swollen with pride, holding everyone else in contempt. Using Hehuan Sect's banner, they've been running amok. Everyone fears Hehuan Sect's reputation and is unwilling to offend them."

"No wonder they're strutting about like this," said someone from the table beside them. "Just dogs that go around biting others because their master is powerful..."

"Shh, careful that you don't talk yourself into trouble! Martially, they're quite strong. Last time, even Tianshan's Yujian-zi ended up humiliated at that loudmouth's hands!"

"Huh?!" There was a sharp gasp of surprise. "But as a martial expert, Tianshan's Yujian-zi was only a little below first rate!"

"Right? How could they strut about like that otherwise? That loudmouth is Taohua Pier Master's younger brother. His moniker is the 'Stream-Severing Saber.'"

"Oh, I've heard of him. The Stream-Severing Saber, Er Deming. So it was him!"

Though the conversation from the table beside them wasn't loud, Yan Wushi and Shen Qiao still heard it. That loudmouth had already pushed aside the innkeeper and was now striding toward them.

Fan Yuanbai and Zhou Yexue were young and impetuous, so upon seeing this, they were about to rise and stop the man. Naturally, they had no interest in protecting Yan Wushi, but Shen Qiao was a good man, and he had done a great kindness to Bixia Sect. In the six months he stayed on Mount Tai, his relationship with everyone there had only grown closer. He wasn't like Yan Wushi, who'd pass judgments whenever the whim came—instead, he would amiably answer every question asked of him. Whenever he taught his disciples, he'd also let Fan Yuanbai and the others watch on the sidelines. All of this had greatly benefited Bixia Sect. Fan Yuanbai and the others all saw him as a teacher or an older brother, so they were naturally displeased to see someone else be so rude and disrespectful toward him.

In the end, Zhao Chiying was more experienced and reserved. She didn't move at all; instead, she called out loudly, "Innkeeper, where is the mutton stew I ordered for table six? Why haven't you delivered it to them yet? Huanyue Sect Leader Yan and Daoist Master Shen Qiao have been waiting for a long time!"

The moment these two names were spoken—especially the first of them—it was like a frigid wind had blown through the hall. Everyone froze.

That loudmouth's foot stopped, frozen in midair and unable to move another inch.

Entering Chunyang Monastery

THE SHEER POWER contained within the name "Yan Wushi" was clear from the reactions of everyone on the scene.

Any one of the five experts who'd ambushed Yan Wushi would have been enough to crush everyone there, let alone Yan Wushi himself—someone who'd gone through that kind of ambush and been declared dead, only to reappear alive and kicking in front of everyone afterward. He'd practically become the kind of monster only heard of in legends.

The innkeeper was a sharp man. When he saw how powerful that single sentence of Zhao Chiying's was, so much so that it'd frozen everyone in the room, he rushed to nod and bow. "This lowly one forgot," he said, smiling. "I will tell the chef to send it over right away. Please wait a moment, just a moment!"

Yan Wushi's fingers caressed the rim of his cup for a moment, but Shen Qiao reached over and held them down. He had seen through his intentions with a glance—he'd done this to stop him.

Though that person had wanted to steal their seats, he hadn't done any real harm in the end. If Yan Wushi attacked, the man would certainly be injured, if not killed. Then his companions would want revenge. As they needed to hurry along their way, why seek out trouble for themselves?

Yan Wushi gleaned these notions from Shen Qiao's eyes, and he gave a lazy smile. "I'll spare him this time, for your sake."

Earlier, he'd yet to finish what he was saying when that loud-mouth impudently interrupted him, and so when he had been stroking his cup, he really had possessed murderous intentions. But now he changed his mind. He sent the cup flying with a featherlight touch, and it buried itself right before Er Deming's foot, which was still midstep.

Er Deming's expression had gone stiff the moment he'd heard Yan Wushi's name. He didn't move again, and his face was pale and bloodless.

His companion behind him wasn't blind either—when he saw the situation, he quickly stepped forward and cupped his hands. "Sect Leader Yan, my younger brother is young and ignorant, as well as rude and reckless. We beg you to forgive his offenses."

Yan Wushi sat completely motionless, calm and composed. Just this was enough that no one doubted his identity. It would take great courage to impersonate the Huanyue Sect Leader. After all, few people in the world could have the guts to offend practically every single major sect as he did, all while those offended sects were unable to do anything to him.

When everyone else saw Er Deming's bearded face described with the words "young and ignorant," they all fought to restrain their laughter.

"Young and ignorant?" Yan Wushi repeated the description, his tone meaningful. "But this venerable one sees a big, burly man. Is he mentally lacking, perhaps? Not right in the head?"

"Pfft!" Immediately, there were people who couldn't hold back their laughter.

"What did you say—" Er Deming was about to explode, but his

older brother sealed his acupoints and grabbed his shoulders, stopping him from moving. Then he smiled apologetically at Yan Wushi. "That's right, my little brother is indeed mentally ill. Sect Leader Yan is a magnanimous man; please do not sink to his level!"

This man was the Taohua Pier Master who'd submitted to Hehuan Sect. They'd been flourishing in the jianghu as of late, but he still knew whom he could and couldn't afford to trifle with. Right now, it looked like Hehuan Sect had suppressed Huanyue Sect, crushing what momentum they had and greatly diminishing Huanyue Sect's power within the demonic discipline. But a starving camel was still larger than a horse. If they angered Yan Wushi—never mind whether or not Hehuan Sect would actually step up to help the two brothers—they'd first have to pay with their humble lives today.

Yan Wushi appeared to have seen through his thoughts. He gave a small smile, and the Taohua Pier Master instantly felt his hair stand on end.

"Since he has mental problems, he should stay home properly instead of running amok outside and offending others in your stead. With him like this, you must be exhausted."

The corners of the pier master's mouth twitched, but he was forced to agree. "Sect Leader Yan is right. This one will discipline him once we get back and command him to reflect on himself. I will be sure to not let him out so carelessly again!"

Now that he'd finished speaking, he was terrified that Yan Wushi might change his mind. He ignored the way his brother was practically boring a hole through him with his stare and quickly dragged the man away.

They'd rolled in like fire or wind, rash and reckless, and only a moment later they were fleeing in disarray. The sheer contrast caused everyone on the scene to glance at each other.

Shen Qiao shook his head. In truth, few people had noticed that when Yan Wushi had sent the cup flying, a tiny shard of porcelain had broken off, which struck right at one of Er Deming's acupoints. The location was so tricky, they probably wouldn't be able to unseal it themselves. Perhaps they'd even have to return to look for Yan Wushi.

"If they return to look for you, would you actually unseal the acupoint for them?" Shen Qiao asked. "Why do something so excessive?"

Yan Wushi smiled. "They won't look for me—they'll go crying to Hehuan Sect. That way, won't it save me the trouble of searching for them?"

Right after saying this, he rose from his seat. Before everyone else could regain their senses, Yan Wushi had already gracefully slipped away. They all assumed that he'd gone to chase after the group from Taohua Pier, and they couldn't help but lament over their misfortune. Why did that group choose to offend this fiend, of all people?

Despite this, due to the arrogant impression Er Deming had left on everyone, some were secretly pleased.

After the meal, the youthful Fan Yuanbai and Zhou Yexue felt somewhat restless. The two informed Zhao Chiying that they were going out on a stroll together. Zhou Yexue also invited Li Qingyu, only to unexpectedly receive a cold rejection. He said he wanted to train in his house, and Zhou Yexue found herself embarrassed. Unable to let go of her pride for the time being, she left with a sullen expression.

Zhao Chiying hadn't known of Yan Wushi's plans. When she saw that he didn't return, she couldn't help her confusion. "Where did Sect Leader Yan go?"

"He has other matters to attend to," said Shen Qiao. "He won't be traveling with us anymore."

Zhao Chiying nodded. Her heart was already heavy with worries, so she didn't have the mind to ask further.

Though Hehuan Sect and the Buddhist discipline were rather influential these days, most sects were unwilling to associate themselves with either faction. Hehuan Sect had a terrible reputation, and though the Buddhist sects had Buddhist Master Xueting and the Zhou Dynasty standing behind them, the Daoist sects, especially major ones like Chunyang Monastery, could never seek influence and connections through them. Thus, the Sword Trial Conference was incredibly timely—as soon as they heard the news, many people hurried there from all over. A fair number of rising stars wanted to use this chance to make a name for themselves. Meanwhile, the various sect leaders, being more experienced and reserved, were considering forming an alliance with Chunyang Monastery to avoid the instant annihilation Zhongnan Sect had suffered.

Having endured that tragic crisis, Bixia Sect had fallen greatly in strength, and they were currently very weak. Zhao Chiying didn't aspire to crush everyone present, but she'd been troubled by the lack of talent at the sect for a while. Hence, she hoped to put on a stunning performance at the Sword Trial Conference and give Bixia Sect's reputation a thunderous boost. This would allow them to restore their strength. But as for how to make this wish come true, they'd need to consider and discuss the matter further.

Fan Yuanbai and Zhou Yexue were only average martial artists— this was easy to see by simply contrasting them to Li Qingyu. He was around the same age they were, yet he'd already entered the ranks of first-rate martial artists. Given some time, he was sure to achieve great things. Zhao Chiying couldn't help but envy Yi Pichen's good fortune once more.

As a sect with some amount of history, Bixia Sect didn't lack for profound martial arts techniques. What they lacked was workable talent capable of comprehending such profound martial arts.

An entire day flashed by as Zhao Chiying remained inundated by thoughts and concerns. Early the next morning, everyone washed up, headed downstairs to eat, then set off for Qingcheng Mountain.

This time, they didn't make any further stops during their journey but arrived at Qingcheng Town, at the base of Qingcheng Mountain, in one push.

The town was already packed full of martial artists on account of the Sword Trial Conference. Chunyang Monastery had sent people to Qingcheng Town to wait to receive them. Upon seeing guests, they'd ask for sect and background and enter it into the registry before escorting them up the mountain, group by group. But there were simply too many people; the scale was beyond their expectations. Many people were forced to line up outside the mountain gates to wait their turn.

Li Qingyu brought Shen Qiao and the others to that gate, then rapped his sheath against the desk to alert the person sitting there, hunched over and writing.

The man raised his head, then gasped and quickly stood. "Li-shidi, you've returned!"

It wasn't just him; the nearby Chunyang Monastery disciples responsible for receiving guests all walked over to greet Li Qingyu.

Li Qingyu cupped his hands. "Zhao-shixiong, Cao-shixiong. Is Shizun on the mountain?"

"He is," said Zhao-shixiong. "The representatives from Linchuan Academy and Kuaji Commandery's Wang family have both arrived. The abbot is currently entertaining them himself."

Li Qingyu nodded. Without another word, he led their party right through the mountain gates.

Zhao-shixiong quickly stopped him. "Li-shidi, who are the ones with you? Please report their sect, that way I can register them. This is my responsibility, so I ask for Shidi's understanding."

Li Qingyu had made great achievements in martial arts. Now, he was already implicitly a leader for Chunyang Monastery's younger generation, so even those two shixiong had to treat him with utmost politeness. Unfortunately, while his martial prowess was incredible, his interpersonal skills were somewhat lacking.

Li Qingyu gave a slight frown. "They're the guests that Shizun asked me to bring."

The clear implication was, "There is no need for you to know any more than that."

Shen Qiao could tell that he was about to upset them, so he spoke up first. "This is Bixia Sect Leader Zhao, and the two behind her are her disciples. This humble Daoist is Shen Qiao, a wandering priest."

Zhao-shixiong showed little reaction to "Bixia Sect," but his expression shifted when he heard the name "Shen Qiao." "May I ask if it's Daoist Master Shen from Xuandu Mountain?"

Shen Qiao nodded. "Indeed."

Zhao-shixiong quickly cupped his hands, his face seeming to glow. "So, it was Daoist Master Shen! This one was disrespectful. Please enter, Daoist Master Shen and our respected guests. I will send someone ahead to report to Shizun!"

"Zhao-shixiong, I can take Daoist Master Shen and the others up the mountain myself."

Zhao-shixiong smiled. "Li-shidi may not know that Shizun left instructions earlier: if we were to see Daoist Master Shen and Sect Leader Zhao, we must send someone to tell him so that his esteemed self can personally greet them. You can take them there via the main path; they can admire the scenery on the way there. I'll send someone along the side path with a report to Shizun."

Though he said, "Daoist Master Shen and Sect Leader Zhao," anyone could tell that his courtesies were entirely directed at Shen Qiao. But as Zhao Chiying possessed a calm and steady mentality, she felt no dissatisfaction at this.

When he heard that it was Shizun's instructions, Li Qingyu naturally said no more.

The people waiting in line saw how they'd been given priority for entering the mountain after only a few words with Chunyang Monastery's disciples, and they inevitably raised a clamor. "We've been waiting here for a long time. So we're less important just because they have personal connections? If you don't understand even the courtesy of 'first come first served,' why is Chunyang Monastery even holding a Sword Trial Conference?"

Zhao-shixiong acted neither haughty nor apologetic. "The good brother has misunderstood. Chunyang Monastery isn't holding the Sword Trial Conference; we're simply lending our venue to Liuli Palace so they can. We are also only here to assist with maintaining order. Since you've come to Qingcheng Mountain, you must follow our rules. As for these guests just now, one of them is Xuandu Mountain's Daoist Master Shen, while another is Bixia Sect Leader Zhao. The third is our own sect's Li Qingyu-shidi. Li-shidi is under Shizun's orders to personally take those honored guests up the mountain. If you have any dissatisfaction, please wait until you meet with my shizun, then you can tell his esteemed self in person."

Qingcheng Mountain's Li Qingyu. The name of this rising star had long been renowned throughout the land. First, he'd dueled the sect leader Yu Ai on Xuandu Mountain, and though he'd lost by a single move, his fame had exploded. Afterward, he wandered the jianghu and fought first-rate experts like Duan Wenyang. Though he hadn't won all his battles, he was good enough to match his opponents. When one considered his age, these were incredible, shocking achievements. Nowadays, the name "Li Qingyu" resounded within the jianghu, bright and clear, not much inferior to the world's top ten. Countless unmarried maidens and powerful jianghu families all saw this young and promising disciple of Chunyang Monastery as an ideal future husband or son-in-law.

However, if the mention of Li Qingyu's name only made people gasp in understanding, it was Shen Qiao's name that shook their expressions entirely. First in disbelief, then some looked on with shining eyes, just like Zhao-shixiong. Naturally, no one complained about Shen Qiao's party being given priority anymore.

In the past half year or so, he'd done many things: killed the man with a fetish for making human-skin masks, Huo Xijing, and sent Kunye to the underworld with his sword on Mount Tai. After Yuwen Xian had entrusted his orphaned son to him, he'd also fought his way out of a heavy siege and brought Yuwen Song to safety, even killing two elders from Hehuan Sect. As news of these events gradually spread, his current reputation had grown to be no less than Li Qingyu's—in fact, it was even greater than when he'd still been the sect leader of Xuandu Mountain.

Though there were also people who didn't trust these reports of Shen Qiao's abilities, thinking that most of the rumors had been exaggerated, some of these incidents had happened in full view of the public such as Shen Qiao fighting his way out of Chang'an as well as him beating back Yu Ai and the others in the royal capital of Tuyuhun. There were quite a few witnesses to these events.

Today, Hehuan Sect was tremendously influential, and they'd crushed many sects and weaker wandering martial artists to the point of misery. As a result, everyone greatly revered and admired Shen Qiao, who had both the ability and courage to oppose Hehuan Sect. Shen Qiao didn't know that during this time, his fame had been rising day by day—the wretched image he'd had in the past had long since vanished completely. Though Liuli Palace had yet to release their rankings, rumors that Shen Qiao's martial arts had recovered completely had been circulating the jianghu for some time. It would be no great upset if he ascended to the top ten rankings.

As Yan Wushi constantly kept track of news from outside through a mutual exchange of information, he naturally knew of these changes. But on Mount Tai, Shen Qiao had remained singularly focused on his own training and on teaching his disciples, thus isolating him from the dust of the mortal world. So he naturally had no idea.

Li Qingyu truly made for a rather poor guide. As he led Shen Qiao and the others up the mountain, he'd offer explanations of the scenery they saw, yet he lacked eloquence, and his explanations were also dull, flat, and without any embellishment whatsoever. The listeners couldn't help but wish to cover their ears—just viewing the scenery by themselves would have made for better entertainment.

It was one thing for Shen Qiao and Zhao Chiying, whose profound discipline and cultivation meant that they'd never forget their manners, but by the time they reached Chunyang Monastery, neither Zhou Yexue nor Fan Yuanbai could hide their expressions of abject misery nor their sighs of relief that it was over.

A middle-aged man dressed in Daoist garb was standing in the monastery square in front of an incense burner. His hair was as black as ink, and he held a horsetail whisk in one hand. Behind him stood several disciples—it wasn't a small welcoming party.

The man in front was, of course, Chunyang Abbot Yi Pichen.

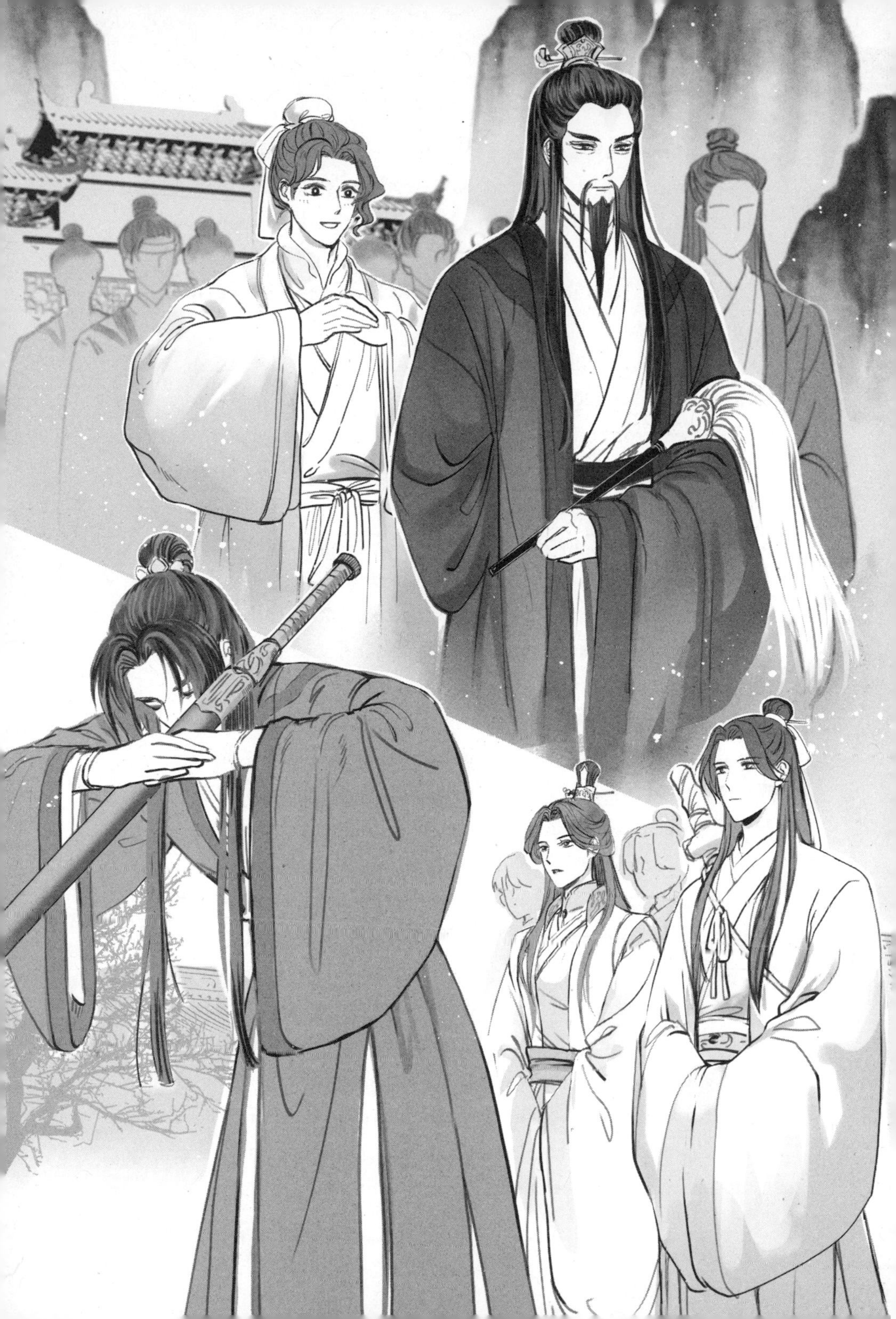

Shen Qiao swept a glance over them and recognized a familiar face behind Yi Pichen: Linchuan Academy's Zhan Ziqian. Zhan Ziqian had also spotted Shen Qiao; he cupped his hands at him and smiled.

Shen Qiao inclined his head toward him, sending a small smile in greeting.

Li Qingyu quickly came forward and gave the deepest of bows. "Shizun, this disciple has returned!"

"No need for courtesies, Mingchen. This trip has been hard on you." Yi Pichen intimately called his beloved disciple by his courtesy name as he pulled him up. Then he walked over and cupped his hands at Shen Qiao and Zhao Chiying. "Daoist Master Shen and Sect Leader Zhao have come a great distance," he said with a smile. "You've graced our humble monastery with your brilliant presence. This humble Daoist is greatly honored and wishes to invite you inside for a chat."

With Yi Pichen's current status, his coming out to receive them personally was an incredible show of respect. Zhao Chiying had even been worried that he'd snub them. While her own personal reputation wasn't an issue, the reputation of Bixia Sect was. Now, as she witnessed Yi Pichen's exemplary conduct, the complete opposite of Li Qingyu's brusqueness, she couldn't help but silently praise his generosity.

After everyone exchanged their pleasantries, Yi Pichen formally introduced Zhan Ziqian to them.

Zhan Ziqian held a fairly high position within Linchuan Academy, but the sect's most favored disciple was Xie Xiang, who hadn't appeared this time. Ruyan Kehui had only sent Zhan Ziqian as his representative, which was enough to indicate a certain attitude.

Yi Pichen led Shen Qiao and the others inside. There they saw that several others were already seated within.

"These are the second and third young masters of Kuaji Commandery's Wang family," said Yi Pichen.

The two young men didn't rise from their seats but only raised their sleeves a little in greeting.

They'd been speaking with Yi Pichen earlier, but when news came that Shen Qiao's group had arrived, only Zhan Ziqian and Yi Pichen had left to welcome them. It was obvious that the Wang family found neither Bixia Sect nor Shen Qiao worthy of association. Their contempt was crystal clear.

A Storm Approaches

A T PRESENT, the Wang clan was no longer the Wang clan from back when "the Wang-Xie's exploits filled the Book of Jin." As the dynasties changed, the powerful families would also rise and fall with the turning of years. Furthermore, the Kuaji Commandery's Wang family who were currently present weren't direct descendants of the Wang clan, but only a branch family—at most, they could claim they were related by blood. As their forefathers had entered the jianghu long ago, though, they were fully accepted as one of the noble families of the jianghu. They ran some businesses on the side and never involved themselves with the imperial court. Hence, they counted among the few powerful and influential families within the jianghu.

Though the Kuaji Commandery's Wang clan was only a branch family, their blood relationship meant they too considered themselves an illustrious, high-ranking family. They naturally thought a small sect like Bixia Sect beneath their attention. As they were guests, if they were unwilling to follow Yi Pichen out in greeting, he couldn't force them.

After exchanging greetings and taking their seats, Yi Pichen first thanked Shen Qiao for helping the Su family when he'd been in Chang'an. Then he said to Zhao Chiying, "When Bixia Sect's crisis took place, this humble Daoist was too far away to help and unable to send you timely aid. Thinking about it now, I am overcome with regret. I ask Sect Leader Zhao not to blame us."

Zhao Chiying sighed. "Abbot Yi is too courteous. Bixia Sect's problems arose from within. We were fortunate enough to weather the crisis, but our numbers have greatly declined, and so we've fallen quite a distance. By contrast, I see that your honored sect is filled with talent, with elites springing forth. It truly fills one with admiration and envy!"

Yi Pichen stroked his beard. "Sect Leader Zhao need not worry so much. Looking at these two disciples of yours, if they're willing to train diligently, they will certainly achieve great things over time."

Even if it was an offhand comment said out of politeness, receiving praise from the master of Chunyang Monastery was enough to make both Zhou Yexue and Fan Yuanbai ecstatic.

When he saw that these pointless courtesies would continue, the Wang family's third son gave a light cough and interrupted them. "May I ask Abbot Yi if other sects will be attending the current Sword Trial Conference?"

"There are many sects who are attending the Sword Trial Conference," said Yi Pichen. "Is Wang-sangongzi searching for someone, or is he seeking a master to apprentice under?"

Wang-sangongzi gave a dry laugh. "The abbot really knows how to joke around! Our Wang family possesses stacks upon stacks of martial arts manuals, so many that I can't even practice them all. How would I have the time to apprentice under a master? If other sect leaders will be attending, we wish to trouble Abbot Yi to introduce us so that we may make their acquaintance."

Zhan Ziqian was decently well-connected, but he wasn't an important figure in Linchuan Academy—he was only here as a messenger.

Bixia Sect had suffered great losses, and Wang-sangongzi deemed them beneath himself.

As for Shen Qiao, though he'd made great martial progress, the two brothers had witnessed his duel on Banbu Peak, and the scene of him falling from the cliff was etched deep into their memories. However high their hopes for the sect leader of Xuandu Mountain had been before, those hopes had plummeted just as far down afterward. They'd long since lost their former admiration and reverence; seeing him now, they only thought of him as mediocre and had no interest in associating with him.

Therefore, the Wang brothers had already excluded everyone present from their list of potential acquaintances.

Everyone loved fame, and the people of the jianghu were no different. Many people attending the Sword Trial Conference were focused on Liuli Palace's rankings, but that wasn't their only motivation: they also wanted to ally with Chunyang Monastery against the Buddhist discipline and Hehuan Sect.

Though the Wang family was from the Chen Kingdom in the south, they had plenty of business dealings in the north as well, so they couldn't ignore Hehuan Sect's influence. As they considered themselves a great and noble clan, how could they work together with a faction like Hehuan Sect? The Wang brothers had arrived with the aim of looking into Chunyang Monastery. If many powerful sects were to cling to Chunyang Monastery this time, they must indeed be powerful and influential, and the Wang family could consider allying with them as well. Otherwise, they could simply work together with Linchuan Academy. Why seek help from distant forces instead of nearby ones?

Their disregard for the others at the scene was clear from this question. Zhao Chiying and Shen Qiao didn't mind, but Fan

Yuanbai and Zhou Yexue couldn't suppress their expressions of anger.

Yi Pichen gave a slight smile and acted like he hadn't understood Wang-sanlang's insinuations. "There are guests from other sects as well, and they're all being settled separately. Others still remain at the base of the mountain. It's no trouble if Wang-sangongzi wishes to see them. Later, I'll send one of my disciples to lead you there. We arranged for everyone's lodgings to be together—we don't discriminate based on status."

Wang-erlang was somewhat disappointed. Yi Pichen's words implied that those much-anticipated martial arts masters of theirs wouldn't be coming.

Wang-sanlang, refusing to give up, continued to pursue the matter. "It's said that great heroes from all over traveled to the Sword Trial Conference ten years ago," he said, "and that it was a gathering of elites, with five or six of the current top ten among them. Could the Sword Trial Conference's influence have fallen to such an extent after only nine years?"

Zhou Yexue couldn't hide her mocking smile. Did this man really think that true martial experts were like cabbages, ready to be picked at their leisure? Being martial experts, they naturally had to put on the appropriate airs. Take the Huanyue Sect Leader, for example: hadn't he disdained to attend such occasions and left halfway through their travels? Only someone as good-natured as Daoist Master Shen would be willing to help Bixia Sect stand out and accompany them to the conference. But who could have expected that someone would be too blind to recognize Mount Tai,[5] taking the pearls before him for fish eyes! It was truly too laughable!

Wang-sanlang saw the sarcastic smile on her face and frowned.

---

5   泰山. Mount Tai is the most important and famous of China's Five Sacred Mountains.

"This lady's expression speaks of her mockery. Does she have any objections to what I said?"

"I dare not," said Zhou Yexue indifferently. "I only thought I saw a monkey just now, one that's lived on a mountain its entire life. It's only ever seen the bit of sky above its own head, yet it believes that its mountain amounts to the entire world!"

Of course, Wang-sanlang picked up that she was calling him shortsighted, and he immediately sneered. "You have quite the clever tongue. I only hope that your skills are just as clever, lest you end up losing your life after offending someone with your nonsense!"

After he said this, his sleeve furled, sending his teacup flying from the table. The full cup of tea swept toward Zhou Yexue, and not a single drop of liquid within spilled.

Since Wang-sanlang dared to look down on Bixia Sect, it was obvious he was fairly capable himself. Upon seeing this move, even Yi Pichen revealed an expression of appreciation. Calling this man "fairly capable" would be selling him short—within the younger generation, one could even call his skills astounding.

Zhou Yexue was shocked. Before the teacup had even reached her, she'd already involuntarily taken a step back.

Zhao Chiying silently shook her head and was about to help, but Shen Qiao's hand stopped her.

Although Shen Qiao's sitting posture remained unchanged, his other hand plucked his own cup off the table. First, he drank the contents, then tossed it outward. It crashed right into Wang-sanlang's cup that was careening over!

The two cups collided with a clatter, yet neither cracked. Due to the tremors, the tea from the first cup spilled into Shen Qiao's, then both cups rebounded off each other and returned to the hands of their respective owners.

It all took place in the blink of an eye. Wang-sanlang's expression remained stunned as he caught his cup, as if in disbelief over what he'd just seen.

Shen Qiao grabbed his own returning cup. After giving it a sniff, he put it down. "It seems that Abbot Yi is impartial. The tea served to Wang-sangongzi is the same as ours. Since that's the case, why was Wang-sangongzi so enthusiastic in insisting we taste his tea?"

That move of Shen Qiao's was far more brilliant than Wang-sanlang's. Though it'd appeared understated and effortless, this level of execution was impossible without profound internal energy and skill. In comparison, what Wang-sanlang had done with Zhou Yexue was like brandishing one's blade before Duke Guan[6]—he'd completely overestimated himself.

Having realized this, the Wang brothers no longer dared to look down on their fellow guests.

Wang-sanlang's expression was feeble as he cupped his hands, and he said nothing. This could be considered his apology.

Always a stronger person, always a higher sky. To think that Shen Qiao, someone they already deemed unworthy of ranking within the top ten, would still be an impassable mountain to them.

Yi Pichen looked on coolly. Seeing that the Wang clan's spirits had plummeted, he didn't speak more on it and simply smiled. "Everyone has traveled a long distance today. I trust that you're all exhausted. Shall this humble Daoist send for someone to take you to your rooms so you can rest?"

The Wang brothers naturally had no objections, and Zhan Ziqian nodded as well. "Then we'll be troubling Abbot Yi."

Once they left the hall, Li Qingyu turned to Shen Qiao and said, "I live in the small building to the east. It's the one that has a

---

6   关公门前舞大刀. *Guan Yu was a general who served under Liu Bei before and during the Three Kingdoms period. A renowned master of the blade.*

nameplate with the character 'Li' on the door. If Daoist Master Shen needs anything, feel free to come find me."

Shen Qiao thanked him, then went with Zhao Chiying, following the Chunyang Monastery disciples as they led them to their lodgings.

Zhao Chiying purposely trailed behind by several steps, letting Fan Yuanbai and the others walk in front. She then grabbed Shen Qiao and whispered into his ear, "When I look back on the situation, Abbot Yi seemed like he wished to say something, but the Wang brothers interrupted him?"

Shen Qiao nodded. "That's indeed the case."

After all, he'd once led a sect as well. Abbot Yi personally coming out to greet them was partially to express his sincerity, but it'd also served as a prologue of sorts—he must have had important matters he wished to discuss with them.

Zhao Chiying pondered to herself. "In your opinion, do you think he wanted to discuss forming an alliance?"

Shen Qiao didn't answer the question but instead asked his own. "If that's the case, how do you plan to respond?"

Zhao Chiying sighed. "Right now, Hehuan Sect and the Buddhist discipline hold immense power. In Bixia Sect's current state, if they try to annex us like the Göktürks did last time, we can only wait to be slaughtered. Forming an alliance might solve this problem."

"From what I see, Abbot Yi is deeply ambitious, and he handles matters with great ease and confidence. Right now, the Buddhists have Xueting to foster them, while the Confucians have Linchuan Academy. Only the Daoists are like scattered sand. It might be a good thing if he can unite the Daoist discipline."

Zhao Chiying was silent for a moment. "At this time, Abbot Yi might find it difficult to achieve his wish. The Sword Trial Conference has always been a grand event in the jianghu, yet

Linchuan Academy only sent a single disciple. The situation doesn't look too promising."

Then she paused before continuing. "Actually, if we're discussing martial skills and moral character, Daoist Master Shen may not be inferior to Abbot Yi. If you're willing to call for action, I would throw Bixia Sect's lot in with you without a second thought."

Shen Qiao shook his head and couldn't help but laugh. "I don't even have a sect beneath me right now. Even if you threw in your lot with me, I wouldn't be able to take you in."

He thought that Zhao Chiying was joking, yet she earnestly said, "How many people in this world can measure up to Daoist Master Shen, who traveled thousands of miles to fulfill a single promise? It's not only my Bixia Sect who is indebted to your kindness. How many of the people who've interacted with you could say they've never received your kindness? Even Sect Leader Yan, who draws no line between good and evil, who acts according to his whims, doesn't he show special regard to you and only you?"

Shen Qiao gave a strained smile. "This special regard...I fear that's only because he wishes to toy with me."

Zhao Chiying smiled slightly back at him. "I think that may not be the case."

As they conversed, they arrived at their lodgings. Their houses happened to be adjacent to each other, which made it easy to keep in contact. The two of them each entered their own residences and washed up.

Shen Qiao had just finished washing his face when he heard a knock on his door.

He'd thought that Zhao Chiying must still have things she wanted to talk about, but when he opened the door, he saw Zhan Ziqian standing outside.

"Has Daoist Master Shen been well?" Zhan Ziqian said, cupping his hands.

Shen Qiao turned sideways so that he could enter. "Please come in, Zhan-langjun."

"I'm ashamed to say this," said Zhan Ziqian. "When I first saw Daoist Master Shen, I was immensely pleased. I even wanted to have a long chat with you and fathom my painting techniques. Unfortunately, my shizun has ordered me to return as quickly as possible, so I could only come to say goodbye."

Shen Qiao was shocked. "That urgent? Isn't the Sword Trial Conference only starting tomorrow?"

Zhan Ziqian gave a wry smile. "It's because it starts tomorrow that I must leave today. At tomorrow's Sword Trial Conference, I fear there will be a rain of blood—even Chunyang Monastery might not be able to save themselves, let alone any kind of alliance. An upright gentleman does not wait amid danger. I really don't wish to see Daoist Master Shen dragged into such matters, so I was wondering if you'd be willing to go to Linchuan Academy with me. Shizun will definitely welcome you, Daoist Master Shen."

Shen Qiao could tell how grave he was and how serious his words were, but there seemed no rhyme or reason to them. He couldn't help but frown. "Just what is going on?"

100

The Sword Trial Conference

EVEN THOUGH THERE WAS Zhou in the north and Chen in the south, each with their own governments, the jianghu wasn't split between north and south. After all, the world itself made no such delineations—it was one.

Therefore, the violent expansion of Hehuan Sect and the Buddhist discipline sent not only the northern sects into a panic, but had alarmed Linchuan Academy as well.

The Sword Trial Conference naturally gave the various sects a fantastic opportunity to make contact and foster friendships. Linchuan Academy wanted to form an alliance, so they'd sent Zhan Ziqian over to test the waters. If Yi Pichen were willing to acknowledge Linchuan Academy as the head, the alliance would form as naturally as waters gathering in a canal. Then this union between Confucians and Daoists would have a great advantage in containing the soaring influence of Hehuan Sect and the Buddhists.

However, Zhan Ziqian's trip hadn't gone smoothly. It had become clear that Yi Pichen was unwilling to accept a subordinate role, so Zhan Ziqian could only return empty-handed.

Without the participation of the Confucian discipline, the Sword Trial Conference would indeed lose quite a bit of luster.

Shen Qiao listened to the ins and outs of this tale, then shook his head. "When everyone shares a common goal, does it matter who's in charge?"

Zhan Ziqian smiled and shook his head. "Not everyone can be like Daoist Master Shen, caring little for hollow and material things. Now that Xuandu Mountain has joined the Göktürks as their limbs, Chunyang Monastery can consider itself the pillar of the Daoist discipline. However, my sect, Linchuan Academy, is the head of the Confucian discipline. Daoism and Confucianism's differences lead them to vie for supremacy, like a battle between dragon and phoenix. In this case, the subordinate faction will fade into the background— who wants to end up a prop for someone else's reputation?"

Shen Qiao frowned but did not speak.

It was exactly as Zhan Ziqian said. Ruyan Kehui and Yi Pichen were both martial experts of the current generation. The weight attached to the position of "alliance leader" wasn't insignificant. No matter who took the seat, the other one would grow uneasy. Worse still, they were both sect leaders, and ones who represented Confucianism and Daoism respectively. Neither of them would rashly place their own sect in an inferior position where they'd be forced to follow someone else's lead. This wasn't only an issue of reputation, but related to the orthodoxy of the schools, their statuses, and the changes of such.

"I trust that Abbot Yi was unwilling to accept this."

"That's right," said Zhan Ziqian. "After Abbot Yi heard the reason behind my arrival, he gracefully refused the suggestion of forming an alliance. I believe my shizun, too, had already expected such a conclusion; that's why he sent only me, and not my shidi or anyone else. But Abbot Yi's desire to form an alliance against Hehuan Sect and the Buddhist discipline isn't a secret. Sooner or later, their side will know. I fear that a storm may descend without warning at the Sword Trial Conference tomorrow. Though you may be a Daoist, you have no relationship with Chunyang Monastery, so why not come with me to Linchuan Academy as a guest? Ever since you parted with the Su family, my shidi has held you in great esteem. Surely he'll be delighted to see your honored self again."

Shen Qiao smiled. "Thank you, Zhan-xiong, for your kindness. However, this humble Daoist will remain here."

Zhan Ziqian was confused. "Why?"

"Everyone within the Daoist discipline is bound by a common cause," said Shen Qiao. "A calamity wouldn't affect only Chunyang Monastery—if Hehuan Sect annexes them, disaster won't be far from the other sects as well. Moreover, I already promised Bixia Sect that I'd help them during the Sword Trial Conference."

Regret washed over Zhan Ziqian's face. "Then there's nothing to be done," he said. "However, I fear that Abbot Yi's desire to promote an alliance this time will come to nothing."

"Currently, Chunyang Monastery is on the rise, and its scope and prestige are no worse than Xuandu Mountain's," Shen Qiao pointed out. "Logically speaking, quite a few people should wish to come and join them."

"That is the case, but everyone has different thoughts. Leaving myself aside, look at the Wang brothers, Daoist Master Shen. Abbot Yi personally invited them to the main hall, hoping to win them over, but they insist that they only came for the Sword Trial Conference and refuse to say anything regarding an alliance. It's obvious that they see Chunyang Monastery as a lone hand trying to clap, unable to make any sound, and so they're only willing to watch from the sidelines—they won't allow themselves to be dragged into the vortex. Forming an alliance is easier said than done."

He was a mild-tempered man, and though he was a disciple of Confucianism, he didn't hold any extreme positions. He even expressed regret for Chunyang Monastery's situation, as if he'd already foreseen that an unceasing tempest would buffet the Sword Trial Conference tomorrow, and that a bleak outcome awaited them at the end. The two of them sighed over this for a while before Zhan Ziqian again brought up painting. He invited Shen Qiao to visit Linchuan Academy another day, and Shen Qiao naturally accepted.

Zhan Ziqian had only just left when the Su brothers came to visit, wanting to thank Shen Qiao for his assistance back in Chang'an. Though the entire Su clan had temporarily fled to Qingcheng Mountain for their safety, they hadn't entirely abandoned their wealth and estates back in Chang'an. Once the time was ripe, they'd return once more.

On top of this, many sects had also sent over visitation requests, wishing to meet with Shen Qiao.

Shen Qiao was now beginning to realize that he was no longer that former sect leader, adrift with nothing to his name, whom everyone had derided. Somehow the fact had crept up and taken him by surprise. When people brought up Shen Qiao now, they were inevitably talking about his battle in Chang'an. Since the sheer speed with which Hehuan Sect was expanding these days was putting everyone on edge, Shen Qiao killing two of their elders made people discuss him with even more relish.

It was a completely unexpected outcome to Shen Qiao, and he was caught between laughing and crying. Using the excuse that it was getting late, he gracefully rejected all these visitation requests. After he'd sent Su Wei and Su Qiao off, he meditated within the house, quietly waiting for morning to arrive.

Not long after the dawn of the next day, someone brought over breakfast and some hot water for washing. Once he sorted everything out, Shen Qiao was about to leave when Zhao Chiying showed up, already knocking on his door. They left for the main hall together.

"Where are Fan Yuanbai and the others?" asked Shen Qiao.

"They've already gone to get their number plates," said Zhao Chiying. "If all goes as expected, they should be in the first round."

Shen Qiao had yet to fully grasp the rules of the Sword Trial Conference, so he took this chance to ask about them.

"When we arrived yesterday, Chunyang Monastery's disciples were already registering everyone's surnames and sects. Today they'll sort the participants according to order of arrival, then hand the list of names over to Liuli Palace. Liuli Palace will also consult everyone's battle chronicles within the jianghu, then group contestants of similar strength together for the competition. If someone didn't mean to participate, they just need to tell Liuli Palace beforehand. Their name will then be removed and replaced with someone else's. However, these rules only apply to regular disciples. Those like us usually won't end up on the list unless we specifically decide to enter and compete."

"Even the person themselves might not have clear knowledge of their battle chronicles," said Shen Qiao. "Liuli Palace are so reclusive—how do they obtain this information?"

Zhao Chiying smiled. "I've also wondered about this. I suppose they must have created a vague tier list based on information received from various other parties. Thoroughly determining the rankings is also one of the goals of the Sword Trial Conference. They say that Liuli Palace possesses dazzling foresight: as long as they see someone's skills, they'll know how that person's martial arts compares in the jianghu. Everyone who's seen it firsthand has been amazed. Ten years ago, I didn't have the chance to see it, so this time I definitely will, to broaden my horizons."

As the two of them talked, they passed through Chunyang Monastery's backyard and arrived in the main hall.

At this time, many people had already arrived. The main hall was different from the wide, empty space they'd seen yesterday—now it was covered with seating cushions and soft mats, all arranged beautifully. The doors of the main hall were open as well, so if one was seated inside the hall, they'd have a clear view of the matches outside, all without needing to be exposed to the sun or rain.

Yesterday, Zhan Ziqian had taken his leave early and the Wang brothers had shown little interest in a potential alliance, so Shen Qiao and Zhao Chiying thought few people would be here today as well. They certainly never expected to see seven to eight-tenths of the hall's seats—which numbered almost a thousand—already occupied. A diverse assortment of sects had come. Not only were there small sects and clans like Feixian Gate and Qingyang Mountain Estate, but there were also organizations that hovered between first and second-rate, like Jiuhua Sect and Chixia Sword Sect. Though the prominent Confucian and Buddhist sects such as Linchuan Academy and Tiantai Sect failed to show up, judging by the current situation, things weren't bad at all.

Zhao Chiying and Shen Qiao took their respective seats. Zhao Chiying whispered, "With Li Qingyu's aptitude, he will definitely take first place today. Should Abbot Yi propose an alliance then, he'll be able to reap large gains with minimal effort."

Shen Qiao nodded, as he thought the same.

Yi Pichen walked over, surrounded by his disciples. He first greeted everyone with some niceties, then said loudly, "Thank you all for taking the time to attend the Sword Trial Conference, which is held every ten years. This time, Liuli Palace has borrowed my humble monastery to use as the venue. Chunyang Monastery is deeply honored. I hope that everyone here can get to know each other through martial arts, but take care not to overdo it, lest we damage the amity between us!"

Yi Pichen's voice was warm and gentle, neither loud nor soft. But as he used internal energy to transmit it, everyone in attendance could hear him with perfect clarity.

After speaking, he withdrew half a step and introduced a purple-garbed woman beside him to the crowd.

"This is Yuan Zixiao from Liuli Palace, or Yuan-niangzi."

Many people had heard of Liuli Palace, yet they'd never seen any of its members in person. Now, they saw that the renowned Liuli Palace had sent a woman to serve as the judge of the Sword Trial Conference, they were all stunned into silence and couldn't help but reveal expressions of skepticism.

"Abbot Yi, we're not trying to embarrass you, but the Sword Trial Conference is held only once every ten years, and everyone in the jianghu is eagerly awaiting its rankings. Now, not only is it being held early, but they have only sent a single woman. Not only does this show their contempt for us, it also demonstrates their disrespect toward you!"

"That's right! Could Liuli Palace be afraid of Hehuan Sect and the Buddhist discipline's influence? That's why they sent only a single, weak woman to deceive us?"

"Precisely! If that's the case, what point does this Sword Trial Conference even have? We might as well just head home and sleep!"

With one person serving as the lead, the rest naturally followed suit. Doubts soon arose all around them, and the situation grew unstable. The Chunyang Monastery disciples couldn't help their anxious expressions as they looked to their shifu.

"Your name is Wei Gaofei, from Feixian Gate. You specialize in the saber, and you've achieved the height of proficiency in a set of Feixian Gate techniques called the 'Inverted Heavenly Void.'" The woman in purple standing next to Yi Pichen suddenly began to speak, her voice ringing out like clinking jade and echoing in the main hall. Though crisp and pleasant, it was cold and devoid of any emotion, let alone any signs of anger and injustice that might have arisen at being questioned.

The young man who'd started the questioning was startled for a moment, then countered, "That's right. So what?"

Yuan Zixiao continued, "But your saber techniques contain a fatal flaw—or rather a hurdle that you've failed to overcome no matter what—so you are unable to bring into play the true essence of your saber techniques. This is the reason you lost to Qi Wei from Longmen Sect last time."

Wei Gaofei's face paled in shock. "How... How did you know about this?"

Yuan Zixiao paid him no heed and instead continued icily, "The saber discipline known as Inverted Heavenly Void demands speed, ruthlessness, and precision, but your wrist isn't nimble enough, so you're unable to achieve that kind of speed. No matter how skilled you are in wielding the saber, you will never become one with it."

At this moment, Wei Gaofei could no longer concern himself with how she knew of his shortcomings. He hastily asked, "Then, may I ask if there's a solution?"

"There is," Yuan Zixiao replied. "Since your body is the limiting factor preventing you from reaching the pinnacle demanded by Inverted Heavenly Void, why persist in pushing yourself down a dead end? It would be better to switch to your sect's other set of saber techniques, the Jade's Glow, which focuses on the slow and steady, and on effortless execution. With your aptitude, it won't be difficult for you to achieve great things there."

"Effortless execution, effortless execution..." Wei Gaofei mumbled, a thoughtful cast to his face as a myriad of expressions passed across it.

Suddenly, he let out a loud cry and bowed deeply to Yuan Zixiao. "Thank you for your guidance. No words can express my gratitude for your great kindness—I will definitely repay you someday!"

With that, he stood, ignoring the others, and quickly left the hall. No matter how his martial brothers called out from behind him, he didn't look back.

Seeing his behavior, the onlookers understood that he must have comprehended something from Yuan Zixiao's words. Martial artists occasionally experienced flashes of inspiration, allowing them to break through a bottleneck. No one was surprised at this; rather, they were envious.

Yuan Zixiao continued to expose the backgrounds, weaknesses, and flaws in the martial arts of several other people, all of whom had just voiced doubts. Now that they were being exposed one by one, their faces also shifted greatly.

At this moment, everyone understood just how formidable Liuli Palace was, and they were terrified that Yuan Zixiao would also reveal martial weaknesses, allowing their opponents insights into their flaws before they even began competing. Naturally, no one dared to make a sound.

Zhao Chiying whispered, "What a formidable woman. Liuli Palace's reputation is well deserved. I trust that she'd know the shortcomings of Bixia Sect's martial arts as well." There was a hint of fear in her voice.

Shen Qiao smiled. "All things beneath the heavens have two sides, yin and yang. Where there are strengths, there will be weaknesses. Even the most brilliant of martial arts have flaws. Her ability to expose each and every one is indeed incredible, but just because someone knows the flaw doesn't mean that they'll be able to exploit it. The greater your martial arts are, the fewer weaknesses they'll have.

Therefore, instead of taking the trouble to remember the weaknesses of others, it's better to improve your own abilities. When you reach the stage of perfect, unobstructed harmony, others will naturally be left with no chances to exploit them."

Zhao Chiying nodded. "Spoken like a true grandmaster. I cannot compare!"

On the other end of the hall, Yi Pichen saw that Yuan Zixiao could hold her own and so said nothing to intervene. Only once everyone quieted down did he speak. "Since you all have no objections, let us continue according to the rules!"

As his words fell, the Chunyang Monastery disciples rang the jade chimes. The clear sound traveled far, indicating the official start of the Sword Trial Conference.

The first battle was between the Wang family's Wang-sanlang and Zhou Yexue.

As this pair had come into conflict earlier, when they met on the field, both looked at each other with displeasure. However, Zhou Yexue was clearly not Wang-sanlang's match. In fact, the result had already been decided before they even began.

Though Zhao Chiying thought this a shame, there was nothing she could do. It was possible that the revitalization of Bixia Sect depended completely on her. Today, she'd made up her mind to enter the competition, but the question of which match to enter depended on her potential opponents. If her opponent was too unskilled, there would be no glory to it even if she won.

Zhou Yexue was an unyielding young maiden. Though she knew the outcome, she refused to surrender without a fight. She still wielded her sword and faced Wang-sanlang. Blades glinted and flashed as they fought, making for an exciting scene, if only temporarily.

The venue was so spacious that, in order to save time, another two pairs had their match at the same time.

Su Qiao was among that pair, and his opponent was Jiuhua Sect's personal disciple. They were the same age, and both rising stars. The battle between the two was even more exciting than that of Zhou Yexue and Wang-sanlang, so most of the crowd's attention was on them. They watched with rapt attention while silently sighing over how the jianghu's talents were like waves pushing forth, the new supplanting the old.

At this moment, a Chunyang Monastery disciple came down the mountain, with another person behind him.

Upon seeing that person's face from afar, Shen Qiao couldn't help but shift slightly. It was clear that he was both extraordinarily surprised, as well as deeply shaken.

Sitting beside him, Zhao Chiying couldn't help noticing his shock. "What is it?"

101

Shimei

THE NEWCOMER WAS DRESSED in plain clothing, yet she was graceful and beautiful beyond compare. Her black hair was pulled into a tall bun and fastened by strings of jade. Shen Qiao wasn't the only person whose attention was caught—most in attendance had their gazes ensnared by the sudden appearance of this unknown woman, and they all turned their heads in her direction.

She carried a longsword on her back, her spirits high and eyes bright. Yet her gait wasn't feminine in the slightest, nor did she grow nervous under the onlookers' gazes. She remained composed and assured, and when she entered together with the disciple from Chunyang Monastery, she swept a glance around. When she saw Shen Qiao, uncontainable surprise first appeared on her face, followed by surprised joy. She didn't wait for the disciple guiding her to take her to Yi Pichen but instead flew toward Shen Qiao with a tap of her toes.

Shen Qiao had also just stood, and two pairs of eyes stared at each other. The girl darted over like a swallow returning to its nest, and she embraced him tightly.

The gazes of the onlookers instantly gained a peculiar slant.

"Zhangjiao⁷-shixiong!" The girl was completely unaware of their thoughts, nor did she care. She held him for a long time, until Shen Qiao patted her back. Only then did she let him go.

---

7 掌教. Literally "sect leader," commonly used for Daoist sects.

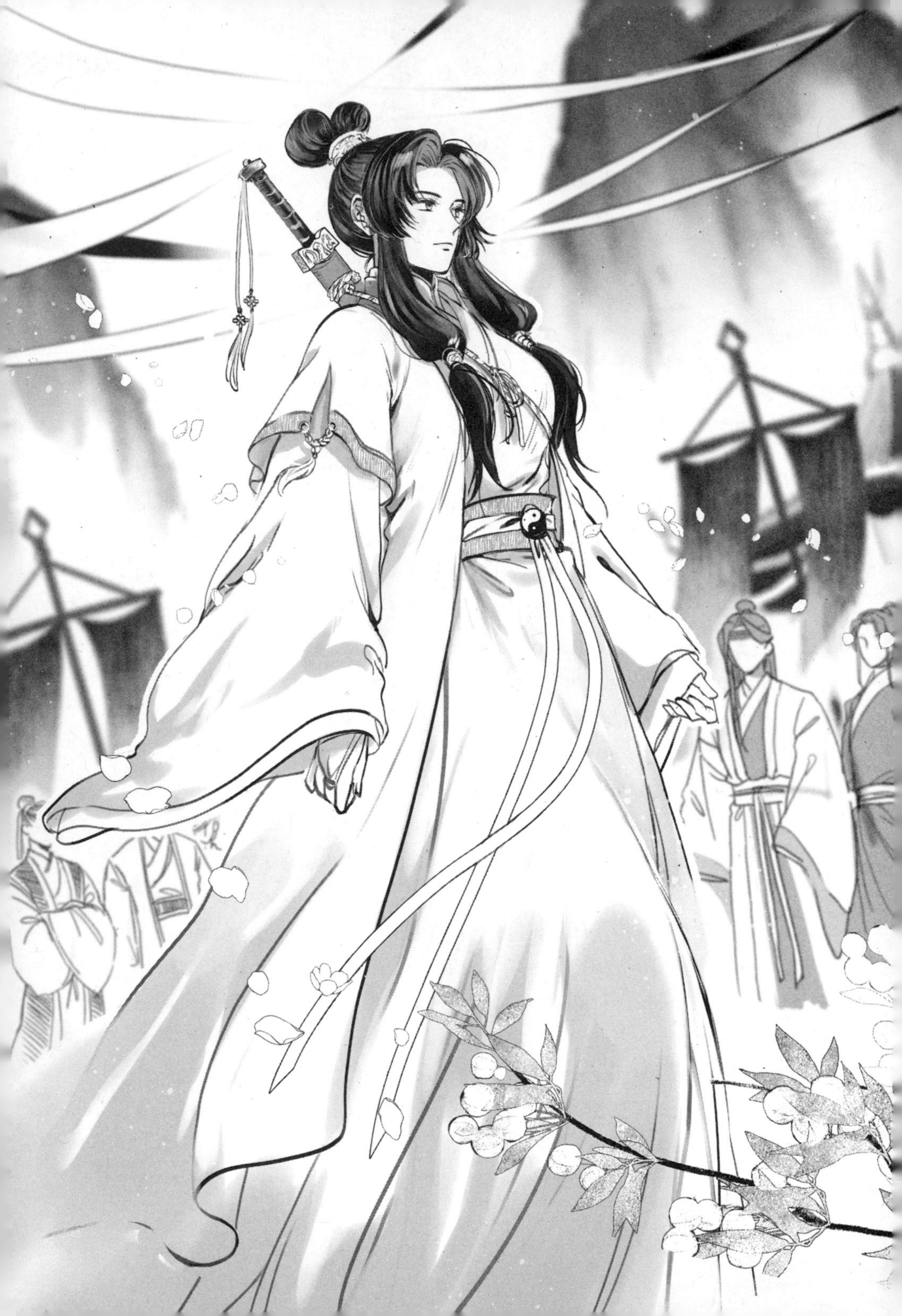

Hearing this address, Zhao Chiying knew that the girl must be a disciple of Xuandu Mountain: Shen Qiao's shimei.

Sure enough, Shen Qiao led her over by hand and introduced her to Zhao Chiying. "This is my fifth shimei, Gu Hengbo. Wuniang,[8] this is Bixia Sect Leader Zhao."

In the past, Zhao Chiying had heard that Qi Fengge had five disciples: Tan Yuanchun, Shen Qiao, Yu Ai, Yuan Ying, and Gu Hengbo. There was only one female disciple, who naturally had to be the Gu Hengbo standing in front of her.

Looking at her now, the girl seemed to be carved of cold, noble jade. The aura of an immortal hung about her, lending Gu Hengbo an outstanding demeanor. She was indeed a lovely young lady.

Gu Hengbo and Zhao Chiying looked at one another, then Gu Hengbo laughed. "Your illustrious reputation precedes you, Sect Leader Zhao, though I didn't expect to meet you here. Wuniang is so fortunate!"

It was clear that she knew her etiquette, but she'd been overcome with excitement when she saw Shen Qiao earlier and had been unable to take anyone else into account.

The two exchanged greetings, then Shen Qiao asked, "Wuniang, when did you arrive? Is Yu Ai here as well?"

Gu Hengbo shook her head. "No, we had a huge argument. I've been away from the mountain for a while, and I wasn't planning to go back in the first place."

Shen Qiao frowned. "What happened? Did he mistreat you?"

Gu Hengbo pursed her lips into a smile, as if the entire matter was of no importance. "It's a long story, why don't we talk about it later? I heard that a Sword Trial Conference was being held here,

---

8   五娘. Literally "fifth daughter." Refers to how Gu Hengbo is the fifth in seniority of her martial siblings.

so I came up the mountain to see for myself. I didn't expect to meet Zhangmen-shixiong here."

When Shen Qiao heard her calling him "Zhangmen-shixiong" as before, he felt a great surge of emotion deep within his heart. "Very well. Let me take you to meet Abbot Yi first."

Gu Hengbo naturally had no objections. She'd entered the sect somewhat late, so there was a significant age gap between her and her shixiong. Being the sect leader, Qi Fengge was incredibly busy, so it was impossible for him to personally guide his disciples each and every day. It had been Tan Yuanchun and Shen Qiao who'd taught Gu Hengbo most of her martial arts, and of the two, Shen Qiao spent more time with her. Therefore, Gu Hengbo treated this shixiong of hers like a brother and father both, and she adored and admired him deeply. They were much closer than the average fellow disciples.

Gu Hengbo was exceptionally beautiful, and many young male disciples couldn't help but stare. Upon seeing how intimate she was with Shen Qiao, they all developed some misunderstandings, and even Yi Pichen was no exception. Only when Shen Qiao introduced her did he understand. "Sect Leader Qi was truly a pride of the heavens—even his disciples are all outstanding," he said. "I was fortunate enough to meet two of them. When I think back to Sect Leader Qi's magnificence in the past, I cannot help but find it heartbreaking!"

He'd always been adept with social situations. When he saw that Gu Hengbo had come alone, he didn't ask the reason. After a few pleasantries, he learned that Shen Qiao and Gu Hengbo had just re-united after a long separation, so they must've had a lot to say to each other. He had someone place another seat cushion beside Shen Qiao, allowing the martial siblings to continue their conversation.

Shen Qiao and Gu Hengbo sat down, but he quickly found that she seemed absent-minded and easily distracted. "What's wrong, Wuniang?" he asked, confused.

Gu Hengbo pulled herself together and shook her head, "It's nothing. A-xiong has suffered a lot these days, haven't you? While I was wandering about outside, I often heard news about you. I'm also at fault for my negligence. Back then on Xuandu Mountain, I was unable to see through that bastard Yu Ai. That's why A-xiong had to suffer so much."

"Back then, even I was completely in the dark, never mind you," Shen Qiao replied. "The matter has already passed, so regrets are now meaningless. But how did you end up arguing so intensely with Yu Ai?"

"After you fell from the cliff, Xuandu Mountain was without a leader, but the situation didn't descend into chaos—instead, it quickly stabilized beneath Yu Ai's leadership. Everything was in good order, and several elders even mentioned that with your status unknown, Xuandu Mountain couldn't be left without a leader for even a day. They decided Yu Ai should take over the position of sect leader."

"It's good that Xuandu Mountain didn't descend into chaos." This was the first time Shen Qiao had heard the event as described by a Xuandu Mountain disciple, with all its inside stories. Even now, he still wasn't very clear on all the details. However, as Gu Hengbo tirelessly spoke, there was a sense of the fog lifting.

"At that time, I was ordered to stay on guard duty at Xuandu Mountain, so I was unable to personally watch your fight," she went on. "When the news came, it was as if I'd been struck by lightning. I was panicked and at a loss, but when I thought about it carefully later, something seemed off, and I felt that there was foul play involved. Because we, or even most of Xuandu Mountain's disciples, were all incredibly heartbroken over your accident, Zhangmen-shixiong. Only Yu Ai was resolute, his actions decisive and sweeping. Even though he looked sad on the surface, his behavior was terribly suspicious.

"After this incident, you returned to Xuandu Mountain once before, but Yu Ai couldn't keep you there. Afterward, he said that you were colluding with members of the demonic discipline. At that time, Da-shixiong was there, but I wasn't. Later, I saw that Da-shixiong seemed preoccupied and restless, so I took the opportunity to ask him, but he just hemmed and hawed and refused to tell me the truth."

Tan Yuanchun had always been indecisive. He was well-known among Xuandu Mountain's disciples for being overly accommodating, and a bit of a doormat. He regretted what had happened to Shen Qiao but was unable to take decisive action against Yu Ai. This wasn't surprising behavior for him.

Gu Hengbo continued, "One time, I heard him talking to Elder Chai. They seemed to have anticipated the outcome of your duel with Kunye. I became even more certain that there was something more going on, that Yu Ai must have hidden something from us. It wasn't until later, when they announced that Xuandu Mountain would be working together with the Göktürks, that I couldn't help myself anymore. I questioned Yu Ai, to ask if he'd been colluding with the Göktürks for a long time, and if your fall from the cliff and severe injuries were related."

Shen Qiao shook his head. "How could he admit to it if you asked him like that?"

Gu Hengbo smiled bitterly. "Of course he didn't admit to it. Not only that, he was only pretending to appease me—that night he snuck into my room and attacked me. However, I realized it in time, then fought him and fled down the mountain. I haven't gone back since."

Shen Qiao was silent for a moment. "You're a skilled martial artist, but you're not a match for Yu Ai," he said. "He also had full control of Xuandu Mountain then, and should have been perfectly capable of capturing you, yet he let you escape from the mountain. He still holds the friendships with his fellow disciples close to his heart, and that's why he let you go."

"Even if it's true, he poisoned you, causing you to fall from the cliff and lose all your martial arts," protested Gu Hengbo. "In my opinion, that little drop of kindness is just like a cat shedding false tears over a mouse. Da-shixiong is unable to tell right from wrong, so he chooses to hold a candle for the devil, assisting Yu Ai in his misdeeds. But I refuse to associate with him."

"Then what about Yuan Ying? What happened to him?"

Gu Hengbo shook her head. "Before I left the mountain, I secretly left Si-shixiong a letter explaining this matter. I don't know if he saw it, but I've heard no news of him since I left Xuandu Mountain."

As the pair of martial siblings chatted, several matches took place at the competition site. Wang-sanlang was an arrogant man, but his martial skills were outstanding among the younger generation. After defeating Zhou Yexue, he won several consecutive matches, and even Su Qiao lost to him by one move; at the moment, he was unstoppable.

Gu Hengbo glanced at the competition site several times, then suddenly said, "When the tiger is absent, the monkey is king. I will fight him too!"

Then, before Shen Qiao could stop her, she entered the site and ran toward Wang-sanlang.

This dazzling beauty's sudden appearance drew the entire audience's attention. Wang-sanlang showed an arrogant attitude toward the others, but in front of Gu Hengbo, he looked flattered at the unexpected attention, and even demonstrated the modesty one expected from a noble family's scion. "Swords and sabers care not who they cut, and I do not wish to hurt this celestial maiden. Why don't we shake hands and make peace instead?"

Gu Hengbo indifferently responded, "So you didn't come here to compete but to simply be a pompous snob?"

Wang-sanlang hadn't anticipated this beauty to be so scathing. Humiliated, he snarled, "Of course not!"

Gu Hengbo drew her sword. "Then please begin!"

Zhao Chiying watched their fight, and though she was surprised, she also felt it was to be expected. "Your shimei is truly extraordinary—renowned masters produce brilliant disciples. She clearly shares the same source as Daoist Master Shen. Having seen both of you in action, you both shine even more!"

"Sect Leader Zhao is too kind," Shen Qiao said modestly. However, he thought to himself that Wuniang wasn't normally this impulsive. Her behavior now was somewhat strange.

Wang-sanlang was naturally no match for Gu Hengbo. A strike from her sword knocked his from his hand, sending it arcing through the air before falling to the ground blade-first, planting itself there. A disciple of Chunyang Monastery declared loudly, "Gu Hengbo from Xuandu Mountain defeats Wang Zhuo from Kuaiji Commandery!"

Only then did everyone realize who Gu Hengbo was. Wang-sanlang's face looked somewhat pale, not only due to his own defeat but also at the news that the other party was actually Qi Fengge's disciple. At a loss, he remained slightly dazed for a while.

Gu Hengbo sheathed her sword and returned to a standing position, but her face was devoid of joy. Instead of returning to Shen Qiao, she walked toward Yuan Zixiao, who was engrossed in scribbling down notes.

"You've been paying attention to Wang-sanlang for such a long time. Now I've won against him, but you won't so much as glance at me?"

Yuan Zixiao didn't even raise her head. Her brush moved over the paper like a swimming dragon. "You winning against him—wasn't that the obvious conclusion?" she said.

Gu Hengbo sneered. "Fangzhang Isle's Liuli Palace is truly so conceited. It's one thing to leave without saying goodbye, but to pretend that you don't know me when we meet? Could it be that I, Gu Hengbo, am too disgraceful for you to acknowledge?"

There was no one around Yuan Zixiao—Yi Pichen had specifically asked everyone to leave some space around her so as not to affect her record-taking. The two of them spoke in low voices, so it was difficult for others to hear clearly. However, this interaction made it obvious that the two were acquainted. They just didn't understand why the conversation seemed so fraught.

At this time, two other matches had also been decided—the victors were Wang-erlang and a disciple of Chixia Sword Sect named Chao Yu. Those two winners were to fight each other next. Nowadays, swordplay was popular and prevalent throughout the land. Most people in the jianghu wielded swords, and these two were no exception.

The Chixia Sword Sect wasn't a major sect, but as Chao Yu was able to stand strong amid many people, the sect must have had its own strengths. Though Wang-erlang possessed a fierce spirit and was a skilled swordsman, he was still unable to best Chao Yu after two hundred moves and ultimately lost to him.

Wang-erlang refused to release his sword; his entire body was shaken by his opponent's internal energy. He staggered several steps back and almost collapsed into a sitting position. Chao Yu was gracious and flew forward to help his opponent, saving him from embarrassment. Though Wang-erlang was dissatisfied, he knew that there would always be someone better than himself. He cupped his hands and left the site unhappily.

The Kuaji Commandery's Wang brothers had marched in like thunder, and now they were leaving with their tails between their legs. Compared to their previous appearance in the main hall, when they'd had their noses stuck straight up in the air, the difference was like heaven and earth.

Strength was everything in the jianghu, and it was clear that these fledglings had yet to acclimate to this. They might have had the backing of the Wang family, but in the end, their martial arts needed to do the talking. If they were lacking there, even if the heavens themselves came to support them, they'd still find themselves unable to lift their heads.

Wang-erlang looked at his younger brother with his stark-white face, then saw Shen Qiao sitting in the distance, motionless as a mountain and entirely at ease. He felt the sudden urge to ask Shen Qiao: back when Kunye defeated him in full view of the public, how had he managed to endure that sense of humiliation?

But other than the Wang brothers themselves, everyone else's attention quickly shifted elsewhere. Chao Yu didn't seek out Gu Hengbo but instead cupped his hands in the direction of the Chunyang Monastery's disciples and said in a loud voice, "Chao Yu from the Chixia Sword Sect. Could I have the fortune of seeking guidance from Li-shaoxia?"[9]

---

9   少侠. Literally "young hero." A general address for martial artists from the jianghu.

This was an open challenge to Li Qingyu!

When the crowd heard this, excitement spread, and they all turned to look at Li Qingyu.

Chao Yu's goals were very clear. Although Gu Hengbo was young, she was Qi Fengge's disciple, which placed her in the same generation as Shen Qiao, and, strictly speaking, even Yi Pichen. Moreover, Gu Hengbo rarely appeared in the jianghu, so she wasn't well-known. Even if he defeated her, few people would marvel, but Li Qingyu was different.

In the current jianghu, Li Qingyu was the younger generation's most outstanding member. Previously, he had gone to Xuandu Mountain and lost by only one move to Yu Ai, which practically everyone had heard of. Later, at the Su residence, he'd also faced off against the Göktürk expert Duan Wenyang, who was the disciple of Hulugu himself. Li Qingyu had also lost by a narrow margin then, and Duan Wenyang was one of the world's top ten. Though Li Qingyu wasn't strong enough for the top ten, he clearly wasn't far from it either.

When the challenge had named him, Li Qingyu naturally had no reason to avoid the fight. He picked up his sword and slowly stood up, then walked out from the crowd.

"Though your swordplay is indeed formidable," he said to Chao Yu, "you still wouldn't be able to defeat me within a hundred moves."

Chao Yu had excellent self-restraint, but he still couldn't help his expression of indignation when he heard these words. "I respect Li-shaoxia's superb swordsmanship," he said, "but aren't these words a bit too much?"

"He's correct." A voice filled with laughter suddenly rang out in the venue, oozing ceaseless charm and numbing everyone down to their bones. "You are not his match. There are many things that can be discerned even without competing. Out of concern for your reputation, Abbot Yi can't speak up easily and insult you. You need to have more self-awareness."

Everyone turned to see a woman walking up the stone mountain steps. She was as dignified as a lotus, her demeanor elegant and ethereal. Yet at the same time, her words came with a touch of teasing and frivolity, a complete contrast with her appearance. The sheer discord between the two left the watchers temporarily disoriented.

"This one is...?" Zhao Chiying rarely left her mountain, so she naturally didn't know who the woman was.

Shen Qiao said severely, "Hehuan Sect Leader Yuan Xiuxiu."

Zhao Chiying jolted slightly. The name had struck her like piercing thunder.

At the same time, Yi Pichen also stood. "Sect Leader Yuan graces us with her presence. This humble Daoist wasn't able to greet you personally; he begs your forgiveness."

The moment Yi Pichen exposed the woman's identity, many people's faces suddenly twisted in shock.

The demonic discipline carried a resounding reputation, but if the one arriving had been Huanyue Sect or Fajing Sect, the others might not have reacted like this. That reaction was due to Hehuan Sect's fondness for parasitic cultivation, where they consumed others' yin energy to nourish their own yang, or vice versa. Who knew how many lives they'd taken this way? Moreover, due to the gargantuan power and influence the sect wielded, no one wanted to provoke them. Nowadays, when it came to Hehuan Sect, they had no need to fear others, but everyone else feared them.

Yuan Xiuxiu gave a lovely smile. "The ignorant are never guilty. Since the Sword Trial Conference is open to everyone in all the land, Abbot Yi will surely welcome me and not turn me away?"

One can never trust the enemy who comes with a smile. Behind her followed several disciples, all well-known members of Hehuan Sect—many people in the jianghu also recognized them.

Yi Pichen gave a slow nod. "All who come are guests; you are naturally welcome."

Yuan Xiuxiu smiled. "Wonderful. There are quite a few old friends here today, and this one happened to be in the vicinity. I heard that some people believe our Hehuan Sect to be too aggressive and wish to form an alliance opposing us. Is this matter true? What do you think, Abbot Yi?"

If Yi Pichen confirmed it, he would fall into her trap. However, if he denied it, he'd look like too much of a coward, and others were certain to question his abilities. Yuan Xiuxiu's actions made it clear she was here to stir up trouble.

When they heard her question, anger appeared on the faces of many, but their fear of Hehuan Sect's power prevented them from speaking up.

At that moment, someone else said, "There's no need for Abbot Yi to respond; this humble Daoist can reply on his behalf. Is Sect Leader Yuan asking these words out of guilt? Do you also feel that Hehuan Sect's actions are inappropriate, and fear inciting the wrath of the public and igniting an uncontrollable fire? Is that why, after hearing the news, you quickly ascended the mountain so that you could quench the flames?"

The voice was calm, gentle, and reassuring, without feeling aggressive or forceful at all.

Yi Pichen understood that, as the host of the Sword Trial Conference and leader of the Chunyang Monastery, his identity made it difficult for him to reply. At this time, Shen Qiao hadn't spoken to steal the limelight but to give him a way out. He immediately sent him a grateful glance.

Yuan Xiuxiu sneered. "How brave you are, Daoist Master Shen. You killed two elders from my Hehuan Sect, and I haven't even come here to settle those scores. Instead, you dared to come up to me first?"

Someone else suddenly interrupted. "How strange. Why can't someone kill people from your Hehuan Sect? It's a pity I wasn't present when Daoist Master Shen killed them, or I'd have cheered him on with gongs and drums! Everyone, if you really wish to form an alliance against Hehuan Sect, please allow our Huanyue Sect to join in as well. In my opinion, Daoist Master Shen is of noble character and prestige—he's the most suitable choice as alliance leader!"

Accompanying this new voice, a young man appeared on the stone steps, waving a fan.

And who the hell was this, now?

Everyone felt that their eyes were getting overloaded.

But Shen Qiao's head suddenly began to throb.

102

Uninvited Guests

DURING THE SWORD TRIAL CONFERENCE, Chunyang Monastery had to be wary of anyone trying to stir up trouble. Disciples were stationed at the foot of the mountain on sentry duty, and Yi Pichen had even sent an elder down there, just in case. Yet now these people were coming up the mountain one by one, as if they were entering some no-man's land. It was obvious that the screening set up below the mountain had become completely useless.

The moment this young man appeared, the already chaotic situation only grew more so—especially when he'd brought up Shen Qiao's name. "May I ask this distinguished master his identity in Huanyue Sect?"

He was clearly far too young to be Yan Wushi.

As expected, the man said, "This one is Yu Shengyuan, a disciple under Huanyue Sect Leader Yan. I heard that Qingcheng Mountain was very lively today, so I came up to take a look. I'm sure that Abbot Yi wouldn't drive me away, would he?"

"All who come are guests," said Yi Pichen. "This humble Daoist would never turn anyone away at the gates. Someone, come and prepare a few more seats for these honored guests."

"No need to trouble Abbot Yi," said Yuan Xiuxiu in a gentle voice. "Everyone around us is about to attack. If I sit down now, I'll have to stand again right after—that's far too troublesome!"

But Yu Shengyan laughed and said, "If you don't want to sit, that's your business. I haven't seen Daoist Master Shen in a long time, so I can't suppress my excitement and joy! I wish to go and reminisce about the past with him."

With that, he walked over to Shen Qiao and sat down in the seat Gu Hengbo had vacated earlier. He turned his head and smiled at Shen Qiao. "I trust you have been well, Shidi!"

When this "Shidi" slipped out so smoothly, the nearby Zhao Chiying was beyond astonished. She thought to herself that even if Shen Qiao was close to Yan Wushi, surely it wasn't to the point that he'd abandon his own sect and join him instead?

Shen Qiao didn't know whether to laugh or to cry. "Why did you come, Yu-gongzi? Where is Sect Leader Yan?"

Yu Shengyan joked, "Why is Shidi acting like we're strangers? No matter what, I was the one who carried you back from Banbu Peak—for over an hour! That time, you were so dazed as you called me Yu-shixiong, and it was downright adorable. How could you forget? You're breaking my heart!"

With the arrival of Hehuan Sect's party, Yu Shengyan's lone presence wasn't enough for people to drop their guard. Even though he'd shown up out of nowhere and interrupted Yuan Xiuxiu, the atmosphere didn't ease in the slightest.

Li Qingyu rose, his expression indifferent. "If Sect Leader Yuan is here as a guest, we will naturally give her a warm welcome," he said, "but if she isn't here in good faith, please forgive Chunyang Monastery for being unable to entertain her."

Yuan Xiuxiu smiled. "What a temper you have, Li-gongzi. This one was merely asking a question. Since anyone can participate in the Sword Trial Conference, surely Hehuan Sect can as well."

She swept her lovely eyes about her, and her gaze fell on Yuan Zixiao. "Is this the Young Palace Mistress of Liuli Palace? I've long heard that the disciples of the Liuli Palace are wonderfully broad-minded, and that you know the martial arts rankings as well as your own fingertips. May I ask Young Palace Mistress Yuan if Hehuan Sect also has a spot on your ranking list?"

Everyone knew that Yuan Zixiao was a disciple of Liuli Palace, but they didn't know that she was the young palace mistress herself. Yet Yuan Xiuxiu had exposed her identity right away. No one would believe Hehuan Sect if they said they'd come without preparations.

Yuan Zixiao remained sitting, her sleeves tucked together. After Yuan Xiuxiu's words, she began reciting a stream of information without batting an eyelid. "Hehuan Sect's Yuan Xiuxiu, ranked ninth in the jianghu. Her disciple is Xiao Se, who uses fans as blades. He defeated Zhongnan Sect Leader Guo Xun, Liuhe Guild's Hall Master Shangguan Xingchen, as well as Linchuan Academy's Zhan Ziqian. Though his martial arts are not yet first-rate, they are already exceedingly impressive. Hehuan Sect's Sang Jingxing, ranked sixth in the jianghu. His disciple is Bai Rong, who's skilled in palm techniques. Due to cultivating with the secret techniques of Hehuan Sect, her martial arts have improved by leaps and bounds. He also has Xia Hanqiu, Ji Shuang'er, and Zhou Cuiyue as disciples; though their skills pale in comparison to Bai Rong's, they are still figures among the rising stars in the jianghu that cannot be underestimated."

It wasn't just other people, even Yuan Xiuxiu looked surprised. "As expected of Liuli Palace," she said. "Even I didn't know that Xiao Se once defeated a disciple from Linchuan Academy. Yet Young Palace Mistress Yuan has it memorized so well, this information is practically at her fingertips!"

Yuan Zixiao did not show the slightest hint of pride, only continued indifferently, "Knowing such things isn't hard. There are no secrets—it only involves asking a few extra people and traveling to a few extra places."

At this time, someone in the crowd cut in, "Yuan-niangzi, is the ranking you speak of the one from ten years ago? Or the one now?"

"Naturally, it's the current ranking."

The speaker was unconvinced. "The Sword Trial Conference isn't even half over, and many experts haven't even shown up. So how was this top ten ranking conceived?"

"How can a single Sword Trial Conference take into account all the experts in the land?" replied Yuan Zixiao. "Today is just an opportunity for the elites of the jianghu to spar. If one or two astonishing masters appear for the first time, the rankings will of course change accordingly. And if not, the rankings will proceed as was previously determined."

"Then may I ask the identities of the top ten martial artists? Could Young Palace Mistress Yuan regale us with this information?"

Yuan Zixiao continued to answer every question: "At first, the rank of tenth in the jianghu was unstable. Previously, it was the former sect leader of Xuandu Mountain, Shen Qiao. Later, Shen Qiao was defeated at Banbu Peak and replaced by Kunye. And after that, Kunye's shixiong Duan Wenyang came to the Central Plains, and thus Kunye was replaced by Duan Wenyang. Shen Qiao and Duan Wenyang also dueled at the Su residence in Chang'an. Though both sides were evenly matched, Duan Wenyang had first fought with Chunyang Monastery's Li Qingyu before fighting Shen Qiao. Thus, Shen Qiao had an advantage, so tenth place remains Duan Wenyang."

Gu Hengbo couldn't help but frown. "Your ranking is too biased," she protested. "My Shen-shixiong is a heaven-blessed genius and inherited our shizun's mantle. His defeat at Banbu Peak was due to a plot against him. After that happened, his martial ability was greatly reduced. That's why he suffered setback after setback. If we're talking about his original level of power, he was naturally more formidable than both Duan Wenyang and Kunye, so how could he fail to even make it into the top ten?"

Yuan Zixiao glanced at her. "People won't just spin their wheels forever. There is always the chance of moving forward or backward for one reason or another. You refused to let me finish speaking and leapt to interrupt—was that not biased of you?"

Gu Hengbo knew that she was wrong and didn't reply, though her eyes flashed faintly as she gazed at Yuan Zixiao.

Yuan Zixiao ignored her and continued, "Ninth in the jianghu, as I just mentioned, is Hehuan Sect Leader Yuan Xiuxiu. Eighth is Tuyuhun's Kosa Sage."

Most people knew of Tuyuhun's Kosa Sage but had never seen him, so they knew very little about him. One of the onlookers asked, "The Kosa Sage has never set foot in the jianghu of the Central Plains, so how did this ranking come about?"

"Among the three demonic sects, only Fajing Sect has traveled far into the Western Regions, but they've been operating in Tuyuhun for many years. The Kosa Sage fought Fajing Sect Leader Guang Lingsan, and he was defeated by a hair's breadth and has remained in seclusion since then. Guang Lingsan previously commented on his martial arts, saying that the Kosa Sage was on par with him as a fighter and that his victory was due to luck."

Hearing that she was ranked ninth, only ahead of Duan Wenyang, didn't seem to make Yuan Xiuxiu angry; instead, she showed great interest. "Then according to Young Palace Mistress Yuan, seventh place must be Fajing Sect Leader Guang Lingsan?" she asked.

"Correct," said Yuan Zixiao.

Regardless of how accurate this ranking really was, it at least sounded like it was based on evidence instead of being drawn up at random. The higher up on the list Yuan Zixiao went, the more interested people became in the names at the top of the ranking.

Those who didn't pursue benefits would pursue fame. One could never be free from those two things. Everyone possessed a sense of vanity and curiosity; the only difference was in whether it was big or small, excessive or restrained. Even martial grandmasters like Yi Pichen couldn't stop their growing interest after hearing Yuan Zixiao's comments on the land's elites.

"And further up the list?" While Yi Pichen could still restrain himself, the others couldn't take it and continued to ask for more details.

Yuan Zixiao continued, "Further up, starting from the sixth place, those can be considered experts who have achieved grandmaster status. These people, regardless of their moral character, words, or actions, are already more than capable of establishing their own sect and disseminating their own teachings."

Earlier, she'd said that Sang Jingxing placed sixth. It was clear that the grandmaster-level experts included him in their ranks.

Yuan Xiuxiu smiled with her eyes. "It seems that Young Palace Mistress Yuan has a very high opinion of Elder Sang!"

"Sect Leader Yuan has no reason for dissatisfaction," Yuan Zixiao said coolly. "Everyone knows that there are two separate factions within Hehuan Sect. If you could deal with Sang Jingxing, why have you allowed him to hamstring you?"

Yuan Zixiao's words had exposed the internal strife within her sect. Though Yuan Xiuxiu smile remained unchanged, murderous intent flashed across her face.

"Chunyang Monastery now stands above the rest of the Daoist sects. I trust that the top five of Liuli Palace's rankings must have a place for Abbot Yi?" The person who posed this question obviously wished to curry favor with Chunyang Monastery.

"Correct," said Yuan Zixiao. "At fifth place in the jianghu should be the current state preceptor of Zhou, Buddhist Master Xueting. However, the former sect leader of Xuandu Mountain, Shen Qiao, has made great advances in his martial arts and hence may be able to contend with him for fifth place. As for fourth and third, they should be Linchuan Academy Master Ruyan Kehui and Chunyang Abbot Yi, but as I've never seen them duel, it's difficult to determine which one is the stronger."

"Then first and second place?" asked someone, unable to wait any longer.

"Huanyue Sect Leader Yan Wushi might be able to contend for second place. As for number one in the world..." She wasn't a timid person, nor someone prone to faltering, but for some reason, she didn't continue speaking and only shook her head.

The crowd was shocked that Yan Wushi was ranked that high, but when they thought about it, they had to acknowledge that few in the world could withstand a group ambush from five of the best martial artists in the world and emerge unscathed. Furthermore, three out of the five experts who'd participated in the ambush were within the top ten. From this, it was clear that Yan Wushi's strength was indeed astonishing. It wasn't too hard to accept that he was number two in all the land.

Someone challenged her. "Ten years ago, Qi Fengge was number one in the world. Could his death mean that first place must remain vacant? Has there really been no one who could surpass Qi Fengge in the last ten years?"

But regardless of how others questioned her, Yuan Zixiao spoke no more.

Someone tried to provoke her. "Liuli Palace's ranking might not even be accurate. What's there to discuss if they can't even determine who's in first?"

"If you don't believe me," said Yuan Zixiao frostily, "you're welcome to challenge every name on the ranking, one by one. If you can defeat them all, the title of world's number one will naturally be yours."

Yuan Xiuxiu was all smiles. "In my opinion, whether this ranking is accurate or not ultimately depends on strength. Though quite a few people are missing today, I, Abbot Yi, and Daoist Master Shen are all here. Of the top ten, three are present. Why don't we duel to our heart's content?"

"You're not worthy of fighting Shizun," Li Qingyu said with a cold face. "Defeat me first, then you can talk."

With that, he drew his sword. Qiushui was as a stream of rippling autumn water, quavering within his hands.

Though Li Qingyu was a formidable fighter, he didn't place in the top ten, so Yuan Xiuxiu had no reason to fear him. Even before she could speak, Xiao Se gave a bright laugh from behind her. "Why trouble our sect leader to fight? I'll battle you instead!"

At those words, both sides swept toward each other with a tap of their toes, immediately tangling as they began to fight.

Though Yuan Zixiao had just ranked her second to last, Yuan Xiuxiu didn't actually take the ranking seriously. To her, Yuan Zixiao's words were just a prelude to the main act. Now, she smiled and said, "Abbot Yi, since our disciples are already dueling, as their masters, shouldn't we set an example for them as well?"

Her goal in coming here this time was very clear: to capture some thieves, one had to capture their leader first. As long as she defeated

Yi Pichen, both the Sword Trial Conference and any prospective alliance would crumple in an instant. Even if other sects wanted to oppose Hehuan Sect, after she made an example and warning out of Yi Pichen, they would be roundly intimidated and too afraid to create more trouble.

Seeing that this battle was unavoidable, Yi Pichen put down his whisk and took the longsword his disciple presented to him. He nodded and said, "Then this humble Daoist shall seek guidance from Sect Leader Yuan."

At this development, Yu Shengyan leaned over and whispered into Shen Qiao's ear. "Shidi, you shouldn't be too eager to play hero. Wait until Yi Pichen is defeated, then you can step in. That way you'll be able to effortlessly snatch the position of alliance leader for yourself."

Shen Qiao didn't know whether to laugh or cry. "I never wanted to be the alliance leader!"

Yu Shengyan was confused. "Shizun ordered me to come and help you. If you don't want to be alliance leader, why did he instruct me to do so?"

Shen Qiao thought to himself, *Your shizun just does as he pleases, and his actions and words couldn't be further from a normal person's. How am I supposed to know what he's thinking?*

Yu Shengyan knew little of what had happened between Yan Wushi and Shen Qiao, let alone his shifu's change of heart. He only thought that Shizun was unwilling to give up his interest in Shen Qiao and had come up with some other idea. He hadn't asked much, and now he'd misunderstood everything. He was even interacting with Shen Qiao the way he had in the past.

103

Intimate Associate

MEANWHILE, Xiao Se and Li Qingyu had already begun dueling, with both sides relying on speed—the two of them had practically transformed into blurred afterimages. A mediocre practitioner would find it near-impossible to see how they fought, how they exchanged blows, and how each neutralized the other party's attacks.

The moment they started fighting, it was of course impossible for them to constrain it to the competition site. A mere moment later and the two had fought from the ground to atop the nearby stone wall, using their momentum to spar in midair, then they swept over to the bamboo forest on the other side and continued dueling above it. They both had phenomenal qinggong—a tap of their toes allowed them to jump yards into the air. Li Qingyu's sword glare and the blades of Xiao Se's fan only enhanced each other's brilliance; the clang of weapons rang out ceaselessly, shaking everyone's hearts. It was a scene that was impossible to follow.

In Shen Qiao's opinion, Li Qingyu was the best of Chunyang Monastery's current generation, and he'd almost caught up to the world's top ten in terms of strength. Though Xiao Se was also an excellent fighter, he still fell short of Li Qingyu. Winning wouldn't be easy. Eventually, Yuan Xiuxiu would have to come to her disciple's aid. Then, when Yi Pichen took true action, how would Yuan Xiuxiu handle him?

If Yuan Xiuxiu was the only lynchpin of Hehuan's plan to cause chaos here, it would certainly fall through.

When he thought of this, Shen Qiao couldn't help but ask, "Yu-gongzi, what do you think? The Hehuan Sect came prepared on this visit. Then, might they have a contingency plan?"

Yu Shengyan laughed. "Why do you still call me Yu-gongzi? It sounds so awkward. I'd rather you call me Shixiong!"

Shen Qiao smiled but remained silent. Though he and Yu Shengyan had come into conflict over the matter of killing the Yan family, it'd only been due to their different stances and views, not any deep hatred. Furthermore, after he'd fallen from Banbu Peak, this young man had carried him on his back for quite some time. No matter what, one should never be ungrateful. Hence, he never shifted his wariness toward Yan Wushi onto Yu Shengyan, and instead treated him with the indulgence an older brother would show his younger one.

In the end, Yu Shengyan was young and couldn't restrain himself completely. He said, "It's like how Xiang Zhuang's sword dance was a front for assassinating the Duke of Pei.[10] Hehuan Sect's aggressive arrival only looked like it was directed at Chunyang Monastery—their true targets were all the sects holding Hehuan Sect in contempt. Nowadays, the emperor of Zhou only believes in Buddhism, not Daoism. He wishes to foster the Buddhist faction so they can counter Hehuan Sect. This is how emperors protect their imperial power, but he has no such needs from Daoism. Therefore, he simply ignores them, leaving them at the mercy of Hehuan Sect."

---

10   项庄舞剑，意在沛公. *Xiang Zhuang was a general of Chu. In 206 B.C.E., the start of the Chu-Han contention, he hatched a plot to assassinate the future Emperor Gaozu of Han, then known as the Duke of Pei, at a feast.*

Next to them, Zhao Chiying had been listening for a while. She didn't know much about the current world situation, but she could tell that Yu Shengyan spoke with incredible eloquence despite his young age and that his words made a fair amount of sense. She then thought about Yan Wushi's impressive demeanor—it was indeed true that disciples would take after their master. She couldn't help but lament even more that Bixia Sect had no worthy successors.

Yu Shengyan continued, "If she can defeat Yi Pichen this time and paint him as mediocre, he naturally won't be a concern anymore. Then she can take the opportunity to subdue the other forces present at the Sword Trial Conference in one fell swoop. In fact, I bet that old bald donkey Xueting must be terribly envious of her, but he needs to worry about reputation and face—he can't do these shameless things, for they'd damage the reputation of Buddhism, but that's not an issue for Hehuan Sect. Now that they've come today, they absolutely must succeed—they cannot be lukewarm and give up halfway. Yuan Xiuxiu isn't enough to take on Yi Pichen by herself, so Sang Jingxing might be on his way already."

Yuan Zixiao said earlier that Sang Jingxing ranked sixth in the jianghu, while Yi Pichen was between three and four. However, those rankings were only a rough approximation. Those on the list would never stop improving, so their rankings would occasionally change. Sang Jingxing placing sixth didn't mean that he was certain to lose to Yi Pichen. One couldn't calculate things this way. The battlefield could change a thousand times in an instant, and the slightest deviation could turn the tides completely. When experts exchanged blows, even a hopeless situation could still reverse, so the weak defeating the strong was always a possibility.

However, Xiao Se and Li Qingyu was clearly not a case of the weak defeating the strong. Li Qingyu's attacks were steady, and after a hundred moves, he channeled his strength into Qiushui. His swordplay rained down like the scattered flowers from a celestial maiden, and his sword qi overflowed with a dazzling light. Xiao Se was clearly outmatched—though the blades of his fan were formidable, his openings gradually revealed themselves. The skilled spectators like Yi Pichen, Shen Qiao, and Zhao Chiying could all see those openings, so how could Li Qingyu miss them? He summoned a sword screen like rain that blotted out everything, leaving Xiao Se with nowhere to move. He was forced to retreat several steps, and once he found his footing, he conceded defeat.

"They say that Chunyang Monastery boasts fantastic swordplay, far surpassing that of Xuandu Mountain," he said. "Now that I've seen it, its reputation is truly well deserved!"

Xiao Se had praised Chunyang Monastery, not Li Qingyu, implying Li Qingyu's power came not from himself but from his sect. He even tried to implicate Xuandu Mountain, hoping to sow discord between Shen Qiao and Yi Pichen.

Unfortunately, he'd targeted the wrong person with his scheming. Li Qingyu remained expressionless, looking at Xiao Se like he was merely a tree. He had no emotional fluctuations to speak of, and even his tone was flat. "Originally, your talents weren't mediocre, but unfortunately, you have too many things on your mind, so you're unable to focus on the martial path. It'll be difficult for you to make further progress."

Xiao Se was so furious he laughed instead. "This distinguished master need not trouble himself over my potential progress!"

Li Qingyu's gaze shifted away from him, falling on Yuan Xiuxiu instead. After what Yuan Xiuxiu had said to Yi Pichen just before, neither of them had moved. It was unclear whether they were waiting for the outcome of Li Qingyu and Xiao Se's match first.

"May Li Qingyu have a bout with Sect Leader Yuan?" he asked.

Yuan Xiuxiu pursed her lips and smiled. "You're no match for me."

"Match or not, we can't say so without trying."

Still smiling, Yuan Xiuxiu said nothing. She suddenly flung her sleeves outward, splitting her energy into two streams that surged toward him. Caught off guard, Li Qingyu was forced to step back. But Yuan Xiuxiu flew forward, pursuing him relentlessly.

Chunyang Monastery's qinggong was incredible, but Yuan Xiuxiu's was on another level. Her clothes fluttered as her sleeves billowed like clouds. At first glance, she looked like the reincarnation of the nymph of the Luo River—not at all like a demoness from Hehuan Sect.

Li Qingyu had never fought Yuan Xiuxiu before; he'd assessed her abilities through her disciple. Previously, he assumed that even if Yuan Xiuxiu was stronger than Xiao Se, she couldn't be *much* stronger. There were also the rumors that Hehuan Sect took shortcuts to increase their internal energy through parasitic cultivation, which everyone held in disdain. But unexpectedly, certain things only became clear with a fight. It wasn't only Li Qingyu who was surprised; even the spectators were stunned as they completely dropped their previous contempt.

Zhao Chiying couldn't help but exclaim, "Yuan Xiuxiu is indeed formidable enough to be a sect leader!"

When she had listened to Yuan Zixiao rank the world's heroes, placing Yuan Xiuxiu in ninth place while she herself failed to rank at all, though she hadn't said anything aloud, Zhao Chiying's heart had been unconvinced. Now that she saw her fight, however, it was clear that the ranking was grounded in fact. If she were the one dueling Yuan Xiuxiu now, she might perform no better than Li Qingyu.

As Zhao Chiying spoke, Yuan Xiuxiu had already used her preemptive advantage to force Li Qingyu to the cliff's edge. Just as he was about to launch a counterattack, she suddenly withdrew her hand and retreated. She drifted airily away, falling back dozens of paces in an instant before landing on a flag that Chunyang Monastery had staked into the ground.

The flag's soft fabric fluttered in the wind, yet she was able to stand atop it, as if she weighed nothing. This display of skill was so astonishing it drew dumbfounded stares from all around. Before this, some people had underestimated her because she was a woman or because they were unconvinced that she could rank within the world's top ten. But now they saw just how wrong they'd been.

"As I already said, you're no match for my venerable self." Yuan Xiuxiu's tone was gentle, but her words were imperious beyond compare.

"Qingyu is indeed inferior to Sect Leader Yuan. He's embarrassed himself before her." The speaker was Yi Pichen. "Let this humble Daoist seek guidance instead."

If it weren't for the recent match between Li Qingyu and Yuan Xiuxiu, no one would have expected much from a duel between Yuan Xiuxiu and Yi Pichen. But now that they'd seen Yuan Xiuxiu's strength, everyone was eagerly anticipating this next match.

However, the moment Yi Pichen finished speaking, another group of people came up the mountain. At the front was a man, and behind him were several girls, one of them someone Shen Qiao was deeply familiar with: Bai Rong.

As for the man in front, he wasn't a stranger to Shen Qiao either. He'd fought him in the outskirts of Chang'an once. In the end, one man had been severely injured while the other had lost all their martial arts.

As he recognized the man, the man naturally recognized him as well. Their eyes met from afar, and Sang Jingxing's gaze was filled with an almost graphic lasciviousness. It scanned Shen Qiao from head to toe, and there was also a marked kind of cruelty and rage within those eyes.

Shen Qiao possessed an extraordinary appearance; that was beyond all doubt. At first glance, he looked gentle as a spring breeze, and only those who'd encountered him before would know that a cold and indestructible pride lay within his bones. Having fought Shen Qiao before, how could Sang Jingxing not know this? Last time, he'd thought the other man soft, harmless, and weak. Never had he expected there to be nothing but steely bone, and he'd ended up with a mouthful of sand.

But this had only aroused Sang Jingxing's thirst for conquest and sadism. Up until now, he hadn't recklessly sought out Shen Qiao. For one thing, Shen Qiao's whereabouts were elusive and difficult to ascertain. For another, he'd heard that his martial arts had greatly advanced, that he'd even killed a couple of Hehuan Sect's elders. Though Sang Jingxing had a deep love for beauties, he had no interest in losing his life for one.

It'd been a long time, yet a single glance was enough for Sang Jingxing to identify Shen Qiao in the crowd. He only felt that the other man had grown even more gorgeous, with the aura of an immortal and appearance like ice and snow. Even without accounting for clothes and adornments, there was something remarkably pure and transcendental about him. It made Sang Jingxing want to strip him naked and play with him in full view of everyone, watch his face fall as he cried for mercy. How refreshing would that be?

Thinking of this, an indescribable flame blazed to life within his heart.

Sang Jingxing's gaze was incredibly obscene; everyone could see it. But Shen Qiao remained like an old monk in meditation, his eyes half-closed as he treated Sang Jingxing like air.

Yu Shengyan rose and moved to stand in front of Shen Qiao. "To think that a great and lofty elder of Hehuan Sect would act like a starving dog in front of a meaty bone! How shameful!"

Standing up for Shen Qiao was only his secondary aim. Huanyue Sect and Hehuan Sect had always been at odds, and after Yan Wushi had left the capital and fallen to the ambush, Hehuan Sect had defected from Qi and thrown themselves into the arms of Yuwen Yun. With the emperor's support, they'd absorbed Huanyue Sect's authority. Yu Shengyan had long disdained Hehuan Sect—it would have been stranger for him to say nothing at all.

Sang Jingxing sneered. "Even your shifu Yan Wushi wouldn't dare to speak to me like that!"

His words were infused with internal energy, similar to the Buddhist discipline's Vajra Lion Roar technique, but Sang Jingxing's was far superior. It reached the ears of everyone present without exception, and they felt their ears throb, especially Yu Shengyan. When he'd spoken those words, he'd been prepared for a swift attack from Sang Jingxing, but he was shocked to find that he'd still underestimated him. With Sang Jingxing targeting him, the force behind the voice he heard was many times greater than what the rest of the crowd experienced. His face instantly paled as his heart jolted, and he almost coughed up blood.

Fortunately, a hand reached out to steady him in time, accompanied by a stream of true qi. It flowed through him like a murmuring stream, immediately alleviating Yu Shengyan's discomfort.

"Posturing before a junior? I trust that Elder Sang must feel quite ashamed of himself," Shen Qiao said coolly.

His words were also imbued with internal energy, but it wasn't wild and unrestrained like Sang Jingxing's. Rather, he focused his voice straight ahead, sending it directly at Sang Jingxing.

Sang Jingxing lifted his sleeve and shook it once, negating the better part of Shen Qiao's attack. As for the remaining fraction, he relied on his powerful and profound internal cultivation to take it head-on, forcibly absorbing it.

In the blink of an eye, the two had already exchanged a round of attacks without batting an eyelid, but it was impossible to tell who was stronger or weaker with only those incomplete moves.

Sang Jingxing could feel that Shen Qiao's martial arts had greatly improved, and Shen Qiao also felt that Sang Jingxing was worthy of Yuan Zixiao's ranking him as a grandmaster-level expert. They looked at each other, then Sang Jingxing suddenly smiled and said, "Now that Daoist Master Shen has regained his vision, his eyes have become bright and spirited, making him even more captivating. Eyes are indeed the windows to the soul: no matter how lovely a beauty is, they still need a pair of good eyes."

Since he'd ascended the mountain, Sang Jingxing's attention had been fully focused on Shen Qiao. Yuan Xiuxiu silently frowned to herself about how he was ruining things, then followed up with a smile. "In the Young Palace Mistress's words, Elder Sang is ranked sixth in the world, while I am only ninth. Therefore, it would be too humiliating to Abbot Yi if I were to fight him."

Sang Jingxing then shifted his gaze from Shen Qiao to Yi Pichen. "Since I am ranked sixth," he said to Yuan Xiuxiu, "may I ask what place Abbot Yi holds?"

"Just now, Liuli Palace's Young Mistress Yuan said that Abbot Yi's martial arts rank in either third or fourth place, yet to be determined," she replied.

Sang Jingxing gave a mocking laugh. "In that case, if I defeat Abbot Yi, wouldn't the position of third place in the world become mine?"

Yuan Xiuxiu smiled. "Since today is the Sword Trial Conference, the Hehuan Sect should also follow the rules of the jianghu and fight one on one. That way people won't gossip that our Hehuan Sect are territory-trashing thugs who only know how to flaunt our superior numbers. Our humble sect's Elder Sang wishes to seek guidance from Abbot Yi. Would he be willing?"

Yi Pichen already knew that Hehuan Sect had come well-prepared and that there was no way they'd let the matter rest so easily. To him, there was little difference between Sang Jingxing or Yuan Xiuxiu. Regardless of which it was, he had to beat Hehuan Sect into retreating. If he couldn't intimidate them, then forget about winning over people's hearts—the alliance would fall through completely. The people from other sects would be greatly disappointed in Chunyang Monastery.

Although Sang Jingxing had a reputation for being lecherous and cruel, that couldn't conceal the fact that he was an expert of the highest order. If someone were to underestimate him based on his reputation, they would be the only one who'd end up suffering.

Yi Pichen held his sword in hand and gave a small smile. "Since the Sword Trial Conference is open to everyone, naturally, we won't turn Hehuan Sect away at the door. I have long heard of the famous Carving Dragon Palm, so today this humble Daoist wishes to seek guidance."

Though Sang Jingxing was egotistical, he still dared not underestimate the master of Chunyang Monastery. "As you wish. Please start, Abbot Chen."

Before Yuan Zixiao had ranked the world's martial experts, people considered Yi Pichen for top three in the world. Though

Yuan Zixiao now said that Yi Pichen's martial abilities ranked between third and fourth, this slightly lowered ranking didn't diminish his status and prestige in everyone's eyes. It would have been fine for him not to act, but now that he had agreed to the challenge, it would surely be an earth-shaking battle.

Sang Jingxing was famous for his Carving Dragon Palm, but that didn't mean he didn't know how to use a sword. At this moment, he extended his hand behind him, and Bai Rong immediately presented a longsword to him with both hands. The sheath was old-fashioned and plain, and Sang Jingxing didn't take it either. Instead, he drew the sword directly. The blade glinted as it was revealed, akin to the evening sun piercing through mist. Just one look was enough to see that it was a good sword.

He flicked the sword downward, and his true qi immediately traveled through the blade and into the ground, sending dust and sand flying everywhere. Stones rose off the ground, as if drawn by his true qi, and then surged toward Yi Pichen in a massive wave. Sang Jingxing followed right after them, flying forward, his figure and sword merging into one. It was a dazzling sight, the epitome of perfection.

At this point, the people who'd been certain Yi Pichen would win dared not stand by this conclusion. The crowd watched the battle before them with wide eyes, deeply afraid of missing a single second of this magnificence.

Shen Qiao was watching the battle intently when Yuan Xiuxiu walked toward him, a smile on her face. "It's already been several years since my last fight with Daoist Master Shen. I heard that the Daoist Master has made great martial progress. May Xiuxiu have the fortune of seeking guidance?"

According to the rules of the jianghu, if someone initiated a challenge, that challenge couldn't be declined, for doing so would make you look like a coward avoiding the fight. Even if the person challenged didn't care about their reputation, others would inevitably hold them in contempt and ridicule them in the future. Moreover, since Yuan Zixiao had just ranked Shen Qiao ahead of Yuan Xiuxiu, it was even more impossible for him to decline the challenge—otherwise he'd look unworthy of his reputation.

Before Shen Qiao could answer, though, Yu Shengyan stood up and said, "Why bother Daoist Master Shen? I'm willing to have a duel with Sect Leader Yuan."

At any other time, he would have happily watched the show from the sidelines. Demonic practitioners were not that kind and benevolent. Even if Yu Shengyan was close to Shen Qiao, it was impossible for him to shield Shen Qiao whenever something happened. However, before his visit this time, Yan Wushi had instructed him, saying that he should "absorb some troubles for Shen Qiao when needed." Though Yu Shengyan hadn't understood what he was thinking, he had to strictly carry out his shizun's instructions.

But of course, Yuan Xiuxiu didn't take him seriously. "If your shizun came himself, I would be forced to cede some ground to him."

The clear implication behind her words: When you're the only one? You should just step aside!

Of course, Yu Shengyan understood. He just wanted Yuan Xiuxiu to back off, so he name-dropped Yan Wushi more directly: "Shizun isn't far from here. He'll arrive soon."

Yuan Xiuxiu smiled sweetly. "Did Daoist Master Shen sell himself to Yan Wushi? To the point that he needs his consent to fight? If he's not here, is Daoist Master Shen too afraid to make a move?"

Shen Qiao inclined his head slightly. "Since Sect Leader Yuan has invited this humble Daoist, he shall accompany her."

He did not fall victim to Yuan Xiuxiu's provocations. Though Hehuan Sect had impressive numbers, not all of them were grandmaster-level experts. In the end, the only true threats were Yuan Xiuxiu and Sang Jingxing. Sang Jingxing was fighting Yi Pichen, and their relative strengths had yet to be determined. However, Yuan Xiuxiu was undoubtedly superior to Li Qingyu. Among all present, it seemed that no one other than Shen Qiao could deal with Yuan Xiuxiu.

If Shen Qiao didn't make his move today, then there was no doubt he'd witness Hehuan Sect sabotaging the Sword Trial Conference. And if Yi Pichen made any mistakes in his battle, even more people in the jianghu would be too fearful to oppose Hehuan Sect in the future.

"Truly a decisive person, Daoist Master Shen!" Yuan Xiuxiu smiled, and her figure suddenly rose from the ground as she spoke these gentle words. Two streams of black swept out of her sleeves and shot toward Shen Qiao, so quickly they left no time to react!

Those with sharp eyes could tell that the two streaks of black were a pair of longswords, but the rest were unable to see anything— they could only assume they were powerful concealed weapons of some sort.

In the blink of an eye, the flying swords were already in front of Shen Qiao, just inches from his eyelids!

His opponent's movements were really too swift!

Fan Yuanbai and Zhou Yexue couldn't help but yell in surprise. It seemed that Yuan Xiuxiu had held back during her duel with Li Qingyu and left him some leeway. But now she was attacking with her full strength, and as distant bystanders, they were completely unable to react in time, let alone think of how Shen Qiao should respond.

Shen Qiao didn't draw his sword. He shook his sleeves, and his true qi surged out in two streams, rushing toward his opponent's black swords. As the swords whistled through the air, they were blocked by a powerful wall of true qi that stopped them in their tracks. For an instant, they froze in midair.

And using just this instant, Shen Qiao drew the longsword from behind him and slashed at the air!

The sword glare was like the layered petals of a flower, blooming ring upon ring. Its magnificent beauty concealed a razor-sharp edge, one that made others afraid to look, that left them unable to meet it head-on.

Agitated by the sword qi, the black swords reversed directions and flew back, no longer under Yuan Xiuxiu's control. Giggling, she simply grabbed both swords, then swept directly toward Shen Qiao.

Their fight was different from that of Yi Pichen and Sang Jingxing. The latter two used their presences to pressure each other—not only were they competing in swordplay, they were also sparring over whose internal energy was more profound. However, Shen Qiao and Yuan Xiuxiu were both masters of the sword. Although their internal energy was clashing and vying for supremacy, this was accompanied by their sword qi and sword mastery, and not one could be missing. Their fight drew the eye even more than the duel between Sang Jingxing and Yi Pichen, and not by a small margin. Though the crowd's attention wavered between both fights, most were more inclined to watch Shen Qiao's battle.

But fighting wasn't dancing: it couldn't be contained to a particular area, and this was no spar. Although the two of them weren't staking their lives on the fight, they were bringing their full power to bear. Shen Qiao had already achieved the echelon of sword heart. Even leaving aside Yuan Xiuxiu, there were but a few people in the world who could compare with him. However, Yuan Xiuxiu was no pushover. Against her full might, Shen Qiao couldn't prevail with just a few moves. If he could, that would only prove that Yuan Xiuxiu's strength didn't live up to her reputation or that she didn't want to fight at all.

So the two of them fought from the gates of Chunyang Monastery to the roof, and then from the roof to the stone wall. Both parties' qinggong had already attained the pinnacle—they immediately descended along the stone wall, their sword qi overlapping. From afar, they looked like paper dolls affixed to the stone wall, but this was, in truth, a manifestation of their formidable, transcendent qinggong.

Not only was the younger generation left dumbfounded—even Yu Shengyan couldn't believe his eyes. After all, when he'd first picked up Shen Qiao, the man had lost almost all his martial arts, on top of being grievously injured and blind. Now, only a short time after, he'd already become this powerful. If this was the true strength of a grandmaster-level expert, then, never mind Yuan Xiuxiu—Shen Qiao might even have a chance facing off against his shifu Yan Wushi. And Yu Shengyan had just been blindly trying to make Shen Qiao call him shixiong! Thank goodness for Shen Qiao's excellent temper, otherwise he would have never let it slide!

Zhao Chiying gave a quiet sigh. "Looks like Daoist Master Shen has been going easy on us during our sparring sessions!"

Shen Qiao was gentle and approachable, but his sword qi was exceptionally imperious and powerful. Shanhe Tongbei hummed within his hand, accompanied by its sword glare. With enough power to overturn the oceans, it resonated with heaven and earth. Though Yuan Xiuxiu seemed to have a numerical advantage by wielding two swords, Shen Qiao grew bolder as he fought while she found him increasingly strenuous to handle. That powerful, imperious sword glare was almost bearing down on her head, the pressure on her multiplying many times over.

The two of them continued fighting, from the mountaintop to the foot of the mountain. It was impossible for everyone to follow them down the mountain to continue observing. When Yuan Xiuxiu saw that no one was around them, she couldn't help but call out to him, "Wait a minute, Daoist Master Shen. I have something to say!"

Since she'd told him to stop, of course she couldn't keep fighting. She immediately swept back, breathing a sigh of relief when Shen Qiao ceased his pursuit and feeling the immense pressure bearing down on her head suddenly disappear.

With a smile, Yuan Xiuxiu said, "When I first heard that Daoist Master Shen had killed two of our sect elders, I still couldn't quite believe it. Looking at it now, I was indeed too blind to recognize Mount Tai."

Though she looked relaxed, she knew in her heart that if the fight continued, she definitely would not be Shen Qiao's match.

Shen Qiao's heart was as clear as a mirror, open-minded and transparent. "Sect Leader Yuan deliberately led me down the mountain. I trust that it wasn't to praise my martial arts?"

Yuan Xiuxiu pursed her lips and smiled. "Daoist Master Shen is indeed wise. I'll be honest with you. I do have a good offer for you. Are you interested?"

"Please speak," said Shen Qiao.

"I know you and Sang Jingxing loathe each other deeply," she said. "He's cruel, bloodthirsty, and lustful to the bone. There's also Chen Gong, who repays kindness with enmity, who's repeatedly made trouble for you, but now he's colluding with Sang Jingxing. He even used Tai'e to ingratiate himself for an aristocratic title. He is truly a scoundrel, through and through. I also detest him. If Daoist Master Shen is willing to leave here today, to stay on the sidelines and avoid interfering with the affairs of Chunyang Monastery, I'll hand Chen Gong over to you and help you kill Sang Jingxing as well. How about it?"

Shen Qiao slowly shook his head.

Yuan Xiuxiu raised her eyebrows and said, "What, is this not an excellent offer?"

"It's indeed an excellent offer for me."

"Then why did Daoist Master Shen reject it?"

"There is a long-standing enmity between Sang Jingxing and Sect Leader Yuan," Shen Qiao replied. "Sect Leader Yuan wishes to get rid of him, but she's had this notion for a long time. So why use this humble Daoist as an excuse? As for Chen Gong, though he is indeed a scoundrel, we don't particularly hate each other. Even if it turns out I need to take care of him, I will find him myself, so Sect Leader Yuan need not trouble herself."

Yuan Xiuxiu sneered. "You are so close to Yan Wushi yet refuse to cooperate with me. It seems that Daoist Master Shen is not only a hypocrite but also looks down on women!"

Shen Qiao sighed and said, "Sect Leader Yuan, your words are excessive. There's a reason behind my relationship with Sect Leader Yan, but it's a long story and inconvenient to elaborate on. I've never held any thought of looking down on Sect Leader Yuan. The world values men over women, and even if the jianghu has fewer restrictions, it's still a hundred times more difficult for women to establish themselves within it compared to men. This is one of the main reasons why Hehuan Sect has been a repeated target for the secular world. However, under Sect Leader Yuan, Hehuan Sect has stood firm, which is naturally proof of Sect Leader Yuan's abilities.

Though this humble Daoist has also served as sect leader, my performance was far inferior to yours."

Yuan Xiuxiu was a bit surprised. She hadn't expected Shen Qiao to speak in her favor. Ever since she'd entered the jianghu, there had always been people who'd call her witch or demoness. Later, as her martial arts grew powerful, they no longer dared say it to her face but continued to do so behind her back. Hehuan Sect knew no taboo when it came to murder, and they took ruthless action. But if one asked around the jianghu, was there anyone who hadn't killed before? And of the three demonic sects, Hehuan Sect wasn't the only ruthless one. Instead, a large part of Hehuan Sect's notoriety lay in their parasitic and sexual cultivation practices, which gave the rest of the world an impression of extreme depravity.

Her eyes sparkled brilliantly as her expression softened a little. "Daoist Master Shen's words have touched me deeply. It's rare to hear someone speak on behalf of Hehuan Sect. In the beginning, when Bai Rong kept showing you mercy, I thought that she was simply young and easily deceived. But now I see that she really possesses a good eye!"

Shen Qiao smiled. "I'm not speaking on behalf of Sect Leader Yuan; I was only being impartial. To tell the truth, I do not like how your honored sect conducts itself. The likes of Sang Jingxing and Huo Xijing deserve far more than death, and they are unworthy of sympathy. Those who walk different paths cannot work together, and that's why I will never cooperate with Hehuan Sect. Right now, you are trying to stop the Sword Trial Conference, so I absolutely cannot follow your wishes. We hold different stances and viewpoints, so it's natural that we'll end up meeting on the battlefield."

Yuan Xiuxiu's appearance didn't show her age—she looked like a young woman in her twenties, which gave her smile even more charm. "Daoist Master Shen is so considerate that even I can't hold on any longer. Would you be willing to become an intimate associate of mine? If you don't like the Hehuan Sect, you won't have to deal with anyone beneath me. I also have several villas elsewhere, if Daoist Master Shen is willing...to keep our relationship a secret. No one else will know."

How did the two of them transition from fighting to discussing matters of romantic love? Shen Qiao truly didn't understand, but he was a sincere person, so he couldn't use cutting remarks the way Yan Wushi did to force others to back down. Instead, he simply cupped his hands. "Thank you, Sect Leader Yuan, for your loving kindness."

After speaking, he turned around, about to leave.

Yuan Xiuxiu smiled slightly, then flashed in front of him, blocking his path.

"Why is Daoist Master Shen in such a hurry to leave? We were having a good conversation just now! Looking at you, surely Yan Wushi hasn't taken you to his tent. It seems to me that he doesn't enjoy that kind of thing either. Or do you like Bai Rong more? I think that little girl also likes you a great deal. Why don't I help the two of you get together?"

Shen Qiao felt that Yuan Xiuxiu's attitude was somewhat odd. A flash of understanding hit him, and he blurted out, "Are you trying to stall for time, to keep me here on purpose?"

104

Back from the Dead

YUAN XIUXIU SAID CALMLY, "I simply realized that I was very compatible with Daoist Master Shen, so I put in a few extra words. Where did you get that thought of stalling for time?"

Shen Qiao didn't want to say any more to her. He turned to head back up the mountain, but Yuan Xiuxiu flashed in front of him once more.

"Is Daoist Master Shen that displeased at seeing me? Why are you running away after only a few words? If you don't wish to be intimate associates, we can just be ordinary friends!"

Yuan Xiuxiu gave a faint smile, one that was like thousands of red flowers abloom, or a million purple blossoms returning with spring. Anyone else would at least pause, even if their hearts weren't swayed entirely. However, Shen Qiao didn't halt his steps in the slightest and continued walking forward, completely unhindered by her beauty. Having this level of focus, one could truly call Shen Qiao half-immortal. Other than that freak Yan Wushi, when else had Yuan Xiuxiu seen someone like this?

Shen Qiao saw that she was about to strike and said coolly, "Though my cultivation path doesn't revel in reckless slaughter, that doesn't mean I can't kill. That day, Sect Leader Yuan personally witnessed her honored sect's Huo Xijing perish at my hands. Has Sect

Leader Yuan considered carefully what price she might have to pay for trying to stop me?"

Yuan Xiuxiu smiled. "Shen-lang need not get angry. I never intended for us to be enemies, but as a precaution, I need to keep you here so that you don't end up ruining things. However, even if you head up now, I fear that you won't be able to change anything. Out of consideration for our compatibility, this one will advise you: you are not a member of Chunyang Monastery. Even if you wish to make a name for yourself this time, Yi Pichen will remain ahead of you. So why must Shen-lang wade into these muddy waters himself?"

Her tone was soft, affectionate, and meandering, but would the great and lofty Hehuan Sect Leader say heartfelt words just because she took a liking to someone? Shen Qiao only wished to do the best for others while being unwilling to cause trouble. This did not mean that he was stupid or easy to deceive. He didn't listen to her and swept straight up the mountain.

Yuan Xiuxiu originally wanted to stop him, but Shen Qiao used "A Rainbow Stretches Across the Heavens," executing it to the utmost. Before she could catch up, he'd turned into a wisp of blue, leaving Yuan Xiuxiu with nothing but dust.

An ordinary person would take at least half a day to climb the mountain, but a martial expert would need only an hour. With a qinggong of Shen Qiao's level, it only took fifteen minutes.

But since Yuan Xiuxiu had said, "Even if you head up now, you won't be able to change anything," it meant that some unexpected crisis had already occurred.

The Chunyang Monastery disciples who'd been on sentry duty at the mountain gate had already been defeated by Hehuan Sect when they came up. Now, as Shen Qiao climbed the mountain again, his path was completely unobstructed. But his unease only grew worse, all the way until he finally reached the summit and returned to the field before Chunyang Monastery's main hall. There, he just happened to see Yi Pichen meet palms with someone under the full view of the crowd. The other party remained firmly in place while Yi Pichen took three steps back.

He took another look at the crowd around him—their expressions seemed to be frozen, fixed in a moment of great shock.

The person facing off against Yi Pichen was unfamiliar—Shen Qiao didn't recognize him. However, the man in question had a prominent nose and deep-set eyes, and although he was handsome, with a heroic spirit, a glance told Shen Qiao that he wasn't young. He was dressed in foreign garb, and at this moment, he pulled his hands back and stood tall, his expression indifferent. It was clear that he was a person of few words, but around him was a powerful, imperious aura of suppression that caused everyone to fall silent, like cicadas in late autumn.

Shen Qiao internally trembled; he didn't need to ask the man's name, for he too knew who this was.

The number one Göktürk martial expert, Hulugu!

Even though he'd mentally prepared himself, on suddenly seeing this person, a sense of disbelief still rose within his heart.

It really was him.

But how could it be him?

He really hadn't died?

Sang Jingxing, who'd always been arrogant and egotistical, was currently standing respectfully behind the foreigner. When he saw him beat back Yi Pichen with a palm strike, he stepped forward with a smile, then said brightly, "This Abbot Yi is one of the best martial experts in the world, and he's also an esteemed Daoist, yet he is unable to last even a round against Qianbei. It can be seen that the so-called 'World's Top Ten' ranking is unfounded and untrustworthy. Qianbei's grasp of martial arts is already far beyond the reach of mortals, so he truly deserves to be called the world's true number one, backed up by merit!"

Hulugu showed no appreciation for his flattery, however—his face remained cool and empty of all emotion whatsoever. "I came to challenge Yi Pichen; that's my business," he said. "It has nothing to do with Hehuan Sect, and I don't need you to take the lead for me either."

Sang Jingxing's expression didn't waver. "Qianbei's words are too much," he said, still smiling. "We also came to take a look because we heard that there was a Sword Trial Conference here. We didn't expect that Qianbei would arrive right after we did."

If he'd heard Sang Jingxing's words only, Shen Qiao might have really believed that both parties just happened to simultaneously arrive in their bid to wreck the place. But what he'd heard from Yuan Xiuxiu at the foot of the mountain was a reminder that it couldn't be the case. Hehuan Sect had clearly known that Hulugu would come, so they'd arrived in advance. First to exhaust some of Yi Pichen's fighting spirit, increasing Hulugu's chances of victory, and second to pick up some benefits for cheap.

As for why Hehuan Sect wanted to take the lead for Hulugu, that was easy to understand. Yuwen Yong's empress, Lady Ashina, must have also contributed to Yuwen Yun's ascension to the throne. Though she wasn't Yuwen Yun's biological mother, Yuwen Yun had always loved to go against his father. Since the late emperor had kept the Göktürks at a respectful distance, Yuwen Yun must pursue a close relationship with them instead. In that case, it wasn't surprising that Hehuan Sect, with Yuwen Yun as their backer, had also allied with the Göktürks.

Yi Pichen's face betrayed nothing. He'd taken only three steps back, and that alone was incredibly impressive. Hulugu wasn't an ordinary expert; he was the man who'd fought Qi Fengge over twenty years ago. Then two decades had passed, and everyone thought he was dead—even Duan Wenyang, as he walked through the Central Plains, had released false news of his master's death. Who knew that the situation would suddenly change, bringing a legendary character back from the dead? Of course everyone would find it shocking.

Many of the people present had yet to figure out Hulugu's identity. And those who'd vaguely guessed it probably still felt it as impossible as seeing a ghost in broad daylight.

But Shen Qiao was paying close attention to Yi Pichen, and he noticed that the man's face had turned red for a moment just now. It was obvious that he'd suffered internal injuries—he wasn't as unscathed as he appeared on the surface.

And if he could tell, naturally so could Hulugu.

Hulugu's gaze fell on Yi Pichen, and he said coldly, "I heard that Chunyang Monastery is now known as the world's leader for Daoism, but as a martial artist, you're inferior to Qi Fengge from back then."

It was incredible that Yi Pichen could still maintain his smile and composure under such crushing pressure. "Chunyang Monastery has never claimed to be the leader of Daoism, and I've never compared myself to esteemed Daoist Master Qi. Your martial arts are superb—this humble Daoist admires you greatly. May I ask if your distinguished self came to participate in the Sword Trial Conference? Or did you come for Chunyang Monastery?"

The former meant a normal spar, the latter meant that he was here to gatecrash and out for revenge.

Hulugu answered coolly, "The Sword Trial Conference's sole purpose is for reputation fishing. Those who possess true strength would feel no need to participate. I originally thought that since the reputations of Chunyang Monastery and Yi Pichen resounded like thunder, they must have had some outstanding abilities. But as it turns out, they're merely mediocre."

He'd come to someone else's territory and spoken such disparaging words—Yi Pichen could endure it, but the Chunyang Monastery disciples behind him couldn't. Someone instantly stepped forward and said, "Your distinguished self is incredibly capable, yet you were defeated by esteemed Daoist Master Qi and cowered like a turtle outside the Great Wall for over twenty years. Only now when he's gone did you rush back to sow misfortune in the jianghu of the Central Plains. What kind of hero are..."

As he was about to say the final "you," Hulugu swept him a cold glance, and the speaker was so terrified he lost his voice entirely. He swallowed the word back, and his face instantly flushed red.

Hulugu didn't speak, but Duan Wenyang behind him did. "Even after twenty years, your jianghu of the Central Plains couldn't even find an opponent worthy of being Shizun's rival, yet you have the guts to talk that big? If I were you, I'd be so ashamed I'd just bash open my head and die. What honored Daoist? In my opinion, of your entire jianghu, only Qi Fengge could match my shizun—if only he were still alive. To think that my shizun still believed the Central Plains to be flourishing with heroes. We heard that there was a Sword Trial Conference and rushed here with great enthusiasm. Tsk! Truly unworthy of your reputation!"

Under his mockery, Chunyang Monastery wished to sink into the ground out of shame, and most of the jianghu members in the crowd were rendered completely speechless.

They'd seen Yi Pichen's martial arts, and seen them very clearly. His recent battle with Sang Jingxing had been a brilliant spectacle, and Yi Pichen was undoubtedly far superior to Hehuan Sect. But they hadn't gotten the chance to be happy for long when Hulugu appeared.

Now that this man was here, regardless of whether it was Yi Pichen or Sang Jingxing, they all had to lower their heads.

For ordinary people, Sang Jingxing and Yi Pichen were already far beyond their own existence, and now this Hulugu had arrived as well. He was a moon suspended in the nine heavens, so far out of reach that despair filled their hearts.

People with aspirations were reminded even more of that battle twenty-odd years ago. They lamented that they'd been too young to catch it. The Qi Fengge of back then had been able to defeat even Hulugu—how magnificent he must have been!

But not everyone present was the kind who cheered for others while putting themselves down. Someone who was displeased with Duan Wenyang's words stepped forward and said loudly, "You came to Chunyang Monastery, yet dare to spread such blasphemy, saying that the Central Plains lacks talent. Don't you know how many experts exist in the land? There are the Buddhist sects in the north, Confucian sects in the south. Unless you've challenged them all? Just now, Liuli Palace has ranked the world's elites, yet Hulugu's name never appeared. Your esteemed master and disciple are just singing your own praises—how fun that must be! All you're doing is providing others more fodder for jokes!"

Hulugu's face remained placid, but Duan Wenyang narrowed his eyes. "What is your surname, and which sect are you from?"

The man's heart trembled, but how could he let himself be intimidated in full view of the public? So he raised his voice and reported his background: "Wang Zhuo of Kuaji Commandery's Wang family!"

His Wang family relied on neither Hehuan Sect nor the Göktürks for their survival, so why should he be afraid? With this in mind, Wang-sanlang couldn't help but further bolster his courage.

Duan Wenyang arched an eyebrow, and the pitch of his voice rose slightly. "Oh, Kuaji Commandery's Wang family?"

While he spoke, his hand darted out, quick as lightning. A whip's silhouette appeared out of nowhere at the same time, sweeping straight toward Wang-sanlang!

Wang-sanlang watched helplessly as the other party attacked; he didn't even have the time to draw his sword. He could only retreat to avoid it. But his speed was no match for Duan Wenyang's. He hadn't backed up very far when that whip had already curled around his wrist, twisting until he was overcome with agony and almost shattering his bones.

"Ah!" He let out a loud scream, and the longsword fell from his hand.

"Sanlang!" Wang-erlang's eyes bulged with rage. He flew forward to save his brother.

But someone moved even faster than he did. They drew their sword and slashed at the air, and their sword qi flowed forth, instantly enveloping Duan Wenyang. Duan Wenyang made a sound of surprise, as if he hadn't expected such strength from his opponent's helper. He was forced to withdraw his whip and focus on the newcomer, and only then did he realize that the other party was a beautiful young woman.

When it came to martial arts, only speed was king. Duan Wenyang's whip lashed out again and again, flurry after flurry, leaving his opponent no breathing room whatsoever. Yet despite such crushing pressure, the girl seemed to handle herself with effortless skill, never falling behind. One could tell that she must have come from a famous sect, trained by an extraordinary expert. With time, she might grow to achieve great things.

But Duan Wenyang ranked within the world's top ten; even if he was last in the list, it was no empty title. Though this girl was skilled, her greenness showed, and she lacked actual combat experience. After a couple of moves, Duan Wenyang gradually discovered her openings, and he took the chance to strike, sending his whip right at them.

The girl didn't seek to continue. Her original goal had been to help Wang-sanlang out of his predicament. Now that she'd achieved it, she retreated backward and drifted to the ground, refusing to confront Duan Wenyang head-on.

"Thank you, Gu-niangzi, for your help!" Wang-sanlang was a bit excited. He'd been taken with this beauty at first sight, but she'd only spoken bluntly to him. Yet when he was in danger just now, it was this beauty who'd extended a helping hand.

"Don't mention it." Gu Hengbo's expression was indifferent.

Although Wang-sanlang's behavior was reckless, it could not be said that he was wrong. Everyone had remained as silent as cicadas in late autumn in the face of Hulugu, and Wang-sanlang's speaking out had demonstrated his courage. If someone had been able to save him, yet chose not to, it would only encourage that trend in the future.

Gu Hengbo truly proved that she'd been raised by Shen Qiao—her viewpoint was very much in line with her Zhangjiao-shixiong's.

Though Wang-sanlang hadn't sustained many injuries thanks to Gu Hengbo's intervention, upon seeing that the master and disciple both possessed exceptional martial arts, everyone knew that they couldn't even defeat the disciple, let alone the master. They couldn't help but feel, from the bottom of their hearts, that they were look-ing at people who were out of reach, so much so that they could only see the dust they left in their wake.

To some extent, the plan of Chunyang Monastery to unite the various factions against Hehuan Sect and the Buddhist discipline had already failed.

Li Qingyu's hand was already on the hilt of his sword, but another hand reached out and firmly grasped his arm.

That hand belonged to Yi Pichen.

Meanwhile, Hulugu looked at Gu Hengbo and suddenly asked, "Who was Qi Fengge to you?"

Gu Hengbo had noticed Shen Qiao standing at the edge of the stone platform sometime earlier. At this moment, she couldn't help but glance at him, then said, "He was my master."

Upon hearing about her relationship with Qi Fengge, Hulugu's ex-pression finally shifted a little. Even though he'd just faced Yi Pichen, he had not looked at him straight-on. At this moment, he scrutinized Gu Hengbo, then regained his calm and serene expression.

A disciple would know their master best. Duan Wenyang smiled and said, "Shizun, why do you find it a pity? If this disciple is not mistaken, this woman is Gu Hengbo, Qi Fengge's sole female disciple. Though she's lacking as a martial artist, she still has several shixiong, one of whom inherited the position of Xuandu Mountain's sect leader, and even killed my shidi Kunye with his sword. Coincidentally, he's also here today."

With that, he looked in Shen Qiao's direction and said, "Daoist Master Shen, I haven't seen you for some time. Have you been well?"

In that instant, everyone's gazes followed his voice and fell on Shen Qiao.

Shen Qiao was originally standing off to the side like an invisible man, but now he couldn't remain a bystander any longer. He lifted his sword and slowly walked forward, stopping when he was a short distance away from the other man.

"Thank you very much for your concern. Fortunately, I have mostly been well." His tone was very calm, without a hint of any nervousness caused by Hulugu's appearance.

"So, you are Shen Qiao." Hulugu's gaze moved away from his face and onto Shanhe Tongbei, gripped in Shen Qiao's hand. A trace of nostalgia swept across his face.

"Correct," he replied, "this humble Daoist is Shen Qiao. I am fortunate enough to finally meet Qianbei in person today. Unfortunately, my master has passed away; otherwise, if he knew that Qianbei still walks among the living, I'm sure he'd have been overjoyed."

Duan Wenyang suspected that Shen Qiao was mocking him, saying that his shifu had feigned death and cowered like a turtle in the Khaganate for over twenty years, only daring to emerge with Qi Fengge's death. However, looking at Shen Qiao's gentle expression, which seemed the picture of benevolence, it was hard to believe that was the case.

"You are greatly talented, but you are not my match yet. If you'd had another three to five years, you might have been able to fight me. But since you killed Kunye, I cannot let you leave this mountain alive now that I have met you today." Hulugu's face was indifferent, but his words suggested that he was already grasping Shen Qiao's life in his hands.

Shen Qiao smiled and replied with a single word: "Really?"

In this kind of situation, further verbal disputes were meaningless. His expression might have been calm, but that didn't necessarily mean he wasn't nervous. The onlookers might simply be watching for the excitement, but only the person standing in the thick of it could feel the pressure and aura from Hulugu's powerful presence.

Before, when Yi Pichen had exchanged blows with him, he too must have suffered through this torment.

Hulugu's strength had already reached some kind of nameless, indescribable echelon.

Heaven encompasses all phenomena, and it was a mystery of mysteries. One could only perceive it, but not express it.

Could he win?

Shen Qiao looked at the person in front of him, lowering his breath until he was barely breathing at all.

This would be the most difficult battle he'd ever fought in the jianghu. The level of peril he was facing now was not inferior to when he'd battled Sang Jingxing.

He was a disciple of Qi Fengge, and from the moment he'd taken over his shizun's mantle, his destiny had been set: this battle was inevitable.

105

The World's Number Two

DUAN WENYANG was a whip user, but his shifu Hulugu was not.

More than twenty years ago, when Hulugu fought against Qi Fengge, they had both used swords. However, Hulugu did not hold a sword today. Perhaps he'd decided to tread a new martial path since then, or maybe he no longer liked to use swords. Now he faced Shen Qiao, who raised his sword against the wind, his robes rustling. Sword qi arced like a rainbow piercing the clouds, and like a crane soaring into the sky, it surged straight toward Hulugu. The crowd only heard a thunderous noise exploding in their ears, like the sound of a thousand horses galloping or the endless crashing waves of the boundless sea. They couldn't help but stare in shock. The mediocre practitioners even felt their ears throb—some couldn't withstand it and had to quickly circulate their energy in resistance.

During the Sword Trial Conference, Shen Qiao had first only watched from the sidelines. Everyone knew that he was an exceptional martial artist, but he looked like a handsome Daoist priest through and through, cultured and elegant. There had seemed nothing formidable about him. It wasn't until he'd confronted Yuan Xiuxiu that everyone realized the meaning of "don't judge a book by its cover." But only now was the audience truly shaken.

Shen Qiao's slash was imperious and fierce as it stole the initiative, surging forth like a mighty torrent. Shanhe Tongbei was true to its name: it indeed evoked the image of mountains and rivers, all grieving as one.

Though the onlookers were frightened and awed, Shen Qiao knew very well that while this move of his, using nine-tenths of his full power, might have given him a chance against Yi Pichen, it was still no match for Hulugu.

It might not be clear to onlookers, but when experts dueled, they only needed one exchange of blows for both parties to understand the eventual outcome.

By assessing someone's qi, you could determine how profound their internal energy was by perceiving the atmosphere around them. Perhaps Shen Qiao hadn't made blistering progress even after cultivating the *Zhuyang Strategy*'s true qi and rebuilding his foundations, but he was still on an entirely different level compared to before. Given enough time, he might have been able to match Hulugu in strength.

However, Hulugu had several decades' worth of martial training over Shen Qiao, and he was someone who'd been able to vie with Qi Fengge for supremacy. Furthermore, Shen Qiao didn't know what sort of opportunities Hulugu might have had in the past two decades, or what echelons he'd managed to break through to. Now that he'd left seclusion and returned to the jianghu, the title of the world's number one martial artist could only be his. In the entire jianghu, there seemed to be no one who could be his opponent—even Yi Pichen had fallen beneath his hands. If Shen Qiao wanted to win, the chances for that were slim.

But just because the chances were slim didn't mean that he'd roll over and await capture.

The battlefield could change multiple times in an instant; if he could grab at even the smallest of lifelines, he might be able to escape the jaws of death and transform defeat into victory. Shen Qiao acknowledged that there was a gap between himself and Hulugu, but this gap wasn't large enough to make him sit and resign himself to death.

His sword qi was boundless, surging toward Hulugu like waves crashing against the shore. In an instant, it was right before him, and Duan Wenyang couldn't withstand it and took a few steps back. However, Hulugu remained utterly motionless, though a faint layer of solemn dignity now tinted his eyes, a slight change from their previous nonchalance.

Hulugu suddenly raised his sleeves, then slammed them downward, crushing that surging, imperious sword qi. Then his entire person soared into the air, seemingly spontaneously, and flew toward Shen Qiao while his right hand sent out a palm strike.

It was an ordinary palm strike, not flashy at all, but Shen Qiao felt the sword qi from his swing suddenly slam into something akin to an indestructible stone wall. Instead of crumbling the stone, it rebounded off it, returning to Shen Qiao with several times the power of his own true qi.

Shen Qiao had already anticipated this, so he showed no shock. He didn't take this attack head-on but instead avoided its keen edge—he used his opponent's true qi to soar several feet into the air, then merged into one with his sword as he swept straight down toward Hulugu.

The onlookers couldn't tell where the sword ended and the man began. Shen Qiao's speed was far beyond an arrow in flight, and more like a thundering storm. Yet his figure was light and agile, with a momentum that had nothing in common with thunder, closer to a wisp of smoke or mist. It appeared entirely effortless—the greatest of music was silent, and the greatest of phenomena were formless.

On the sidelines, Duan Wenyang saw everything clearly and couldn't help but startle. Shen Qiao's progress was both rapid and frightening. Just this move itself was far more formidable than anything Duan Wenyang could do.

In truth, Shen Qiao's martial arts were still a little inferior to what he'd possessed before his poisoning. It was only because he'd been cultivating the *Zhuyang Strategy*'s true qi that he appeared to have made astonishing progress. If Duan Wenyang had seen Shen Qiao at his previous level, he wouldn't have been so surprised now.

However, ultimately, Hulugu was still Hulugu. This move of Shen Qiao's still couldn't do anything to him. The man stepped lightly with his foot, and the dark tiles all around it splintered, then burst out of the ground, drawn by the true qi around his body. The shards all transformed into sharp blades and shot straight toward Shen Qiao.

Tiles and stones collided with sword qi, crumbling into even finer fragments and spraying everywhere. The two streams of true qi combined and exploded with an even stronger force. Many people could neither dodge nor block with their qi in time—or perhaps their martial abilities were simply insufficient, so they couldn't block it at all. Terrified, they tried to evade anyway, and some even screamed in horror. Debris scratched faces and necks, causing blood to stream down—a wretched sight.

As for Duan Wenyang, Yi Pichen, and others, the debris simply fell to the ground when it came within half a foot of their bodies. They were completely unscathed but frowned in unison.

Duan Wenyang frowned because he'd originally thought that his shifu would be able to deal with Shen Qiao easily. After all, Yuan Zixiao had ranked the man even lower than Yi Pichen. He hadn't expected that his master would grow serious and stop holding back after exchanging several blows.

Yi Pichen had naturally realized this too, and he furrowed his brow hard. Based on his own experience of fighting Hulugu earlier, he knew Shen Qiao must be having a difficult time at the moment, and, more importantly, his chances of victory were slim.

Within the circle of battle, Shen Qiao was feeling a crushing, mountainous pressure. His swordsmanship had achieved the realm of sword heart, which allowed him to look down on all things from above. However, his internal energy was still an unchanging flaw; it couldn't even be mentioned in the same breath as that of a monster like Hulugu.

His sword's edge was swift as lighting as it swung down on Hulugu, but, surrounded by true qi capable of overturning the oceans, he felt like he was trying to paddle upstream. Standing amid this, Shen Qiao found that it only grew more arduous, to the point he couldn't advance an inch.

At the same time, Hulugu's entire body was radiating with boundless energy. His robes billowed high as his true qi swirled in a vortex of layers. He leapt into the air and struck downward at Shen Qiao. Wherever the wind from his palm reached, it was like a fierce, ravenous beast, overwhelming all of Shen Qiao's sword qi and sword glares as it devoured them all.

The stars and the firmament, the churning of clouds and rain—all of it was happening within this very instant.

Shen Qiao closed his eyes and pushed his internal energy to the limit while clearing his mind of all distractions. Only one thought remained: he must defeat Hulugu!

This battle wasn't only for himself but also for his shizun Qi Fengge. He couldn't let others say that Qi Fengge had been blind, taking in disciples unfit to inherit his aspirations, who even lost to his former opponent.

Shen Qiao didn't care about something as vain as fame, but he couldn't afford to ignore Qi Fengge's legacy!

The sword heart was clear and single-minded; thus, it understood the key. One must strive for victory, but they must not be too eager. At the same time, this was a fight, so it was inevitable that there'd be a superior and an inferior. No one in this world would choose defeat over victory.

Even if one claimed they were seeking defeat, that wasn't truly seeking defeat, but rather that they were so conceited that they believed that few could match them as their opponent.

Shen Qiao suddenly opened his eyes, and his sword was so swift, it'd already transformed into an afterimage.

However, his gaze wasn't on the sword but on the man before him. Hu. Lu. Gu.

His opponent had also raised his palms to receive the strike. The true qi around their bodies swept forth like wild tempests above the great sea. Heaven and earth churned the waves in their rage, as if they wanted to destroy all of creation within the dark ocean depths. Like enemies on a narrow bridge, it was an inevitable encounter, and the victor would be crowned king.

Shen Qiao felt a gargantuan force rush in his direction, immense enough to engulf him. His blood and qi roiled within his heart, as if they were desperately trying to escape his very body. As internal and external energy intersected, his body felt like it was about to be crushed as flat as paper, and his meridians and bones screamed in pain.

He was a person of incredible forbearance. In the past, Shen Qiao had endured the severe injuries from the cliff's fall, the intense pain from his meridians being reshaped. And now, though Hulugu's palm strike caused him horrendous agony, Shen Qiao bore it without a sound. Only after he struck out with his sword did he withdraw and land back on the ground.

But after enduring and enduring, he couldn't suppress it anymore. He coughed up a huge mouthful of blood, which splattered all over his robes and the ground.

Hulugu's face remained impassive. He only took a few steps back without spitting up any blood.

Shen Qiao had put all his strength into that one sword strike, and he knew that he'd finally injured Hulugu. Of course, his opponent's injuries weren't as severe as his own, but it was nonetheless true that he was now wounded.

Zhao Chiying and Gu Hengbo had been waiting for the two to stop, and now that they finally had, they rushed forward to support Shen Qiao.

Yu Shengyan had intended to carry out his shifu's orders, but based on his own martial arts, he knew he was no match for Hulugu—rashly challenging him would only mean his death. As he watched the two of them fight, he had grown increasingly anxious. Now he saw his chance and intervened. "I have long heard of Hulugu of the Göktürks. Watching him fight two great experts, one after another, I see that his reputation is well deserved."

Hulugu had never looked at him directly, and even now he only glanced at him. His filial disciple Duan Wenyang came forward to explain who Yu Shengyan was. After listening, Hulugu said, "I heard that Yan Wushi is in the Central Plains and is considered an expert. They say that his strength isn't far from Qi Fengge's in the past."

"'Not far' is an understatement," said Sang Jingxing with a smile, deliberately adding fuel to the fire. "I heard that Liuli Palace has just ranked the entire jianghu and that Yan Wushi is in second place!"

Hulugu stilled for a moment, then asked, "Who's in first?"

Sang Jingxing smiled at Yuan Zixiao. "You must ask the Liuli Palace's Young Mistress Yuan."

Yuan Zixiao was once again the focus of the whole audience, but her face remained impassive, without a trace of panic. She said to Hulugu, "Originally, first place wasn't you."

"Originally?" asked Hulugu.

"Even now, it seems you are still a level below Qi Fengge."

Hulugu's eyes narrowed slightly. It'd been over twenty years, yet the three characters "Qi Fengge" had never faded from his heart, becoming a complex knot he could never unravel. Unfortunately, the man was dead—even if Hulugu wished to fight him, he could no longer be found.

Duan Wenyang sneered. "Qi Fengge is already dead. Is the world's first place available to even the dead? If that's so, then shouldn't Tao Hongjing and Cui Youwang be ranked as well?"

Yuan Zixiao nodded and said coolly, "So I said that it wasn't you originally. Since Qi Fengge is dead, first place is now yours, probably."

She'd even added a "probably" at the end. Even though her tone was completely flat, it was enough to send someone to their grave from rage.

But Hulugu hadn't fallen so low that he'd argue with a little girl. Duan Wenyang's face darkened, and he looked like he wanted to speak. But Hulugu only swept a glance at Yuan Zixiao's face, then turned his gaze back to Shen Qiao.

"You're really quite good," he said.

"Qianbei is too kind," said Shen Qiao, "but it was only a stroke of luck. Your distinguished self just fought Abbot Yi, so in truth, this humble Daoist had an advantage."

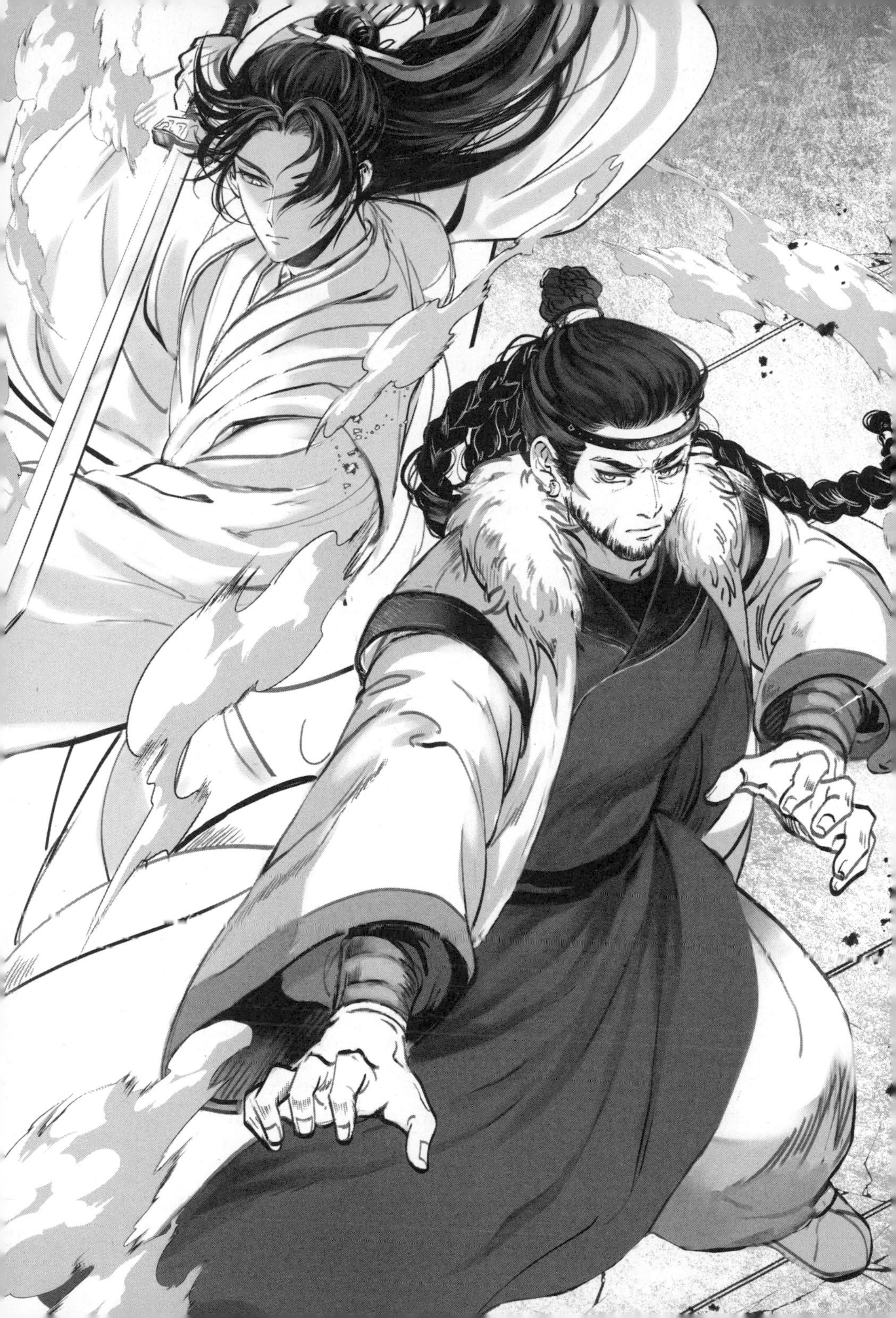

Hulugu revealed a faint smile. His eyes and brows were razor-sharp, like they'd been carved with a knife, and he looked terribly unapproachable when he didn't smile. But within this smile was a faint gentleness, contrasting his words which grew even colder: "Normally, I'd disdain attacking the defeated and would stop here today. But you killed Kunye. If I let you live, my disciple might feel lonely deep down in the underworld. You should go keep him company!"

As he spoke, he slowly stalked toward Shen Qiao. Even a normal strolling speed would have been faster, yet he emanated an invisible chill that made others tremble.

Though Zhao Chiying and Gu Hengbo were no match for Hulugu, they thought to themselves that it wouldn't be too hard to hold him off, just long enough to give Shen Qiao a chance to escape. They turned back to Shen Qiao and said lowly, "Hurry up and go!"

At the same time, they drew their swords.

As a demonic practitioner, Yu Shengyan had never been a selfless hero who could sacrifice himself for others, but Yan Wushi's words still lingered in his ears. He gritted his teeth, then also ran in front of Shen Qiao.

Li Qingyu, Su Qiao, Fan Yuanbai, and Zhou Yexue all came over as well, and they stood in front of Shen Qiao.

At this moment, one could see the good karma that Shen Qiao had accumulated.

Yi Pichen was seriously injured, but he couldn't stand by and let Hulugu kill Shen Qiao here and now; otherwise Chunyang Monastery could forget about their standing in the jianghu. He immediately raised his sword and rushed over, his voice stern. "Stop at once! The Sword Trial Conference is only a competition, not a place for fighting and revenge!"

But why would Hulugu take him seriously? Without him having to do anything, Duan Wenyang and Sang Jingxing had already stepped forward to stop Yi Pichen. The disciples of Chunyang Monastery all rushed forward to help, but the members of Hehuan Sect didn't lag behind either. The scene instantly descended into chaos.

As for the people from the other sects, some couldn't resist intervening to help while the rest looked at each other, at a loss and unsure what they should do.

Thinking of how Gu Hengbo had stepped in to protect him earlier, not to mention his admiration for her beauty, Wang-sanlang too rolled up his sleeves and ran over to help. His brother stomped his foot at this but ultimately could only follow him.

Yet Hulugu didn't pause. He continued to stalk over to Shen Qiao, one step at a time. His expression was indifferent and placid, devoid of any ripples. In his eyes, these people were no more than dead or withered objects, unworthy of his attention.

Shen Qiao said softly, "Thank you, everyone, for your earnest support, but this matter is between him and me. Don't intervene."

So saying, he used a light wind from his palm to push the crowd aside.

"Shixiong!" cried Gu Hengbo anxiously.

Hulugu was already slowly lifting his palm. Shen Qiao clutched tightly at the sword hilt in his hand.

At this moment, a sneer exploded in everyone's ears. "This is someone who belongs to my venerable self, and you think you can kill him as you please?"

Shocked, Yu Shengyan yelled, "Shizun!"

As soon as he said this, everyone knew the identity of the newcomer. But they only saw a phantom appear out of thin air, like an immortal descending from the heavens; untethered and unrestrained, elegant and carefree.

He didn't meet Hulugu head-on as everyone expected, though. Instead, he grabbed Shen Qiao's waist and simply swept him away.

He did it with such swiftness that even Hulugu couldn't stop him in time.

Everyone was dumbfounded.

Nighttime Chat

NO ONE HAD EXPECTED Yan Wushi to suddenly appear. He'd uttered such dramatic words, everyone assumed he was about to duel Hulugu to the death. Instead, in the blink of an eye, he simply grabbed Shen Qiao and ran, even ignoring his disciple.

Xuandu Mountain's "A Rainbow Stretches Across the Heavens" was unparalleled, but while Huanyue Sect's qinggong wasn't as famous, Yan Wushi vanished in an instant as soon as he started moving. Even Hulugu was left in his dust, never mind anyone else.

Of course, it was also possible that Hulugu had never anticipated meeting a martial grandmaster so shameless.

Shen Qiao hadn't anticipated it either.

He was still injured, his blood roiling, meaning it was difficult for him to move rashly. Yan Wushi carried him for more than ten miles, but his steps remained as stable as if he were walking on flat ground, without any turbulence whatsoever. His face was relaxed, and the hint of a smile even hung on his lips. Clearly, he found this effortless.

Shen Qiao finally collected himself to try and speak. With difficulty, he swallowed down the glob of blood in his throat, then coughed twice. "Put me down…"

Yan Wushi was unperturbed. "What's the hurry? I just left the mountain. If Hulugu catches up, wouldn't my entire trip have been in vain?"

There was a beauty in his arms, so what was the harm in carrying him another few dozen miles?

It's not that Yan Wushi had suddenly become an upright gentleman after meeting Shen Qiao, but more that he understood Shen Qiao's personality well. This Daoist master could be coaxed but not cowed. If he tried to force him, he could forget about getting anywhere with him in this life, but he couldn't rely only on coaxing either. This beautiful Daoist was purehearted, ascetic, and serenely detached. He never indulged in any worldly desires and had cultivated himself into keeping his distance from the secular world. But even the most steadfast of pampas grass would be powerless to move bedrock.[11]

However, Yan Wushi thought himself completely beyond the likes of dull bedrock. For if he wanted to, he could pluck even the stars from the heavens.

Shen Qiao was somewhat at a loss for words. "I thought you were going to fight Hulugu."

Yan Wushi smiled. "If I fight him now, I fear that I'll still come up a little short. Why should I waste energy on a poor outcome? If I am to fight, it must be when I'm confident I'll win. My venerable self does not engage in meaningless actions like drawing water with a bamboo basket."

He never shied away from telling the truth, but even this truth exuded Yan Wushi's trademark egotism and imperiousness.

Shen Qiao didn't reply. In truth, the last fight had sapped all his strength, and he'd suffered internal injuries. He was beyond

---

11   A reference to a very old and famous poem, "The Peacock Flies Southwest." In it, the newlywed bride exalts their marriage and love, describing herself as the pampas grass, flexible yet steadfast, to her husband's bedrock, solid and immovable. Yan Wushi is poking fun at the analogy.

exhausted. Before he could realize it, his eyes slid shut, and he fell into a deep slumber.

Yan Wushi looked down, a smile on his lips. He held the man to himself and walked steadily out of Qingcheng Town, heading northeast.

It'd been a long time since Shen Qiao had last slept properly, the way a normal person would.

That wasn't to say that he didn't need sleep. It was just that for martial artists, sleep was training, and training could also double as sleep—by circulating true qi through their bodies, they could cultivate and rest at the same time. Though Shen Qiao cared little for success or failure, he also understood the principle that being strong meant he wouldn't be at the mercy of others. Ever since he'd reshaped his foundations, he'd been training diligently. When resting at night, he'd relax by meditating.

In his recent battle with Hulugu, he'd exhausted his internal energy, draining his heart and mind both. For the time being, his Dantian was completely empty. At night he'd usually spare a portion of his awareness to watch the outside world, but he couldn't do it this time. The moment he closed his eyes, he lost all consciousness, entering a strange and surreal dream.

When he woke up, he was already lying on a bed. He turned his head and saw that it was dark outside the window—the only light came from the flickering flame of a few candles on the nightstand, illuminating the room in a faint glow.

Before Shen Qiao could frown and expel the memories of his dream, a teasing voice came from next to his ear. "Which wonderful dream did you have that you're still savoring it after waking up?"

Only then did Shen Qiao realize something was wrong. The object he was leaning against was clearly not a pillow, but...

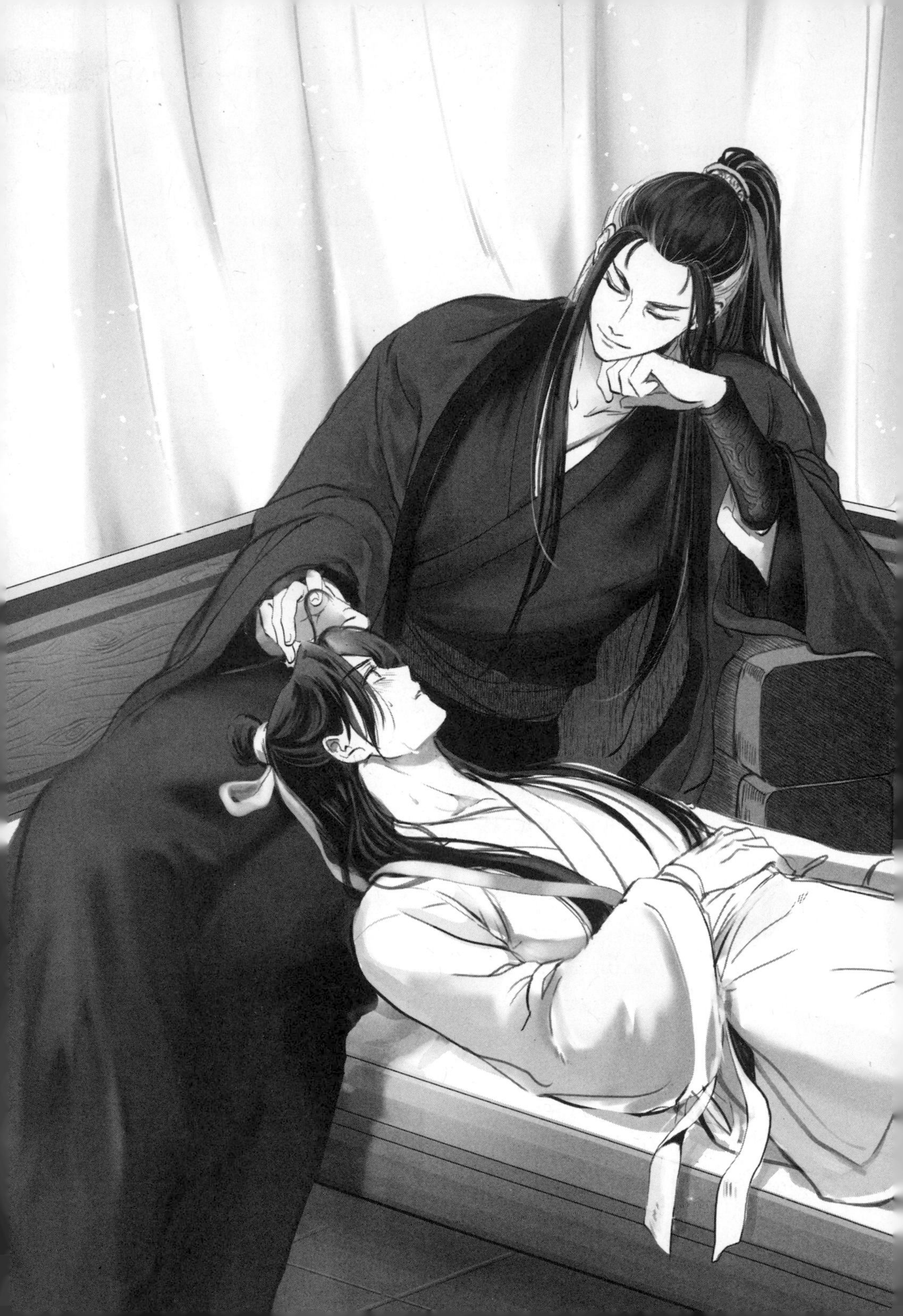

Yan Wushi's thigh.

He'd woken up with his head pillowed on Yan Wushi's thigh.

No matter how composed Shen Qiao was, a realization like this was still unsettling. He braced his arm against the bed, ready to get up, but Yan Wushi pushed his shoulders down. "You still have internal injuries, so you shouldn't move about recklessly."

There was indeed a faint pain in Shen Qiao's chest, and his qi circulation was sluggish. But that didn't mean he lacked even the strength to sit up. He insisted on propping up his torso and moving himself to the edge of the bed.

When he felt a solid surface against his back, he gave a sigh of relief. In the end, leaning against the bed gave him more peace of mind.

Yan Wushi observed him with great interest. "What kind of dream did you have? Your face is flushed like a peach blossom, and your eyes are so dewy."

Shen Qiao was speechless.

Upon hearing this description, those who didn't know better would think he'd had a wet dream.

Yan Wushi reached out to touch his face. "Your face is so warm," he said. "It must have been a wet dream. Did you dream of my venerable self?"

The corners of Shen Qiao's lips twitched. "No, I fear I must disappoint Sect Leader Yan. It was a dream where I fought many people. Even after waking up, I feel exhausted."

He would never say that Yan Wushi was among the people he fought. Who knew what the other man would say?

However, he'd clearly underestimated how shameless this Huanyue Sect Leader was. Even without him giving an inch, Yan Wushi could still manage to say the most embarrassing things. "Fighting? Fighting where? Was it in bed?"

"If you continue to say such frivolous things," Shen Qiao said angrily, "I won't speak to you anymore!"

His A-Qiao was always threatening him, but he was so soft, it was completely ineffective as a deterrent. Yan Wushi laughed and said, "All right, I won't say any more, really. Then you should say something instead. I'll let you talk first!"

Shen Qiao composed himself and said, "How long was I asleep for?"

"That's easy to answer," said Yan Wushi. "An entire day and night."

Shen Qiao was slightly surprised. He hadn't expected to sleep so long. His injuries wouldn't recover for a while, but after waking up, the pains of his body were greatly lessened. It seemed as though Yan Wushi had helped while he was asleep.

He cupped his hands. "Thank you very much, Sect Leader Yan. In the future, if Sect Leader Yan needs anything, as long as it isn't criminal or inhumane, Shen Qiao will definitely do his utmost to help."

Then he thought about how absurd and unreliable the other man's words and actions tended to be, and how staggering his behavior at Bixia Sect had been. Feeling uneasy, he added, "It also can't be anything too preposterous, or offensive to public sensibilities."

Though Shen Qiao wasn't the leader of the Xuandu Mountain Sect any longer, he was still one of the world's top ten martial arts grandmasters. Combined with his moral character, a promise from him was worth more than a thousand gold.

Yan Wushi smiled but lightly declined the offer. "No need. I already collected my reward just now, so you need not be so courteous. Besides, with our relationship, you don't need to behave like such a stranger with my venerable self."

What relationship? Why don't I know? Shen Qiao was dumbfounded. Yan Wushi must have spent these years cultivating the thickness of his face on top of his martial arts and sect administration.

Yan Wushi looked at him with a bright smile. "Is A-Qiao thirsty?"

Shen Qiao involuntarily replied, "I am not. Thank you, Sect Leader Yan, for your concern."

"I thought so," said Yan Wushi. "While you were sleeping, I already fed you some honey water."

Shen Qiao had a bad feeling about this. "How did you feed me?"

Yan Wushi gave him a strange look. "By placing a cup against your mouth, of course. How else should I have fed you?" Before Shen Qiao could answer, an expression of dawning understanding appeared on his face. "Did you think I fed you mouth-to-mouth? A-Qiao, you used to be such an upright gentleman... When did you become so vulgar and indecent?"

Shen Qiao said nothing.

He'd already been rendered speechless by this man. Even with how well-mannered Daoist Master Shen was, he couldn't help but roll his eyes.

Yan Wushi even consoled him. "It's not your fault. I already told you that Hehuan Sect is full of bad people, and that's why you shouldn't mingle with that trash. Like those demonesses, Yuan Xiuxiu and Bai Rong; just stay away when you see them in the future. My A-Qiao is a pure and spirited beauty. How can I let them tarnish you?"

Not like the reputation of your Huanyue Sect is any better than that of Hehuan Sect.

Also, what do you mean, "my A-Qiao"? Who's your A-Qiao?!

Shen Qiao furiously protested in his heart, but he knew he wasn't Yan Wushi's match in a verbal dispute. If he made one retort, Yan Wushi would have ten more waiting for him.

Before, he'd been injured and in a dazed slumber, so there wasn't much he could do. But now that he was awake, Shen Qiao's first thought was to worry about the people still on Qingcheng Mountain.

"I wonder how Sect Leader Zhao and the others are doing. I'll go back tomorrow and check."

Yan Wushi sneered. "Hulugu was targeting you. The moment you were gone, why would he pay any attention to the rest? As long as they didn't rush to their own deaths themselves, that is. With how proud Hulugu is, there's no way he'd go out of his way to kill those who are worthless in his eyes."

Hulugu was conscious of his status as a grandmaster, so he considered murder and slaughter beneath himself. However, Duan Wenyang and the Hehuan Sect, who were trying to profit off disaster, weren't as easy to get rid of. Still, that was within Chunyang Monastery's territory, and Zhao Chiying and the others weren't powerless children. If they couldn't even defend themselves from that, there'd be no place for them in the jianghu anyway.

"Yu Shengyan is still on Qingcheng Mountain," Shen Qiao reminded him.

Yan Wushi was even more direct: "If he can't handle even this tiny amount of trouble, he's not qualified to be my venerable self's disciple!"

In Yan Wushi's eyes, the incompetent would never be worthy of his attention. Counting decades into the past, there'd been one exception in Shen Qiao, but there was only one Shen Qiao. No one else deserved any extra concern from him, even if they were his disciples. He'd already taught his disciples his skills; if they needed his protection in everything, why bother wandering the jianghu? They might as well bash open their heads and die.

It was clear that Shen Qiao didn't agree with this view of his. On a rational level, he agreed with Yan Wushi's words, but while

Zhao Chiying, Li Qingyu, and the others might be able to protect themselves, Fan Yuanbai and Zhou Yexue were far less skilled. If a fight really did break out, their masters might not be able to protect them in time, and they'd inevitably be injured.

Yan Wushi saw that Shen Qiao's mind was wandering, so he reached out to pinch his cheek. "When can you change your bad habit of worrying about everyone in the world?" he scolded. "You're injured. If you go back, you'll only be a burden. And you still want to save people? Besides, an entire day and night has passed; even if there had been a fight, it'd have finished by now. What's the point in going?"

Shen Qiao was caught off guard by the pinching and instinctively leaned back to avoid him. "Sect Leader Yan, please have some self-respect!"

Yan Wushi was all smiles. "A-Qiao is so unreasonable. I've already hugged, caressed, and fed you. What part of your body is left for my venerable self to touch? What's wrong with letting me pinch you? I can see that you're not like the boudoir girls who apply makeup and powder, but your cheeks are as smooth and delicate as theirs. If you dressed up as a woman, you'd surely be a first-class beauty."

Shen Qiao was currently thinking about proper and serious matters, so he took Yan Wushi's words as nonsense and let them flow in one ear and out the other. He frowned a little and said, "Sect Leader Yan was like a prophet when he said that Hulugu might still be alive. I had a hard time believing it then, but it really came true. Hulugu has once again appeared in the jianghu, while my shizun has already passed. Looking at the world now, no one is capable of defeating him. The Göktürks have grown close to Yuwen Yun, and Yuwen Yun has been conspiring with Hehuan Sect and the Buddhist discipline. The Sword Trial Conference came to an untimely demise and collapsed entirely, and Chunyang Monastery was met with a crisis. I fear that the peaceful days of the jianghu are no more."

"Why are you worrying so much about others?" said Yan Wushi lazily, leaning on the bed. "Isn't the decline of Chunyang Monastery a good opportunity for Xuandu Mountain to make its comeback? With your current strength, you could have flattened Yu Ai a while ago. Storming into Xuandu Mountain and taking back the sect leader's position wouldn't be difficult at all. Why do thankless work for others? If you want to do it, I will help you."

Shen Qiao glanced at him, then finally, having endured it for so long, he couldn't take it anymore. "If you want to talk, just talk," he said helplessly. "Can you stop putting your hand on my thigh? It's incredibly undignified."

If not for his injuries and how he was sleeping against the wall, he would have long rolled off the bed.

Yan Wushi patted him twice and chuckled. "Oh, so this was actually your leg. I thought it was a cushion."

He reached under the bedding and pulled out a cushion from next to Shen Qiao's leg. Then he placed his hand on top and patted it some more.

So shameless, thought Shen Qiao.

107

Beloved

IN THE END, Shen Qiao didn't return to Qingcheng Mountain, if only because Yan Wushi had been correct. By now, a day and night had already passed since the Sword Trial Conference. Any conflict would have long ended, so it would be useless to rush there now. Many sects had already left the mountain, one after another. He asked someone for information and was told that after Yan Wushi had taken him away, Hulugu left as well. However, Duan Wenyang didn't—he'd stayed behind to help Hehuan Sect against Chunyang Monastery.

But Chunyang Monastery were no pushovers. Yi Pichen was injured, but the remainder—including Li Qingyu, Gu Hengbo, Zhao Chiying—were not that much weaker than Duan Wenyang, even if they didn't place in the top ten. And on seeing the biggest threat gone, most of the people who'd come to participate in the Sword Trial Conference were unwilling to throw away their reputations by fleeing. Naturally, they had to help Chunyang Monastery, and a brawl ensued.

Yuan Xiuxiu was at odds with Sang Jingxing, so her faction didn't try very hard. She even sabotaged him several times during the scuffle. In the end, while Chunyang Monastery did sustain damage, Hehuan Sect hadn't gained much for their trouble either. Neither side ultimately came out on top, and both had suffered great losses.

Of course, quite a few lives were lost to this fight, but in the jianghu, your life was the least valuable thing you had. It was no exaggeration to say the jianghu was a dog-eat-dog world. Those who were unskilled and died to others had no one else to blame. If their descendants were powerful enough, they could go seek revenge and kill that enemy, and there was nothing an outsider could say. These were the rules of the jianghu.

The one closest to Shen Qiao was naturally his shimei Gu Hengbo. Shen Qiao had practically raised her from childhood. She was skilled, and she wasn't stupid. If she couldn't defeat an enemy, she knew to run, so Shen Qiao didn't worry about her. As for everyone in Bixia Sect, only Fan Yuanbai and Zhou Yexue were likely to be in danger, but to Shen Qiao's great relief, he heard someone leaving the mountain say that there no were casualties from Bixia Sect.

There was one more reason Shen Qiao did not go back: Yan Wushi had received a letter from Chang'an.

It was a letter pleading for help. And it was sent by Yan Wushi's eldest disciple, Bian Yanmei.

Since the death of Yuwen Yong and Yuwen Yun's subsequent ascension to the throne, Huanyue Sect in Chang'an had been in a state of suspicion and apprehension. Bian Yanmei had previously received orders from Yan Wushi to pack up at once if the situation looked dire, leaving behind their superficial connections for Hehuan Sect and the Buddhist discipline to skirmish over while their own people went into hiding. When Shen Qiao had fought his way out of the siege by armed troops with Yuwen Song and Dou Yan, it was partially due to Bian Yanmei's efforts that he had been able to escape without any soldiers in pursuit.

However, the person seeking help in the letter was not Bian Yanmei but Puliuru Jian.

Puliuru Jian's eldest daughter was married to Yuwen Yun. After Yuwen Yun ascended the throne, she became the queen, thus making Puliuru Jian the imperial father-in-law. One would expect that his life should have become more prosperous, but the reality was completely different.

The last time Shen Qiao was in Chang'an, he'd already heard about Yuwen Yun's absurd deeds. Now, when he heard that Puliuru Jian was asking for help, he was still somewhat surprised. "Yuwen Yun won't even spare his father-in-law?"

Yan Wushi chuckled. "Yuwen Yun dared to kill even his own father. What's a father-in-law?"

He'd almost forgotten about it. Shen Qiao frowned and said, "Yuwen Yun committed patricide because he couldn't wait any longer and wanted to ascend early. But what's his issue with Puliuru Jian?"

"If the emperor wants to kill someone, he must believe that they deserve to die," said Yan Wushi. "All his reasons and justifications are just excuses. Puliuru Jian comes from a wealthy noble family. His father followed Emperor Taizu of Zhou in insurrection and setting up the new regime, and he also earned a great deal of prestige and influence within the military. These have passed into Puliuru Jian's hands, as he excels in administration. Now, he already has a small faction within both the military and court. Though it hasn't grown to the point that he can threaten the imperial authority, which emperor could remain indifferent to this? Let alone a crazed lunatic of an emperor."

Yan Wushi possessed no trace of reverence for the imperial authority. He'd called Yuwen Yong by his name back then, and now he was even more scathing toward Yuwen Yun.

He sighed again. "A-Qiao, with your personality, it's fortunate that you weren't born into an official's family. Otherwise, how would you be able to contend in court, with all its political infighting? I fear that you'd have been gobbled up until even your bones were gone!"

This was an oblique way of calling him stupid, but it didn't anger Shen Qiao. Instead, he smiled. "If it's my personality, forget about contending in court; even as a sect leader within the jianghu, I still fell to the schemes of others."

Yan Wushi smiled brightly. "Now you're just belittling yourself. Your personality is intrinsically unsuited for playing mind games, but you have your own strengths. Though you're no longer the sect leader of Xuandu Mountain, there are still many people who wish to associate with you. What they see is your person, not your status. However, even if you're still easily susceptible to scheming, that's not a problem either—you have me, after all. With my venerable self watching out for you on the side, you need not fear being deceived by others!"

So, in the end, this man just wanted to praise himself?

Shen Qiao was somewhat at a loss for words, and his hair stood on end beneath his clothes. He quickly switched back to the original topic. "So what exactly is Puliuru Jian asking for help with?"

Yan Wushi carelessly said, "Yuwen Yun is suspicious of his daughter, so she's been taken hostage and is trapped inside the palace. All comings and goings in the Sui residence are being monitored by the emperor's spies, and the potential destruction of his clan depends on the emperor's whims. Puliuru Jian himself has a guilty conscience due to his actions; why wouldn't he be afraid?"

Yuwen Yun indulged himself in pleasure, and the various absurdities he'd committed after his ascension to the throne needed no mention. First, he'd killed Yuwen Xian and others, all so that he could eliminate the relatives of the imperial family who might threaten his claim to the throne. Now that those threats were dead, he passed the throne to his son, Yuwen Chan, so that he could continue living a life free of restraints while still manipulating the court from behind the scenes.

He was reaping the benefits of being an emperor without having to bear its responsibilities nor endure remonstrations from his ministers—he'd killed two birds with one stone. He was very pleased with himself for this move, but he was deeply mistrustful as well. After eliminating the threat posed by the imperial family, he began to suspect the more capable officials who might have the ability to revolt. Puliuru Jian, being the imperial father-in-law and pillar of the nation, became the first target. Yuwen Yun took extra "care" of him, and now he couldn't eat during the day nor sleep at night—there was a blade constantly hanging above his head, and his heart was plagued with worries.

Shen Qiao had met Puliuru Jian several times before, and he had a good impression of the man's frank, upright nature. He'd also learned after the fact that his escape from Chang'an with Yuwen Song might not have gone so smoothly if not for Puliuru Jian's efforts. Buddhism placed a great deal of emphasis on the concept of karma, but Daoism valued it as well. If you owed someone a favor, you must find an opportunity to repay it, otherwise it would hinder your cultivation and state of mind.

But helping someone was just one part of the whole. There were many other matters that needed clarification.

Shen Qiao wasn't a fool. He could understand the interplay between benefits, interests, and losses. He just wouldn't use that kind of thing to harm or scheme against others.

"That he'd send a letter requesting help, which Bian Yanmei delivered to you, indicates that Huanyue Sect has a fairly good relationship with Puliuru Jian," he said. "Previously, you told me that Yuwen Xian could be an enlightened ruler, but when Yuwen Xian died afterward, you didn't seem particularly sad. I trust that you already found a recourse. Is Puliuru Jian that recourse?"

At present, Yan Wushi was renting a courtyard from an inn in Sui Province, and Shen Qiao was recovering from his injuries there. He'd always had a quiet temperament, and he rarely went out while he was recuperating. Most of the time, he took advantage of the good weather outside by bringing a book and sitting under the grape vines in the courtyard. When he didn't speak, the scene already looked like a gorgeous painting, let alone when he did.

The sun's rays spilled down, shining through the grape leaves and dappling Shen Qiao's body. Even the contours of his cheeks and neck seemed to be cast in a delicate and soft glow. Beholding this scene made a one's heart itch to pick up this beauty and bring him home to hide him there like a treasure, so that in the future, only they'd be privy to seeing him.

Yan Wushi was a man who'd experienced all kinds of beauties. The fact that he could lose himself by simply watching Shen Qiao showed that Shen Qiao himself was truly extraordinary.

But Yan Wushi concealed his thoughts well. As these wanton desires swept through his heart like a storm, his gaze simply lingered on Shen Qiao for a moment before he lazily smiled and said, "That's right, but your use of the word 'recourse' here is incorrect. Even if there were no Puliuru Jian, Huanyue Sect would not fall. But if Huanyue Sect didn't exist, it'd be much harder for Puliuru Jian to achieve his goals. That's why Huanyue Sect is his recourse instead."

Shen Qiao trusted Yan Wushi's insight when it came to politics, but that didn't mean that he thought the man was infallible. In the past, he'd also approved of having Yuwen Yong end these turbulent times by unifying the lands, but only because he'd met Yuwen Yong himself. He'd seen that the man was indeed a great leader, possessing both talent and vision. Even if his rule was severe, he was accomplished when it came to state and military affairs both. Because of him, the wars in the north had ceased, giving the citizens respite, and the north itself had been unified by his hands. If he'd had more time, he might have completely put an end to the hundreds of years of turmoil.

It was a pity that these unforeseen circumstances had arisen. Yuwen Yong had been wise and brilliant to the very end, but his son was a misfortune. Yan Wushi was faster than anyone else when it came to adapting to and taking advantage of a situation; he'd even abandoned Yuwen Xian in the blink of an eye to collude with Puliuru Jian. But how could he be certain that Puliuru Jian would make for an enlightened ruler in the future? *Aren't you worried that this man might be overly ambitious and end up failing instead of succeeding?* thought Shen Qiao.

His expression said that he didn't quite understand what Yan Wushi was thinking.

Seeing the doubt written all over his face, Yan Wushi slowly said, "A-Qiao has his own judgment. I can speak thousands of words, but as you've yet to talk to him, you wouldn't believe me. He has Yuwen Xian's abilities, but none of his shortcomings, and he even possesses the ambition that Yuwen Xian lacked. Back then, Yuwen Xian didn't dare to revolt, and so his entire family was annihilated. Puliuru Jian is not the sort to passively wait for his death. However, he's currently in a very disadvantageous situation. If I can help him, Huanyue Sect will certainly receive great benefits in the future. More importantly…"

Shen Qiao saw that he still wished to say something. Thinking that there must be a more important reason that he hadn't stated, he put down his book and listened attentively.

Yan Wushi slowly uttered the latter half of his sentence: "More importantly, I find him quite pleasing to the eye!"

Shen Qiao couldn't help but stare at him.

Yan Wushi smiled. "I think that it's better if you don't stare at people in the future," he said. "If you want to stare, you can just stare at me, otherwise people will think that you're flirting with them."

When had it started? When had Yan Wushi begun to always use this teasing tone when talking to Shen Qiao? Shen Qiao thought back for a moment. In the past, when he'd been blind and grievously injured, Yan Wushi would carry him in and out of places, purposely leading others to get the wrong idea. Of course, he'd also been all intimate words and inappropriate actions then, wanting everyone to think that the former Xuandu Mountain Sect Leader had become the Huanyue Sect Leader's kept man. Now his words were even more intimate, but he didn't make any overt moves in front of others. Instead, he only grew so talkative and prone to laughing when in private.

Shen Qiao had initially paid no attention to these subtle changes, but at this point, he couldn't keep ignoring them.

He rubbed between his brows. He felt like everything was a mess.

Yan Wushi instinctively reached out and pressed his palm against Shen Qiao's brow, the other on the back of his head, preventing his escape. "Don't you Daoists value the concept of following one's fate?" he said. It was as if he could read Shen Qiao's thoughts. "Are we not a match made in heaven, destined to be? So why does A-Qiao look so troubled?"

"...Following one's fate is a Buddhist saying," said Shen Qiao. "We only talk about following nature's course. Besides, all we're destined for is calamity. Please don't throw words around so indiscriminately, Sect Leader Yan!"

He went to brush Yan Wushi's hand away, and in an instant, the two of them had already exchanged several blows. Yan Wushi had no self-awareness when it came to taking advantage of others when they were sick, and in the end, he directly tapped on Shen Qiao's acupoint, then pulled the beauty into his arms and stroked him. With a gleeful smile, he said, "Good destinies, awful destinies—they're all destinies, nonetheless. Could it be that even after cultivating for so many years, you're still obsessed with superficial qualities? Since Qi Fengge is already dead, I'll have to straighten your thoughts out on your shizun's behalf."

Once he finished, he lowered his head and kissed the beauty thoroughly until Shen Qiao was out of breath, all while enjoying his entire body through their clothes. Though he'd gotten quite a sweet deal while Shen Qiao was in his dazed slumber, Yan Wushi had always been a proud man. If he were to take advantage of someone, he wanted the person to be fully aware of it. Even more, he knew exactly how far to take things, always stopping at the fine line between what Shen Qiao could tolerate and what would make him explode into a rage. This level of precision was truly infuriating.

Shen Qiao's face was flushed red as he panted. The flush was out of rage, and the panting was due to the lecher's harassment.

Yan Wushi's gaze swept over the lips he'd just sucked on, which were glistening and blushing even redder than the rest of Shen Qiao's face. His heart was satisfied, and he finally said in a leisurely tone, "You see, you're feeling it too, so why torment and repress yourself. Why continue denying it?"

Shen Qiao didn't speak.

Clearly, it wasn't that he couldn't speak, but rather that he was so angry he refused to.

Yan Wushi smiled again and said, "A-Qiao, when you were in trouble, I traveled thousands of miles just to save you. Isn't that enough to prove this venerable one's feelings for you?"

He spoke with such tenderness, but he refused to unseal Shen Qiao's acupoints. He knew that the moment he unsealed them, Shen Qiao would immediately leave. There was no way he'd be here still listening to his nonsense.

"I know you bear many grudges against me due to what happened in the past," Yan Wushi went on, "but toward you, my heart has already changed completely. As the saying goes, given enough time, one can see someone's true feelings. Haven't you realized it as well?"

Shen Qiao calmed his breathing and said coldly, "I have never seen Sect Leader Yan's heart before. How should I know whether your heart's changed completely?"

Yan Wushi grabbed his hand and brought it to his own heart. He said softly, "If you don't believe me, you can dig it out and see for yourself, then you'll know. From today onward, this is all yours."

The corners of Shen Qiao's mouth twitched as the saccharine words sent a wave of chills down his spine. He felt that this man's face was thicker than the Great Wall—he'd never be able to match Yan Wushi here no matter how he tried. If he attempted reasoning with him, Yan Wushi would fire back with his own twisted logic. Shen Qiao couldn't be Yan Wushi's match here even if he grew ten more mouths.

"Let go of me first," he said.

"No can do," said Yan Wushi with a smile. "As soon as I unseal your acupoints, you'll run away. I don't want to force you too much, but you shouldn't get any notions about going our separate, happy ways. Even if the person I want hides in Qi Fengge's grave, I will dig them out!"

Shen Qiao turned his face away. "This humble Daoist is one who cultivates the Dao. I will never involve myself in romance, nor get married, for my entire life."

Yan Wushi said, "We're not talking romance. You're too superficial. We're cultivation partners who share the same Dao and walk the same path. I never intended on marrying into your family by force. If you prefer, you can marry into mine instead."

It was like he was teasing a cat, wanting to see its hackles rise, before smiling and soothing it. He undid Shen Qiao's acupoints and said, "All right. I was just joking. Why are you so angry? Back to the main point, Puliuru Jian has run into a big problem this time. Whether he's an enlightened ruler or whether you're willing to support him, we can discuss these matters later. I'm asking you to come with me because there will be great benefits for you."

The moment Shen Qiao's acupoints were cleared, he stood up and retreated until he was over three feet away from Yan Wushi. "Please clarify more, Sect Leader Yan."

Yan Wushi blinked at him and said, "I won't keep you in suspense. In any case, you wanted to repay him too, didn't you? Surely there's no issue in coming with me to Chang'an for a look?"

My god, he's even pretending to be cute!

Shen Qiao covered the injury on his chest, which was faintly throbbing in pain. He turned his head, unable to bear looking at him; he had yet to rid his mind of the man's imperious and offensive actions from earlier. Both anger and helplessness roiled inside him.

"I can go with Sect Leader Yan, but we'll need to establish some guidelines and treat each other with proper etiquette. If Sect Leader Yan it is unable to, I would rather go alone."

And if I follow you, Yan Wushi thought, *how would you get rid of me?*

But he only gave him a small smile and generously agreed. "We can."

108

Sophistry

YAN WUSHI CONTINUED TEASING Shen Qiao, and his attitude changed day by day. Shen Qiao couldn't say that he was completely unaware, but truly, from the bottom of his heart, he didn't feel that he had any beauty or charm to speak of.

For a man to live righteously in this world, the most important thing was his character. As for looks, women adorned themselves for their admirers, and handsome men like Zou Ji or Song Yu also valued their appearances. However, Shen Qiao was a priest, so he'd never placed any importance on such things; hence, he didn't understand what Yan Wushi liked about him.

Due to these doubts, he interpreted Yan Wushi's attitude as a passing whim. After all, there had already been a precedent to this. If he left himself unguarded, he might end up being sold off again. Shen Qiao knew that he wasn't Yan Wushi's match when it came to scheming, and because of this, deep down inside, he was always afraid. A shred of suspicion remained constant within his heart, so he wouldn't dare believe Yan Wushi so easily.

In the end, Yan Wushi had brought this misfortune upon himself.

Back then, Shen Qiao had already regarded him as a friend. The heavens and earth could testify that his heart had been pure as ice, but Yan Wushi had sneered at him, then discarded him like a worn-out shoe. While speaking and smiling gently to him, he'd been in secret contact with Sang Jingxing. In the blink of an eye, he'd presented Shen Qiao to him, then thrown Shen Qiao's sincere heart to the ground and stomped it into powder. Now he wished to salvage it, but a broken mirror was difficult to repair, and spilled water impossible to recover. Perhaps he should have been considered fortunate that it was Shen Qiao he liked, for if anyone else had gone through what he had, even if they didn't undergo a drastic change in personality, they'd surely spend all day plotting revenge on Yan Wushi. At the very least, they wouldn't show Yan Wushi the slightest hint of trust or goodwill.

But Shen Qiao was an exception. This man treated people with utmost sincerity: if someone showed him kindness, he would absolutely repay it ten or even twelve-fold.

Outside the royal capital of Tuyuhun, Yan Wushi had developed multiple personalities due to his severe injuries. And due to the Chen Gong incident, Yan Wushi and Shen Qiao had gone deep underground in Ruoqiang, which had resulted in various entanglements. Later, when Hehuan Sect caught wind of the news and came to kill them, Yan Wushi had decisively chosen to use himself as bait and lure away their most dangerous enemy, Sang Jingxing. This had given Shen Qiao the room to escape. Though Shen Qiao knew very well that the cunning Yan Wushi wouldn't have gone in unprepared, he'd seen the other man's resolve as he left. He couldn't help being shaken by this.

Even when Yan Wushi later recalled this move, he was very proud of it.

With his heart now set on Shen Qiao, he wanted even more to explore this person's words and actions until he knew them inside out and grasped them entirely.

If anyone else had to put up with Yan Wushi's teasing and mocking, and his many frivolous remarks, they would have been pondering how to best escape from him—that is, if they didn't just fly into a rage. However, Shen Qiao was different.

To Shen Qiao, Yan Wushi had just saved him on Qingcheng Mountain, so this kindness was one reason. Then there was Puliuru Jian's letter begging for help. If Shen Qiao hadn't known, it'd be one thing, but now that he did know about it, he had to make the trip, so he and Yan Wushi shared the same destination anyway. This was the second reason.

These two reasons together were much more important than "I don't want to get tangled up by this man's words and actions," so Shen Qiao would first put aside his personal feelings and prioritize what was truly important.

This level of seriousness and rigor could make one look old-fashioned, or even hypocritical. However, when it came to Shen Qiao, many people would feel that this was just the way things were and that there was nothing contradictory about his character.

Back when this person had been the Xuandu Mountain Sect Leader, his reputation hadn't been prominent. When others mentioned him, they would add at most one more sentence: "Qi Fengge's favorite disciple." Nothing else. Yet now that he wandered the jianghu, his identity as Shen Qiao was foremost in people's minds.

Yan Wushi took so much pride in spending most of his life free from the influence of others, that he lived carefree and unrestrained and did as he pleased. Never could he have imagined that, ultimately, this person would put an end to all of that.

He'd always believed that human nature was evil, that true goodness didn't exist. That even if it did exist, it'd only look like weakness when he saw it.

And yet Shen Qiao was an exception. Yan Wushi, who'd never compromised himself for anyone, was willing to concede a little for Shen Qiao's sake.

Yan Wushi had never believed in the people the world thought were good, and he considered them beneath his contempt. And if Yan Wushi found someone he thought was good, and the people of the world thought so as well, he naturally had to snatch this person for himself first. Whether through extortion or by silently nurturing the relationship, he must first gather that person into his arms, then carefully tune them until the other party was finally won over.

All in all, so far, progress had been fairly smooth.

Even Yan Wushi couldn't help but feel quite satisfied with himself. His venerable self had been in the jianghu for decades. Even if he didn't use his status or martial prowess to oppress others, there were countless men and women who'd cling to him of their own volition. This was the first time in his life that he'd had to put so much effort into someone. If he couldn't capture this person, then he'd have wasted the rest of his life. In that case, he might as well bash his head open and die.

So, when Shen Qiao proposed his three rules of "treat each other with courtesy," "never disregard etiquette," and "no frivolous behavior allowed," Yan Wushi naturally agreed. His easy agreement made Shen Qiao somewhat suspicious, but since he *had* already agreed, if he continued to pester him over it, Shen Qiao would come off as the unreasonable one.

The next morning, the two of them set off on their journey. Whenever they happened to pass by a town at night, they would rest there. It was common for people of the jianghu to brave the wind and dew, but if they had a choice, anyone would much rather have a warm and comfortable place to stay. Unless there was really no other option, even martial experts would prefer to stay at an inn. Yan Wushi and Shen Qiao were no exception.

They traveled at a brisk pace, and in just two days they arrived in Xining Town, not far from Chang'an.

With Chang'an in sight, they could finally slow their pace somewhat. They'd be able to enter the city tomorrow.

"Though Puliuru Jian's situation is critical, it's not so urgent that we can't pause for a moment," said Yan Wushi. "It's already evening, so let's rest here for now."

Shen Qiao knew that Yan Wushi had always attached great importance to his appearance. Every time he showed up somewhere, his figure had to be dignified and majestic; there was no telling how much time he spent preparing himself. Of course, the Huanyue Sect Leader would refuse to enter the city travel-worn and caked in dust, so Shen Qiao agreed.

They chose a fairly large inn, and the two of them walked inside. Shen Qiao was afraid that Yan Wushi would again say something about sleeping together, so when the innkeeper asked, "Two separate rooms?" he quickly stepped in front of Yan Wushi and replied, "Yes."

Yan Wushi didn't refute him, but simply smiled happily and let him take the lead.

The innkeeper couldn't help but smile and say, "The two gentlemen here are brothers, correct? You're very close."

"We're not brothers," said Yan Wushi.

"Ah," said the innkeeper as he hesitated a little. "Then...father and son?"

Yan Wushi didn't say anything, only smiled suggestively at him. Then he glanced at Shen Qiao, before smiling again at the innkeeper.

The shopkeeper had seen all types of people before, and dawning realization soon surfaced on his face.

"It can't be helped," Yan Wushi said. "He's been difficult the past few days, and we haven't been getting along."

The innkeeper was incredibly adaptable. "They all say, with ten years of virtue, you'll share the same ship of destiny, with a hundred years of virtue you'll...you know.[12] As the two of you are dragons and phoenixes among men, your friendship is likely extraordinary as well. Since you already have this shared destiny, you should make some concessions to each other. You know what they say: amiability is the key to prosperity!"

Shen Qiao was silent. *What do you mean, "you know?" Say it clearly!*

But the innkeeper had chosen to follow Yan Wushi's lead in being vague. Shen Qiao couldn't go and deliberately correct him. The denial would just make him look even more guilty.

The innkeeper booked a room for them, but Yan Wushi requested another private room and ordered some food and wine to go with it.

There were four dining tables in the private room, all arranged on one side. The other side was for performances as guests could call for some singing and dancing to entertain them during dinner. There was no one dancing at the moment, though, making the room seem a bit empty.

Shen Qiao sat down at the table by the door, but Yan Wushi didn't sit down at the next table over. Instead, he sat down at the table closest to the corner, leaving two tables in between them.

"Why do this, Sect Leader Yan?" Shen Qiao didn't understand.

"The moment I saw your face, I wanted to touch it, but since I promised to treat you with courtesy, it's better if I stay away. Otherwise, you'll see me as a dishonest scoundrel again."

---

12   十年修得同船渡，百年修得共枕眠. A Chinese idiom. Literally, "After ten years of virtue, you'll share the same ship crossing; after a hundred years of virtue, you'll share a pillow."

Yan Wushi's words not only sounded innocent, they dripped with righteousness. Those who didn't know better would have thought that Shen Qiao was the one being indecent toward him.

Shen Qiao was a bit speechless, and after a moment he recalled what had happened just now. "You intentionally misled the innkeeper by saying those things. How is this treating each other with courtesy?"

Yan Wushi acted even more innocent. "Where was I being misleading? I only said two lines the entire time, and you heard them clearly too. We aren't brothers. Is there anything wrong with this sentence? Unless A-Qiao actually wants to be my brother? And the second sentence is even more faultless, is it not? What is there to argue about? The shopkeeper had indecent thoughts, so he came to an indecent conclusion. You can't blame me for that."

Shen Qiao already possessed a profound understanding of Yan Wushi's knack for verbal debates. Hearing this, he only felt a sense of helplessness.

Yan Wushi smiled. "I have done everything you requested. Why are you still unsatisfied?" After a pause, he spoke softly again: "A-Qiao, there aren't many people who can receive my venerable regard in this lifetime, and there are even fewer people for whom I'd make concessions. You are the only one."

Within the softness was a hint of steel underneath the gentle words lay an unyielding stubbornness. It was truly enough to leave a person at the end of their rope.

Shen Qiao frowned. "I would rather not be that special."

That's not up to you. Yan Wushi smiled but did not answer.

Shen Qiao thought for a moment and solemnly said, "Sect Leader Yan's intentions are unpredictable, truly difficult to fathom. And I know even less how my exceedingly ordinary qualifications managed to attract Sect Leader Yan's attention. Since we're being candid today, can I please ask Lord Yan to speak honestly on this matter?"

"A-Qiao, you have many good qualities. So many that I wouldn't be able to list them all even if I spoke for three days and three nights." He'd begun with a joke. Seeing Shen Qiao speechless, he smiled and said, "Just in your softheartedness alone, no one in this world can compare to you."

"I don't know when being softhearted became a good quality," said Shen Qiao glumly. "I only remember that Sect Leader Yan has always detested those who are kind and softhearted."

Yan Wushi gave an easy smile. "Why else would they say, 'In your lover's eyes, you become Xi Shi?'"[13]

All right, so basically, Shen Qiao had been tricked again. He knew he wouldn't be able to get a straight answer out of Yan Wushi.

He was even more certain now that the other man was just acting on a whim, which meant there were only two paths ahead for Shen Qiao. The first was to wait for Yan Wushi's interest to subside so that he'd stop pestering him. Then his ears would finally know peace. Alternatively, he could wait until he could surpass Yan Wushi in martial arts, then pummel him flat. That way Yan Wushi wouldn't dare to pester him anymore.

The wine and food were served, and both of them fell silent and began to eat.

Halfway through the meal, Yan Wushi took a sip of wine and smiled. "If you like someone, must you say a reason? It's like when you hate someone to the point that their face fills you with disgust, but you can't say why. Isn't that the same thing? Just because I enjoy teasing you doesn't mean you can treat my sincerity as fake. My heart won't be able to take it."

---

13   西施. One of the renowned Four Beauties of ancient China.

At first, those words sounded rather earnest, but it was just more twisted logic. *Why is it so difficult to have a proper conversation with this person?* Shen Qiao thought to himself.

The words he wanted to say turned in his stomach a few times, and just as he was about to say them, he heard a slight sound coming from Yan Wushi's table. He couldn't help but raise his head, just in time to see Yan Wushi's head drop low as he coughed up blood.

Shen Qiao's face contorted in horror. All else flew from his mind as he hurriedly leapt up to support him. "What's wrong? Was the wine poisoned?!"

As Shen Qiao hadn't touched the jug of wine, he immediately thought that the wine was the issue.

And because this reminded him of his own experience with Joyful Reunion, his complexion looked even worse than Yan Wushi's.

But then, Yan Wushi suddenly smiled and pulled him into his arms. "Your panic reveals your concern. A-Qiao, your words truly don't match your heart!"

Shen Qiao stared at him. "You...you weren't poisoned?"

Yan Wushi wiped the bloodstain from the corner of his lips and said, "I accidentally bit my lip while chewing. I might have been too agitated."

Agitated to the point of vomiting blood?

To hell with your lies!

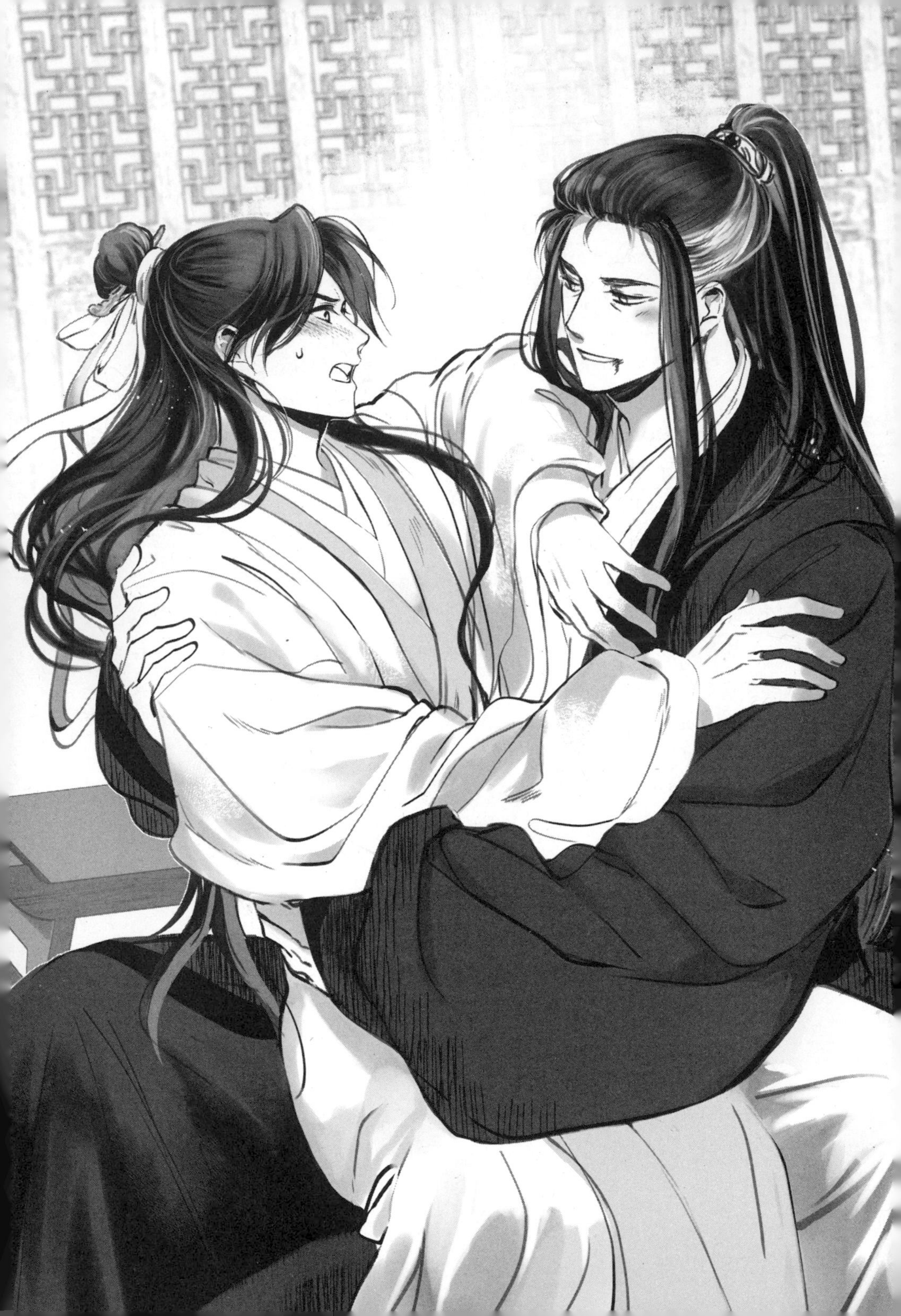

109

Hostages

R EALIZING YAN WUSHI had tricked him by pretending to vomit blood, Shen Qiao refused to say a single word to Yan Wushi the rest of the way to Chang'an and the Duke of Sui's residence.

In his heart, this man and the word "cunning" were already irreversibly linked. His mind held more schemes than a honeycomb had cells. Shen Qiao knew that even if he used every trick he had, he still wouldn't be Yan Wushi's match. Hence, silence was golden—he simply refused to speak. No matter what Yan Wushi said, Shen Qiao only answered with "Mm," or "Oh." He refused to believe that the man could find any openings this way.

Yan Wushi also knew that he'd gone too far. Though he'd forced Shen Qiao to show his concern with his moment of panic, no one enjoyed being embarrassed. Even with someone as good-natured as Shen Qiao, exposing them like that would of course make them angry. It'd be stranger if he wasn't angry.

Chang'an was the same as always, with its tall city walls and majestic grandeur. Thousands of sights combined into a single scene—truly worthy of its status as the imperial capital. Shen Qiao had never seen such a stolid, awe-inspiring aura in even the capital of the Southern Dynasty, Jiankang.

Jiankang could be considered as the capital of several dynasties.

It had been established since the time of Sun Wu, during the Three Kingdoms era. The palace had three outer walls and three inner walls, with the river Qinhuai to the south and the lake Houhu to the north. When Yuwen Yong entrusted Yan Wushi with escorting the Zhou envoys to the Southern Dynasty, Shen Qiao also stayed in Jiankang. Comparing the two capitals, Jiankang had more splendor and charm but lacked Chang'an's power and gravity. There was a saying that "The presence of kingly qi determines the location of the capital. For where the kingly qi resides, the dragon's vein—the flow of fortune—will be found." These words carried a strong whiff of superstition, but there was a grain of truth in them. Though Daoists didn't practice divination, some cursory dabbling was inevitable, and Shen Qiao too knew a thing or two about observing and interpreting qi. Back then, when he'd examined Yuwen Yong's qi and complexion, he'd felt that Yuwen Yong didn't have much longer to live. Now, when comparing Jiankang with Chang'an, he also felt that the former was a little lacking in kingly qi compared to the latter. Perhaps it was this little gap that could determine a dynasty's fate.

But such talk of the supernatural was better kept to himself. Even if the emperor believed them, few emperors would actually move their capital over something like this.

Ultimately, a dynasty's fortunes relied on correct timing, geographical advantages, and human harmony. None of these could be missing. Now that the Zhou Dynasty had lost Yuwen Yong, what use was the correct timing and geographical advantage? They were already pointless; the yellow flowers of tomorrow.

"Why is A-Qiao's expression so grave?" Yan Wushi's voice sounded from beside him, destroying the mood.

Shen Qiao didn't even want to acknowledge him. He pretended he'd heard nothing.

Yan Wushi kept his bright smile despite being given the cold shoulder—there was no hint of displeasure. He followed Shen Qiao and entered the city.

Shen Qiao protecting Yuwen Song while fighting his way out of the siege had left a deep impression on the people. He hadn't even changed his attire for this visit; he was still dressed in a blue Daoist robe, a longsword on his back. With his exceptional face, even the guards immediately recognized him. They watched helplessly as he casually entered the city. Not a single one had the courage to stop or interrogate him.

Most people would admire the truly capable. Shen Qiao's actions that day had been so dazzling, even the low-ranking foot soldiers who'd participated in the siege felt nothing but heartfelt respect for this Daoist priest. After all, he'd managed to escape from a city full of archers and countless martial experts using only his own strength. Though they'd later heard the emperor had been furious over failing to kill his uncle's entire family, having let his younger cousin escape like a fish from a net, they all privately gave Shen Qiao a thumbs-up. Accounts of that brilliant battle had long been pieced into a story that was circulating around the markets. The common folk might not have heard of the world's number one martial artist Qi Fengge, but they definitely knew of this supremely righteous and powerful Daoist Master Shen.

But Chang'an was Chang'an, not anywhere else. Since entering the city, countless eyes and ears had been alerted to their presence. However, Yan Wushi showed no concern, nor did he alert Shen Qiao. He simply took him straight to the Junior Preceptor's residence in the city.

Though Huanyue Sect had lost its influence, Yan Wushi was not a court criminal. Shen Qiao had fled with Yuwen Song, but Yuwen

Yun had come to the conclusion that a single seven- to eight-year-old child couldn't cause too much trouble. In any case, he spent all day indulging in pleasure, so he lacked the time to concern himself with other matters and didn't bother to pursue them further. Thus, though these two people had entered the city and attracted all sorts of attention, no one came to arrest them. One reason was that there was no legitimate reason to do so, and the second was that even if anyone wanted to arrest them, they wouldn't have been able to do so.

Ever since the new emperor's ascension to the throne, the Junior Preceptor's residence had been sealed off. The gates were locked and covered with paper seals. Yan Wushi gently tugged at them with both hands, and even the heavy chains snapped with a clang, to say nothing of the seals. He pushed the gates and entered. The sight of his complete disregard for the court's ban made Shen Qiao's mouth twitch as he watched.

Was this because he'd already resolved to support Puliuru Jian, so he saw no need to avoid suspicion, even in broad daylight?

Shen Qiao wanted to ask, but after opening his mouth, he restrained himself.

Yan Wushi didn't look back, but it was like he had eyes on the back of his head, for he said, "At the Sword Trial Conference, Hehuan Sect went to harass Chunyang Monastery, and Sang Jingxing and Yuan Xiuxiu must have been injured in the ensuing scuffle. The handful of small fry remaining aren't even worth mentioning. Currently in Chang'an, the only one worthy of my concern is Xueting, but that old bald donkey relies too much on the Buddhist orthodoxy and clings to his face, so he can't do anything underhanded like espionage. As for Yuwen Yun, I also used to instruct him when he was the crown prince. He knew he couldn't provoke me, and in any case he was only interested in having fun. He would never act recklessly until he was completely certain. If someone were to accuse me in front of him, he'd just turn a blind eye."

Shen Qiao frowned. From what Yan Wushi was saying, Yuwen Yun also didn't seem entirely incompetent. But to annihilate his uncles' families right after ascending the throne... These actions were truly chilling.

Yan Wushi seemed to notice his thoughts again. "Yuwen Yun elevates Buddhism, but he also brought in Hehuan Sect. He clearly doesn't want the Buddhist discipline to be the sole dominant faction, and he does have some skill when it comes to controlling his subordinates; he was able to disperse the various sources of power over multiple factions. If he truly lacked competence, he couldn't have kept up the act in front of Yuwen Yong for so many years without being deposed. But these are the limits of his abilities. If Yuwen Yong had listened to me and established Yuwen Xian as ruler instead, the Zhou Dynasty could have enjoyed three more generations of stability."

Shen Qiao hadn't expected that Yan Wushi would have suggested that to Yuwen Yong. No wonder Yuwen Yun had immediately targeted Huanyue Sect upon ascending to the throne. He probably loathed Yan Wushi to the bone. Unfortunately, this emperor didn't use his smarts on official matters, instead wasting it on pointless things.

At present, the Göktürk Khaganate was in the north, while the Southern Dynasty was in the south. Even the conquest of the north itself had been due to the late emperor. However, a normal emperor, even one who didn't want to unify the lands eventually, wouldn't do something like abdicating the throne for his son and taking the position of emperor emeritus instead. Even when Shen Qiao was in Xining Town, he'd heard about the emperor's large-scale construction of imperial gardens, as well as about him engaging in inappropriate behavior with his concubines and palace maids in broad daylight. If Yuwen Yong in the underworld found out that his son was ruining the empire that he'd spent decades of blood, sweat, and tears on this way, he'd probably come back to life out of sheer rage.

Yan Wushi added, "Yuwen Xian was weak, but he was skilled with military administration, as well as an excellent commander. Even if he couldn't have inherited Yuwen Yong's legacy, he wouldn't have squandered the family's wealth entirely. Unfortunately, Yuwen Yong couldn't break free from the shackles of tradition and insisted on his son inheriting the throne. His vision was far too narrow and shallow. He labored his entire life and ended up being killed by his son, and all his hard work has come to nothing. Such misfortune he brought upon himself!"

He showed little respect for the previous emperor, his criticisms flowing forth the moment he opened his mouth. Anyone else hearing this would have been terrified out of their wits, but Shen Qiao couldn't help but internally roll his eyes. He thought, *Didn't you get ambushed by those martial experts in the capital of Tuyuhun? You even ended up with a crack in your skull and almost lost your life. You call Yuwen Yong shallow, but where was your foresight then?*

Yan Wushi didn't even turn back as he joked, "A-Qiao, I didn't expect you, an upright gentleman, to develop the bad habit of silently cursing someone behind his back. That's not good!"

Shen Qiao knew Yan Wushi was trying to provoke him into talking, but this only made him clam up more.

By now, the two had already passed through the atrium and arrived in the backyard.

Shen Qiao didn't know why Yan Wushi had brought him here, but looking at the surrounding vegetation and furnishings, there was no sign of the neglect or disarray that should come from the owner's absence. Instead, everything was neatly maintained, indicating that someone had been coming over frequently to take care of the place. Yet the seals and locks outside had been untouched, which was rather intriguing.

Yan Wushi pushed open a door to the house, but the inside wasn't empty—several people were waiting.

Upon their arrival, those people all stood up to greet them. The person in the middle took a few steps forward and cupped his hands, saying, "I heard that Sect Leader Yan has encountered many crises while outside lately. Alas, I am not from the jianghu and was unable to help at all. It is fortunate that you are safe and sound. I can finally lay my worries to rest."

He then greeted Shen Qiao and said, "Daoist Master Shen was utterly brilliant that day, practically unforgettable. The people of Chang'an are still discussing it with relish even now. Seeing you again, your magnificence has only increased!"

This man was an old acquaintance, so Shen Qiao naturally recognized him. Moreover, Yan Wushi had already mentioned him in advance, so he'd come mentally prepared. Now, he also cupped his hands and smiled. "Duke of Sui," he greeted him, "I heard that when I left the capital with Qilang that day, the Duke of Sui had been secretly assisting us, and that's why we were able to escape safely. This humble Daoist has yet to thank the Duke of Sui for this."

Puliuru Jian gave a hearty laugh. "I only lifted a finger! No need to let it linger on your mind!"

He introduced the person with him to Shen Qiao: "This is Zheng Yi, a senior official from the Department of Internal History."

And there was another person here who needed no introduction but was also an old acquaintance—Yan Wushi's eldest disciple, Bian Yanmei. The moment Yan Wushi had entered, Bian Yanmei had come forward and bowed. When he saw Shen Qiao looking at him, he smiled and cupped his hands at him as well.

Despite Yan Wushi's pride, he dispensed with his usual posturing and spoke pleasantly to Puliuru Jian. "While outside, I received a letter from Dalang, saying that there was some trouble on your end."

Everyone took a seat, and Puliuru Jian gave a bitter smile. "Yes, there has indeed been some trouble. I've thought long and hard but still cannot find a way, so I can only presumptuously bother Sect Leader Yan."

Yuwen Yun was rather lacking when it came to governing the country, but he was quite adept with tactics for protecting his imperial power. After killing several of his uncles in succession, he turned his attention to his officials. The first to receive his attention was his own father-in-law, the Duke of Sui, Puliuru Jian.

Puliuru Jian wasn't Yuwen Xian. He refused to simply sit and wait for death, or perhaps he'd already intended to revolt. Faced with an emperor like Yuwen Yun, he couldn't possibly be happy to submit himself and serve as his minister. Therefore, though he appeared respectful on the surface, he'd been making many preparations in secret. First, he'd contacted the military to attempt to take over the remnants of Yuwen Xian's troops. After Yuwen Xian's death, those who were originally loyal to him had been subject to the emperor's suspicions and oppression, leaving them in a state of constant fear. When they saw Puliuru Jian offering an olive branch, they naturally rushed to take it. As Puliuru Jian worked, many people in the court also fell to his side, becoming the backbone of his faction. Zheng Yi was one of them.

However, Yuwen Yun was not completely unaware. Puliuru Jian's daughter was Yuwen Yun's empress. Yuwen Yun was unable to grasp any of Puliuru Jian's weaknesses, and so his attitude toward the empress had deteriorated. He would verbally abuse and browbeat her at every turn, even threatening her with death several times. It was only thanks to Puliuru Jian's wife, Lady Dugu, entering the palace and pleading for mercy that she'd narrowly escaped with her life.

Puliuru Jian sighed. "A few days ago, it was the empress's birthday. His Majesty had no intention of arranging any grand celebrations, but only bestowed a few gifts on her and allowed my wife to visit. However, a message came from the palace, saying that the empress wanted to see her brothers, so my wife brought our first and second sons into the palace to celebrate her birthday. But after she met with the empress, someone lured my wife away with an excuse, and when she returned, she was told that the empress missed her brothers and wished to have them stay for a meal. My wife asked to see the empress, but to no avail, so she pleaded with His Majesty and was expelled from the palace. Since then, I have seen neither the empress nor my sons. I did all I could, but His Majesty refuses to let anyone go. I don't even know if they're alive or dead."

In other words, two of Puliuru Jian's sons and one of his daughters had been taken hostage by Yuwen Yun.

Puliuru Jian had five sons. The eldest, one of the sons who'd been taken to the palace, was only nine years old.

At this point, his face was filled with distress, his earnest love for his sons pouring into his words. "I've done everything I could. I even begged His Majesty, but he wouldn't let anyone go. He insists that it was my sons who wanted to remain in the palace so that they could keep the empress company. Buddhist Master Xueting is watching over the palace, and martial experts have gathered there like storm clouds. If I use force, I can't guarantee that my children will remain unharmed. I never imagined that Yuwen Yun would suddenly launch an attack, even resorting to a method like this. I truly have no alternative but to beg Sect Leader Yan for help!"

The room was so quiet, one could have heard a pin drop. Yan Wushi smiled a little and said with perfect composure, "I'll put it bluntly. All the necessary preparations are complete, Duke of Sui. You need only wait for the perfect opportunity. Even without those two sons, you still have three, so it doesn't hinder the overall situation. As long as you remain firm, Yuwen Yun cannot use this to threaten you."

110

A Grand Gift

THESE WORDS WERE FULL of Yan Wushi's characteristic callous ruthlessness. Throughout the ages, he was saying, those with great accomplishments could abandon even their parents and disregard their siblings, never mind their children. In any case, those two weren't Puliuru Jian's only sons—he had another three. Moreover, Puliuru Jian was in his prime, so having more sons and daughters wouldn't be difficult. There was no need to have his hands tied just because two of his sons were in Yuwen Yun's hands—he should still do what he had to do.

Though Shen Qiao did not agree with these words, he didn't find them strange or unexpected. He knew this was the kind of person Yan Wushi was. On the contrary, the various special treatments he'd been getting from Yan Wushi lately were far more disturbing and bizarre.

Other than Shen Qiao, Zheng Yi and Bian Yanmei were also present. Bian Yanmei was Yan Wushi's disciple and a demonic practitioner; his methods were also unconventional and unpredictable, so he wouldn't see anything inappropriate in what Yan Wushi said. As Zheng Ying was considered a trusted confidant by Puliuru Jian, he couldn't have been too gentle a person either. So, though he said nothing, he also agreed with Yan Wushi's words.

Puliuru Jian smiled bitterly. "Though those with great achievements do not concern themselves with trivial details, how can I forsake my own flesh and blood so easily? Emperor Gaozu of Han asked Xiang Yu to share the meat soup made from his father's flesh. I can't do that. If I can abandon even my own kin, I trust that Sect Leader Yan would also look down on me, would he not?"

It was indeed a canny statement. Though he was clearly asking for Yan Wushi's help in rescuing his children, he managed to give off an impression that was both devoted and righteous. An emperor as kind and soft as Yuwen Xian would naturally be able to achieve very little, but one like Gou Jian, who disposed of subjects the moment their purpose was fulfilled, would instead be too horrifying. Puliuru Jian was offering reassurance to his followers, implying that he would never forget their kindness in the future either.

Shen Qiao vaguely understood why Yan Wushi had changed to supporting Puliuru Jian.

Yan Wushi smiled for a moment, but he didn't continue the topic of whether to rescue them or not. Instead, he said, "Are you sure that they're still alive, inside the palace?"

Puliuru Jian understood that this was Yan Wushi tacitly promising to save them, so he quickly collected his spirits and said, "I am sure. The empress risked her life to secretly send someone to us with a letter, saying that His Majesty had detained my sons in the empress's palace, and the empress herself is under house arrest and cannot leave. It's already been more than ten days. I think that His Majesty wants to use them as hostages to prevent me from acting rashly."

Carrying out a rebellion wasn't like eating food or drinking water. Though Puliuru Jian had already made many preparations, he hadn't completely made up his mind before this development. If anything, the emperor's coercion had forced out his determination. The moment his children were saved, he'd launch a coup without a second thought.

"To rescue your children, you need to be prepared to turn against Yuwen Yun," said Yan Wushi. "There are people from the Buddhist sects overseeing the palace, and Hehuan Sect has members there as well. Even if they can't defeat me, there's little to stop them from killing your children out of spite."

Puliuru Jian sighed. "Yes, this has been weighing on my mind as well. I'm feeling quite anxious. Does Sect Leader Yan have any good ideas?"

Yan Wushi pondered for a moment. "Yuwen Yun refused to let anyone go, but in the end, he hasn't turned on you in public," he said. "You can send gifts to your children as a pretext for entering the palace, then wait for an opportunity to save them. This is the only way."

Bian Yanmei quickly understood. "This disciple is willing to accept this task. I can disguise myself and sneak into the palace, then wait for the opportunity to rescue someone."

Surprisingly, Yan Wushi rejected him. "Your martial arts are still lacking. If you end up facing Xueting, only death awaits you."

Bian Yanmei rubbed his nose but went silent.

"Meanwhile, my stature is too eye-catching," said Yan Wushi, "and I've never practiced the Bone Shrinking Technique. If I disguise myself, maybe others won't notice anything unusual, but that bald old donkey Xueting would see right through it. It would only backfire. If we wish to save those boys, we must find an exceptional martial artist who is able to adapt to the situation accordingly. When the time comes, I'll coordinate with them from outside the palace."

To Puliuru Jian, Bian Yanmei was already a powerful martial artist, but Yan Wushi had deemed him insufficient, saying they needed better. If they had to prepare for the possibility of fighting Xueting, then they needed a grandmaster-level martial expert.

However, grandmasters didn't grow from the ground like cabbages, and Puliuru Jian wasn't the emperor yet either. Even if he were, he'd still have to treat this hypothetical martial artist with extra courtesy and respect. Where could he find one on such short notice?

When several pairs of eyes fell on him, Shen Qiao gave a sigh. "This humble Daoist lacks talent," he said gently, "but saving someone's life is worth a thousand merits. I would be willing to try, but I'm not familiar with the palace's layout. Once I'm inside, I'll be as good as blind. I fear that I might lose my way before I could rescue anyone."

Puliuru Jian had just been considering Shen Qiao, but this was different from asking for help from Yan Wushi. He shared no deep friendship with Shen Qiao, so if he didn't offer, Puliuru Jian couldn't be so shameless as to ask. Now that Shen Qiao had volunteered, he was naturally overjoyed.

"Daoist Master Shen taking the field is more than Jian could ask for," he said. "But infiltrating the palace will be terribly treacherous. Though I am worried about my loved ones, I dare not rashly put Daoist Master Shen in danger. I've heard that on Buddha's Birthday, the eighth of April, Xueting will head to the city's Qingliang Temple to pray for blessings. With him gone, the remaining forces should be much easier to deal with. At that time, I will send more people to accompany Daoist Master Shen—first to lead the way, and second as backup in case something goes wrong. They can also serve as your helpers."

"Quality over quantity," said Bian Yanmei. "Let me accompany Daoist Master Shen into the palace, as I'm also familiar with its layout. Then sending just two more maids will be enough. Yuwen Yun isn't a fool—if there are too many people, he will also grow suspicious."

Shen Qiao nodded and said nothing more.

After further discussion of the time and location, both parties agreed that Puliuru Jian should first submit a letter requesting to visit. If Yuwen Yun refused, they would enter the palace to deliver gifts under the name of the empress's mother, Lady Dugu. Shen Qiao and the others arranged to meet on the seventh of April at the Duke of Sui's residence, where they would disguise themselves as servants from the Duke of Sui's residence who were visiting the empress. Inside, they'd wait for the opportunity to stage the rescue.

By now, the news had doubtless already been reported that Yan Wushi and Shen Qiao had entered the Junior Preceptor's Mansion, thus ignoring the ban and trespassing. They couldn't remain here for too long. After the matter was decided, everyone dispersed. Puliuru Jian followed a secret passage out of the Junior Preceptor's residence and returned to the Duke of Sui's residence while Bian Yanmei brought Yan Wushi and Shen Qiao to another residence in the city.

The residence was not the one Shen Qiao had lived in but another one that he'd never set foot in before. "The wily rabbit has three burrows." The demonic practitioners, especially Huanyue Sect, exemplified this saying. Shen Qiao suspected that Bian Yanmei had secretly bought as many as ten residences as contingencies, and when one was discovered, he'd abandon that one and relocate to the next. In any case, Huanyue Sect had made a lot of money back when Yuwen Yong had supported them, and even now, they still ran numerous businesses. While they didn't operate on as large a scale as the Liuhe Guild, Yan Wushi certainly wasn't lacking in wealth.

Bian Yanmei introduced the building to them. "This is a private residence under the surname of Li. To the outside world, it is a merchant's residence, so Hehuan Sect won't be able to find this place for the time being. Shizun and Daoist Master Shen can rest assured."

He didn't know what kind of relationship Shen Qiao had with his shifu now. Close friends? They didn't look like it. And with his master's temperament, forget about Shen Qiao—even if the world's number one martial artist wanted to be his friend, Yan Wushi might still consider it pointless. Bian Yanmei still remembered that his master had always brought Shen Qiao along with him, but only to amuse himself—there'd been no sense of friendship between them.

Bian Yanmei's powers of observation were much sharper than those of his shidi Yu Shengyan. He was naturally able to see that Yan Wushi's treatment of Shen Qiao was highly unusual, and very different from before. But he couldn't say exactly what the difference was—even if he racked his brains, he couldn't imagine his own shifu having such thoughts. Though Shen Qiao was gentle and handsome, it was impossible to imagine him as a kept man being showered in favors. Besides, Liuli Palace had just released the rankings of the martial artists throughout the land, and Daoist Master Shen ranked in the top ten. Who in the world dared to harbor impure intentions toward martial grandmasters?

Yan Wushi dared.

But Bian Yanmei didn't expect his master to dare.

In any case, since Yan Wushi was showing Shen Qiao special regard, someone as artful as Bian Yanmei could never snub Shen Qiao. And though he took after his shifu in his own lack of scruples, he held genuine admiration for Shen Qiao's character within his heart. There were many scoundrels and hypocrites in this world, and no shortage of people who appeared to be morally upright gentlemen but in truth were unable to control themselves in the face of temptation. Bian Yanmei was from the jianghu, but he'd also served in the imperial court of the Northern Zhou for many years, and he'd met all types of people. One such as Shen Qiao could truly be called a person who practiced what he preached—his actions and conscience were one.

As they spoke, the Duke of Sui's residence had secretly sent someone over to deliver something, and it was addressed to Shen Qiao.

Huanyue Sect was allied with the Duke of Sui, so they naturally knew about this location as well, allowing for convenient communication at any time.

Shen Qiao didn't know what it was, so when he opened the bamboo tube, removed the contents, and opened it up to take a look, he let out a quiet gasp of surprise.

Yan Wushi glanced at him and smiled. "Puliuru Jian is truly a clever, incisive man."

This object was one of the *Zhuyang Strategy*'s five scrolls: the one originally concealed within the inner palace of Northern Zhou.

Yan Wushi had read this *Zhuyang Strategy* scroll in the past, but at the time, he'd already realized that its contents were mostly incompatible with the *Fenglin Scriptures*, so he hadn't committed it to memory. Later, after his feelings for Shen Qiao had grown, he'd roughly told him about everything he remembered. However, that couldn't compare to having the complete original delivered to him. Now, with the exception of the scroll in Tiantai Sect, Shen Qiao had obtained full knowledge of the *Zhuyang Strategy*'s contents.

Although the *Zhuyang Strategy* scrolls were precious, Yuwen Yun wasn't a martial artist. After he'd poisoned and killed his father, the court had experienced a great flood of changes. Yuwen Yun hadn't had the time to pay attention to this kind of thing, nor had he cared to. Puliuru Jian had taken advantage of his status to have his daughter smuggle the scroll out of the palace during the chaos. He had stored that scroll away until now, when he'd given it to Shen Qiao.

Having received such a valuable gift, Shen Qiao naturally had to acknowledge his favor because Puliuru Jian conducted himself brilliantly. He hadn't waited until the task was completed to present this gift—instead, he'd delivered it in advance, expressing his own faith in Shen Qiao's character and his confidence that Shen Qiao wouldn't break his promises.

Now, no matter how dangerous the palace would be, Shen Qiao would have to go, and he'd do so willingly, without a shred of reluctance.

So that was why Yan Wushi had said Puliuru Jian was judicious, with an excellent grasp on how to conduct himself socially.

Shen Qiao suddenly realized something. "Before, you said that meeting with Puliuru Jian would bring great benefits," he said. "Is this what you meant? Did you expect Puliuru Jian to give me the *Zhuyang Strategy* scroll?"

Yan Wushi smiled. "I'm not a god or an immortal. How could I possibly predict the future? But the scroll was with Puliuru Jian, and I knew that if he wanted your help, he'd at least have to show you his sincerity. The full recovery of your martial arts appears imminent, but since the entire *Zhuyang Strategy* shares the same source, as long as any part is missing, it'll ultimately remain flawed. Perhaps you might have missed some key point, which isn't conductive to cultivation. Even if this incident hadn't occurred, I'd have gotten the scroll from him anyway and given it to you."

Shen Qiao couldn't help but send him a glance.

If Yan Wushi wanted to be good to someone, he wouldn't just be "good," he'd be exceptional. He would offer them the entire world's treasures and openly tell them, "I'm willing to do this for you."

Noticing Shen Qiao's gaze, Yan Wushi smiled slightly and said, "A-Qiao, there's no need to be so moved. I've already told you about this volume's contents. Puliuru Jian's gesture now is just an extra touch, like adding flowers to brocade. Next time, I'll give you something even better, and you can save being moved until then!"

Shen Qiao truly wanted to collapse with laughter at this man's shamelessness. He quickly withdrew his gaze, afraid that Yan Wushi would come up with something even more horrifying to say.

On the seventh of April, as agreed upon, Yan Wushi, Shen Qiao, and Bian Yanmei arrived at the Duke of Sui's residence.

Puliuru Jian had already submitted a request to allow Lady Dugu to visit their daughter in the palace, and it was indeed rejected by the emperor. Puliuru Jian then wrote another memorial stating that though Lady Dugu was unable to visit the empress in the palace, the love between mother and child was strong, so she hoped to gift the empress some food and letters from home as a token of a mother's longing for her children.

Perhaps the emperor did not wish to make his disagreement with the Duke of Sui public, for this time, he agreed.

Puliuru Jian picked two intelligent and capable maids, then made preparations for them to accompany Shen Qiao and Bian Yanmei into the palace.

When Shen Qiao saw the attire he was to wear to enter the palace, his expression darkened. Turning to Yan Wushi, he asked, "Why didn't you tell me you wanted me to dress up as a woman?"

Yan Wushi looked surprised and asked him his own question in return. "How could an outsider casually enter the palace, let alone the imperial harem? I thought that you already knew!"

Shen Qiao was at a loss for words.

He felt that Yan Wushi was probably still holding a grudge for the time Shen Qiao had dressed *him* up as a woman, but Yan Wushi's reasoning sounded so insincerely dignified that he couldn't refute him.

"It's all right," Bian Yanmei consoled him. "I will also be wearing women's clothes."

They were already at this point. Since Shen Qiao had agreed to help, he naturally couldn't renege. He could only accept his fate and let the maids change his clothes, then start daubing makeup on his face.

The maid who put on his makeup was not an ordinary maid but a disciple of Huanyue Sect brought here by Bian Yanmei. She had some insights into disguising oneself and changing one's appearance.

Previously, Shen Qiao had thought that disguise techniques were all like the kind Huo Xijing used, where one would directly cover their face with a human-skin mask, then use some secret technique after, but Bian Yanmei told him that this was not the case.

"Huo Xijing's face-changing technique requires the use of countless medicinal herbs to first process the human skin, then more secret techniques to refine it further," he explained. "It would take over half a year to complete. First, we don't have the time, and second, I don't know what kind of secret technique it is. Third, the mask must fit the wearer well—the contours have to match. There are many requirements. If there is even a slight discrepancy, others will easily notice the flaws, and it won't look convincing at all. So, it's better to use other methods."

The maid smiled as she painted Shen Qiao's face. "This Daoist master is already so handsome and beautiful. With just some slight embellishments, he will make a beauty capable of toppling nations!"

Shen Qiao was baffled. "Unlike women, men have a protrusion in their throats, which can't be concealed no matter how high the collar is. Anyone paying attention would see through it at once. How will you hide it?"

The maid smiled brightly. "Just leave things to us, Daoist Master!"

Beside him, Bian Yanmei gave them a reminder. "Don't make Daoist Master Shen too beautiful. It'll be terrible if the emperor takes a liking to him."

Shen Qiao was speechless.

The maid sputtered a laugh. "There's nothing we can do about that," she said. "No matter how hard we try, we can't cover up the Daoist Master's bearing itself. At best, we can only make his face look a bit more ordinary!"

After finishing up their faces and necks, they brought two sets of maids' attire from the Duke of Sui's residence for Shen Qiao and Bian Yanmei to change into.

The preparations were all finished, but there was an uneasiness to Shen Qiao's expression. Bian Yanmei, on the other hand, was confident and unperturbed. He even playfully imitated the way maids covered their mouths, thumb and middle finger touching in an orchid gesture as he giggled. "Shen-jiejie, look, aren't I pretty?"

The corner of Shen Qiao's mouth twitched.

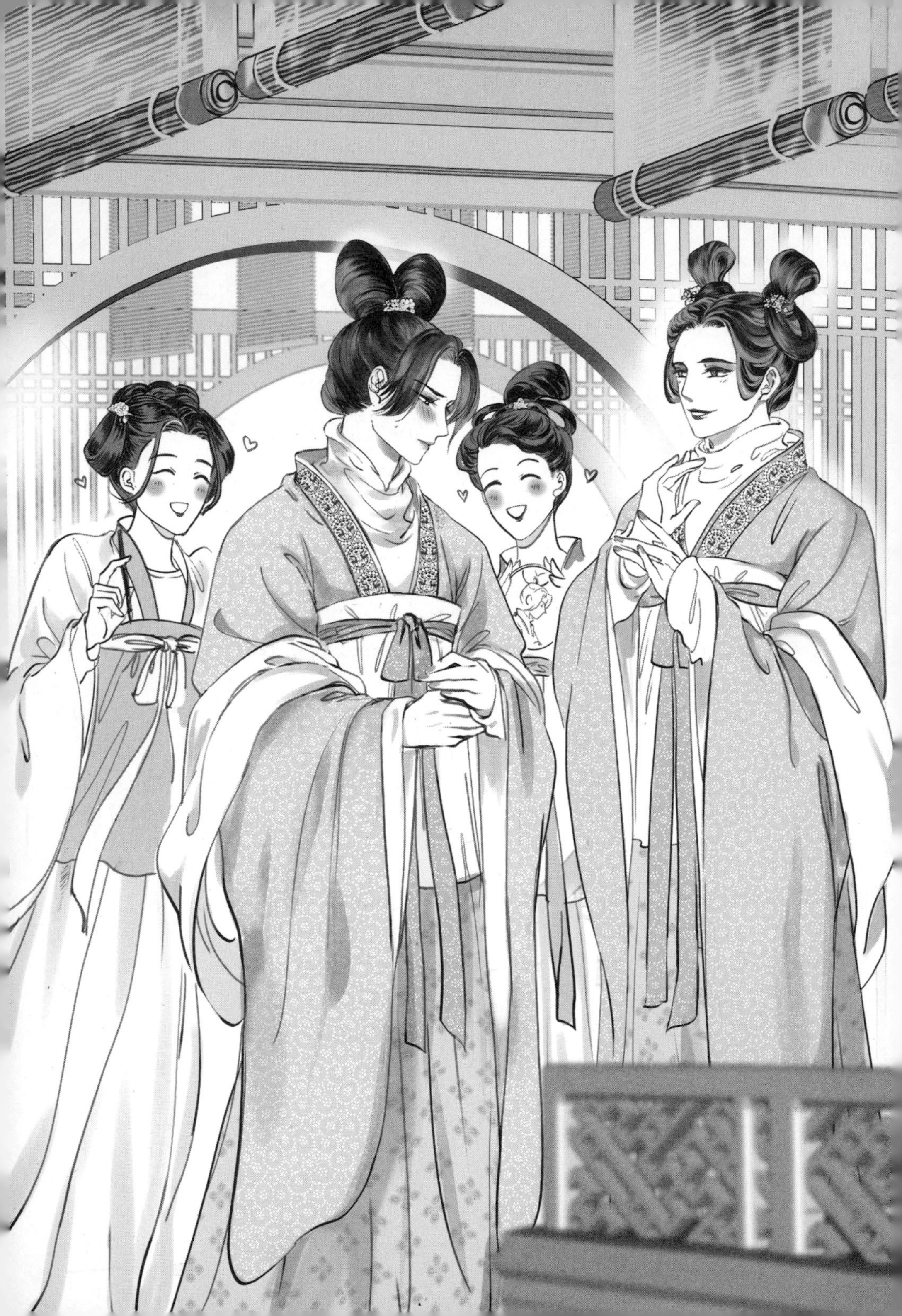

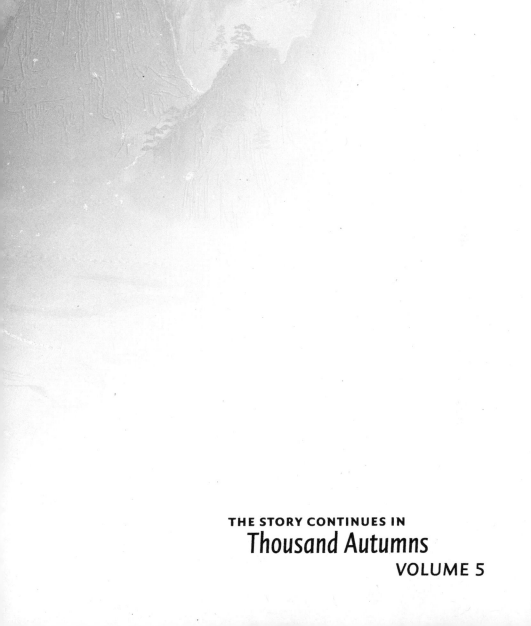

THE STORY CONTINUES IN
Thousand Autumns
VOLUME 5

Characters
and
Associated
Factions

CHARACTERS
AND ASSOCIATED FACTIONS

The identity of certain characters may be a spoiler; use this guide with caution on your first read of the novel.

A sizable portion of *Thousand Autumns'* cast are based on real-life historical figures, though they have all been fictionalized to some degree. The names of those with real-life counterparts but without an entry of their own are indicated by **bold text**.

MAIN CHARACTERS

Shen Qiao (沈峤)

TITLE(S): Sect Leader of Xuandu's Violet Palace

CHARACTER BASIS: Fictional

As the chosen successor of the legendary Qi Fengge, and the reclusive leader of the land's foremost Daoist sect, Shen Qiao seemed to have it all: first-rate talent, a world-class master, a loving family, and a kind heart devoted completely to the tenets of Daoism. But a duel atop Banbu Peak changed everything for him.

The *qiao* in Shen Qiao's name is a rare character, referring to a tall and precipitous mountain peak. He was named after a verse in "Ode to Zhou: On Tour" (周颂·时迈), recorded in the *Shijing*—a song written in commemoration of King Wu of Zhou. The verse extols how he traveled the land after vanquishing the Shang in 11th century B.C.E. He offered sacrifices to the many gods, including those in the rivers and tallest mountains.

Yan Wushi (晏无师)

TITLE(S): Huanyue Sect Leader, Junior Preceptor of the Crown
Prince of Zhou (former), Demon Lord

CHARACTER BASIS: Fictional

The egotistical and capricious leader of the demonic Huanyue Sect.
A terrifying martial artist who some sources claim was on par with
Qi Fengge, Yan Wushi is also ambitious, shrewd, and above all,
a committed misanthrope. In Yan Wushi's eyes, there are no good
people, only evil people disguised as good people. As far as he's
concerned, anyone who thinks otherwise is either a liar or a fool.

Or at least, so he thought.

Yan Wushi's personal name means "has no master." The *ling* in his
old name, Xie Ling (谢岭), means "mountain range."

XUANDU MOUNTAIN (玄都山)

The world's foremost Daoist sect, located on the border intersection
of Northern Qi, Southern Chen, and Northern Zhou. Sect Leader
Qi Fengge built their legendary reputation, but despite this prestige
and influence, he chose to seclude Xuandu Mountain away from
the world, closing its gates and withdrawing from all outside affairs.
After his death, his mantle passed to Shen Qiao, who held fast to
his shizun's isolationist stance. When Shen Qiao fell during his duel
with Kunye, Yu Ai took the reins as Acting Sect Leader.

Officially, Xuandu Mountain is a location—the actual sect is
called Xuandu's Violet Palace (玄都紫府, *xuandu zifu*), named after
Taishang Laojun's abode on the mythical Daluo Mountain. *Xuandu*
("black city") refers to Daluo Mountain's immortal realm, while *zifu*
("violet residence") refers to the Bajing Palace supposedly located
within it. The sect leader of Xuandu's Violet Palace is known as

the *zhangjiao* (掌教), a term more specific to Daoism compared to *zongzhu* (宗主), which is how Yan Wushi is addressed in Chinese.

Qi Fengge (祁凤阁)

TITLE(S): Sect Leader of Xuandu's Violet Palace, World's Number One Martial Expert

CHARACTER BASIS: Fictional

The number one martial artist in all the land before his passing and Shen Qiao's master, Qi Fengge is held in high esteem by the entire world to this day. Two decades ago, he won a duel with Hulugu of the Göktürks. In lieu of a reward for his victory, he made Hulugu swear to stay out of the Central Plains for the next twenty years. He had five disciples in total: Tan Yuanchun, Shen Qiao, Yu Ai, Yuan Ying, and Gu Hengbo.

Yu Ai (郁蔼)

TITLE(S): Acting Sect Leader of Xuandu's Violet Palace

CHARACTER BASIS: Fictional

One of Qi Fengge's disciples and Shen Qiao's shidi, though two years older than him. Originally the closest to Shen Qiao out of all his martial siblings, he collaborated with Kunye to poison Shen Qiao, which led to Shen Qiao's crushing defeat on Banbu Peak. Afterward, he took over leadership of Xuandu Mountain and involved the sect in the ongoing power struggles of the current regimes, cooperating with Göktürk Khaganate. One of the five martial artists who participated in the group ambush on Yan Wushi.

Gu Hengbo (顾横波)

CHARACTER BASIS: Fictional

The youngest of Qi Fengge's disciples, though she was primarily taught by Shen Qiao. Forthright, with a strong sense of justice.

HUANYUE SECT (浣月宗)

One of the three demonic sects, established and led by Yan Wushi after the collapse of Riyue Sect. Though wealthy and influential, they tend to keep a low profile and are the key supporters of Yuwen Yong's rule in Zhou. Like the rest of the demonic sects, their final goal is to reunite the sects of the demonic discipline. After Yuwen Yong's death, they have been driven into hiding by Yuwen Yun.

Yu Shengyan (玉生烟)

CHARACTER BASIS: Fictional

Yan Wushi's youngest disciple. A quick-witted and charismatic young man.

Bian Yanmei (边沿梅)

CHARACTER BASIS: Fictional

Yan Wushi's first disciple. Shrewd and insightful, he's a key to Huanyue Sect's continued survival under Yuwen Yun's regime.

HEHUAN SECT (合欢宗)

One of three demonic sects born from Riyue Sect's fall, Hehuan Sect specializes in charm techniques and parasitic cultivation, where the practitioner drains qi and energy from their sexual partners to strengthen their own martial arts. Hehuan Sect was established and led by Yuan Xiuxiu, but her lover Sang Jingxing is known to hold great power within it as well. Once highly influential in Qi, after Qi's downfall and Yuwen Yun's ascension, they gained his favor and great power in Zhou, replacing Huanyue Sect.

Bai Rong (白茸)

CHARACTER BASIS: Fictional

One of Hehuan Sect's most prominent disciples under Sang Jingxing. Cunning and devious. Though deeply fond of Shen Qiao, she has her own goals for herself.

Yuan Xiuxiu (元秀秀)

TITLE(S): Hehuan Sect Leader

CHARACTER BASIS: Fictional

The leader of Hehuan Sect, rumored to have gotten her position due to her relationship with Sang Jingxing. Despite this, they do not get along, but constantly seek to undermine—even kill—each other.

Sang Jingxing (桑景行)

CHARACTER BASIS: Fictional

An exalted elder in Hehuan Sect, Cui Youwang's disciple, and Yuan Xiuxiu's supposed lover. A twisted martial artist with a horrific reputation, as well as an appetite for beauties and parasitic cultivation. He was grievously injured by Shen Qiao when the latter destroyed his own martial arts to take him down and loathes both Shen Qiao and Yan Wushi.

Xiao Se (萧瑟)

CHARACTER BASIS: Fictional

Yuan Xiuxiu's disciple, but seeks to earn favor with Sang Jingxing. Specializes in fighting with fans.

Yan Shou (阎狩)

TITLE(S): The Buddha with the Blood-Soaked Hand
CHARACTER BASIS: Fictional
An elder in Hehuan Sect. Keeps his head shaved like a monk's but has a reputation for murder. Shen Qiao chopped off one of his arms in a failed bid to kill him.

Baoyun (宝云)

Character Basis: Fictional
An elder in Hehuan Sect, who enjoys deceiving women by pretending to be a monk.

FAJING SECT (法镜宗)

One of the three demonic sects born from Riyue Sect's fall. Unable to compete with the other two branches, the sect now primarily operates within Tuyuhun, though they still hold ambitions for the Central Plains. Their sect leader is Guang Lingsan.

Guang Lingsan (广陵散)

TITLE(S): Fajing Sect Leader
CHARACTER BASIS: Fictional
The leader of Fajing Sect, who moved their operations to Tuyuhun ten years ago due to overwhelming pressure from Huanyue Sect and Hehuan Sect. A master of the zither who uses music to harm and confound his opponents. To boost his sect, he participated in the group ambush on Yan Wushi.

RIYUE SECT (日月宗)

The origin of the "Noble Discipline" (demonic discipline to outsiders). Once located in Fenglin Province, it vanished after splintering into three: Huanyue Sect, Hehuan Sect, and Fajing Sect. Their last sect leader was Sang Jingxing's master, Cui Youwang.

BIXIA SECT (碧霞宗)

A Daoist sect located on Zhunan Peak of Mount Tai, it narrowly escaped destruction with the help of Shen Qiao. The current sect leader is Zhao Chiying.

Zhao Chiying (赵持盈)

CHARACTER BASIS: Fictional

TITLE(S): Bixia Sect Leader

The current leader of Bixia Sect and known to be highly talented. After Bixia Sect's crisis, of which only six of their disciples survived, she's been greatly worried about their sect's future.

Yue Kunchi (岳昆池)

CHARACTER BASIS: Fictional

TITLE(S): Bixia Sect Acting Sect Leader

The current acting leader of Bixia Sect and Zhao Chiying's shixiong. A mediocre martial artist who puts all his energies into administration.

Fan Yuanbai (范元白)

CHARACTER BASIS: Fictional

Yue Kunchi's disciple who survived the massacre at Bixia Sect. Greatly admires Shen Qiao.

Zhou Yexue (周夜雪)

CHARACTER BASIS: Fictional

Another surviving disciple of Yue Kunchi's. She also deeply reveres Shen Qiao, seeing him as an older brother figure.

Shiwu (十五)

CHARACTER BASIS: Fictional

Shen Qiao's first disciple who he accepted after Shiwu's master's death. Sweet and gentle.

CHUNYANG MONASTERY (纯阳观)

The powerful Daoist sect led by Yi Pichen, one of the top ten martial artists in the world. Their sect shares close ties with Bixia Sect.

Yi Pichen (易辟尘)

TITLE(S): Abbot of Chunyang Monastery

CHARACTER BASIS: Fictional

The leader of Chunyang Monastery. Like the rest of the jianghu, he considers Hehuan Sect and the Buddhist discipline's rising influence a great concern.

Li Qingyu (李青鱼)

TITLE(S): One of the Twin Jades of Qingcheng

CHARACTER BASIS: Fictional

Yi Pichen's beloved final disciple, a rising star who shook the world with his various impressive feats. A brilliant swordsman but a poor conversationalist.

LINCHUAN ACADEMY (临川学宫)

The leading Confucian sect and the main force backing the Emperor of Chen. Their leader is Academy Master Ruyan Kehui, one of the world's top ten martial artists.

Ruyan Kehui (汝鄢克惠)

TITLE(S): Linchuan Academy Master

CHARACTER BASIS: Fictional

The leader of Linchuan Academy. A powerful and cultured martial artist who ranks in the top ten, he believes wholeheartedly in the superiority of Confucianism and the Han's right to rule, and therefore sought to undermine Yuwen Yong's Zhou Dynasty. Was part of the plot to ambush Yan Wushi.

Zhan Ziqian (展子虔)

CHARACTER BASIS: Historical

One of Ruyan Kehui's disciples and a talented painter. He met and began admiring Shen Qiao at the earlier birthday banquet.

LIULI PALACE (琉璃宫)

A famous but reclusive sect located on the isolated island of Fangzhang Province. Their members are not skilled martial artists but possess extraordinary knowledge of the jianghu and uncanny powers of observation. They produce the official rankings for the jianghu, including the highly revered "World's Top Ten Martial Artists."

Yuan Zixiao (袁紫霄)

TITLE(S): Young Palace Mistress of Liuli Palace
CHARACTER BASIS: Fictional
The future leader of Liuli Palace, responsible for the current iteration of the "World's Top Ten Martial Artists."

LIUHE GUILD (六合帮)

One of the largest martial arts organizations in the Central Plains, whose reach extends both north and south of the Yangtze River. Led by guild leader Dou Yanshan and deputy leader Yun Fuyi, they deal in all kinds of business, from escort missions to spy work, and they were a key player in the group ambush on Yan Wushi. However, friction has been growing between the two heads.

QI DYNASTY (齐朝)

Also known as Northern Qi, the country occupies the land northeast of the Yangtze River and was founded by **Gao Huan**. Originally warlike and powerful, the reign of Gao Huan's successors, especially the incompetent and frivolous **Gao Wei**, has put the kingdom into a steady decline. Its capital was Yecheng (located at the south of modern-day Hebei). The nation was eventually annexed by Zhou under **Yuwen Yong**, who also executed Gao Wei.

ZHOU DYNASTY (周朝)

The country that occupies the region northwest of the Yangtze, also known as Northern Zhou. Its capital is Chang'an (now known as Xi'an). Though it was established by **Yuwen Tai** before his death, for years his nephew **Yuwen Hu** held power as regent, killing off Yuwen Tai's puppet-ruler sons whenever he perceived them as a threat. The third such son, **Yuwen Yong**, managed to feign obedience for years before finally ambushing and killing Yuwen Hu, officially seizing back his imperial authority.

After Yuwen Yong's death, his son **Yuwen Yun** has taken the throne. With his unstable, mistrustful personality and deep grudge toward his father, his influence has rapidly driven Zhou into a decline.

Xueting (雪庭)

TITLE(S): State Preceptor of Zhou (former)

CHARACTER BASIS: Fictional

One of the top ten martial artists of the world and a former member of the Buddhist Tiantai Sect. Originally heavily favored by Yuwen Hu, who honored Buddhism, the late emperor Yuwen Yong's oppressive anti-Buddhist stance led to him taking drastic measures to eliminate him and his supporter Yan Wushi. One of the participants in the group ambush.

With Yuwen Yun's ascension, he and Buddhism have regained their previous glory in Zhou.

Puliuru Jian (普六茹坚)

TITLE(S): Duke of Sui

CHARACTER BASIS: Historical

A learned, high-ranking official of Zhou whom Shen Qiao met at an earlier birthday banquet. He assists Shen Qiao in rescuing Yuwen Song and Dou Yan from Yuwen Yun.

Chen Gong (陈恭)

TITLE(S): Duke of Zhao

CHARACTER BASIS: Fictional

Once a homeless youth who Shen Qiao met in Funing County, he was later bestowed the title of county duke by Gao Wei, then grand duke by Yuwen Yun. Opportunistic and possesses the outstanding ability to remember everything he hears and reads.

Yuwen Song (宇文诵)

CHARACTER BASIS: Fictional

The youngest son of Yuwen Xian. After killing his father Yuwen Xian in a plot, Yuwen Yun seeks to eliminate him as well.

Dou Yan (窦言)

CHARACTER BASIS: Historical

The young daughter of the noble Dou family, and Yuwen Yong's niece. Ran away from home after witnessing his murder by Yuwen Yun and is being persecuted by him for it.

CHEN DYNASTY (陈朝)

The country south of the Yangtze River, founded by **Chen Baxian**, also called Southern Chen. Unlike Qi and Zhou where most of the upper class are of Xianbei descent, the Chen Dynasty is dominated by the Han. Its capital is Jiankang (modern-day Nanjing), and the current ruler is Emperor **Chen Xu**.

GÖKTÜRK KHAGANATE (突厥)

A powerful Turkic empire north of the Great Wall, led by **Taspar Khagan**. Their people have been at odds with the nations of the Central Plains for years—relations between them are uneasy and tinged with hostility.

Hulugu (狐鹿估)

CHARACTER BASIS: Fictional

Once the most powerful martial artist of the Göktürk Khaganate, he was narrowly defeated by Qi Fengge twenty years ago. Qi Fengge then made him swear not to set foot in the Central Plains.

Duan Wenyang (段文鸯)

CHARACTER BASIS: Fictional

Hulugu's disciple and Kunye's shixiong, a shrewd and ambitious whip user. An active agent in spreading the Khaganate's influence after his master's death, he's one of the five martial artists who participated in the group ambush on Yan Wushi.

OTHER CHARACTERS

Characters who aren't associated with a particular faction, regardless of where they live.

Tao Hongjing (陶弘景)

CHARACTER BASIS: Historical

The legendary creator of the *Zhuyang Strategy*. Before his death, he was known as a great genius and the one true master of martial arts for his success in marrying the principles of all three schools of thought.

PRONUNCIATION GUIDE

Mandarin Chinese is the official state language of mainland China, and pinyin is the official system of romanization in which it is written. As Mandarin is a tonal language, pinyin uses diacritical marks (e.g., ā, á, ǎ, à) to indicate these tonal inflections. Most words use one of four tones, though some (as in "de" in the title below) are a neutral tone. Furthermore, regional variance can change the way native Chinese speakers pronounce the same word. For those reasons and more, please consider the guide below a simplified introduction to pronunciation of select character names and sounds from the world of *Thousand Autumns*.

More resources are available at sevenseasdanmei.com

NOTE ON SPELLING: Romanized Mandarin Chinese words with identical spelling in pinyin—and even pronunciation—may well have different meanings. These words are more easily differentiated in written Chinese, which uses characters.

CHARACTER NAMES

Qiān Qiū

Qiān, approximately **chee-yen**, but as a single syllable.
Qiu, as in **choke**.

Shěn Qiáo

Shěn, as in the second half of ma**son**.
Qiáo, as in **chow**.

Yàn Wúshī

Yàn, as in **yen**.

Wú, as in **oo**.

Shī, a little like **shh**. The **-i** is more of a buzzed continuation for the **sh-** consonant than any equivalent English vowel. See the General Consonants section for more information on the **sh-** consonant.

Qí Fènggé

Qí, as in **chee**se.

Fèng, a little like **fun**, but with the nasal **ng** one would find in so**ng**.

Gé, a little like **guh**.

Bái Róng

Bái, as in **bye**.

Róng, a little like the last part of chape**rone**. See the General Consonants section for more information on the **r-** consonant.

GENERAL CONSONANTS

Some Mandarin Chinese consonants sound very similar, such as z/c/s and zh/ch/sh. Audio samples will provide the best opportunity to learn the difference between them.

X: somewhere between the **sh** in **sh**eep and **s** in **s**ilk

Q: a very aspirated **ch** as in **ch**eat

C: **ts** as in pan**ts**

Z: **ds** as in su**ds**

S: **s** as in **s**ilk

CH: very close to **c-**, but with the tongue rolled up to touch the palate.

ZH: very close to **z-**, but with the tongue rolled up to touch the palate.

SH: very close to **s-**, but with the tongue rolled up to touch the palate. Because of this, it can give the impression of **shh**, but it's a different sound compared to the **x-** consonant.

G: hard **g** as in **g**raphic

R: partway between the **r** in **r**un and the **s** in measure. The tongue should be rolled up to touch the palate.

GENERAL VOWELS

The pronunciation of a vowel may depend on its preceding consonant. For example, the "i" in "shi" is distinct from the "i" in "di," where the first is a buzzed continuation for the sh- consonant and the latter a long e sound. Compound vowels are often—though not always—pronounced as conjoined but separate vowels. You'll find a few of the trickier compounds below.

IU: as in **yo**-yo

IE: **ye** as in **ye**s

UO: **war** as in **war**m

APPENDIX

Historical Primer

HISTORICAL PERIOD

While not required reading, this section and those after are intended to offer further context for the historical setting of this story, and give insights into the many concepts and terms utilized throughout the novel. Their goal is to provide a starting point for learning more about the rich culture from which these stories were written.

The following segment is intended to give a brief introduction to the major historical events featured in *Thousand Autumns*.

THE JIN DYNASTY

In 266 C.E., at the close of the tumultuous **Three Kingdoms** era, the central plains were finally united under Sima Yan, founder of the **Jin Dynasty**, also known as **Western Jin**. But when Sima Yan passed away in 290 C.E., his son and heir was deemed unfit to rule. Conflict broke out among members of the imperial court who vied for the throne. This became known as the **War of the Eight Princes**, after the eight members of the Sima royal family who were the principal players.

UPRISING OF THE FIVE BARBARIANS AND THE SIXTEEN KINGDOMS PERIOD

Over a period of fifteen years, the repeated clashes and civil wars greatly weakened the Western Jin Dynasty. During this time, most of the royal princes relied on non-Han nomadic minorities to fight for them, in particular Xiongnu and the **Xianbei**. The Han lumped them together with other foreign ethnicities like the Jie, Di, and Qiang, collectively designating them the **Hu**, sometimes translated as "barbarians." As the Jin Dynasty's control over these minority tribes slipped, instances of rebellion combined with local unrest to usher in the **Uprising of the Five Barbarians** in 304 C.E.

Although it began as a revolt spearheaded by the Hu, the Uprising of the Five Barbarians soon led to the complete collapse of Western Jin as its Han upper class fled south of the Yangtze River. This was the mass **southward migration of the Jin** referenced in *Thousand Autumns*. When the old capital of Chang'an fell, the new emperor reestablished the seat of government in Jiankang, heralding the start of the **Eastern Jin Dynasty**. At the same time, north of the Yangtze River, the Di, Qiang, Xiongnu, and Jie each established their own dynastic kingdoms. Thus began a time of great upheaval known as the **Sixteen Kingdoms** period.

During the turmoil of the Sixteen Kingdoms, regimes formed and collapsed in the blink of an eye as they warred with each other and the Eastern Jin. The strife finally abated when the **Northern Wei Dynasty** conquered the other northern kingdoms in 439 C.E. and unified the lands north of the Yangtze. Meanwhile in the south, Liu Yu usurped the emperor of the Eastern Jin Dynasty and founded the **Liu Song Dynasty**. This marked the beginning of the **Northern-Southern Dynasties** period, during which *Thousand Autumns* is set.

NORTHERN-SOUTHERN DYNASTIES

For a period of almost ninety years, Northern Wei held strong. The first half of their reign was focused on expansion, but when Tuoba Hong rose to power in 471 C.E., he championed the dominance of **Buddhism** and Han culture, going so far as to ban Xianbei clothing from the court and assigning one-character family names to Xianbei nobility (Tuoba Hong himself changed his family name to Yuan).

South of the Yangtze, the regime changed hands three times—from Liu Song to **Southern Qi** to **Liang**, before the **Chen Dynasty** that ruled during *Thousand Autumns* was finally established in 557 C.E.

In the north, Northern Wei held strong for almost ninety years. While the first half of their reign was focused on expansion, when Tuoba Hong rose to power in 471 C.E., he championed the dominance of Buddhism and Han culture, going so far as to ban Xianbei clothing from the court and assigning one-character family names to Xianbei nobility.

A rift slowly developed in Northern Wei between the increasingly Han-acculturated aristocracy and their own armies who adhered more to the traditional, nomadic lifestyle. A series of rebellions escalated into all-out revolt, and by 535 C.E. the kingdom had split in half. **Western Wei** was ruled by Yuwen Tai, and **Eastern Wei** by Gao Huan. In the space of a generation, they would depose the last of the old leadership and become the kingdoms of **Northern Zhou** and **Northern Qi**. In the Zhou Dynasty to the west, rule favored the Han-acculturated nobles, while in the Qi Dynasty to the east, the traditional tribes came into power.

Qi's military superiority over both Zhou and Chen began to diminish due to corruption and incompetence in the ruling class, and particularly that of the emperor's grandson, **Gao Wei**. After a politically turbulent period of regency in Zhou, **Yuwen Yong** took power in 572 C.E. and made a point of bolstering state administration and military affairs.

By 575 C.E., where *Thousand Autumns* begins, a new maelstrom is already brewing...

THE THREE SCHOOLS OF THOUGHT

This section hopes to provide some basic context as to the major schools of thought that inform the background of *Thousand Autumns*, so that readers may explore the topic in more depth on their own. Note that with their long period of coexistence, the schools have all influenced each other deeply, and their ideals have become rooted in Chinese culture itself, even among non-practitioners.

Daoism (道)

Daoism revolves around the concept of **Dao**, or "Ways": the courses things follow as they undergo change. Though there are many Dao a human can choose from, there is one primordial "great Dao" (大道), the source of the universe and origin of all things—the void of infinite potential. The course all things in the universe follow is the "heavenly Dao" (天道), the natural order.

According to Daoist principles, by imposing constraints and artifice, humanity strays from the primordial Dao and stagnates.

In particular, the rigid social roles enforced by society are seen as unnatural and an example of degradation. For humans to flourish, they must revert themselves, disengaging from these tendencies in order to return to the primordial Dao. This is sometimes known as "becoming one with heaven" (天人合一). The method of disengaging is called **wuwei** (无为), sometimes translated as inaction or non-interference.

Expanding on this idea, Daoism has the concepts of **Xiantian** (先天, "Early Heaven") and **Houtian** (后天, "Later Heaven"). The prenatal Xiantian state is closer to the primordial Dao, and thus is both purer than and superior to the postnatal Houtian state. The Houtian state is created at birth, along with the **conscious mind** that thinks and perceives and which in turn suppresses the primordial mind. This is what gives rise to sources of suffering: anger, worry, doubt, desire, and fatigue.

The goal of *wuwei* is to reverse the changes brought on by Houtian and return to the primordial state of Xiantian. To conflict with nature is to stray from it, and to intervene in the natural order—as society does—is to perpetuate degradation. Disengaging from all of these influences requires rejecting social conventions and detaching from the mundane world altogether, so seclusion and asceticism are common practices. Emptying oneself of all emotion and freeing oneself from all artifice is the only way to achieve union with heaven and surpass life and death itself.

When it came to politics, Daoism was often seen as a justification for small, *laissez-faire* governments—in fact, *laissez-faire* is one of the possible translations of *wuwei*—supporting low taxes and low intervention. The anti-authority implications of its philosophies were not lost on its followers, nor on their rulers. As a result, it wasn't uncommon for Daoism to struggle to find its footing politically, despite its cultural pervasiveness.

Buddhism (佛/释)

Founded by Gautama Buddha in India, Buddhism only arrived in China during the Han Dynasty, well after Confucianism and Daoism. Despite early pushback and social friction, its parallels with Daoism eventually helped it gain widespread influence.

Buddhism is rooted in the concepts of reincarnation, karma, and **Maya**—the illusion of existence. Attachment to Maya keeps living beings rooted in the cycle of reincarnation, where they are beholden to the principle of karma that determines their future rebirths. Buddha claimed that this eternal cycle is the root of all suffering and that the only escape is through achieving **Nirvana**, or enlightenment. To achieve enlightenment is to fully accept that all things within existence are false. It then follows that any emotions, attachments, or thoughts that one develops while interacting with and perceiving the world are equally false. This philosophy extends to the attitude toward karma—the ideal Buddhist does good deeds and kind acts without any expectation of reward or satisfaction, material or otherwise.

Despite these selfless ideals, it also wasn't uncommon to see Buddhist temples amass land, authority, and wealth through donations, worship, and the offerings of those seeking better futures or rebirths. Combined with the men who'd leave their homes to join these temples as monks, this sometimes made the relationship between Buddhism and rulers a tricky, precarious one.

Confucianism (儒)

Unlike Buddhism and Daoism, Confucianism focuses on the moral betterment of the individual as the foundation for the ideal society. The founder Confucius envisioned a rigidly hierarchical system wherein the lower ranks have the moral duty to obey the higher ranks, and those in superior positions likewise have the moral responsibility to care for their subordinates. This social contract is applied to everything from the family unit to the nation itself—the emperor is the father to his people, and they in turn must show him absolute obedience.

To foster such a society, Confucians extol the **five constant virtues** (五常): **benevolence** (仁), **righteousness** (义), **propriety** (礼), **wisdom** (智), and **integrity** (信). Paragons who embody all five virtues are called **junzi** (君子), sometimes translated as "gentlemen" or "noble men," while their direct opposites are *xiaoren*, literally "petty people," and sometimes translated as "scoundrels."

Throughout most of history, mainstream Confucians believed in the goodness inherent in humanity, that people can better themselves through education and learning from their superiors. The ideal ruler must be the ultimate *junzi* himself and lead by example, thereby uplifting all of society. In the same vein, Confucius expected officials to be virtuous parental figures, held to a higher moral standard than ordinary citizens.

Due to its emphasis on social order, Confucianism was easily the most influential and politically favored of the three schools throughout history. Its social contract was so absolute that even dynastic takeovers had to be performed in a way that did not "break it." Usurpers who acted otherwise ran the risk of being seen as illegitimate in the eyes of the people. Famously, the old emperor had to offer the new emperor his position multiple times, with the new ruler declining three times (三让) before finally accepting.

Bonus: Legalism (法)

Though not regarded as one of the "big three" and although it received far less overt support, Legalism was enormously influential for one key reason: it served as the foundation for the entire Chinese government tradition for two thousand years, regardless of dynasty.

Unlike the three schools, which are each in pursuit of an ideal, Legalism is entirely utilitarian and concerned only with efficacy. This is reflected in its Chinese name, the "house of methods." Core to its beliefs is the idea that human nature is selfish and evil, and so people must be motivated through reward and punishment. Morality is inconsequential, the ends justify the means, and the most effective administration must minimize corruption by restricting its subordinate administrators as much as possible.

It was with these tenets that the first unified Chinese empire, the Qin Dynasty, dismantled the existing feudalist system and established in its place a centralized government overseen by the emperor. After the Qin's collapse—brought about in part due to how harsh a fully Legalist regime was on the people—the succeeding Han Dynasty under Emperor Wu of Han made sure to suppress Legalism as a philosophy. However, they inherited the entire Legalist government structure mostly unchanged, though their policies were softened by a push toward Confucianism. This trend of furtively repackaging Legalist tendencies within the leading school of thought (usually Confucianism) continued almost uninterrupted for this period of two thousand years, and rulers continued to study Legalist texts like the *Han Feizi*.

OTHER IMPORTANT CONCEPTS

DAOIST CULTIVATION, THE ZHUYANG STRATEGY, AND THE POWER OF FIVE

In real life, the scholar Tao Hongjing compiled the famous, three-volume *Concealed Instructions for the Ascent to Perfection* (登真隱訣, translated in the novel as "Dengzhen Concealed Instructions"). For *Thousand Autumns*, Meng Xi Shi invented an extra associated manual, called the *Strategy of Vermillion Yang* (朱陽策, translated in the novel as "Zhuyang Strategy") after the real-life Monastery of Vermillion Yang on Mount Mao where Tao Hongjing secluded himself.

The *Zhuyang Strategy* draws heavily from classical concepts of Daoist cultivation and pulls together many ideas from Chinese culture. Primarily, they are based on the *Wuqi Chaoyuan* (五气朝元, roughly "Returning the Five Qi to the Origin"). The first lines of each of the *Zhuyang Strategy*'s five volumes correspond exactly to the *Wuqi Chaoyuan*'s five principles:

1. The heart conceals the mind; Houtian begets the conscious mind, while Xiantian begets propriety; once emptied of sorrow, the mind is settled, and the Fire from the Crimson Emperor of the South returns to the Origin.
2. The liver conceals the soul; Houtian begets the lost soul, while Xiantian begets benevolence; once emptied of joy, the soul is settled, and the Wood from the Azure Emperor of the East returns to the Origin.

3. The pancreas conceals the thought; Houtian begets the deluded thought, while Xiantian begets integrity; once emptied of desire, the thought is settled, and the Earth from the Yellow Emperor of the Center returns to the Origin.

4. The lungs conceal the anima; Houtian begets the corrupted anima, while Xiantian begets righteousness; once emptied of rage, the anima is settled, and the Metal from the White Emperor of the West returns to the Origin.

5. The kidneys conceal the essence; Houtian begets the clouded essence, while Xiantian begets wisdom; once emptied of cheer, the will is settled, and the Water from the Black Emperor of the North returns to the Origin.

The traditional Chinese worldview includes the **Five Phases**, the **Deities of the Five Regions** (also known as the **Five Emperors**), the five constant virtues, the **Five Spirits**, and the five major internal organs. The *Wuqi Chaoyuan* links all these ideas together, unifying them into a doctrine that explains how one can achieve immortal status or "godhood." For those who are interested, we provide here a brief introduction to several of these concepts in hopes that readers can further appreciate the world of *Thousand Autumns*.

THE FIVE PHASES

The **Wuxing** (五行), sometimes translated as Five Agents or Five Elements, are a cornerstone of Daoist philosophy. Unlike the Four Elements proposed by Aristotle, the Five Phases—**Metal** (金), **Wood** (木), **Water** (水), **Fire** (火), and **Earth** (土)—are seen as dynamic, interdependent forces. Each phase can give rise to another (生), or suppress another (克). As Daoism dictates that all entities are bound by the natural order, the Five Phases can be seen as an overarching rule set that governs all aspects of nature. Most things are regarded as corresponding to a certain phase, including but not limited to planets, seasons, cardinal directions, organs, colors, and types of qi.

FIVE EMPERORS, FIVE REGIONS, FIVE COLORS

In Daoism, the **Wufang Shangdi** (五方上帝), or High Emperors of the Five Regions, are the fivefold manifestation of the **Supreme Emperor of Heaven** (天皇大帝), or simply **Heaven** (天). As they correspond to the Five Phases, each emperor has an associated cardinal direction, as well as a color that informs his namesake.

FIVE SPIRITS, FIVE ORGANS

The traditional Chinese conception of the spirit divides it into five separate aspects: **mind** (神), **soul** (魂), **thought** (意), **anima** (魄), and **will** (志). These classifications may not be a perfect match with their western definitions. For example, the will—which arises from the **essence** (精)—is responsible for memory, as well as discernment and judgment. A strong will is generally associated with clear-mindedness. In another example, the anima governs instincts, impulses, and reflex reactions, and is said to dissipate on death, unlike the soul.

Each of the five aspects is said to reside in one of the five major internal organs—heart, liver, pancreas (includes the spleen), lungs, and kidneys, which in turn also correspond to the Five Phases. The *Wuqi Chaoyuan* claims that part of ascending to immortality is learning how to "return" the true qi of each aspect to one's Dantian, or "Origin."

THE FOUR OCCUPATIONS

The 士农工商 classification of citizens as *shi* (eventually **gentry scholars**), *nong* (**farmers**), *gong* (**artisans**), and *shang* (**merchants**), was a cornerstone of ancient Chinese social hierarchy strongly associated with both Confucianism and Legalism.

As the upper class and decision-makers, the *shi* naturally ranked the highest, followed by the peasant farmers who were valued as the backbone of the nation. Merchant businessmen were seen as agents of exploitation who profited from price fluctuations, so they were placed lowest.

In practice, these hierarchical rankings shaped cultural attitudes more than they dictated political clout. Even though merchants were looked down upon, the much-needed cash flow they provided made them far more influential than the artisan and farmer classes. This created a curious situation—merchants were both sought after and derided by the *shi* in charge of governance. In later dynasties some merchants went so far as to purchase positions within the imperial court, making them honorary *shi* and granting them legal protections.

Though the *shi* remained firmly at the top of the social hierarchy regardless of the period, the membership of the class changed over time. Originally, the *shi* were warrior aristocrats not unlike western knights, but they became obsolete when the Warring States period mobilized the common folk for warfare. With the rise of philosophy, the warriors slowly gave way to scholars. Later, during the harsh Legalist regime of the Qin Dynasty, the emperor began assigning administrative responsibilities to learned scholars who showed promise and merit. To weaken the authority of the noble class, he dismantled the existing feudalist system in favor of a centralized bureaucracy of dedicated officials.

Though the Qin's system of governance persisted well after the dynasty's collapse, the importance of family lines meant that prominent scholar-officials effectively became the new aristocracy. Their wealth and influence almost always guaranteed their descendants the resources to land their own positions within the imperial court. *Thousand Autumns* includes examples of powerful clans like the Su and the Xie; one talented ancestor could elevate their entire family for generations to come. It wasn't until the Tang Dynasty that a true merit-based system was introduced—the civil service exams—that would give capable commoners the chance to find their place in governance.

APPENDIX

Glossary

GLOSSARY

GENRES

DANMEI (耽美, "INDULGENCE IN BEAUTY"): A Chinese fiction genre focused on romanticized tales of love and attraction between men. It is analogous to the BL (boys' love) genre in Japanese media and is better understood as a genre of plot rather than a genre of setting. For example, though many danmei novels feature wuxia or xianxia settings, others are better understood as tales of sci-fi, fantasy, or horror.

WUXIA (武侠, "MARTIAL HEROES"): One of the oldest Chinese literary genres and usually consists of tales of noble heroes fighting evil and injustice. It often follows martial artists, monks, or rogues who live apart from the ruling government. These societal outcasts—both voluntary and otherwise—settle disputes among themselves, adhering to their own moral codes over the law.

Characters in wuxia focus primarily on human concerns, such as political strife between factions and advancing their own personal sense of justice. True wuxia is low on magical or supernatural elements. To Western moviegoers, a well-known example is *Crouching Tiger, Hidden Dragon*.

NAMES, HONORIFICS, AND TITLES

Diminutives, Nicknames, and Name Tags

A-: Friendly diminutive. Always a prefix. Usually for monosyllabic names, or one syllable out of a two-syllable name.

DA-: A prefix meaning "eldest."

LAO-: A prefix meaning "old." A casual but still respectful way to address an older man.

-ER: A word for "son" or "child." When added to a name as a suffix, it expresses affection.

XIAO-: A prefix meaning "small" or "youngest." When added to a name, it expresses affection.

GE/GEGE: A word meaning "big brother." When added as a suffix, it becomes an affectionate address for any older male, with the -gege variant expressing even more affection.

Cultivation Sects

SHIZUN: Teacher/master. For one's master in one's own sect. Gender-neutral. Literal meaning is "honored/venerable master" and is a more respectful address, though Shifu is not disrespectful.

SHIXIONG: Older martial brother. For senior male members of one's own sect. When not bound by sect, speakers may also append "-xiong" as a suffix for names, as a friendly but courteous way of addressing a man of equal rank.

SHIJIE: Older martial sister. For senior female members of one's own sect.

SHIDI: Younger martial brother. For junior male members of one's own sect. When not bound by sect, speakers may also append "-di" as a friendly suffix to names, with "-laodi" being a more casual variant.

SHIMEI: Younger martial sister. For junior female members of one's own sect.

SHIZHI: Martial nephew or niece. For disciples of the speaker's martial sibling.

QIANBEI: A respectful title or suffix for someone older, more experienced, or more skilled in a particular discipline. Not to be used for blood relatives.

Other

DAFU: A general but respectful address for court officials.

DAOYOU: An address used by Daoists, for fellow Daoists.

GONGZI: A respectful address for young men, originally only for those from affluent households. Though appropriate in all formal occasions, it's often preferred when the addressee outranks the speaker.

LANG/LANGJUN: A general term for "man." "-lang" can be appended as a suffix for a woman's male lover or husband, but it can also be used to politely address a man by pairing it with other characters that denote his place within a certain family. For example, "dalang," "erlang," and "sanlang" mean "eldest son," "second son," and "third son" respectively. "Langjun" is a polite address for any man, similar to "gentleman."

NIANG/NIANGZI: A general term for "woman," and has the same pairing rules as "lang." "Niangzi" is a polite address for women, both married and unmarried.

SHAOXIA: Literally "young hero." A general way to address a younger martial artist from the jianghu.

XIANSHENG: A polite address for men, originally only for those of great learning or those who had made significant contributions to society. Sometimes seen as an equivalent to "Mr." in English.

XIONGZHANG: A very respectful address for an older man the speaker is close to. Approximately means "esteemed elder brother."

TERMINOLOGY

FACE (脸/面子): A person's face is an important concept in Chinese society. It is a metaphor for someone's reputation or dignity and can be extended into further descriptive metaphors. For example, "having face" refers to having a good reputation and "losing face" refers to having one's reputation damaged.

INTERNAL CULTIVATION (内功): Internal cultivation or *neigong* refers to the breathing, qi, and meditation practices a martial artist must undertake in order to properly harness and utilize their "outer cultivation" of combat techniques and footwork. As Daoism considers qi and breathing irrevocably linked, a large part of internal cultivation centers on achieving the advanced state of **internal breathing** (内息). Practitioners focus on regulating and coordinating their breaths until it becomes second nature. This then grants them the ability to freely manipulate their qi with little effort or conscious thought.

In wuxia, the capabilities of internal cultivation are usually exaggerated. Martial artists are often portrayed as being able to fly with qinggong, generate powerful force fields, manipulate objects across space without physical contact, or harden their bodies and make themselves impervious to physical damage.

JIANGHU (江湖, "RIVERS AND LAKES"): A staple of wuxia, the jianghu describes the greater underground society of martial artists and associates that spans the entire setting. Members of the jianghu self-govern and settle issues among themselves based on the tenets of strength and honor, though this may not stop them from exerting influence over conventional society too.

MARRIAGE: In Chinese culture, the woman traditionally marries into the man's family when she takes his surname. Because of the importance placed on lineages and ancestors, this concept remains even if either side has lost, disowned, or never knew their family at all.

MERIDIANS: The means by which qi travels through the body, like a bloodstream. Some medical and combat techniques target the meridians at specific points on the body, known as acupoints, which allows them to redirect, manipulate, or halt qi circulation. Halting a cultivator's qi circulation prevents them from using their internal cultivation until the block is lifted.

NAMES: When men and women came of age in ancient China, they received a new name for others of the same generation to refer to them by, known as a **courtesy name**. Use of their original or **personal name** was normally reserved only for respected elders and the person themselves—using it otherwise would be very rude and overfamiliar.

Using an emperor's personal name was even more disrespectful. Rulers were usually addressed by the dynasty they led, and they each had a formal title to distinguish themselves from their predecessors or successors. For example, Yuwen Yong's official title was "Emperor Wu of Northern Zhou" (北周武帝).

PAIR CULTIVATION (双修): Also translated as dual cultivation, this is a cultivation practice that uses sex between participants to improve cultivation prowess. Can also be used as a simple euphemism for sex.

PARASITIC CULTIVATION (采补, "HARVEST AND SUPPLEMENT"): The practice of draining life energy and qi from a host to strengthen one's martial arts. As the bodies of men are believed to hold more *yang* qi while women hold more *yin* qi, the person in question will often "harvest" from the other sex to "supplement" themselves, which gives the practice its association with sexual cultivation.

QINGGONG (轻功): A real-life training discipline. In wuxia, the feats of qinggong are highly exaggerated, allowing practitioners to glide through the air, run straight up walls and over water, jump through trees, or travel dozens of steps in an instant.

SECLUSION (闭关): Also known as "closed door meditation," seclusion or secluded cultivation is when a martial artist isolates themselves from the rest of the world to meditate and further their internal cultivation for the purpose of healing injuries or taking their martial arts to the next level.

SHARED DESTINY/FATE (缘): In Chinese culture, the fate and destiny associated with relationships has its own word, called yuan. Two people with good yuan are destined to be friends or lovers, depending on the type, while two with calamitous yuan are ill-fated. The well-known Red String of Fate is based on this idea.

TRUE QI AND CORES: True qi (真气) is a more precise term for the "qi" commonly seen in Chinese media. In Daoism, one's true qi or life force is believed to be the fusion of Xiantian qi and Houtian qi.

True qi is refined in the lower Dantian (丹田, "elixir field") within the abdomen, which also holds the foundations of a person's martial arts, called the core. In *Thousand Autumns*, Daoist cores and demonic cores are mentioned, differentiated by the discipline (and hence Dao) the practitioner chose. All internal cultivation and breathing builds off these foundations—losing or destroying them is tantamount to losing all of one's martial arts.

In wuxia, a practitioner with superb internal cultivation can perform superhuman feats with their true qi. On top of what is covered under internal cultivation above, martial artists can channel true qi into swords to generate sword qi, imbue simple movements and objects with destructive energy, project their voices across great distances, heal lesser injuries, or enhance the five senses.

YIN AND YANG (阴阳): In Daoism, the concept of *yin* and *yang* is another set of complementary, interdependent forces that govern the cosmos. It represents the duality present in many aspects of nature, such as dark and light, earth and heaven, or female and male. *Yin* is the passive principle, while *yang* is the active one.

WARRING STATES PERIOD: An era in ancient Chinese history characterized by heavy military activity between seven dominant states. The rise of schools of thought like Daoism, Confucianism, and Legalism was partially in response to the extreme turmoil and suffering that were rampant during this time. It lasted from around 475 B.C.E. to 221 B.C.E., when the Qin state annexed the rest and established the first unified Chinese empire: the Qin Dynasty.

WEIQI (围棋): Also known by its Japanese name, *go*. Sometimes called "Chinese chess," it is the oldest known board game in human history. The board consists of a many-lined grid upon which opponents play unmarked black and white stones as game pieces to claim territory.

ZOROASTRIANISM: A religion from ancient Persia founded by the prophet Zoroaster.